THE SPY

SOPHIE LARK

*For Jenne,
♡ Sophie Lark*

This one is for Mr Lark, aka Business Daddy, because this story would not exist without him.

He came up with the whole concept for "The Spy", and helped me with so many of the most difficult parts. To say nothing of the constant encouragement, foot rubs, all the dishes he washed, and kids he cared for so I could get this thing done on time, all while continuing to handle the entire business side of self-publishing.

I would be nothing and nowhere without you Ry. You're the Ivan to my Sloane. We're invincible together 🖤

– Sophie

The Spy Official Soundtrack

Spotify → geni.us/spy-spotify

Apple Music → geni.us/spy-apple

1. Siren - Kailee Morgue
2. Wolves (feat. Post Malone) - Big Sean
3. Snake - Halflives
4. Lonely Boy - The Black Keys
5. Runaway - AURORA
6. Wolf - Boy Epic
7. Daddy Issues - Sophia Gonzon
8. Gangsta - Kehlani
9. Uprising - Muse
10. Desire - Meg Myers
11. High - Sivik
12. Start a War - Klergy
13. Gold - Kiiara
14. Bang Bang - GRAE
15. Beat Up Kidz - The OBGMs
16. Nightmare - Halsey
17. I Feel Like I'm Drowning - Two Feet
18. Why Do You Love Me - Charlotte Lawrence
19. Trouble - Valerie Broussard
20. Shimmy Shimmy Ya - El Michels Affair
21. Seven Nation Army - The White Stripes

22. Watch Me Burn - Michele Morrone
23. Born For This - The Score
24. Follow You - Imagine Dragons
25. Home - Edward Sharpe & The Magnetic Zeros

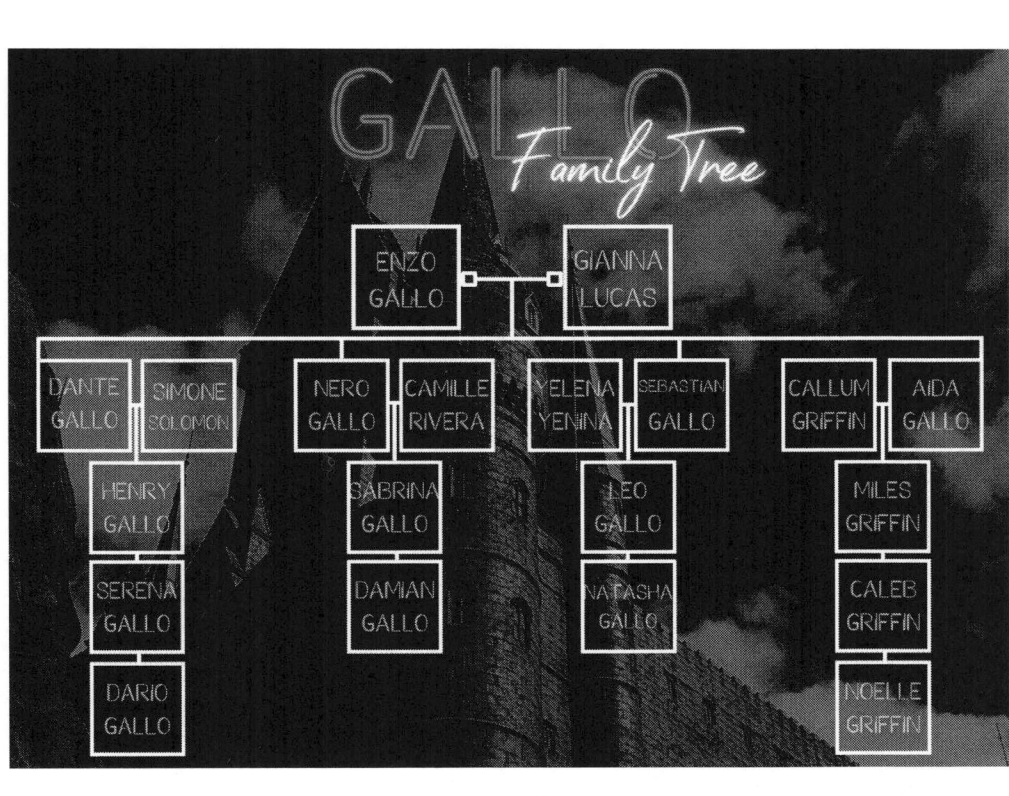

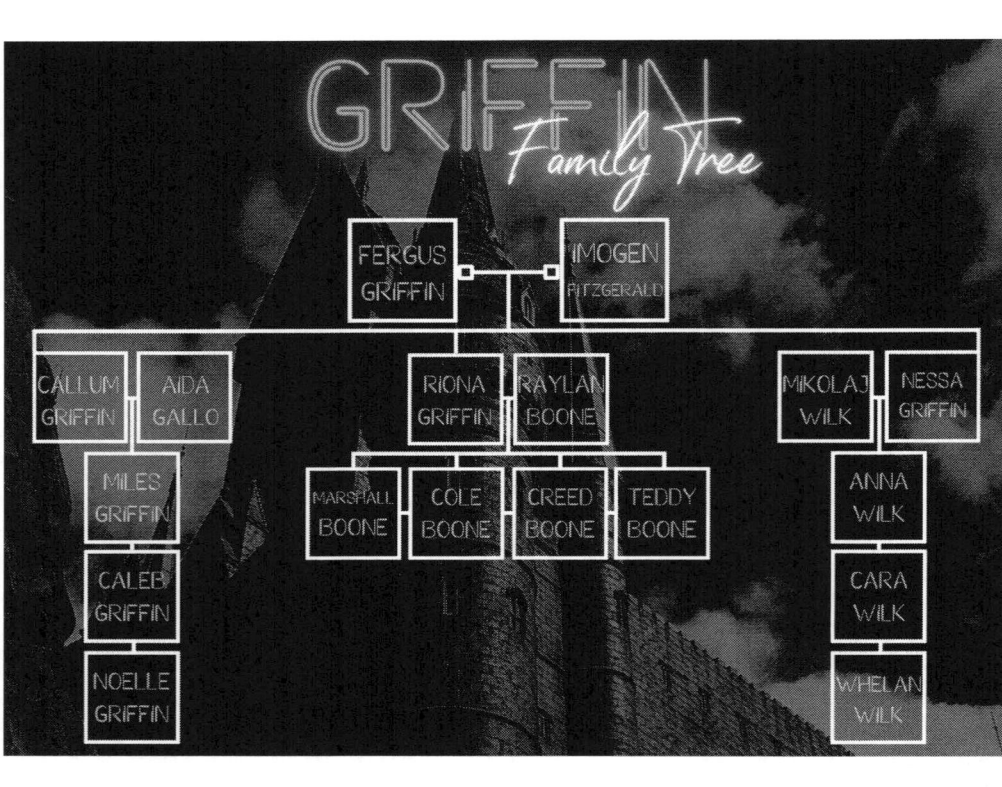

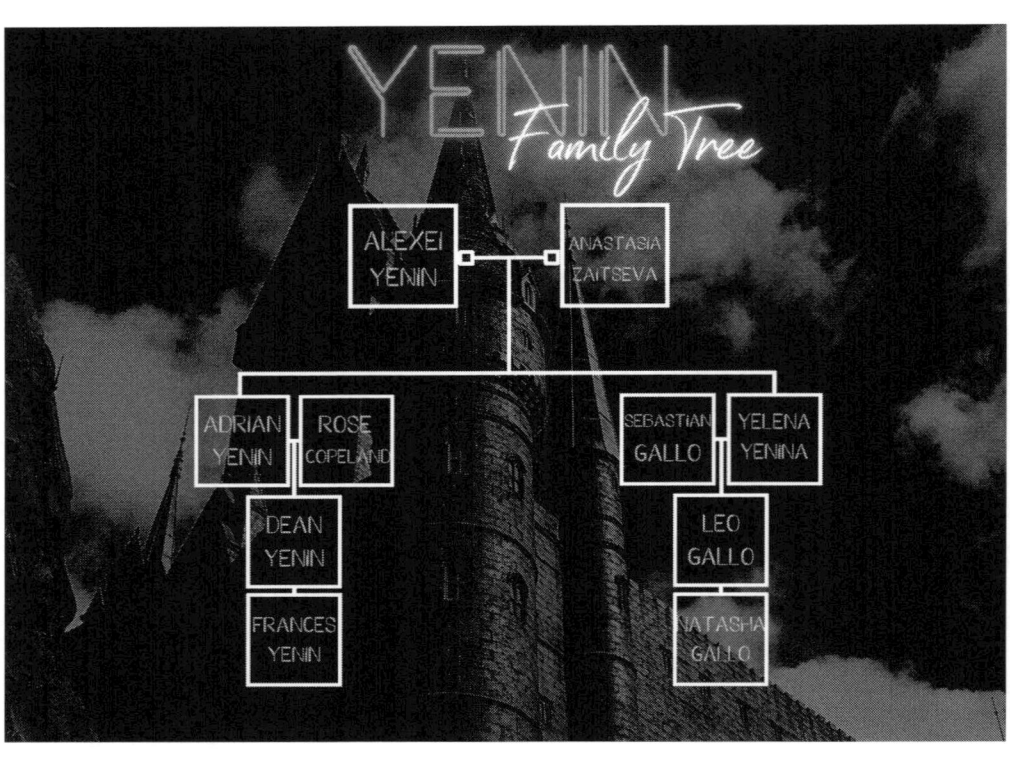

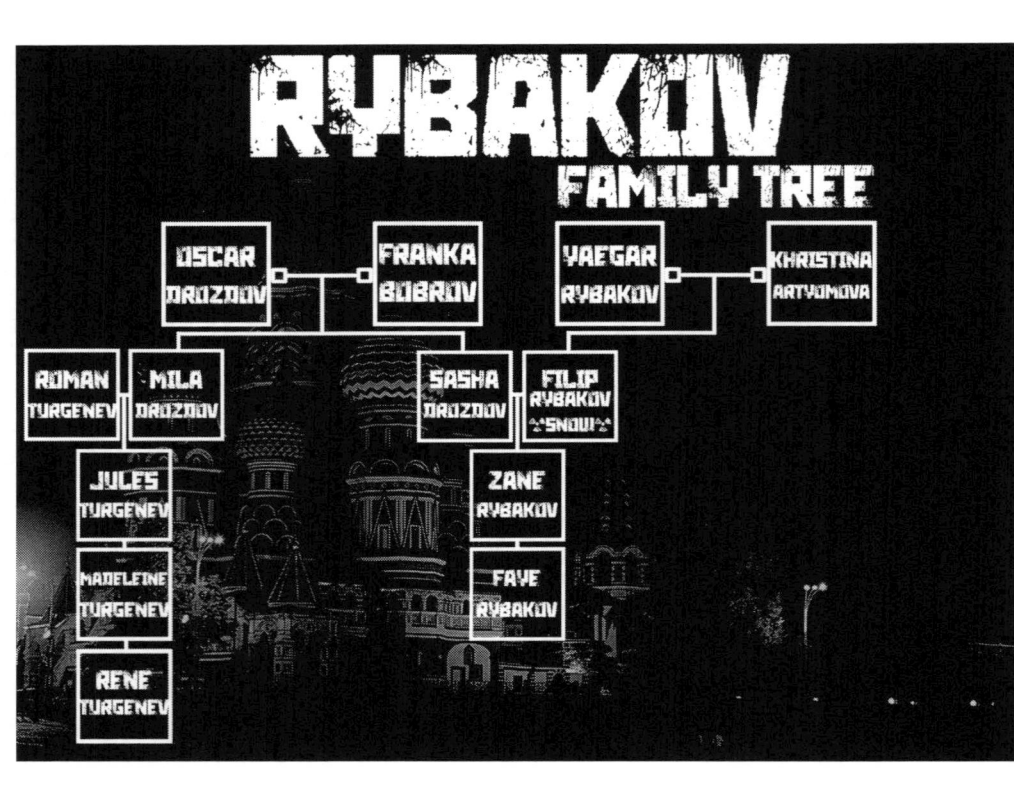

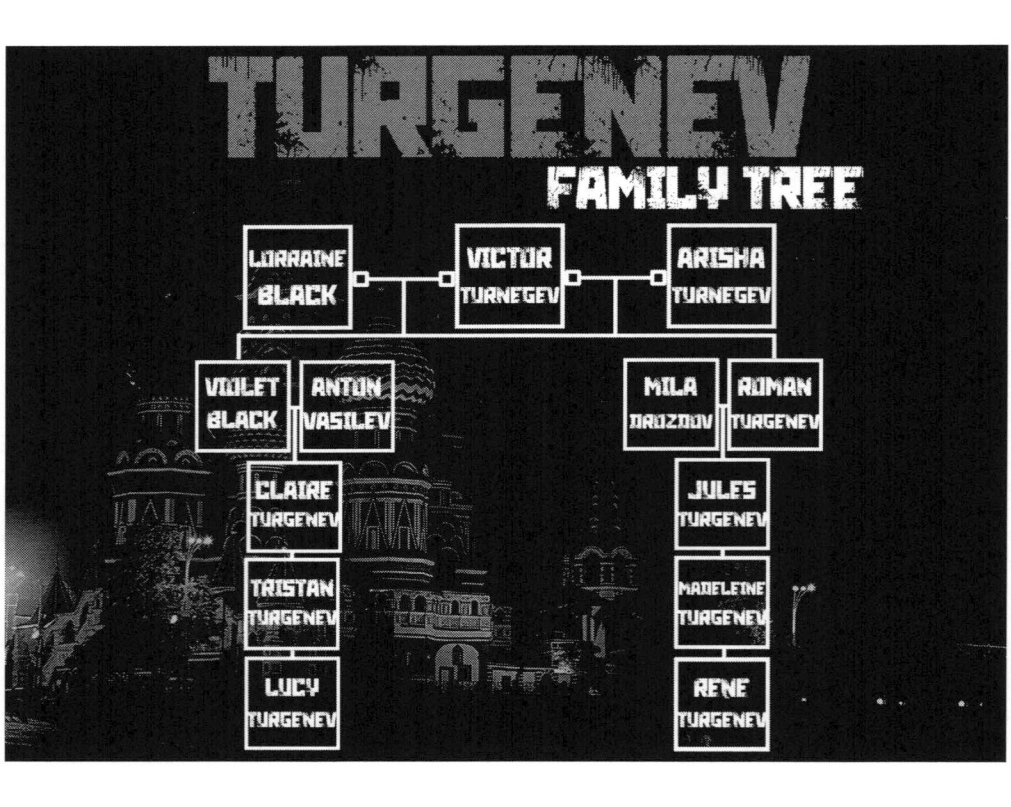

1

THE SPY

Three Years Ago

I wake to my mother's hand clamped over my mouth.

"There's someone in the house," she murmurs in my ear.

I slide out from under the light summer sheet, moving silently and listening for whatever sound might have alerted her. I hear nothing at all—not even the whir of a fan or the mild hum of the appliances down in the kitchen. Glancing at the digital clock on my nightstand, I see only a dark face.

The power's been cut.

That's what she heard—not a noise, but the sudden absence of sound as everything in the house shut off.

I'm wearing boxer shorts and an undershirt. It's been sweltering in Poseidonia, the sea breeze barely managing to cool the villa by midnight. I bend to retrieve my shoes. My mother gives a swift shake of her head.

She's barefoot beneath her silk pajamas, padding noiselessly toward the window. She checks the garden below, and the deck to the left, without ever bobbing her face into view. Then she motions for me to follow her toward the door, staying against the wall where the boards are less likely to creak. She glides along like a shadow, her dark hair tousled with sleep.

She's left the door cracked. I join her, waiting for her to scan the hallway in both directions before we move.

She's about to head toward my sister's room when I grab her shoulder.

"She's not in there," I murmur. "She fell asleep in the study."

I saw Freya passed out on the chaise with an open book splayed across her chest. I covered her with a blanket before I went to bed myself.

My mother curses silently. The study is at the very top of the villa, accessible only by the staircase on the other side of the house.

Changing direction, she heads toward those stairs.

My father intercepts us, dressed in sweatpants and no shirt. His broad chest is heavily inked with the tattoos I know as well as my own face, crossed by the strap of the AR hung over his shoulder. He passes a second rifle to my mother, who sets the stock against her shoulder and assumes a low, ready position.

They split apart, creeping down the hallway with my father in the lead, my mother covering him. They duck under each window we pass. I'm careful to do the same.

I still haven't heard anything. I'm hopeful that my father's soldiers will deal with the threat down on the grounds. We always bring at least six men with us, even when we come to the summer house. As my father's wealth has increased, so has his caution.

We've almost reached the stairs.

I hear the creak of someone coming up. My father motions for us to fall back. He gets low, his rifle pointed at the doorway.

The hulking figure holding a Beretta is instantly recognizable to me—my father's cousin Efrem, big and bear-like, with an incongruous set of spectacles perched on his nose. His shoulders drop in relief when he sees the three of us.

"Where's Timo and Maks?" my father demands.

"Unresponsive," Efrem says, tapping the radio on his belt.

My father's face darkens. That's not good.

"We need to—" Efrem starts.

He's cut off by the sharp crack of shattering glass and a thudding sound. My father grabs me by the shoulder, yanking me to the ground as an explosion blasts through the house. The whole floor heaves beneath me, a wave of pressure and heat roaring out from the direction of our bedrooms.

Now that the silence is broken, the night comes alive with gunfire and shouting. The sharp staccato of automatic weapons bursts up all around us, seemingly from every corner of the grounds. I smell smoke. Not pleasant campfire smoke—the acrid stench of paint and fabric and carpet burning.

"We've got to get to the helicopter!" Efrem says, trying to grab my mother's arm.

She shakes him off impatiently. "That's where they'll expect us to go," she says.

We flew in on the helicopter. It's parked on our private pad on the west side of the grounds. But my mother is surely right—anyone attacking the house would have blocked that route first.

"The garage, then," my father says.

Several vehicles are parked in the underground garage, including Efrem's Land Rover.

"No," my mother says quietly. "The gardener's shed."

I don't understand at first. Then I remember that the gardener has his own ancient Jeep, and the shed is located directly beneath the study. We still have to retrieve my sister.

My father heads up the staircase, trusting my mother's judgment.

We follow after him, Efrem guarding the rear.

As we reach the top floor, I see two figures ducking into the study. These are not my father's men—they're dressed in tactical gear with balaclavas over their heads and rifles on their shoulders.

My mother gestures for me to follow her. While my father and Efrem circle around behind the men, she and I exit onto the balcony. We creep along the open deck, carefully avoiding the lounge chairs, and the empty glasses and sun-bleached books my sister forgot to bring back inside with her.

I peek through the French doors. Freya is no longer asleep on the chaise. She's nowhere to be seen at all. The two men are searching the room, using the lights mounted on their scopes.

My mother covers them with her rifle, but she isn't firing. She knows any noise will draw the whole invading army down on us. She's giving my father a chance to handle them quietly.

In tandem, my father and Efrem sneak up on the men. Efrem's knife is already drawn. My father is bare-handed. He seizes the first soldier from behind, ripping the man's own Bowie knife from his belt and cutting his throat in one slash.

Efrem's opponent swings his gun around. Efrem is forced to drop his knife so he can yank the man's hand away from the trigger.

My mother readies her rifle, barrel pointed directly between the soldier's eyes.

Then an arm darts out from under the chaise, stabbing a letter opener down through the top of the soldier's boot, pinning his foot to the floor. My sister rolls out from under the chaise, leaping to her feet. My father snatches up Efrem's knife and finishes disposing of the second soldier.

My mother cracks the French doors, hissing, "Come on!" to the others.

Freya joins us on the balcony, followed close behind by Efrem and my father.

"What the fuck is happening?" she whispers to me.

Unlike my mother, Freya's hair is pin-straight, barely a strand out of place despite her exertions. It gleams blue-black in the moonlight, a dark veil around her pale face.

My mother motions for us all to stay silent.

I can still hear fighting down on the grounds, on the west side where the helicopter is located, and also at the front of the house where we would have gone to access the garage. My mother was right—she's always right.

Meanwhile, shouting and thundering feet seem to be coming from every direction inside the house. They're searching for us, room by room.

My mother vaults the railing, descending the trellis. She's light and nimble, as is Freya. I'm not sure the spindly wood will hold my weight. I hesitate, wanting to let the women get down first, but my father pushes me forward.

"Go, son," he murmurs.

As soon as my mother's feet touch the ground, she sprints for the gardener's shed, Freya close behind. She keeps her rifle ready. A soldier rounds the corner of the shed, and she shoots him between the eyes.

He falls backward, his finger jerking convulsively on the trigger of his AR. A burst of bullets fire up to the sky.

"*Blyad*," my father hisses behind me.

Now I hear more shouting and more men sprinting toward us. My father drops to one knee, calling to me, "Keep running!"

One of the soldiers points his gun at me, before being blasted off his feet by my father.

The doors of the shed burst outward as my mother drives right through them, bumping over the grass and screeching to a halt directly in front of me.

I jump in the open back of the Jeep, followed closely after by Efrem. As he leaps over the tailgate, he's shot from behind. He falls heavily onto my lap, a dark stain blossoming on his back with awful speed.

My father fires twice more, hitting the man who shot Efrem, then he jumps into the back with me.

"Go!" he shouts to my mother.

She floors the accelerator, speeding not toward the front of the house, but over the grass and through the lemon trees toward the side gate.

Freya takes my mother's rifle so she can cover our right side, while my father watches behind us. I try to prop Efrem up, ripping off my shirt so I can use it to apply pressure to the wound.

"I'm sorry," he says to my father.

"It's not your fault, *moy drug*," my father says with surprising gentleness.

It's the kindness in my father's voice, more than the horrible waxy color of Efrem's face, that tells me my uncle is going to die.

I press harder against the wound, the wadded shirt already soaked through with blood.

Efrem pushes his Beretta into my hand. His dark eyes meet mine for a moment, and he tries to say something through colorless lips. Instead, he lets out a long, rattling breath and his head falls back, his glasses slipping askew and eyes staring blindly upward at the night sky. Each bump of the Jeep jolts his limp body.

"Nine o'clock!" my mother barks, wrenching the wheel to the left to give my father and sister a better angle. They fire at the three soldiers guarding the side gate.

The gate is chained shut and padlocked. Gripping Efrem's Beretta tight, I roll out of the back of the Jeep and crouch behind the tire. Once my father and sister have dropped the first two soldiers, I shoot the third one in the chest, then I run to the gate. I empty the clip at the padlock until it's destroyed, ripping away the chain and shoving the gate open.

My mother drives forward, only pausing long enough for me to leap in once more before she roars down the dark, winding road that leads along the sea cliffs.

I'm about to say, "We made it!" when two black SUVs screech out onto the road behind us, speeding after us at a reckless pace. A heavily tattooed man in tactical gear leans out the passenger side window to fire at us.

"Stay low!" my mother shouts back at us.

With its wide-open back, we're poorly protected in the ancient Jeep. Worse, the newer and better-maintained SUVs are gaining on us.

"Who are they?" I ask my father. "Bratva?"

Their tattoos look like my father's.

He shakes his head.

"Malina," he hisses through his teeth.

My skin freezes.

The Ukrainians are every bit as ruthless as the Bratva—maybe even more so. They're our dark twins, our twisted doppelgängers. Never have they been more dangerous than since Marko Moroz solidified his control of Kyiv by stabbing a pen through the eye of his own former mentor.

"Look!" Freya calls back to us, pointing up into the sky.

Our helicopter swoops up over the villa, passing over the stone walls in our direction.

"Who's flying it, though?" my father mutters.

The radio on Efrem's hip crackles.

I snatch it up.

"*I'm coming to get you, boss . . .*" a familiar voice says.

I grin. It's Maks, my father's *Avtoritet,* and a close friend to me, despite the twenty years between us. I'm almost as pleased to hear that he's still alive as I am to see him flying to the rescue.

Until I hear a booming shot ring out, and I watch a bright flare arcing across the sky, from the top of the villa directly toward the helicopter.

Like a deadly firework, it hits the tail of the chopper and explodes outward in all directions. The helicopter whirls around and around, the body now wrenched along by the blades. It crashes down to the ground where it erupts into a fireball so immense that I feel the heat blast hit my stunned face moments later.

"NOOO!" I shout.

My father shoves me down as more gunfire whizzes over our heads from the pursuing SUVs. Still, I catch a last glimpse of the lone man standing atop our villa, an MK 153 resting casually across his shoulder.

Even at this distance, there can be no doubt of the identity of that goliath figure. It's Marko Moroz.

My father fires back toward the SUVs, keeping them at bay. He hits a tire and the Escalade fishtails back and forth across the road, but it doesn't roll. The driver recovers, still following after us.

"Get ready!" my mother shouts.

She yanks the wheel to the left again, pulling us into the overlook above the marina. Directly below, a dozen boats are moored, including our cruiser.

She grabs her rifle back from Freya and she and my father take cover behind the Jeep, firing toward the approaching SUVs.

"No time to climb down!" she shouts at me and Freya. "You'll have to jump!"

"Go with them!" my father tells her. "I'll cover you."

"No!" she says fiercely, her dark eyes glinting in the glare of the Jeep's headlights. "I'm with you until the end."

My sister is already climbing over the seawall while the SUVs screech to a halt in front of us, their headlights blinding, their doors opening. My father fires toward the windows, driving the men back inside.

Then, teeth gritted, he seizes my mother's rifle and wrenches it out of her hands.

"I'm sorry, my love," he says.

He picks her up bodily and chucks her over the wall.

I hear her howl of fury as she falls.

"Go!" he says, shoving me after her. "Make her leave!"

As I leap over the wall, I catch one last glimpse of my father firing in several directions at once as the Ukrainians close in on him. I see his body jerk as he's hit in the shoulder and the leg, but he won't stop shooting.

I fall down, down through the black night toward the freezing water. I plunge into the sea, sinking so deep that I have to swim upward with all my might to break the surface again. As soon as my head pops up, I stroke hard for our boat.

Freya has already climbed in. She casts off and starts the engine.

I see my mother's dark head. She's not swimming for the boat—she's trying to reach the pier so she can climb back up to my father.

It will never work. He'll be dead long before she gets there.

I seize a handful of her hair and haul her backward.

"LET GO OF ME!" she shrieks, twisting around in the water.

The last person in the world I would want to fight is my mother. And not out of respect—because she's fucking terrifying. Still, I have to obey my father.

"IT'S TOO LATE!" I bellow. "You're going to get us all killed!"

I see the wild look in her eyes, that savage determination that I've never seen falter, never once in my life.

Then reality hits her harder than any hammer.

Her face slackens, and she looks back toward the cliff with pure misery instead.

"Come on," I say, grabbing her hand and swimming for the boat.

I've barely managed to haul her in before the Malina reach the edge of the cliff and begin firing down on us. Splinters explode off the railing. A bullet hits the deck an inch from my foot.

Freya opens the throttle, speeding us out of the harbor.

I look back at the flashes of gunfire still lining the cliff.

My father can't protect us anymore.

2

Nix Moroz

Present Day

I was born on an island in the Black Sea.

My mother had come boar hunting with my father and his men. She didn't know she was pregnant.

She had always been a tremendous athlete—hurdles, high jump, and the four-hundred-meter dash. Later she turned to long-distance swimming.

She swam the English Channel in less than eight hours and set a record for the 25 km open water race at the European Aquatics Championships. She swam from Florida to Cuba without a shark cage, stung on the face and hands three separate times by jellyfish, but never stopping.

That's how she met my father—when she returned to Kyiv, she was invited to a dinner hosted by the Minister of Foreign Affairs. She was a country girl, and though she didn't mind donning a gown for formal affairs, she found the conversation tedious and the canapés highly unsatisfying for someone accustomed to eating a lunch of twenty potato pancakes smothered in sour cream and fried onions, and then an entire herring for dinner.

My father had never seen a woman like that, with a back almost too broad to zip into a dress, and welts from the jellyfish tentacles still marking her cheeks and throat and the backs of her hands like whiplashes. She was scowling at everyone because she was hungry.

When he tried to approach her, she rudely rebuffed him, having no idea that she was speaking to a man far more powerful than the minister hosting the party.

"Where's your manners, girl?" my father said.

"I don't have any manners," she replied, tossing down her drink in one gulp. "I never said I did."

He liked her boldness and the strong column of her throat as she threw back that drink.

"How did it feel swimming with all those sharks?" he demanded.

My mother had been followed for several miles of the swim by two hammerheads, and later by an ugly bull shark.

She regarded my father and his two lieutenants with a cool stare. "It felt very like this," she said. "Only my wetsuit was more comfortable."

My father had already decided he would marry her. He simply had to convince her to come to dinner with him first.

She said she would, if he took her somewhere with proper Georgian food.

"None of this foreign shit," she said, sniffing at a passing tray of spinach puffs.

They married within the year. My mother agreed to it on the condition that my father wouldn't interfere with her athletic pursuits. She had dreams of crossing the Adriatic next.

In the meantime, she joined my father skiing in Bukovel and hunting red deer in Manchuria. She was six feet tall, built like an Amazon, and so relentlessly active that she hadn't menstruated in years.

That, combined with her love of food, meant that she disregarded any changes to her figure, thinking that the bit of belly she had grown was simply the result of my father spoiling her with honey cake and toffee.

The boar hunting was closer to home—on Dzharylhach island, which some call the Ukrainian Maldives because of the clear turquoise water. Warm sea, clean sand, and four hundred salty lakes scattered all over the island—a lonely and beautiful place, perfect for pig-sticking.

They hunted the boars in the old way, with spears. The spears had a cross guard to prevent the enraged pig from driving its own body further down the spear so it could at least have the satisfaction of mauling you as it died.

By that time, my father knew my mother well enough to be concerned when she failed to charge after the boars with her spear upraised, fleet as Artemis on the hunt.

Instead, she pressed her hand against the cramp on her side, telling my father to go on with the men. She planned to sit and soak in one of the warm, salty pools.

She thought it was indigestion. As the cramps worsened, she considered that perhaps she was about to have the long-delayed period in spectacular fashion.

It was only when the pain overtook her to the point that she could no longer stand that she began to realize how deserted the long section of beach really was, with barely a gull in sight, let alone any humans.

She wondered if her appendix was the issue, or her gallbladder. The sight of blood in the salt pool disgusted her more than it alarmed her. She forced herself to hobble down to the ocean instead, where the waves would wash her clean.

The steady surf was immensely soothing to her, the rhythm of the waves as familiar as her own heartbeat.

And then, out of nowhere, the irresistible impulse to bear down . . .

The birth itself took less than ten minutes.

She reached between her legs and felt the curve of the infant skull—my skull—with comical surprise. She made a sound halfway between a shriek and a laugh of pure astonishment. It seemed like I had played a trick on her, appearing out of nowhere, uninvited, and unexpected.

She lifted me out of the water, as if it were the sea that had birthed me. The placenta she left for the crabs to eat.

Though she had never seen it done before, she successfully knotted the cord and severed it with the edge of a scallop shell.

When my father returned an hour later, triumphant with a bloody boar carcass strung up on a pole, he found his new bride sitting topless in the sand, her shirt wrapped around the infant at her breast.

I was small, having arrived, by the doctor's estimate, at least a month early.

My father thought it was just as good a joke as my mother.

He marveled at my copper-colored hair and appetite all out of proportion to my size.

He wanted to name me after his grandmother.

But my mother had already named me Nix, the word for a water sprite that can shift back and forth to human form.

My father liked that even better. He said, without any evidence to the contrary, and whether I shared his red hair or not, he could never be entirely sure that my mother hadn't found me on the beach.

That's the first bedtime story I remember: the story of how I was born.

It was my favorite, and I begged to hear it again and again, though my father had dozens of tales to tell, all equally full of mystery and adventure. He's a fantastic storyteller to this day. Even his men shout for their favorites when they've all been drinking together.

My father's stories center on himself and his soldiers: legendary tales of bravery, bloodshed, and revenge, epic in scale and rich in detail.

My father looks like he should be carved on the side of a mountain. He's seven feet tall with a ginger mane of hair and a flaming red beard. He's ferocious and clever. All girls idolize their fathers I suppose, but none with better reason than me.

Right now, however, we're in a hell of a fight.

He doesn't want me going to Kingmakers.

It's not the first fight we've had, but it's the most vicious.

It's not like the time I broke the ankle of his favorite horse, or the time he said I ought to stay a virgin until I was married and I laughed in his face and told him that ship had already sailed.

This time, it seems that we're both ready to defend this particular hill until all else is a flaming ruin.

"I told you, I won't discuss it again!" he roars at me, storming around the oak-slab table in the huge farmhouse kitchen.

I'm leaned back in my chair, arms crossed, feet propped up on the table to annoy him.

"It doesn't need any more discussion," I say. "Because I'm going."

"Good luck getting on the ship without my fingerprint on that contract!" he growls, disdainfully flinging down the handwritten list of rules and regulations to attend Kingmakers.

I leap to my feet, knocking my chair backward on the flagstone floor.

"Enjoy growing old and decrepit all alone without me if you won't!" I holler back at him.

"Where do you think you're going to go?" he snorts, folding his cable-like arms across his broad chest.

"Anywhere *you're* not! You can't keep me a prisoner here!" I shout.

"You're not a prisoner! You've got a hundred acres of land, horses, dune buggies, a private plane in which I've taken you all over the goddamned world! You're spoiled," he says, in a disgusted tone.

"And you're a coward! You've gotten as paranoid as an old woman—why shouldn't I go to school, the same school you went to yourself?"

Stepan Pavluk comes into the kitchen, then makes an about-face so abrupt that he must have given himself whiplash. He hustles back out again, not wanting to get in the middle of another epic row between me and my father.

Too late—Dad already saw him.

He shouts, "Get back here, Stepan. Explain to Nix why it's the worst possible time for her to go swanning off to school all on her own with no bodyguards and no security whatsoever."

Stepan winces, looking back and forth between my father's furious face and mine. He's only a bookkeeper, though a damn good one. He prefers the silence of pen and paper to the smashed dishes and hurled insults that are surely about to erupt between my father and me.

"Nix," he says carefully, "with your father's deal with the Princes and Romeros, and his expansion of—"

"Don't tell me it's not a good time," I hiss at my father, completely ignoring Stepan. "It's never a good time. When will it be the right time for me to go to college? When exactly are you planning to retire?"

"When I'm dead," he barks.

"Exactly! So either I'm going to school, or I guess I'll have to fucking kill you!" I yell.

Stepan is trying to sneak away again. This time my father lets him go, distracted by this new outrage coming out of my mouth.

"You think that's funny, girl?" he snarls. "I'd cut out a soldier's tongue if he said that to me."

"I'm not one of your soldiers," I remind him. "I know you forget that sometimes."

This is how we fight—with wild accusations and savage personal attacks. In an hour we might eat a bowl of ice cream together, but right now we want to strangle each other.

That's what happens when you grow up in a family of two, always together, no time or space apart.

Which I know will be his next point of attack.

Sure enough, the very next thing out of his mouth is, "If something were to happen to you on that island where I can't protect you, your mother would never forgive—"

"Oh, don't bring her into this!" I shout. "First of all, you know damn well she wanted me to get an education. And second, she doesn't get a vote because she doesn't exist anymore."

Now my dad is really pissed. He raises one thick finger and points it right in my face, warning me.

"*Don't,*" he snarls.

He likes to think my mother is waiting for him in his version of Valhalla.

I take a deep breath, trying to bring us back to sanity before we both say something we regret—worse than the usual things.

"You know she would want me to go to school," I say quietly. "And you know if she were in my position . . . nothing and no one would stop her from going to Kingmakers."

This is the best way to appeal to him. To remind him that my mother was just as stubborn and adventurous as I am, and he loved her for it.

I can see the war taking place inside of him—his inability to counter my point, battling with his overprotective impulses, and his absolute abhorrence at the idea of letting me out of his sight. Not to mention his refusal to ever back down or admit when he's wrong.

His face is almost as red as his beard, his fists balled up like Christmas hams.

It's now or never. School starts in a week.

Pushing hard one last time, I say, "The whole damn island is only eight miles across. You'll know exactly where I am the whole time. You might as well have me in a snow globe in your pocket. It's the safest place on earth, isn't it?"

"Rocco Prince was killed there only a year ago!" my father barks.

"Dieter Prince isn't you. Nobody would lay a finger on *your* daughter." I grin. "Even when I want them to."

My father snorts. He's well aware that my dating opportunities have been as dismal as the rest of my social life, and it's his fault.

Making him laugh is the second-best way to get what I want.

The best way is straight up begging.

"Please, Dad," I say. "I want to go to school. I want to be normal, for once in my life. Or normal-adjacent, at least."

He sighs, his massive shoulders dropping an inch. "I'll think about it," he says.

I heroically resist the urge to jump up and down.

"Thank you, Dad!"

"I said I'll *think* about it!" he reminds me.

"I know," I say, righting the kitchen chair and stepping up on the seat so I can kiss him on the cheek.

We both know that means I'm going.

3

Nix

Freshman students board the ship to Kingmakers from the port in Dubrovnik, the first week of September.

I hadn't realized we were supposed to put on our uniforms already, so I come down to the dock dressed in my usual tank top, cargo pants, and combat boots. My father's men outfit themselves from the same military warehouse that supplies the Spetsnaz, and I'll admit, that's where I do most of my shopping. It's all top-quality tactical materials, in consistent sizes. I like to be comfortable.

I'm not looking forward to wearing the uniforms, and I sure as fuck have no intention of putting on one of those plaid skirts. I bought the boy's trousers instead.

I'm not trying to *be* a boy. Not trying to "be the son my father never had" or whatever the fuck. I just want to be able to run around and sit any way I like without worrying about my underwear showing.

I'll admit, I feel a little scrubby compared to all the other students who dressed up for the first day of school—fresh haircuts and shiny shoes and all the works.

I thought I was really doing something just washing my hair last night. But it's a lot more humid here than in Kyiv, and my curls are forming rebellious twists that are halfway between a dreadlock and something Medusa would have growing all over her head.

Meanwhile, the rest of the students are sleek and polished, and a lot of them seem to know each other already. They're forming excited little bunches, eagerly chatting about the upcoming school year.

I throw my duffle bag down in the pile of luggage waiting to be loaded on the ship. Then I square my shoulders, looking around for one of those groups to sidle up and join. After all, the whole point of coming here was to try to make friends.

I've been isolated, growing up on my father's private compound with nobody around except his army of men. Don't get me wrong, it's great having thirty rowdy uncles at your beck and call, but it's not the same as your own peers.

I'm feeling pretty confident, though. I'm smart and funny, and always down to try something new—what's not to like?

So I stroll up to the first person I see: a tall Asian girl with retro-framed glasses and hot-pink lipstick. She's got a group of friends around her and she looks cool.

"Hi!" I say. "I'm Nix. Where are you guys from?"

"I'm from Hong Kong," the girl says, holding out a slim hand to shake. "Alyssa Chan."

Before I can take her hand, her friend mutters something in her ear in rapid Cantonese.

Alyssa drops her hand and tucks it into the pocket of her skirt, as if she never meant to shake. At the same time, she takes an unconscious step back from me.

"Nix... what was it?" she says.

"Nix Moroz," I say, trying to pretend I didn't notice the cock-block from her friend.

Alyssa nods, her face smooth and impassive. "Nice to meet you," she says, coolly. Then she turns back to her friends, in a silent but perfectly articulate rebuff to any further conversation.

Well, fuck.

Either I'm sweatier than I thought in the Croatian sunshine, or maybe these girls feel like they have enough friends already.

Trying not to feel self-conscious, I look around for somebody else who might be more welcoming.

Maybe it's my imagination, but I feel like a couple of kids are whispering to each other now, casting looks back in my direction. A ripple runs through the crowd of students, a message passed from ear to ear while I stand here, alone and stupidly gaping.

When I take a step toward a group of Irish students, they immediately split apart and head in opposite directions, some boarding the ship and others feeling a pressing impulse to check on their luggage.

What the fuck is going on?

Well, it doesn't matter—the ship's crew are hollering for everybody to board. I join the stream of students ascending the gangplank to the deck.

The barquentine is beautiful, with crisp white, navy, and gold paint, and taut sails snapping in the breeze. I watch the sailors with interest, seeing how they work together to manipulate the ropes and rigging, which are too heavy for one man to handle, no matter his experience or brawn.

Once every last student is onboard, the sailors cast off. The ship begins to move, with aching slowness at first, and then surprising speed as the sails fill with wind and the ship turns into the optimum angle for tacking.

The students settle in across the deck—some playing cards or dice games, a few reading, and others turning their faces to the blazing sun to catch a tan.

Everybody seems to have at least one person to talk to.

Except one girl.

She's sitting on the railing of the ship, heedless of the fact that one rough buck of the waves could chuck her backward into the water. Her dark hair streams over her shoulder in the wind. Every male within a twenty-foot radius is staring transfixed at the long expanse of tanned thighs bared beneath the short hem of her skirt.

She looks boldly back at them, daring them to approach. None has gathered up the balls to do it yet, probably because she's the most beautiful girl I've ever seen. Her skin is deeply tanned, her figure outrageously sensual, her lips full and pouting, and her eyes an unusual shade of foggy gray. Her eyebrows are dark slashes, slightly tilted up at the outer edges, giving her a fierce expression, though she's actually smiling slightly.

It's no wonder that none of the girls have gone near her, either. I see a few casting her envious or wistful looks. I don't believe that girls hate pretty girls—they're drawn to them, more often. But this kind of beauty is terrifying and fundamentally unfair to most people's eyes.

I'm fascinated by her. Maybe it's because I do so much hunting with my father—I can't help but view this girl as a rare specimen.

Besides, I never expected to be the prettiest girl around. I'm a little odd-looking, quite frankly. Almost as tall as my mother was, with this wild hair and skin that will never take the slightest bit of sunshine, always remaining as cadaverous as if I lived full-time in a cave. I've got a raspy voice, and I laugh too loud. I turn heads for the wrong reasons.

So I stride right up to this girl and I say, "Is everybody too scared to talk to you because you're gorgeous, or are you a secret serial killer?"

The girl gives me a wicked grin, saying, "I'm not a *secret* anything."

"Nix Moroz," I say, holding out my hand.

She slides off the railing so she can shake. Once she lands on her feet and realizes she's a good four inches shorter than me, she says, "Goddamnit! I hate looking up at people."

But she gives my hand a good squeeze anyway. Hers is surprisingly strong, and I notice that her fingers are stained with something dark. Her perfume is tinged with a heady chemical scent—oil or gasoline. It makes my head spin.

"Sabrina Gallo," she says.

"Where are you from?" I ask her.

Maybe it's rude to ask everybody that question, but I'm wildly curious, with students coming to Kingmakers from every corner of the globe.

"Born and raised in Chicago," she says. "You?"

"Kyiv."

"Oh yeah," she nods. "I was gonna guess Russian—the accent sounds the same."

"To you." I grin. "Not to us."

"Fair enough." Sabrina smiles back at me.

There's an easy comfort between us already—the kind that springs up between people who are blunt. It's so much easier to know where you stand with someone who says whatever pops into their head, rude or not.

"Are you excited to go to Kingmakers?" I ask her.

"Hell yeah," she says. "I've been jealous as fuck of all the fun my cousins have been having."

"I'm jealous you've got cousins," I say. "I don't know anybody here."

"You will soon enough. There's less than a hundred people in our year. By Christmas you'll know them all, and by springtime you'll be sick of them."

"That sounds . . . pretty nice," I laugh.

"I recognize a few people," Sabrina says, her eyes sweeping the bunches of students all over the deck. "That's Leah Weiss over there—she's from Chicago. Her older brother Jacob's in the Spy division. I think she said she was gonna be an Accountant. Fucking kill me—I'd rather scrub toilets than balance books. No offense, if you're one."

"I wouldn't mind it," I say. "I like numbers. I'm an Heir, though."

"Me too," Sabrina says easily. Then, continuing her survey of the students, she adds, "That kid over there, I've seen him before, he's from one of the Italian families in New York, but I can't remember which one. Oh, and there's the rest of my cousins!"

She waves to a boy with dark, curly hair and a friendly grin, who's pushing his way through the crowd of students to join us. Right behind him follows a pretty brunette girl with delicate coloring and a reserved expression.

"There you are!" the boy says to Sabrina, puffing slightly.

"There *I* am!" she laughs. "Where the hell have you two been? I thought you were gonna meet me at the airport?"

"We missed the flight," he winces. "It was my fault. Got pulled over—might have been speeding a bit 'cause I was late picking Cara up from her house. Almost missed the boat too, quite honestly. They re-routed us through Madrid and then Bern. With the layovers, we only arrived an hour ago."

Sure enough, both Caleb and Cara look rumpled and sleep-exhausted.

Cara seems to accept her cousin's fuck-up with equanimity. Serenely, she says, "We made it, though."

Caleb is less gracious. "Thanks for NOT waiting for us on the dock!" he accuses Sabrina.

Sabrina laughs carelessly. "How was I supposed to know what happened to you? I left my phone at home, remember? No cellphones on the island. I wasn't about to miss the boat out of solidarity."

"Anyway," Cara says to me, interrupting the pleasant bickering, "I'm Cara Wilk. This is Caleb Griffin."

"You know Sabrina?" Caleb asks me.

"For about ten minutes," I say. "I'm Nix Moroz."

I think I see a strange expression pass over Caleb's face, but he smooths it away as quickly as it came.

"Nice to meet you," he says.

"What division will you guys be in?" I ask them.

"Enforcer," Caleb says. "My brother Mi—I've got an older brother who's Heir."

"I'll be with the Accountants," Cara says.

"She's actually a writer, though," Sabrina says.

"Oh, really?" I say, curiosity piqued.

"I'm a last-minute addition to Kingmakers," Cara says. "I'd planned to go to normal college. Take literature courses and all that. But then I thought . . . learning about the world might be more useful than studying writing." She smiles. "Or maybe I just couldn't stand the thought of pretending to understand *Beowulf* yet again."

"I came last minute as well," I say. "My dad didn't want me here."

"Why's that?" Caleb asks, eyeing me closely.

"He's overprotective," I say. "Or I dunno, maybe it's the right amount of protective, considering the kind of things that go on in our world. But it feels like I'm in a box with a lid. And I just . . . want to know what it's like to walk around without somebody watching me every minute of the day."

"I don't know if you came to the right place for freedom," Sabrina says, casting a glance around at all the uniformed students. "You saw the list of rules they sent us for this place."

"Don't pretend like you intend to follow any of them," Caleb snorts.

"Oh shut the fuck up, you kettle-calling pot." Sabrina tosses her dark hair back over her shoulder. "Neither will you."

Since the cousins obviously have the scoop on Kingmakers, I pepper them with questions they're happy to answer.

Caleb tells us that he's most excited to compete in the *Quartum Bellum,* the annual challenge where all four years of students are pitted against one another for supremacy.

"What kind of challenges?" I ask him.

Caleb shrugs. "It's different every year. There's no sports at Kingmakers, so that's it in terms of athletics. I mean, other than Combat training and all that shit."

"I dunno how I'm going to do in the classes," I say. "I didn't go to a normal high school; I had a tutor."

"Who learns anything in high school?" Sabrina says airily. "Besides, the classes here are completely different. It won't matter if you passed trigonometry or not."

That cheers me up a little. Even as I see another boy standing against the mast of the ship giving me an absolutely filthy glare. Some of my fellow students are pretty damned unfriendly.

Well, I don't need a million friends—one or two would be more than I had before.

Sabrina and Caleb are talking about the motorcycle Sabrina has been fixing up with her mom, which will belong to her alone if they can ever get it running.

"You know, when you buy them new, they already work," Caleb teases her.

"They don't make the Indian Four anymore," Sabrina says, rolling her eyes at his ignorance. "That's pretty much the whole point."

Meanwhile, the boy at the mast has been joined by a couple of friends. They're all looking over at me, muttering.

I try to ignore them.

"You like fixing cars?" I ask Sabrina.

"Not as much as bikes," she says. "The Indian Four has this upside-down engine and it—"

The three boys interrupt her, pushing between Sabrina and me.

"*Podyvit'sya, khto tse.*" *Look who it is,* the biggest one says in Ukrainian.

He was the one leaned up against the mast, the one watching me the longest. He has a heavy, sullen-looking face, a shaved head, and earrings in both ears.

His friends—one skinny and heavily tattooed, the other handsome in a sloppy, unshaven sort of way—are both leering at me like they know me.

"*Khto vy, chort zabyray?*" I demand. *Who the hell are you?*

"Are you serious?" the big one says, looking at his friends and laughing derisively.

Sabrina is watching in confusion, but Cara seems to have understood at least part of what was said. She asks the boys, "Well? Are you going to answer the question?"

The skinny one sneers at me. "He's your cousin, you dumb shit."

"I don't have any cousins," I scoff.

"Second cousin, then. Same fuckin' difference," the scruffy one says.

"You really don't know who I am?" the big one says, dark eyes narrowed. "You don't know the Lomachenkos?"

"You're Odessa Mafia . . ." I say slowly.

I am, of course, aware that a chapter of the Ukrainian Mafia operates out of Brighton Beach in New York. I knew my father had dealings with them at times, but I didn't know that we were blood-related—if this idiot's even telling the truth.

"Estas Lomachenko," he says, puffing up his chest. "I suppose I shouldn't be surprised that *Marko* doesn't want to remember what he did to my brother."

I've never heard of Estas or his brother, but I don't like what he's insinuating. And I definitely don't like the sneering way he says my father's name. No fucking way would he have the balls to call my dad "Marko" to his face.

"I have no idea what you're talking about," I say coldly.

"He's got a lot of nerve sending you here," Estas sneers, his nose so close to mine that his spit hits my cheeks. He bumps me with his chest, pushing me backward. "Does he think the Rule of Recompense is gonna protect you? We can make your life a living hell without ever putting a finger on you . . ."

"Get the fuck out of my face," I snarl back at him. "And don't you say a word about my father or I'll twist your head around like a fuckin' dandelion!"

"I'll say whatever I like about that lying, murderous piece of—"

I haul off and punch Estas right in the nose, hard as I can.

I do it without thought or any kind of plan. I know we're not supposed to fight at Kingmakers, but technically we're not *at* Kingmakers yet, and also, fuck this lying sack of shit trying to start something with me on the first day of school!

Disloyalty to family is the worst accusation you can make in the mafia world. This motherfucker's gonna learn real quick the consequences of slandering my father.

His skinny friend tries to grab me and put me in a headlock, which turns into a tussle on the deck, me punching and kicking every piece of him I can reach, while the skinny guy hangs on like a spider monkey. Estas, snarling with blood all over his teeth, tries to jump on me too. To my surprise, the lovely Sabrina Gallo punches him in almost exactly the same place that I did, turning his bloody nose into a spurting fountain.

Caleb grabs her arms and hauls her back, shouting, "Dude! How am *I* the responsible one here?"

The rest of the fight is swiftly broken up by several burly deckhands who rip Estas and me apart, tie our hands in front of us, and dump us down on opposite ends of the deck.

Unfortunately, Sabrina gets the same treatment, deposited right next to me with Estas' blood still on her knuckles.

"NO FIGHTING!" the first mate howls at us, pointing his thick finger right in our faces. "You fucking sit there and don't move an inch, any of you!"

Estas and his skinny friend glower at us from the stern, but under the first mate's glare, they keep their mouths shut.

Caleb, at least, isn't in trouble because he only tried to hold Sabrina back. He watches us from several feet away, frowning and worried, held back by the prowling first mate. Cara Wilk gives us a sympathetic shrug.

"I'm sorry," I say to Sabrina guiltily.

"Ah, it's fine," she says. "He started it."

"I don't even know him!" I cry. "I don't know what the fuck his problem is."

"Hm," Sabrina says noncommittally.

"What?" I demand, turning to face her.

"Nothing." She shrugs.

"No, it's not nothing," I say. "Everybody's looking at me weird. You know something about it—go on and spit it out."

Sabrina cocks one soot-black eyebrow, looking at me with her cool gray eyes.

"You didn't seem too open to constructive criticism from our friend Estas over there," she says.

My face goes hot. I swallow back the retort that immediately springs to mind. I'm in fight mode right now, and I don't want to turn that on Sabrina. She was trying to help me.

"I want to know what's going on," I tell her.

Sabrina holds up her bound hands, in a silent, *Well, if that's what you really want...*

"Your dad's got a bad reputation," she says.

I frown.

"Everybody has a bad reputation. We're a bunch of criminals."

"Even in a school full of bad guys . . . he's known as a pretty bad guy," Sabrina says.

I want to tell Sabrina to fuck off. That's my father she's talking about—the man who adored me and raised me and taught me everything I know. My dad's brilliant and ambitious. Yes he has a temper, and yes we fight like hell sometimes, but I admire him wholeheartedly.

On the other hand . . . Sabrina's not really the person saying this. The message is screamed at me in the cold disdain of every student I meet.

Sabrina Gallo's the only person who doesn't seem to hate my guts on sight. So it would be pretty stupid to bite her head off as the bearer of bad news.

"I've never heard that before," I say stiffly. "Obviously I think he's great."

"Of course you do," Sabrina says.

I sit there fuming for a minute, pissed that all these kids think they have the right to judge my family, when they're from thieving, murdering stock, just the same as me.

"Why'd you help me, then?" I demand. "If you think Estas is right?"

"I didn't say I thought he was right," Sabrina says. "I don't know your dad; I've never met him. You seem cool, and Estas seems like an asshole. And quite honestly, I didn't put that much thought into it before I decked him. It just felt right in the moment."

That's about the same amount of forethought I was using.

Our eyes meet, and I can't help snorting. Sabrina starts laughing, too.

It's embarrassing as hell arriving in the port of Visine Dvorca tied up like prisoners. But it's also kind of funny how badly I managed to fuck up the first day of school.

Caleb Griffin sees us laughing. He shakes his head at us like we've lost our damned minds. Cara Wilk watches us solemnly.

"She's definitely gonna write a short story about this later," I whisper to Sabrina.

Sabrina hides her face in the cave formed by her arms and her drawn-up knees, shoulders shaking with laughter.

"Thank god my parents won't care if we get expelled before we've even started," she says.

"My dad will throw a party," I say. "He never wanted me to come in the first place."

That thought wipes the smile off my face.

"What's wrong?" Sabrina says. "Isn't that a good thing?"

"Yeah . . ." I say. "I just don't want to give him the satisfaction of thinking he was right."

That's not it, though.

What actually disturbs me is the realization that there's more than one reason my father didn't want me coming to Kingmakers.

4

Nix

The ship has to change directions several times to shoot the gap into the protected harbor of Visine Dvorca. This is the lowest point of the island, encircled by the small village that students are permitted to visit if they don't mind the long walk down from the school.

We'll be riding in wagons on the way up.

I had hoped that the crew would untie us, and the whole first-day fistfight could be forgotten. No such luck—it appears that the punishment will be following us up to Kingmakers.

Sabrina and I are marched onto the luggage wagon, ignominiously seated apart from the other students like convicted criminals.

To my utter outrage, Estas Lomachenko *is* released and allowed to join the rest of the Freshmen like nothing happened.

"What the hell?" I demand of the first mate. "How come he's not in trouble?"

" 'Cause you fuckin' started it," the first mate says. "And 'cause he's the one bleedin' all over himself while you don't have a scratch on you."

The front of Estas' dress shirt is soaked red. He looks extremely grumpy as he unsuccessfully tries to staunch the flow from his nose with a filthy-looking handkerchief provided by the crew.

That's the only comfort I get as the wagons lurch up the unpaved road—that at least Estas looks almost as stupid as Sabrina and me.

Sabrina doesn't seem to mind. I guess she's used to attention. She sits tall and proud on the bench seat, glancing around curiously as we pass through farms and vineyards, thick pine forest, and then wide-open fields, fragrant with the last of the sweet summer hay.

Kingmakers looms on the highest point of the island, a vast stone fortress with bone-pale walls and dark gables. Its gates are guarded by two monolithic figures: a knight with an ax to our left, and a winged woman with an upraised sword to our right. Their stone faces look down on us, coldly forbidding.

The inscription over the entrance reads:

Necessitas Non Habet Legem

Necessity Has No Law

The temperature inside Kingmakers is at least ten degrees colder. The grounds are shadowed by the thick stone walls, not to mention the many towers, parapets, and interior structures that make up the castle. It's like a secret city, whole and entire unto itself, with vast glass greenhouses and terraced gardens and students striding around with a sense of purpose and self-possession that has entirely abandoned me at the moment.

A group of four Seniors wait for us just outside the main Keep. The rest of the students file out of the wagons, called to attention by a bright-eyed blonde girl wearing a pair of pink rhinestone cowboy boots with her school uniform. Even though she's 5'4 at best and could be mistaken for a sorority sister, her tone more closely resembles a drill sergeant. She shouts, "Hurry up fresh meat! We haven't got all day!"

She tips a wink at Cara Wilk, apparently recognizing her.

Then she frowns at the sight of Sabrina Gallo, hands tied, perched in the back of the luggage wagon.

"What's this about?" she demands of the driver.

"Those two gotta go see the Chancellor," he says.

"What for?" the blonde girl cries.

The driver shrugs.

The blonde gives him an irritated scowl but doesn't argue further. Instead, she calls the rest of the students to order as the driver begins to unload the luggage.

"Welcome to Kingmakers!" she shouts. "I'm Chay Wagner, and this is Bodashka Kushnir,"—she nods toward a hulking boy with a blocky jaw and a dull expression—"Matteo Ragusa"—a slim boy with close-cropped dark hair, who gives the Freshmen a wave—"and Isabel Dixon"—a clever-looking black-haired girl with a crooked smile and horribly-bitten fingernails.

"I'm going to be taking charge of the Heirs today. My fellow guides will show the rest of you to your dorms. I should hope you know your own division by now, but just in case you're completely stupid, I'm gonna call your name and you can grab your suitcase and go stand by your guide."

Chay begins with the Accountants, reading the names off her list with the speed of an impatient auctioneer.

Cara Wilk is already retrieving her single suitcase. She gives us a worried look.

"What should I do?" she whispers up to Sabrina. "Should I try to call someone?"

"I'll be fine," Sabrina says, tossing her dark hair back over her shoulders. "Go on, don't stress."

Reluctantly, Cara joins Matteo Ragusa and the rest of the Accountants.

Caleb Griffin is next to depart, splitting off with the brawny and boisterous Enforcers under the care of Bodashka Kushnir. Caleb is less concerned than Cara, only sparing us one last amused glance before galloping off with his new dormmates.

Isabel Dixon takes charge of the Spies.

It's interesting to see the clear physical differences amongst the divisions. The Enforcers are almost entirely male, with a clear preference for size and athleticism. The Accountants are, for lack of a better word, *neat*. They show the most deference to the school dress code, and every one of them appears to have woken up in time to shower this morning. The Spies, by contrast, look like they might have spent the night clubbing, chugged down a Bloody Mary, then pulled their uniforms on over whatever they were wearing before. One of the girls has a leather corset under her school blouse, and one of the guys bears several smeared stamps on the back of his hand from his last outing in civilization.

The Heirs are a mixed bag. Alyssa Chan—the Asian girl who snubbed me on the ship—Sabrina Gallo, and I are the only female Heirs in our year. The rest are an assortment of boys of every nationality whose only unifying characteristic is cocky confidence.

"You looking for a new roommate?" a redheaded Scot asks Chay, sidling up next to her and giving her a seductive grin.

"Afraid not," Chay says. "No dogs allowed in the Solar."

The rest of the male Heirs chortle at the brush-off, but Chay wastes no time wiping the smiles off their faces.

"I'll walk you over to your dorms in the Octagon Tower," she says, "Dean Yenin will take charge of you then—he's not nearly as nice as me, so watch the lip or he'll knock you on your ass."

Estas Lomachenko joins the Heirs, picking up his suitcase and spitting a mouthful of blood out on the grass.

"I hope the Chancellor chucks you off the fucking cliff," he snarls up at us.

"Aww, does your wittle nose hurt?" Sabrina mocks him.

Chay cuts between us before Estas can lunge at Sabrina.

"Join the Heirs," she tells him sternly. Then, looking up at Sabrina, she says, "I'll come up to Chancellor's office as soon as I drop off the Freshmen."

"Don't worry about it," Sabrina says blithely. "You saw that big fuckin' baby, he's not even hurt."

"Well," Chay says, unconvinced. "I'll still come check on you."

Once we're alone with the driver, Sabrina impatiently orders, "Will you untie us already? We're not gonna run away. Where the fuck would we go?"

"Just doing what the first mate said to do," the driver replies stubbornly. He chucks the reigns, encouraging his droopy gray horse to stumble forward again.

Rolling her eyes in annoyance, Sabrina starts wriggling her wrists free of the rope.

It's not too difficult for me to do the same. While the sailors' knots are impressive, the rope itself is too thick for the purpose. We had only remained bound out of a desire to avoid getting in any more trouble.

The driver takes us in a slow half-circle around the Keep, bringing the horse to a stop only twenty yards from where we were sitting before.

"We're here," he says.

"We could have just walked over!" Sabrina shouts at him, utterly annoyed.

"Just doing my job," the driver says.

I can tell Sabrina wants to pop *him* in the nose too, but this time she restrains herself. She shakes the ropes off her wrists and jumps down from the wagon. I follow after her, likewise free, at least for the moment.

"Where's the Chancellor?" Sabrina demands imperiously.

"Top floor," the driver says. "I'm taking you up."

"I'll tell him myself what happened," Sabrina says.

This girl is fucking insane, and I'm loving it.

I always prefer action over waiting, boldness over apology.

"Let's get this over with," I say to Sabrina, grinning.

The driver's horse waits patiently. The driver himself shuffles along behind us, clutching a folded piece of paper that I can only assume is a letter from the first mate tattling on our misdeeds.

We climb five sets of stairs to the topmost floor of the Keep, the driver puffing along behind us. He either smokes or he's even older than he looks.

This is my first time inside one of the Kingmakers buildings. I'm impressed with the luxurious furnishings. Thick carpets blanket the stone floors, the walls are hung with tapestries and oil paintings, and elegant statuary fills the recessed niches in the hallway.

The closer we get, the less I want to meet the Chancellor. I only know Luther Hugo from his foreboding acceptance letter—I didn't get the sense that he was an indulgent headmaster.

Sabrina reaches the double doors of the Chancellor's office, rapping her knuckles against the wood. The driver drags himself up the last few steps, annoyed that he had to hustle to keep up with us.

After a brief pause, a sonorous voice calls, "You may enter."

Sabrina turns the handle.

The room beyond is much larger than I expected. The office appears to be a combination living quarters and working space, including several sitting areas, endless bookshelves, artwork, and personal photographs, and of course, the dark and imposing desk behind which the Chancellor waits.

The rich colors, the fur throws, and the deep fireplace remind me of a hunting lodge—if that lodge were owned by a sultan.

The driver seems determined not to let Sabrina control this part of the proceedings. He practically sprints across the long expanse of carpet to thrust the letter into the Chancellor's hands, saying, "Here! These girls got into trouble on the ship ride over."

Luther Hugo takes the letter.

"Thank you," he says to the driver. "You may go."

The driver looks mildly affronted by this swift dismissal. He was looking forward to watching the hammer fall on our heads. However, the Chancellor's black stare leaves no room for argument.

"Yes, sir. Enjoy the rest of your afternoon," he says humbly, exiting the office with one last glower at Sabrina and me.

However ballsy Sabrina might have been on the way up here, she quails before the Chancellor's deeply-lined face and heavy black brows. Luther Hugo is broad-shouldered and intimidating, even while seated. His chair is throne-like, his double-breasted suit as richly embroidered as an emperor's. His mane of dark hair and his beard are shot through with silver threads as bright as wire.

We stand silently while Luther scans the letter from the first mate.

Though his gaze is fixed on the paper, the eyes of every photograph on the wall seem to stare down at us. I recognize some of the famous people hobnobbing with the Chancellor. Others look like mafia. To a frame, they're all wealthy and distinguished, the pictures taken in exotic locales: on yachts and estates, at banquets and on golf courses. With the exception of the photograph tucked in the corner behind Luther's desk—this is the only picture featuring a group of students: three frowning boys, and one dark-haired girl who beams in triumph as she shakes the Chancellor's hand.

Luther places the letter facedown on the desk in front of him so we can't read what was written about us.

"You make a poor start at my school," he says in his low, rumbling voice.

"We weren't at your school yet," Sabrina says.

She somehow manages to keep her tone respectful while contradicting the Chancellor.

He raises one pointed eyebrow, his beetle-black eyes fixed on Sabrina.

"Who do you think owns that ship, missy?" he says.

Sabrina is wise enough not to answer that rhetorical question.

I can't stay silent, however.

"It was my fault," I blurt out. "I'm the one who hit Estas. Sabrina got caught in the middle."

"Sabrina didn't hit Estas as well?" the Chancellor inquires, eyebrow still raised.

"Yes, I did," Sabrina says honestly. "But he deserved it. He was threatening Nix and insulting her father."

"And you think that justifies breaking the rules," the Chancellor says.

"Well," Sabrina says, "necessity has no law."

I can't believe she's quoting the school motto at him.

I'm starting to think she *wants* to get us kicked out.

Well, whatever happens, I have to stand by Sabrina like she stood by me.

"We're extremely sorry," I say to the Chancellor. "*Both* of us. I can promise you, it won't happen again."

"Oh, that is a near-certainty," the Chancellor says coolly.

Shit. That doesn't sound good.

Sabrina bites the edge of her full lip, obviously hearing the same note of impending doom. Throwing all caution to the wind, she cries, "You would have done the same thing!"

The Chancellor slowly turns to face her, his expression both threatening and mildly surprised at the sheer audacity of this girl.

Sabrina persists, knowing that it's all-or-nothing in this moment.

"You'd never let someone slander the Hugo name! We're mafia— we follow no law but our own. All we have is our word and our honor. If we don't defend it, if we don't show it matters to us . . . then no one would trust us. No business could be done."

Sabrina's cheeks are flushed, her eyes as electric as storm clouds. She refuses to drop the Chancellor's dark stare.

I keep my mouth shut, knowing better than to interrupt their battle of wills.

"Sabrina Gallo . . ." the Chancellor says softly. "Cousin to Leo Gallo and Miles Griffin."

"That's right," Sabrina says, chin up-tilted.

"I'm beginning to regret extending admission to any of your family," he says.

"This is not a school for the meek and submissive," Sabrina says.

"No," the Chancellor agrees. "But it *is* a school, and you *will* follow my rules while you are here. Or you will reap the consequences. Is that understood?"

"Yes," Sabrina says.

"Absolutely." I nod.

"Good," he says. And then, his black eyes fixing on me. "You can start with your uniform."

"Sorry," I say, face as scarlet as my hair. "I didn't know we were supposed to wear it on the way over . . ."

Hugo ignores this.

"Get to your dorms," he says. "And hope that we have no more occasion for conversation."

He turns back to his papers, dismissing us.

Sabrina and I hurry out of his office, limp with relief.

As soon as the doors close behind us, I say, "Fucking hell, girl. I don't know how you had the balls to talk to him like that. And I thought my dad was scary..."

A small smile plays at the corners of her mouth.

"There's two kinds of men in the world," she says. "The kind who want to hurt you . . . and the kind who want to be persuaded by you."

I gaze at Sabrina with an entirely new level of admiration. This girl's eighteen years old, and she can bend Luther Hugo around her finger...

"Teach me your ways," I say, breathless and awed.

Sabrina shakes her head, coming back to reality.

"Come on," she says. "We better go grab our bags, if that dickhead driver even left them for us."

We jog back down the stairs, finding my duffle bag and Sabrina's suitcase unceremoniously chucked on the lawn. That's better than the alternative, so we scoop them up happily, high on the relief of not being expelled.

As we're doing so, Chay Wagner and a tall girl with a long sheet of ash-blonde hair and dark gothic makeup come running up to us.

"What happened?" Chay cries.

"Do we need to go talk to the Chancellor?" the goth girl asks.

"No, it's fine," Sabrina says, already recovering her grin. "He let us off with a warning."

"He did?" Chay says, mouth hanging open.

"I think he liked Sabrina," I tell her.

"*Liked* you?" the goth girl says, mystified. "Since when does the Chancellor *like* anybody?"

Sabrina shrugs, already bored of talking about it. "This is Nix Moroz, by the way," she says.

"Anna Wilk," the goth girl replies, giving me that wary and slightly repulsed look that I'm already coming to despise.

In this instance, I can't exactly fault her. I nearly got her cousin expelled within ten minutes of meeting her.

"I'm really sorry about all this," I say, trying to clear the air. "I'm not here to cause problems. I just want to go to class like everybody else."

Anna sighs. "It's Kingmakers," she says. "Causing problems *is* like everybody else. Classes are a secondary pursuit."

"Let's go drop your bags off before we miss dinner," Chay says.

The older girls give us a quick tour of campus as they lead us to our dorm.

"You already saw the Keep," Chay says. "That's where most of your classes will be held, except for the ones in the Smithy, or the Armory, or the shooting range outside the castle walls."

"A shooting range?" I say, perking up.

"You like to shoot?" Anna asks.

"Yeah." I nod. "I go hunting with my dad—bow hunting, mostly. I like archery in general—target shooting, trick shots . . ."

"You'll be good at Marksmanship, then," Chay says.

"That's the Armory over there," Anna points to a low, round building west of the Keep. "That's where all your Combat classes will be held. There's an underground pool under the gym."

Kingmakers is sounding better and better.

"I love swimming," I say.

We're walking to the north end of campus, passing a large, terraced garden fragrant with mint, basil, rosemary, and lavender. Beyond the garden, I see a tall, angular structure that can only be the Octagon Tower.

"That's where the male Heirs have their dorms," Chay says, confirming my guess. "And then over here—" We pass a long, stone platform surrounded by orange trees. "Here's where we stay—the Solar."

The Solar is smaller than the Octagon Tower, likewise bordering the north wall, with its windows looking out over the dizzying drop down the limestone cliffs to the ocean below.

The rooms are bright and airy, the furnishings in delicate shades of blue, silver, and cream. Large mirrors hang on the common room walls, reflecting the clouds and sky from the glass-paned windows.

"These were the private quarters of the Lord and Lady of the castle," Chay explains. "So it's the prettiest part of Kingmakers."

"The Chancellor's office wasn't bad," Sabrina says.

Anna gives her a sharp look. "Be careful, Sabrina. Just because he was lenient once, don't make the mistake of thinking he's all bark. Remember what he did to Ozzy's mom."

I don't know who Ozzy is, or what happened to his mom, but I'm guessing it wasn't good.

"You're right," Sabrina says. And then, with an apologetic look at Chay, "I'm sorry."

"It's okay," Chay says, squaring her shoulders. "Ozzy's doing great. Honestly, I just want to get this damn school year over and done with so we're not long-distance anymore."

"You guys are gonna have to share a room," Anna tells us. "Alyssa Chan demanded the single."

Sabrina laughs. "She was trying to buddy up with me in Dubrovnik—guess she changed her mind."

I feel a little flush of relief that Sabrina doesn't seem to mind rooming with me, even after everything that happened.

Anna is still watching me as the two older girls show us our room on the second floor.

"It's for the best," Chay says. "That single is the size of a closet. Remember poor Zoe trying to squeeze in there?"

Anna laughs. "That seems like a hundred years ago."

I'm reminded again how small my network is, compared to all these people known to Sabrina.

Our dorm room is no closet—it's open and spacious, with twin beds pushed up against opposite walls, a carved wardrobe, and a stunning view.

Anna and Chay look around nostalgically.

"We stayed here first year," Anna says.

"I almost like it better than our room on the top floor," Chay says. "The one we have now is bigger, but the window looks the other way over the grounds. I liked the ocean."

"It's tradition, though," Anna says. "The Seniors get the Lord's room. This one probably belonged to a Lady-In-Waiting."

"Or a mistress." Chay grins.

Anna seems to remember we were supposed to be hurrying.

"Drop your bags off!" she says. "No time to unpack right now. Dinner's only an hour long, and we already missed half of it."

"Which bed do you want?" I ask Sabrina.

"I'll take left," she says.

"I'm right then," I say, throwing my duffle down on the rough gray blanket stretched over the mattress with military precision.

"We'll wait outside for you to change," Chay says, eyeing my cargo pants. "They're not fussed about *how* you wear the uniform, but you are supposed to wear it."

"Right." I nod. "I'll be quick."

5

THE SPY AKA ARES CIRILLO

I'm standing at the window of the Octagon Tower when Anna and Chay cross the lawn, followed closely by two Freshmen girls. Through the bubbled glass I see them: Sabrina Gallo, and the other girl, tall and fit, with a mane of flaming red hair trailing down her back. She's dressed in military gear, an olive-green duffle bag slung over her shoulder.

The loathing that boils up inside of me is immediate and intense.

She looks like her father.

Same bold set to the shoulders, same stride. Same bluish cast to her fair skin that seems to make the coarse, wild hair burn all the brighter by comparison.

Those features are scorched in my memory as the most abhorrent, the most revolting.

The hatred surprises me. I've spent so much time in frustration and waiting that I forgot I could still feel anger this acutely.

It's a good thing.

Because it's finally time to take action.

I've been waiting three years and two months for this moment. Searching, planning, scheming.

Not all predators hunt in the open. The zone-tailed hawk looks exactly like a turkey vulture. It will even fly among a flock of turkey vultures, wheeling and circling like one of their brothers. And then, at a time known only to itself, it will break from formation, attacking one of its former fellows as its prey.

That's how I have to think of myself now.

I've spent three years pretending to be Ares—calm, kind, patient. Humble.

At first it was easy. After all, I know Ares better than anyone. His family's farm abutted our summer house in Poseidonia, our land next to their land with no fence in between. Ares and I grew up together, sailing around Syros in his father's skiff, feeding his fainting goats, our younger siblings playing hide and seek in the vineyards.

Our fathers were friends, and our mothers too. His father loved to read, just like mine. They used to trade books from their libraries, my father's biographies for Galen Cirillo's military histories.

Galen Cirillo was a gentle and intelligent man. He'd think for a long time before speaking. Devoted to his wife and children.

Though the Cirillos are one of the oldest mafia families, Helio Cirillo gave up all his ties to crime when he married Ares' grandmother. Ares' father likewise lived a simple life—sometimes poor, but always happy.

The night we were attacked by the Malina, Galen woke to the sound of gunfire. He took his hunting rifle down from the wall, running across the fields toward our house.

I don't know exactly what happened next. Only what my uncle Dominik found three days later: two of Marko Moroz's men with 7 mm Remington bullets in their skulls. And Galen lying dead in our dining room with his throat cut. I think he was trying to get upstairs to help us.

The Cirillos want revenge for that night just as badly as I do.

Ares wrote to Kingmakers, requesting acceptance for the fall, as is his right as heir of one of the ten founding families.

No one here knows him by sight. The Cirillos are too small, too insignificant. I doubt Marko Moroz even knows that he killed Galen—if he noticed him at all, he might have thought he was our gardener.

But he was our friend. Our ally.

He will be avenged, as will my father.

I took Ares' place on the ship to Kingmakers. I wore his clothes. Carried his backpack. We look alike—our parents used to joke that we were meant to be brothers. The only brother either of us had.

No one recognized me. I'd been living in America where my father was capitalizing on the legalization of marijuana, opening massive dispensaries in Oregon, Colorado, and Nevada. I hadn't been back to St. Petersburg in years.

The very first night in Dubrovnik, Bram Van Der Berg and Valon Hoxha mocked me for my shabby belongings and my weak family name, never realizing that they were speaking to the son of the most powerful Bratva boss in Russia.

I swallowed the taunts. I took the abuse. And I listened—constantly listened for any information on Marko Moroz.

I boarded the ship. I came to this island under my new identity. When class started, I hid my skills. I pretended to be quiet, studious, focused. I pretended to be uninterested in girls or dating. All the while looking for the information I needed.

I've played my part well. No one has ever guessed that I'm not actually Ares Cirillo—that the real Ares has been living in secret in one of my family's properties in Nevada. He's been managing our Las Vegas dispensary, taking in almost a million dollars a day in cash, cash that we desperately need to keep the high table off our asses so they don't suspect that my father is not actually running the business anymore.

If those sharks scented blood in the water . . . they'd rip us to shreds. St. Petersburg is too tempting a prize to expect loyalty from the Bratva.

I hid in plain sight, and I gathered crumbs of information while searching for that one crucial document that we hope is here at Kingmakers.

I never expected it to take this long. I never thought I'd still be here, three years later.

But I am here.

And now, so is Nix Moroz.

If Plan A fails, then we have to go through with Plan B.

I despise Plan B.

Unfortunately, it doesn't matter what I like or what I want. We're far past preferences.

I wait until the new female Heirs have followed Chay and Anna inside the Solar, and then I head west along the north wall, all the way to the Library Tower.

I know this part of campus better than any other—better even than my own dorm room. I come here almost every day.

I know I shouldn't. Miss Robin has warned me several times that I'm being too obvious, taking too many chances.

I can't help it. I never realized the toll it would take on me, lying every single day. Never answering questions honestly, even in casual conversation. Never hearing my own name spoken aloud. Never being hugged by a friend who truly knows me.

I'm separated from everyone I love—except for her.

So I push open the heavy wooden doors to the library, catching the scent of ancient paper, dusty rugs, spiced tea, and a hint of that perfume that reminds me so powerfully of home.

My mother's scent reminds me of my father's. There was always something similar between them. Like coffee and vanilla, or sea salt and cedar . . . things meant to pair together, each enhancing the other.

My parents were made for each other, partners in a way I've never seen in any other coupling. So alike that a novel's worth of words seemed to pass between them in a glance.

Before they met, neither one believed in soulmates. Neither of them was looking for love. They were the most independent people imaginable—my father, a ruthless *Pakhan,* subduing the city of St. Petersburg, smashing any rivals in his path. My mother an assassin for hire, expert in the subtle murder of powerful men without a trace of evidence left behind.

My father was supposed to be another name on her death list.

She breached the security of his monastery. Crept into his bedroom in the dead of night. Held a syringe full of poison to the side of his throat.

And then . . . fate intervened.

His eyes opened and locked on hers.

They fought a desperate, bloody battle in his bedroom, each trying to slay the other.

Each had met their match, for the very first time.

When my father ripped off her balaclava, he saw not an enemy . . . but his own reflection looking back at him, in female form.

I climb the long, spiraling ramp of the Library Tower. Since it's only the first week of school, most of the tables are empty of students. No one is yet burdened with enough homework or enough anxiety of upcoming exams to forgo the pleasures of the sunny day outside.

My mother sits at her desk, dressed in her ridiculous disguise.

It's difficult to hide how beautiful she is. She's dyed her hair a distracting shade of red. The repeated applications have caused her sleek curls to become frizzy and unruly. She wears several layers of chunky woolen cardigans, not only to ward off the chill of the stone tower but also to disguise the athletic figure beneath. Her granny glasses, thick tights, and orthopedic shoes are supposed to make her look older. None of it works, not really. The only thing that can mar her lovely face is the expression of unhappiness that settles over her when no one is looking.

These three years have worn on her even worse than on me. She was bound to my father, body and soul. They never spent a single day apart if they could help it. She's been in constant misery without him.

The only thing that keeps her going is that fire inside of her. It never goes out, not even for a second. My mother never gives up.

Even now, at this moment, she's poring over maps. She's scoured every fucking blueprint in the archives beneath the library, and now she's searching them all again. Because even though she hasn't found what we're looking for, she won't stop.

"Hello, Miss Robin," I say quietly.

She looks up, her eyes red and exhausted behind the thick frames of her glasses. She doesn't seem to have slept.

"Hello, Ares," she replies.

She says we always have to use these names, even if we know for certain we're alone where no one can hear.

She says it's the tiny mistakes that get you caught—the errors that don't seem to matter until all of a sudden they do.

I look around once more, to make sure there's nobody within earshot.

"She's here," I tell her. "I saw her with Chay and Anna, and Sabrina Gallo."

My mother nods slowly.

"Good," she says. "I thought he might not send her, even after they signed the contract. Predators have a sense for traps."

I try to swallow the burning acid in my throat.

"I don't know if I can do this," I say.

She sets down her pencil and takes off her fake glasses, so she can fix me with her ferocious dark eyes.

"You can do whatever you decide to do," she says sternly.

"I hate her," I hiss. "How can I get close to her when I want to strangle her on sight?"

My mother tilts her head to the side, showing the sharp curve of her jaw.

"You get close to her by any means necessary," she says.

My face is hot. "You mean . . . seduce her?"

My mother laughs softly. "Befriend her. Help her. Earn her trust. If she's already associating with Sabrina Gallo, it should be all the easier. Manipulate the circumstances if you have to—create a need and then fill it."

I feel like she's asking me to cuddle up with a viper.

Marko Moroz is the most treacherous counterfeit of a human being I've ever encountered. I don't want to get close to his daughter any more than I'd want to roll around in a pile of his dirty laundry. The thought disgusts me.

Reading my face, my mother says, "She's his weakness. His one vulnerability. You know this can't be done by force—only by subterfuge. Or we'll lose everything. All the time, all the money, all the suffering . . . for nothing."

I force myself to nod. "I'll do it. Whatever it takes," I say.

"I know you will," she says, unblinking. "You are his son through and through."

I swallow hard.

"Loyalty in Blood," I say.

It's the motto inscribed on the gates of our monastery. And on the band of my father's ring, wherever that might be.

"Loyalty in Blood," my mother replies.

6

Nix

My first week at Kingmakers is not at all the scintillating hubbub of social expansion that I'd hoped. If anything, I'm even lonelier than I was at home.

The only Freshman who will talk to me is Sabrina Gallo.

Everybody else avoids me like I'm infected with the plague.

At first I didn't want to believe what Sabrina said—that it was all because of my father and his reputation.

But by the tenth, or twentieth, or thirtieth brush-off, it was pretty fucking clear that my father is feared and loathed to an unusual degree, even by mafia standards.

It's messing with my head.

I don't understand how the man I love and respect more than anyone can be known as a monster.

"What did he do, exactly?" I demand of Sabrina, after yet another class where one of my fellow students hissed at me like a medieval villager warding off a demon.

"I don't really know anything about it," Sabrina says, keeping her steady pace across the commons as we walk from the Armory to the Keep.

Her tone is light, but I can't help feeling that she's lying. She doesn't want to get into it. She's willing to be my friend, but she wants nothing to do with my father and his sordid history.

It's infuriating, feeling like everyone around me knows more about my own family than I do. Feeling like everyone is in on the secret but me.

I suppose I could ask Estas Lomachenko. He seems to think his family was wronged by mine. He's certainly spreading that story to the very few people who weren't already prejudiced against me.

And I'll admit, it looks pretty fucking bad that I don't have friends or allies even amongst the other Ukrainians. At Kingmakers, most of the cliques revolve around mafia groups: the New York

Italians stick together, likewise the Taiwan Triads, and the Dublin Irish.

I have no friends from my father's Malina. In fact, none of his men are allowed to marry or have children. Their loyalty is to him alone.

I'm starting to realize how odd that is compared to other mafia groups that center around family.

This is what really has me twisted up in a pretzel: my father told me that he didn't want me coming to Kingmakers because it wasn't safe. He said he had too many enemies.

Well, that fucking much was true. But I think the real issue is that he didn't want me to know what everyone says about him: that he's a snake, a backstabber. That he has no honor.

I tell myself it can't be true.

After all, there's bad blood between plenty of families. Grudges and feuds are as common as Swiss bank accounts amongst the mafia.

Still, I can't shake this nagging feeling that my father hasn't been completely open with me.

I'm his heir, his only child.

I thought I was his protégé. I thought he trusted me.

Now I worry that he only viewed me as a kid, feeding me the Disney version of his life and business.

My paradigm is cracking. It feels like my skull is splitting apart.

My only release is exercise.

Thank god we're allowed to leave the campus grounds whenever we want. I've been tramping all over the island when class is done.

It makes me feel less alone to hike the paths along the cliffs or to run through the forest trails in the cool green shade of the river bottoms. There I'm surrounded by birds, butterflies, rabbits, and squirrels. Even the occasional deer.

I feel alive when I'm surrounded by living things.

Some people think that hunters don't like animals—nothing could be further from the truth. I see *myself* as an animal. I only kill like a bear or a panther would do—to eat.

I run around like a wild thing until I'm scratched and filthy, until the sky is dark. Only then do I come back to Kingmakers, to the confinement of stone walls and cold stares.

I sleep like the dead, because I'm exhausted in body and brain.

Our classes are incredibly difficult. The Heirs are expected to learn most of what the students in the other divisions will know —everything from bribery and extortion to interrogation and foreign investment. After all, we're the ones who have to run the whole operation. We can't manage our people if we don't know what they're doing.

I thought I understood my father's business. He's taken me to every one of his properties. Every strip club, every casino, every safehouse, every warehouse. I know all his men, not just the inner circle who live on our compound.

Still, the complexity of criminal enterprise is only now becoming apparent to me in the endless lectures, charts, and textbooks meted out by our professors.

I'm drowning in work and classes have just started. I'm dreading exam season even more—thank god my father doesn't particularly care about my grades, unlike the draconian parents who call every week to grill their children on their scores.

Sabrina and I head into our Extortion class, taught by the brilliant Professor Ito. He's a small man, slight, well-dressed in impeccably-tailored black suits. He's the only professor I've seen who wears a tie; his are hand-dyed silk. His lecture style is clear and methodical, which is the only reason I can keep up with the avalanche of information.

Sabrina tells me that he used to operate a Moriarty-level network of crime in Hamamatsu. It was immensely profitable until it attracted the attention of the Yakuza. After a long and bloody battle, Professor Ito sold his holdings for a boggling amount of money and retired to Kingmakers.

"I bet he only teaches here a couple of years," Sabrina whispers to me as Professor Ito takes his place at the front of the classroom. "He's probably waiting for the heat to cool off in Japan. Lots of professors do that. It's a sanctuary here—nobody can attack you. By the time you go back to society, it's all water under the bridge."

I chuckle. "Depending how badly you pissed off your enemies . . ."

"Extortion," Professor Ito says, hands clasped loosely in front of him, and jaw tilted up so his voice rings clear and melodious across the heads of the students. "It is the bedrock of our business. The lifeblood of mafia. The one tool you must always use . . ."

He gazes around at us, his eyes clear and piercing behind the round lenses of his glasses.

I've seen stupid-looking people turn out to be smart. But I've never seen a man with that bright and avian stare who was anything less than a raptor.

"Why is that, do you think?" he barks at us. "Why is extortion so necessary?"

"Well . . . you get money," the pudgy boy sitting next to me says, with the confused expression of someone who knows his answer is too obvious to be correct.

"There are many ways to get money," Professor Ito says. "None is more crucial than the others simply by nature of providing cash."

He waits, the seconds stretching out agonizingly slow. His teaching method always involves questions to the class and torturous pauses afterward. I'm not sure if he's trying to motivate us to learn by burning the memory of our ignorance into our brain, or he really believes we can figure out the answer on our own.

Instead of staring at the blank faces around me, I try to consider his question. What purpose does extortion serve besides money?

"Control," I say aloud.

"That's right," Professor Ito inclines his head toward me. "It is *essential* that you control your entire territory on a fundamental level through its businesses and citizens. Everyone must pay you. Everyone must be involved. And in return—this is the crucial part, ladies and gentlemen! *You must provide a service in return.* Extortion is not robbery! They pay for protection, and you provide that protection to them. Mafia are, in effect, a professional security force. An army controlled by a king. You Heirs will be that king."

I copy his words carefully into my notebook.

Sabrina sits on my other side, arms folded over the chest straining the bounds of a very tight blouse. Her top button is barely hanging on for dear life, a struggle observed with great interest by our male seatmates.

Sabrina never takes notes or reads the textbook. Yet she beats me on every quiz.

Professor Ito continues. "The people accept the rule of the king when the kingdom prospers. Businesses, neighborhoods, families: happy, safe, and thriving. You must never become greedy, demanding too much. And you must never fail to provide the benefit inherent in the extortion contract."

Sabrina raises her hand.

"What about the cops?" she says. "They already consider themselves the 'professional security force.' "

"The police are a rival gang," Professor Ito says. "Never forget that. They don't actually want to destroy you—then they themselves would cease to exist. But they want to be the most powerful gang in the city. If you intend to take that spot, you will have to force homage from them."

He explains how to collaborate with the cops—how to punish rivals and disloyal employees within our own ranks by handing them over to the police as token sacrifices. How to bribe and blackmail officers, and how to liaise with the politicians that control the police force.

While Professor Ito is talking, I'm remembering instances when I saw my father take the actions described. I'm beginning to understand the theory, the process of what I had only known by sight.

It's strangely addictive learning about the world I've always inhabited. Like a hand pulling back a gauze curtain so I can see clearly.

Sabrina seems equally fascinated. She keeps her cool gray stare fixed upon the professor wherever he walks in the room, instead of getting bored and gazing out the window as usual.

She's been a good roommate so far—reasonably tidy, or at least willing to clean up her mess now and then. Communicative and cheerful. I'd say we're becoming friends.

The only problem is that Sabrina already had a bunch of ready-made friends when she got to Kingmakers. I feel awkward horning in on their group when I know they probably don't want me around.

"So remember," Professor Ito says, wrapping up his lecture, "enforce the law of silence. This is the one point on which you must be ruthless: snitching is punished more harshly than non-payment. Silence is control. Silence is collaboration."

He takes off his glasses, polishing them with a silk cloth drawn from his breast pocket. When he puts them on again, the lenses glint like diamond.

"Extortion controls your territory. Other schemes layer on top: drug trafficking, gun running, gambling . . . always remembering that the frosting must not cause the cake to collapse. Never let your city become a war zone. Keep profit and quality of life in balance."

The professor dismisses us.

Sabrina chuckles as she snatches up her school bag.

"What?" I say.

"He almost makes us sound altruistic," she says. "I do intend to be a benevolent queen. Unless somebody fucks with me."

She slings her bag over her shoulder, heading down the deep stone staircase of the Keep.

The hallways are crowded with students. That was the last class of the day—now everybody's heading to the dining hall.

I've got no complaint about the food at Kingmakers. My dad likes to eat, but he has no taste, so none of the chefs at our compound have ever been good.

Also, I'm fucking starving all the time so I'm hardly picky.

I follow Sabrina out into the late-afternoon sunshine. The light turns her skin from tan to gold. It makes every male head in a half-mile radius twist toward us. Only five seconds pass before we're joined by Hedeon Gray, Leo Gallo, and Leo's tall friend who I've seen at a distance but not yet met. The boys are lured in to Sabrina like bees to honey.

"How's class, kiddo?" Leo says, reaching out a long-fingered hand to ruffle Sabrina's hair.

She nimbly slips his grasp, falling into pace next to Hedeon instead. Hedeon pretends not to notice, but pulls his shoulders back all of a sudden, standing taller.

"Class is great," Sabrina replies. "I knew you guys were exaggerating when you said Kingmakers was hard."

"Or you're just smarter than us, is that what you're saying?" Leo laughs, shaking a finger at her.

"I dunno." Sabrina grins at him wickedly, "Can the same cousin be the smartest AND the best looking?"

"No fucking way are you the best-looking cousin!" Leo scoffs, genuinely offended.

"You don't care if I'm the smartest, though," Sabrina snorts.

"Fuck no," Leo says. "That's why I've got Anna here, in case I need to fill out a crossword puzzle."

Anna Wilk has just caught up with us, her fair hair twisted up in a knot on top of her head, and her tights artfully shredded beneath the hem of her black plaid skirt.

Leo grabs her hand and pulls her close so he can kiss her.

They make a striking couple: Leo tall and tan, with a dazzling smile and the easy grace of an athlete, Anna stark and pale, her ice-blue eyes cutting straight to the soul.

This is the other reason I've been nervous to join Sabrina's table in the dining hall—every damn person she associates with is gorgeous. They all have this glamor around them, even Hedeon with his perpetual scowl, and Leo's tall friend in his shabby uniforms and cheap shoes—Ares, I think he's called.

I fall into step by Ares, noticing that our strides are almost exactly the same length. I look up at his face—it's nice to look up to someone again. Makes me miss my dad.

He's got a lean, tanned face. A dark thatch of hair with streaks of sun in it. His eyes are mostly blue with a little green in them. I think Sabrina said he was Greek—he must be, with that name.

"I'm Ares," he confirms.

"Nix," I hold out my hand.

I'd stopped doing that, with the reception I'd been getting from my fellow students. But I forgot, and now I have to watch the shudder of repulsion that crosses his features before he forces himself to take my hand and give it a brief shake.

His hand is warm. I can feel the bones shifting beneath the muscle and skin, like deep tectonic plates.

"You're Sabrina's roommate?" he asks.

"That's right."

"I room with Leo." He nods toward Leo Gallo, who's now whispering something in Anna Wilk's ear, to which Anna grins and agrees.

Ares has a deep and resonating voice. It vibrates across my skin, like a bass speaker set too close.

His eyes, as beautiful a color as they may be, are not pacific in any sense of the word. They're fixed on me with frightful intensity. I'm becoming too used to this to care, but I get the sense that he loathes me. That he hates me on sight, when I've only spoken three words to him.

After we've all filled our trays at the dining hall, I'm surprised that Ares voluntarily sits next to me on the long wooden bench. Sabrina drops down on my other side, Hedeon Gray directly across from her, and Anna Wilk and Leo next to Hedeon.

Cara Wilk arrives a few minutes later, squeezing in beside Anna.

The sisters are a fascinating lesson in genetics: their coloring completely different, but their features almost identical. As if they were formed from the same mold but painted in alternate shades. If they were fairies, Anna would be the ice queen, and

Cara the woodland sprite. Cara's dark hair and hazel eyes were made for the green of the school uniforms.

"How are you doing, Nix?" Cara says to me cheerfully.

I haven't seen much of her since the ship ride over. The Accountants and the Heirs only share a few classes.

"I'm great," I say. And then, more honestly, "Pretty good, at least."

"Kingmakers is an adjustment," Anna Wilk says in her low, clear voice.

She's watching me without the same level of friendliness as her sister. Hedeon likewise seems to find my presence unpleasant. Only Sabrina seems completely relaxed—I guess she figures if I were gonna shank her in her sleep, I would have done it already.

I hate this pariah feeling. It makes me anxious and aggressive, when usually I'm cheerful and aggressive.

How am I supposed to prove I'm a decent person when I feel ready to snap at any moment?

The more I try to act "normal," the more unnatural everything feels. I hardly remember how to hold my fork.

"Have you met everybody?" Sabrina says, looking around the table.

"I think so," I say.

Even as she's asking, a tall blond boy, a petite girl, and a black-haired guy with a scar across his right eye all crowd onto our table.

"We're running out of seats!" the blond boy complains.

"I'm not sitting back over there with Valon," the black-haired one says, jerking his head toward a table on the opposite side of the room. "He chews so fucking loud."

"That's Dean Yenin, Cat Romero, and Bram Van Der Berg," Sabrina helpfully informs me.

Her introduction draws three pairs of eyes in my direction. Bram scowls until the scar across his eye forms one solid line.

"What the fuck is *she* doing here?" he says.

"She's my guest," Sabrina informs him icily.

I've had enough of this shit.

"What do you care where I sit?" I snap. "I don't even fucking know you."

Bram's face fills with blood, his skin flushing red and the scar turning white. He leans across the table, his nails digging into the wood.

"Oh, you don't know me?" he says softly. "You've never heard the name Bram Van Der Berg before?"

"No," I say, frowning.

"What about Frans Van Der Berg? He was my uncle. He taught me how to fight and how to drive. Then he made a deal with your father. And somehow he ended up upside down in a vat of acid, with all his fuckin' teeth pulled out. Does that sound *familiar* to you?"

My stomach feels like it had a rock shoved down inside of it. I can feel everyone at the table watching me.

"I don't know what happened to your uncle," I say stiffly. "And I don't think you know the whole story, either."

"I know what your father did," Bram hisses.

His teeth are bared, his hands trembling like he'd like to wrap them around my throat.

Everyone else at the table is silent, staring at us like Bram is the judge and they're the jury.

To my surprise, it's Ares who intervenes.

"She's not her father," he says. "We all have violent histories. The point of Kingmakers is that you're supposed to leave the grudges at the door."

"Fuck that!" Bram spits, thrusting his tray away from him and standing up. "And fuck *you*," he snarls at me, before turning and stalking out of the dining hall.

Dean Yenin stands up as well. "I'll go talk to him," he says, resting his hand on Cat's shoulder. "Stay and enjoy your dinner, my love."

Cat's cheeks flush pink, drowning out her freckles. She squeezes the hand on her shoulder before letting him go.

I can hardly stand the awkward silence that follows.

"I can leave, too," I say, looking around at them all with a defiant pride I don't really feel.

"Nix," Leo says, the kindness of his voice almost unbearable to me—I'm afraid it's going to make me crack. "You wouldn't believe the shit that's gone down just in our own families. Remember, I've been here three years already. Dean and I wanted to kill each other first year. Now we're friends. Bram will come around . . . and so will everybody else."

Anna looks less convinced, but she nods slowly.

"You'll find your place here," she says to me. "Everyone does."

I don't know if she intends that place to be at her table.

I eat my food silently, while everyone else tries to return to normal conversation.

Though Bram left the dining hall, I can still feel the angry glares and the barely-suppressed mutters of other students.

And I know, I just fucking know, if I look across the dining hall to the Odessa Mafia's table, Estas Lomachenko will be smiling in delight.

Regardless of what Leo said, there doesn't seem to be anything normal about how much everyone hates my family.

7

Ares

Because I'm dreading befriending Nix Moroz, I put it off during the first week of school. I tell myself I'll watch her first and learn more about her.

That's not exactly easy to do, because Freshmen and Seniors don't have any classes together. The one shared class was boxing, but that's over since Snow returned to New York.

Nix is restless and highly active. Any time I catch a glimpse of her outside of school hours, she's heading off for a run in the fields around the castle or making use of the shooting range or the gym. From the dampness of her hair when she leaves the Armory, I'm guessing she also likes to swim.

That's why I find myself rolling out of bed at an ungodly hour on Sunday morning, pulling on the tight black swim trunks provided by the school.

I walk down the wide staircase of the Octagon Tower, skirting the edge of the terraced herb garden, then crossing the deserted grounds toward the Armory. Thick fog blankets the lawn, the buildings looming up unexpectedly like ships moving through the mist. I can smell the salt of the ocean far below us, and I feel the first chill that always comes in the autumn—subtle at first, before tightening its grip on the castle.

Very few students get up early on the weekends. Even fewer of the professors—the mafia world is nocturnal, and old habits die hard. You're more likely to see Professor Lyons or the Chancellor himself strolling the grounds at 2:00 in the morning than at 6:00 a.m.

The squat Armory looks like a hut with its rounded walls and pointed roof. I push my way inside, hearing the steady *thwack* of someone hitting the heavy bag over and over again.

I already know it's Dean Yenin before I see him standing, shirtless and sweating, on the opposite side of the gym. His hands are wrapped. He drives his fists into the swinging bag in relentless rhythm. With his back to me, I can see the ugly scars from the whipping he took last year, all but obliterating the Siberian tiger that once crawled up his spine.

His back looks almost as bad as Hedeon's.

My stomach squirms guiltily.

Hedeon Gray has been digging for clues about his biological parents.

I could tell him everything he wants to know.

Instead I have to pretend to be his friend, his confidante, while secretly blocking him from ever discovering the truth—yet another task assigned to me that I loathe.

Dean hears my footsteps on the padded mats and turns.

"Morning," he says, nodding to me.

"Working hard as ever," I say.

"That's right," Dean says, hitting the bag again. "I used to come in here to blow off steam . . ." he grins. "Now I'm just trying to look good for Cat."

I laugh.

"I don't think you have to worry about that," I say.

Cat can't take her eyes off Dean—she melts like butter every time he comes near her. Leo and Anna are likewise completely besotted with each other. Zoe moved to Los Angeles with Miles. I barely see Chay outside of class hours because she sneaks away to talk to Ozzy on her contraband cellphone.

All my friends have paired off. It's just me left alone. Always alone.

And now I'm supposed to make a new friend—the last person on the fucking planet I want to spend time around.

Sighing, I descend the stone steps to the underground pool beneath the Armory.

Siren — Kailee Morgue
Spotify → geni.us/spy-spotify
Apple Music → geni.us/spy-apple

The pool is a massive sinkhole in the limestone, full of salt water. The cave in which it resides shimmers with green light. Deep ridges and folds score the chalky walls.

I don't hear splashing, so for a moment I think I got up early for nothing. Then I see the long, sleek form cutting across the pool, swift and soundless.

I've already seen her athleticism in the gym.

That's nothing compared to how she moves in the water.

She kicks off from the wall, flipping over and swimming below the surface for ninety yards before resurfacing for breath. Her legs move in fluid tandem like fins, her arms scything through the water without leaving a ripple.

Her motion is hypnotic. I watch her pass back and forth a dozen times before I realize I'm supposed to be getting in the pool myself.

I strip off my shirt, leaving it puddled by the steps on top of my shoes. Then I wade down into the water.

It's cold, but I know I'll warm up soon enough. I begin swimming laps, while keeping Nix in my peripheral view.

The underground pool is several times standard size. Nix and I are far apart from one another, yet it seems unspeakably intimate to be alone together in this private place beneath the school. I can hear her slightest splash in the cavernous space, and even her breathing. I'm sure she can hear mine, too.

I could grab her and drag her under the water. Hold her down while she kicked and thrashed and clawed at me. Keep her under until she drowned.

That would be justice. The ultimate revenge against her father.

You can capture a man. Torture him. Maim him. Kill him, even. But when the violence is over, the pain stops.

But if you kill the only thing he loves . . .

That pain is unending.

I know this for myself. When someone you love is torn away from you, the ache torments you every minute, every hour. You never stop thinking about them. You never stop regretting.

Marko Moroz has no love, no loyalty.

Except for this girl.

She's the only way to hurt him.

I could make it look like an accident. No one knows we're down here, except for Dean. He'd keep my secret, just like he kept Cat's. Just like *I've* kept Cat's secret.

My body blazes with anger so hot that I no longer feel the chill of the water. My heart pounds like a voice in my ears saying, *Do it. Do it. Do it.*

That's not the plan, though.

I have to follow the plan.

The wolf hunts with the pack.

That's what I was taught. The fundamental law of my family: alone we're weak, together strong.

So I force myself to take long, steady breaths. I feel the cool water flow over my skin. I listen to Nix's breathing on the other side of the pool. When I think she's finally beginning to tire of her marathon swim, I cross to the stairs and climb out, grabbing a towel off the stack against the wall.

The Kingmaker's towels are as rough as the blankets. Nothing here was made for luxury, only durability. These stone walls will stand for a thousand years beyond any one of our families.

And none will end sooner than the house of Moroz.

I dry my hair, pretending not to notice as Nix likewise finishes her laps, swimming toward the stairs.

I hear her climbing out. I can't help looking up.

The water streams down her body. The black swimsuit and the dark auburn of her wet hair contrast her pale flesh. Her hair is reedy as seaweed, her skin taking on the queer green cast of the water. Her eyes are long and narrow, iridescent as abalone.

She looks like a mermaid taking human form.

The ancient kind of mermaid—mysterious and malevolent, luring sailors to their death beneath the cold, dark waves.

I hate her, and yet I'm transfixed by her.

I see her father's height, his coloring . . .

Her body is all long, smooth lines: strong shoulders, athletic taper to her waist, and an endless stretch of thighs beneath the high-cut legs of the school swimsuit.

I've never seen a girl look so powerful.

I don't want her powerful.

I want to destroy everything she knows and loves.

She must see some hint of this in my face because she pauses mid-step, droplets pattering down on the white limestone steps.

"Hello, Ares," she says.

She's watching me closely, tense in the shoulders.

I force myself to smile—friendly and disarming. Like Ares would do.

"Here," I say. "Have a towel."

I hand her a fresh folded towel from the stack. My skin crawls when our wet fingers briefly touch.

Nix takes the towel, still eying me warily.

I have to be more careful. I'll never convince her to trust me if I'm holding back a snarl every time I look at her.

"You're an excellent swimmer," I say.

"Thank you," she replies. "You're not bad yourself."

"Well, I grew up on an island."

Now she smiles, relaxing slightly and wrapping the towel around her body. "I was born on one. Born in the ocean."

"Really?"

I didn't know that. And this is why I'm here, after all—to learn about this girl. Every last detail.

"Yeah." She grins, her teeth glinting like pearls. "My mom didn't realize she was pregnant. I was the mother of all surprises."

"You mean the daughter of all surprises," I say.

She gives a throaty laugh. "That's exactly right."

I already know about Nix's mother. I know who she was and what happened to her. I know a lot of things about Nix, while she knows nothing about me. It might seem unfair . . . if the scales weren't already stacked three years and $240 million against me.

"You come down here often?" I ask her.

"Yeah." She nods. "It helps me relax. Away from . . . everybody."

She's the most despised person at this school. Sabrina had to threaten and cajole everyone in our group just to get them to consent to Nix sitting at our table. Bram's still pissed about it.

"It's peaceful down here," I say.

"Like the library," Nix replies.

That startles me. I feel my eyes narrowing.

Nix colors. "Sabrina said you spend a lot of time studying," she says.

I can't tell if she's as naive as she seems, or if this girl is conniving. I find it hard to believe that it was really such a shock to her finding out that her dad is a vicious, backstabbing monster.

Marko Moroz is a master at hiding who he really is until it's too late.

His daughter must be the same.

In Russia, we say, *Kakov pop takov i prihod: What the priest is like, so is the church.*

Whatever Nix pretends to be, deep down, she's as rotten as her father.

I give her the standard Ares story:

"I'm not as well-connected as the rest of the students here," I say. "There's no empire waiting for me. So I guess grades matter more for me than for some people."

"Does that bother you?" Nix asks me, her sea-green eyes fixed on mine. "Do the rest of us seem spoiled, like we don't have to work as hard?"

There's no challenge in the question. She seems genuinely curious. Sympathetic, even.

Even though I'm determined not to trust this girl, not to give her even a shred of honesty, something twitches in my brain.

I can't help thinking how easy it is for everyone else to call their parents on the weekend, to go to parties, practice, and study, with no stakes to anything. No weight on their shoulders. No real consequences to their actions.

And even though I detest this girl, even though I have half a mind to wrap my wet hands around her pale throat and throttle her on these steps, I find myself doing something unexpected.

I tell the truth.

"Yes," I say. "I resent it. I hate being here with everyone else . . . but not *like* everyone else."

Nix nods slowly, her face filled with understanding.

"Me too," she says.

Though I want no connection with her, though we have nothing in common . . .

I see the same loneliness in her eyes.

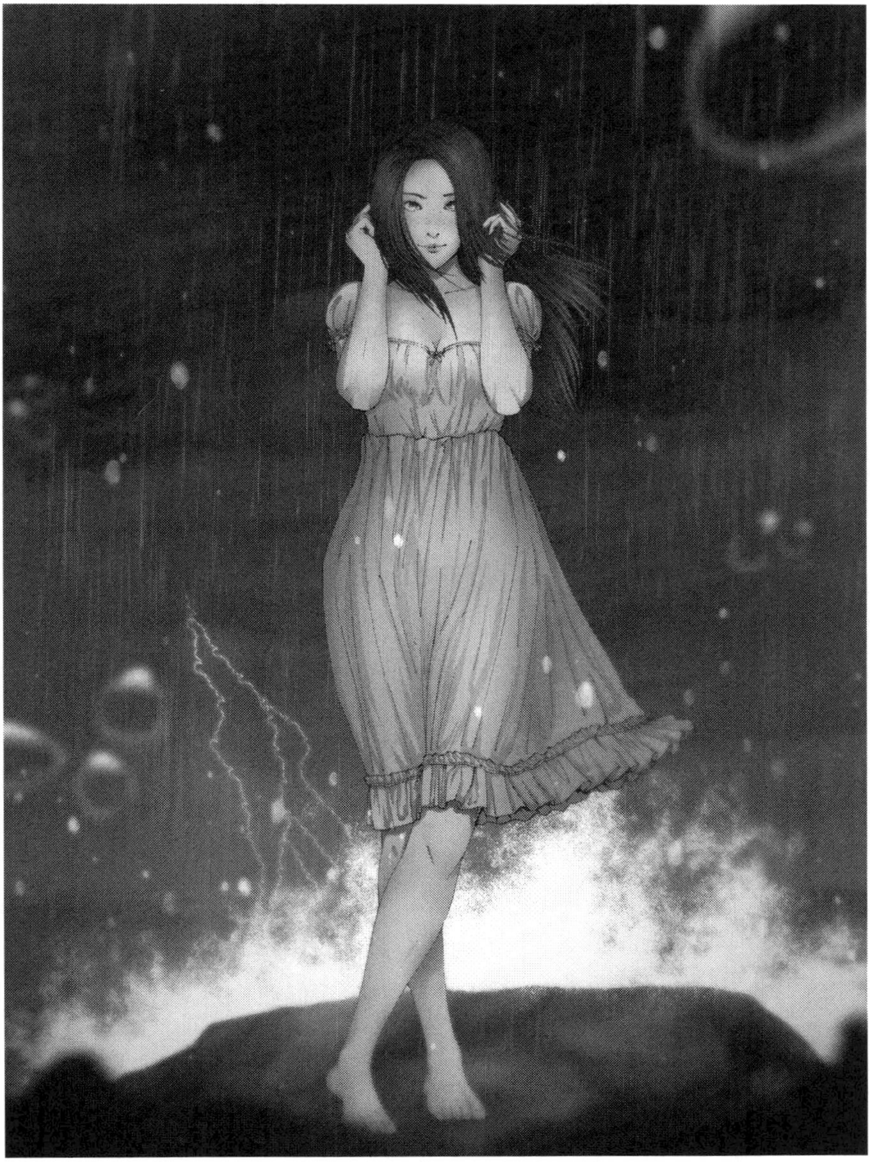

8

Ivan Petrov

Krasnoyarsk

Thirty-two Years Ago

When the big Ukrainian is thrown in amongst the high-security inmates, I know someone will fight him the first day. A man that big always attracts trouble. He has to be taken down, like a hunting trophy. The bosses inside will want to force his fealty.

I've only been at Stark for a year, but I know how things work in the prison camp. This is what I'm learning, rather than the pitiful "educational programs" we're supposed to undergo for rehabilitation. I already know my calculus and my essay-writing—unlike most of the men here, I actually finished school.

This is a new sort of education, provided by my fellow inmates. Go in with a bachelor's in petty drug trafficking, come out with a master's in organized crime.

My father is *Pakhan,* but he's a terrible teacher. Soft-hearted. Too eager for the approval of his own men. His territory has dwindled and dwindled, until even his uncles can no longer keep him in power.

He couldn't keep his own son out of prison.

I'll be a different kind of boss. With what I've learned here, and my brother Dominik at my side, I'm going to crush St. Petersburg under my heel. Not only will I recover every street, every neighborhood we once controlled, but I'm going to punish those families who thought they could swallow us whole, bite by bite. I will make them give back everything they took, and I'll put every one of them under my control.

As soon as I get the fuck out of here.

Luckily, there's only a few more months on my sentence. I was shoved in Stark during one of St. Petersburg's cyclical crackdowns on drug trafficking. It was a harsh punishment for a first-time offense, but I can't exactly blame them, knowing how many offenses I've committed without being caught.

This time I was betrayed.

Two dozen state police swarmed into my warehouse at the perfect moment to find my most recent shipment of powder—one of the only times I take personal possession of product.

I'm not an idiot. It's no coincidence.

I suspect my father's lieutenant.

I caught Rurik Oblast skimming money from his weekly collections. I punished him harshly, against my father's wishes. I suppose this was Rurik's revenge.

He took a year of my life. I'll take all the years remaining from his. One of many action-items on my list as soon as I'm out of here.

For now, I watch the redheaded giant face off against Sobaka, a hulking enforcer who works for one of the incarcerated Moscow bosses.

You don't end up in prison if you're a well-connected Bratva. Being sent here means you're out of favor with the high table, or one of your rivals has succeeded in hamstringing you. It means you're weak, that even the cops and the judges don't fear you.

The bosses inside fight for position even more violently than on the outside. They take no chances, and they show no mercy to unaffiliated prisoners like our Ukrainian friend.

He has no Malina brothers in here.

The only warning of the impending fight is a low whistle from one of Yuri Molotok's men. The older prisoners scatter, and the guards monitoring our "daily exercise" of milling around a cement yard surrounded by chain-link fence suddenly become blind and deaf, turning their backs on us. They receive enough bribes from the bosses to mind their own business.

As long as no one escapes, the guards couldn't care less what happens between these walls. Violent deaths are written down as "natural causes."

When the guards get bored, they use fresh inmates as their own personal punching bags. Only last week, they forced the incoming prisoners to run down a corridor with their hands tied behind their back, while the guards kicked, pummeled, and pushed them from all sides, blasting *Du Hast* at deafening volume, and bellowing with laughter every time one of the guards landed a particularly good hit. One of those prisoners died three hours later of a ruptured spleen.

So I don't expect any sympathy for the Ukrainian. More likely the guards will take bets on what looks to be a particularly entertaining match-up between the redheaded giant and Molotok's most vicious enforcer.

Sobaka circles around the Ukrainian, his shaved head a stubbly bowling ball set directly on his bull-like shoulders, with almost no neck in between. Despite Sobaka's height, he's still a good four inches shorter than the Ukrainian, who might be the biggest man I've ever seen outside of a televised basketball game.

And this Ukrainian is no lanky basketball player. He's got the build of a Viking—broad shoulders, barrel chest, long, ape-like arms. Though his head was shaved during intake like everyone else, the ruddy stubble on his scalp and cheeks still glints in the gray light.

Most interesting of all, he seems to have expected the whistle and the attack that comes without provocation, without warning. He patiently waits in the center of the yard as Sobaka rushes him.

Sobaka is a champion scrapper, veteran of a hundred prison-yard fights in the decade he's been inside. He comes at the Ukrainian with shoulders hunched, fists upraised.

The Ukrainian waits with a dull look on his face, as if he intends to simply take the beating.

Then, as Sobaka draws back his fist for the first blow, the Ukrainian stoops with shocking speed, picks up a chunk of broken concrete, and smashes it into Sobaka's temple.

Sobaka drops to the cement, legs twitching.

Molotok makes a sharp hissing sound to his men. Three more soldiers break free of his pack, running at the Ukrainian.

Fatally, they hesitate. They're scared of the giant. They don't act in coordination.

Like a bear harried by dogs, he swats them aside with devastating blows from his massive fists. He knocks several teeth out of Kruzinsky's mouth, then bodily picks up Yamerin and throws him into Bolski. Both men skid across the yard, the rough cement rubbing their flesh raw.

The Ukrainian opens his arms wide, palms upraised, silently challenging the rest of the prisoners in the yard. When none step forward, he glances from boss to boss, easily picking them out of the crowd without foreknowledge, with only his own observation of where they stand in relation to their men.

His eyes fix on Molotok.

"You don't send the stable boy to break the stallion," the Ukrainian says, in perfect Russian. "Is that really your best?"

Molotok's face congests with blood, his piggy eyes full of rage. I know he's weighing his desire to see this red giant beaten against the possible humiliation of *all* his men failing to accomplish the task.

He satisfies himself with drawing his thumb across his fat neck in one jerky swipe, and then he spits on the ground, sealing his promise to see the Ukrainian dead, one way or another.

The Ukrainian looks utterly unconcerned. He clasps his hands behind his back and completes several more leisurely strolls around the yard before the guards call us back inside.

That night, I find myself next to the Ukrainian in the dinner line as we carry our trays forward to receive our portion of bread and stew.

"Is that all they intend to feed us?" he asks me, glowering at the thin soup.

I shrug. "It's not always stew."

"What else do we get?"

"Sometimes there's hash."

"God almighty, I should have let those idiots kill me."

We're walking toward the tables together.

I should split apart from him. I don't need the target painted on his back extended to mine.

But I'll admit, I find this arrogant giant likable in a strange way. He's a powerful fighter—if he survives the week, he could be a useful ally.

He seems to be thinking the same of me. He looks me over with an appraising eye, saying, "Why aren't you sitting in place of honor in the yard, instead of those fat despots?"

"They leave me alone because I'll be a *Pakhan* in St. Petersburg in short order. But my holdings are weak."

"Time changes all things," the giant says.

"Indeed it does."

He drops down in the seat next to mine without asking permission. Alek and Vassi raise their eyebrows at me, wondering if it's wise to allow the Ukrainian at our table.

I knew Alek on the outside. Vassi shares my cell.

I've built a small crew in prison. Not as big as the gangs amassed by those who have been locked up in here five, ten, twenty years. Still, a half-dozen men answer to me: those I've identified as intelligent, loyal, and useful.

The Ukrainian could be all those things.

"What's your name?" Vassi demands.

"Moroz," the giant says. "Marko Moroz."

"I've never heard of you," Alek says.

"Well you won't forget me now, will you, boy?" Marko grins, pointing his spoon at Alek, its handle completely enveloped by his massive fist and only the battered top protruding.

"How did you end up in Stark?" Vassi inquires.

"Got in a brawl in Tosno. Broke somebody's arm."

"They put you in Stark for that?"

"Well." Marko shrugs. "It was a cop's arm."

"How long did they give you?" I ask him.

"Only six months."

I nod. We'll be out around the same time.

Molotok waits three days to enact his revenge.

He sends four men, this time armed with shanks made from sharpened scrap smuggled out of the metal processing shop.

They come for Marko in the showers.

The guards retreat first, and as soon as they do, the most observant prisoners likewise melt away, having no interest in being present for the bloodbath.

I see Yamerin, Bolski, Alenin, and Dubov striding into the shower room, fully dressed. Yamerin, Bolski, and Alenin clutch their gunmetal gray, wickedly-edged blades, and Dubov a sock with a padlock in the toe that he can swing like a mace.

I'm naked myself, save for a towel. I have no weapon on me. I ought to leave with the others.

And yet, when I see Marko standing under the shower spray, his vast body thick with muscle, I think to myself it would be a waste for him to bleed out on these filthy tiles, stabbed a hundred times by these scavenging rats who could never hope to best him on their own.

They circle around Marko.

He turns off the water, the steam still thick in the air like a poisonous mist. I notice he hasn't rinsed the soap from his skin, and I think I know the reason why.

He takes his towel from the hook. Instead of wrapping it around his waist, he twists the rough material in his hands, forming a rope.

As Yamerin slashes at him with his blade, Marko deftly wraps the towel around the shank and twists hard, jerking it out of Yamerin's grip. Bolski and Dubov lunge at Marko, Bolski slashing him down the arm from shoulder to elbow, Dubov swinging his cosh.

I seize the nearest towel rack and wrench it out of the tile, the metal coming free from the wall with a screeching groan. Before Alenin can even turn, I hit him in the back of the head with the steel bar. He goes down like a felled tree, blood leaking out from under his head onto the wet tiles.

Meanwhile, Marko is wrestling Bolski, his soapy body so slippery that Bolski can't get purchase. Marko flings Bolski against the wall, skull hitting tile with a sound like a dropped melon.

Dubov swings his cosh at me, howling threats for my interference. Marko dives at him from behind, taking out his knees. I bring the metal bar down on Dubov's head.

The fight is over in a matter of minutes. The water running down the drain is as bloody as a biblical plague. And yet, Marko's only injury is the slash on his arm.

He stands, turning the shower head on once more. He has to duck his head to stand beneath the spray, rinsing the last of the soap off his back.

Once he's clean, I throw him a new towel.

"Thank you, my friend," he says.

"Are you in a hurry to go back to Kyiv?" I ask him.

He rubs the towel across the short, coppery stubble on his head.

"Not particularly," he says. "Why?"

"I have plans in St. Petersburg. I could use a man like you," I say.

Marko wraps the towel around his waist, unable to tuck the end in because it barely goes around him.

"I'm no lieutenant," he says. "I mean to become a boss myself." He glances at the men on the floor. "But I do owe you a favor."

"Work with me, then," I say. "As partners. We split the profit. When the time comes, we part as friends. You go back home with the seeds to grow any fruit you like."

There's no need for me to wait until I'm free to begin amassing my army. I can do it right here, inside this prison.

With the exception of my brother, who is still young and learning, my family is weak and scattered. Marko's is non-existent. Neither of us has a network of ready-made soldiers.

We're the two biggest men in this prison. We can protect each other, and I can tighten my hold on the prisoners who already fear and respect me. They'd prefer my leadership to the petty dictatorship of Molotok and his ilk.

I'll train my soldiers here. Once I'm free, St. Petersburg will be mine for the taking.

Marko holds out a hand to me, his fingers gory from the blood dripping down his arm.

"Brothers, then," he says.

I already have a brother. But who says I can't have another?

I take his hand and shake.

"Brothers," I agree.

9

Nix

A res Cirillo is a mystery to me.

When he looks at me, I feel like his stare could burn the flesh off my bones. His restrained, buttoned-up exterior doesn't fool me. I see the intensity behind the facade, an actual living person peering through the eyes of a painting.

Sometimes he seems to be seeking me out.

Other times, I think he hates me.

My first thought, of course, is that there's some dark history between our families. But from what I've heard, his father and grandfather left the mafia life. He has no grudge against me.

We part ways at the door of the Armory, each of us heading off to our respective dorms to shower.

I watch his tall frame loping off across the grass, moving with a fluidity not dissimilar to Leo Gallo.

I was surprised when I saw Ares in his swim trunks. Divested of his baggy school uniform, he's more muscular than I would have guessed — with a much more interesting collection of tattoos.

Everything about him is subtle and understated. This interests me because I'm the opposite: too blunt, too loud, too obvious. Ares is a deep pool . . . I'm curious what's under the water.

I wish it weren't Sunday. As difficult as our classes can be, I'm not looking forward to long hours at loose ends. I could walk down to the village, but on such a mild and sunny day, it's as likely to be stuffed with students as the castle grounds.

I need to call my father.

Sunday is the only day we're allowed to call home. We have to use the banks of phones on the ground floor of the Keep, which offers little privacy.

I wait until lunch hour, when I know there will be fewer students around.

He picks up at once, as if he was waiting.

"There you are," he says. "Having too much fun to remember your dad?"

"Yeah," I say. "Something like that."

"So . . . how has it been?"

I don't know if it's my imagination, but I think I hear an edge of nerves in his question. He's wary of what I might say but doesn't want me to know it, in case I'm still blissfully ignorant.

"It's been eye-opening," I say flatly.

A long pause on the other end of the line.

"What does that mean?" my father says.

"What do you think it means, Dad?"

Another silence.

"I have no idea," he says.

That pisses me off.

"You had no idea that half the people here seem to hate you, and me by extension?"

My father scoffs. "Come on," he says. "You think Kingmakers is a congeniality contest?"

"That's the real reason you didn't want me to come here, isn't it? You didn't want me to know that we're pariahs."

"Bullshit," he snorts. "You're no pampered mafia princess, thinking her daddy owns a chain of hotels. You know how the sausage is made, my girl."

Do I?

I'm not so certain anymore.

"If anyone there has shit to say about me, it's because I don't rub the right elbows or kiss the right rings," he continues. "The Malina are independent—my men are loyal to me, and me alone. I don't bend to some Don like the Italians, or share my money like some Bratva *Pakhan*. The Malina are the lone wolves of the mafia world. And that's how I like it."

I sigh.

Being a lone wolf is . . . lonely.

"They say things about you," I tell him. "Things that upset me."

"What things?" he growls.

My stomach clenches. I don't want to tell him.

My father is a strange mix of brashness and oversensitivity. He's as blunt as I am in telling other people how it is, but when it comes to himself, he's quick to take offense, and he'll hold a grudge till the end of time.

But I've never been able to hide what I feel.

"They say you're duplicitous," I tell him. "Even the other Ukrainians say it. The Odessa Mafia—"

He interrupts me, going into a rage as I knew he would.

"They're JEALOUS!" he roars. "They want to cut me down any way that they can. They hate what I did on my own, without any of them! They'll lie and slander and say whatever they can to try to hide their own weakness, their own failure . . ."

I grip the receiver, frustrated and confused.

I knew he'd react like this. He always does.

When my father is happy, there's no one more charming, more engaging. But when he's angry . . . the switch flips, and there's no talking to him.

It's why we fight so often.

Everything is black and white to him. You're with him, or you're against him.

And if you're against him, you're his enemy.

"You don't believe any of it. Do you?" he demands. "You don't believe their lies?"

"Of course not, Dad," I say.

But I want to know. I want to know what happened with the Odessa Mafia.

"Do you know the Lomachenkos?" I ask him.

He's quiet. I can still hear his heavy breathing from his rant. He's put on weight the last few years—he's not as fast as he once was, though I still wouldn't get too close when he's angry.

"Kyrylo Lomachenko was my cousin," he replies at last.

"*Was?*"

"Someone cut his throat six years ago."

"But it wasn't you. You had nothing to do with it."

"I won't be questioned by you, girl," my father snarls, his temper flaring up again like a fire hit by a blast from the bellows.

"Please, Dad," I say desperately. "Just tell me what happened."

"There's nothing to tell," he says. "I was sending him old Soviet guns in shipping crates. He was smuggling them in past the port authority. I was perfectly happy with our arrangement. Obviously, someone else was not."

There's no hint of a lie in my father's voice. He sounds as honest and certain as ever.

I let out a sigh of relief. "Alright, Dad," I say. "I'm sorry I brought it up."

"What are you letting them give you shit for, anyway?" my father demands, recovering his cheerful bluster. "I thought you were made of stronger stuff, Nix."

Well . . . he's right about that.

I've never been one to roll over in a fight.

"Don't worry about me," I tell him. "I know how to take care of myself."

"That's my girl," he says.

I can almost see his grin, half-hidden by his red beard.

The Spy

THE SECOND WEEK of school is better than the first. For one thing, the pace of our classes is only increasing, which means nobody has much time for hassling me.

Also, anytime anybody gives me a dirty look, I tell them to fuck off with enough vigor that it seems to dissuade the others.

Only Estas seems entrenched in his grudge against me. He mutters insults at me in the hallways and glowers at me everywhere I go.

I don't care as much anymore—I believe my dad, not some random fucking idiot who thinks hoop earrings are a fashion statement. As long as Estas keeps his hands to himself, I'm just gonna ignore him.

At the same time, I pluck up the courage to join Sabrina for lunch again. While Bram Van Der Berg slouches at the far end of the table, seething and silent, only consenting to speak with Dean Yenin and Cat Romero, I still manage to have a reasonably pleasant conversation with Sabrina, Cara Wilk, Hedeon Gray, and Ares.

Well, it's mostly Ares and me talking—Sabrina gets pulled into conversation with a couple of extremely friendly German boys at the next table over.

Cara is writing something in her notebook, her head bent over her pen and her dark hair pooled on the edge of the page. Her script is too cramped to read, but it looks like she's working on a story.

Hedeon is glaring across the dining hall at a table containing several beefy Seniors, including one with the face and proportions of a silverback gorilla.

Hedeon has his hand pressed against his side. He's slumped in the same direction, breathing shallowly.

"What's wrong with you?" I ask him. "You look like your ribs are broken."

I've seen it before—several times in my father's men, and I broke my own ribs once, the same day I ruined my dad's favorite horse when the both of us took a tumble off a ridge ten miles from home. That was a fucking miserable hike back to the house, and not just because of the ribs—I knew my father would be furious that he'd have to shoot the horse.

"They might be," Hedeon admits, wincing.

Cara glances up from her page, pen pressed against her lower lip. Her brows draw together in sympathy as she looks at the mottled purple and yellow bruises running down the side of Hedeon's face.

"Why's he always fighting with you?" Ares asks Hedeon, jerking his head in the direction of the silverback gorilla.

"He's angry that I'm the Heir," Hedeon says.

"That's your brother?" I ask, finally understanding.

"In a manner of speaking," Hedeon replies, as if it pains him to say it.

"That's Silas Gray," Ares explains to me. "The Grays adopted Silas and Hedeon at the same time. They're almost the same age. So the Grays had to pick one son for Heir, and one to be his lieutenant."

Cara absorbs this silently, pen still pressed to her lip and soft hazel eyes watching Hedeon's face.

"How did they choose?" I ask.

For a minute, I don't think Hedeon will answer. He's obviously in pain, and never in the best of moods to begin with. I quickly learned that unlike the rest of the students, Hedeon's foul mood and rude rebuffs have nothing to do with me—it's how he behaves to everyone.

Still, he likes to associate with Sabrina's group, probably because none of them pester him with annoying questions like the one I just asked.

To my surprise, he takes another shallow breath and says, through gritted teeth, "They pitted us against one another. From the time we were small. They forced us to compete, over and over and over again. All kinds of challenges. When we would lose, they'd punish us. I often lost. Silas was always bigger than me, and stronger."

Ares looks startled by Hedeon's answer. I'm guessing this is new information for him, too. Cara's pale pink lips have opened in dismay, the pen dropping to the table.

"The competitions were brutal," Hedeon says. "The punishments for losing even worse. They whipped us. Burned us. Cut us. Made us hold our hands in buckets of ice water until we cried. We were only four when it started. And it went on for . . ." He sighs. "Until we came to Kingmakers."

The dark shadows under Hedeon's blue eyes make them look large in his face, like he's a small boy still, forced to compete against an opponent he knows he can't beat, with the specter of torture always in front of him.

Now I see the scars crawling up the back of his neck, beneath the collar of his white dress shirt. I see the marks on his forearms where his sleeves are rolled up: round, shiny scars from cigarette burns. Long white cuts from the blade of a knife.

My mouth is too dry to speak.

When I look at Ares, his face is frozen in shock and horror, his tan all but bleached away.

"Kenneth Gray wanted Silas to be Heir," Hedeon says, his eyes still fixed on his brother's hulking form. "Silas was faster, stronger, more brutal. I was smarter, but it didn't matter. The tests were never designed for intelligence. Margaret Gray . . . she favored me. Not in the way you would think, not with kindness. I think only to oppose her husband. She drove me on again and again and again, demanding that I win, ordering me to prove myself. Her punishments were worse than his. Because she was angry when I lost."

I notice he calls his adoptive parents by their first names, never calling them "mother" or "father."

Cara holds her hands pressed tight against her mouth. A tear leaks from the corner of her wide eyes, slipping down her cheek.

"You might think it would bring us together, having a mutual enemy," Hedeon says, watching his hulking brother methodically bring food to his mouth. "Children are too young, too easily manipulated. We hated each other exactly as they wanted us to. We fought and clawed and tried to kill each other, just as they wanted. Because really, they only needed one son. The heir and the spare."

Ares, Cara, and I are all transfixed by the horror of what we're hearing. None of us seem able to speak.

I blurt out the only thing I can think to say:

"They picked you in the end?"

"No." Hedeon shakes his head slowly, his dark blue eyes finally coming to land on my face. "I don't think they did. The night our letters came from Kingmakers, Kenneth and Margaret were screaming at each other. You could hear it all over the house. And in the morning, they told me I was accepted to the Heirs division. But neither of them looked happy."

I frown, confused.

"Hedeon," Cara says, softly, laying her hand over the back of his hand.

Hedeon jumps as if he's not used to being touched. But he doesn't pull his hand away.

"I'm so sorry that happened to you," she says, looking up into his face. Dampness sparkles in her lashes like tiny gems.

"I'm sorry, too," Ares says, in a choked voice.

"It doesn't matter," Hedeon replies, the dark veil of anger sweeping back over his features. He takes his hand back from Cara, sitting up straight despite the broken ribs. His jaw is fixed, his teeth bared. "The people responsible will get what they deserve."

He's glaring at Silas once more.

But I get the feeling he's not talking about his brother, or the Grays.

I turn my head, catching sight of Cat Romero at the far end of the table.

Dean Yenin has his arm around her shoulders, and Bram is muttering something to them both. Cat is sitting still, her keen dark eyes fixed upon our group. Though she's so far away, I can't help thinking that she was listening to every word Hedeon said.

Ares follows my gaze, likewise locking eyes with Cat, then quickly looking away.

"They're an interesting couple," I say.

Dean is tall, ferocious, and barely any more polite than Hedeon, while Cat is diminutive, soft-spoken, and much more friendly.

"Don't be fooled," Ares tells me. "Cat is clever. She's no little kitten."

"I would never think that," I say to Ares. "Women are always more than they seem."

10

Ares

I'm sick with guilt, hearing Hedeon's recounting of how the Grays abused him.

I knew the story of his real parentage. But I never knew what had happened to him after he was dumped on the Grays' doorstep.

Now I'm in a hell of a predicament.

I'm increasingly reluctant to keep hiding the information he needs. At the same time, his obvious intention to seek revenge on those who wronged him makes it all the more crucial that Hedeon learns nothing.

Hedeon's revenge is in direct opposition to my own.

Even worse, Cat Romero heard the whole thing. I can tell from that glint in her eye that the wheels are turning in her head.

The more quiet Cat is, the more she's thinking.

Never was someone put in a more appropriate division than when Cat was assigned to the Spies. Luther Hugo has no idea how inspired he was the day he signed those papers.

Cat is relentlessly curious and way too fucking good at putting together the pieces of a mystery that no one else would even notice.

I already know she's suspicious of me, and Miss Robin too. My mother said she knew Cat would be trouble for us the moment she saw her hiding in the library stacks, spying on Rocco Prince.

Everyone is my enemy because I can trust no one.

I can't risk it.

There's too much riding on this last year at school.

I can barely focus on my classes. My grades are slipping, not that it matters. The studying was always just an excuse to see my mom, and a useful distraction from the pressure of my situation.

It's not working anymore.

Every day feels like another cement block laid on my shoulders. I don't know how much more I can take.

I'm not my mother, and I'm not my father, either. They're both brilliant, ruthless, and highly skilled. They taught me and trained me, but deep down, I don't know if I have the strength to take my father's place, to do what he would do if he were here.

I'm walking down to the village every few days to see if there's a letter from Freya. She's on the outside, working with my uncle Dominik. Her job is to make everything seem normal. To help the real Ares keep the dispensaries running, to speak as my mother when calling our allies, even to occasionally post old pictures of me on social media, with sunglasses and tan on the deck of a yacht, as if I'm still engaged in the carefree leisure I enjoyed as a teen.

I can tell the pressure is wearing on Freya, too.

I have our mother here with me, while Freya has only been able to see her over the summers.

I came to school, albeit under another name, while Freya has had to put her life on hold. She has a brilliant head for numbers. She could have come to Kingmakers as an Accountant this year or accepted her scholarship to study Economics at Cambridge.

Instead, she's been working and waiting, trapped in this awful limbo that holds us all imprisoned like insects in amber.

As distracted as I've been, there's no way to skate through Combat class today. In our first two years, we focused on hand-to-hand combat before moving on to weapons training. This year, we're learning to fight with a knife.

"Anything can be a weapon," Professor Howell says, striding across the mats with his usual restless energy, as if his legs are spring-loaded. "You can kill a man with a belt, a fry pan, or even a pen, if that's what you have around you."

Marko Moroz killed his former mentor with a pen. Stabbed him right through the eye, or so I've heard.

Professor Howell continues: "The likeliest and most effective weapon to find at hand is a knife."

Howell is short, compact, and deeply tanned, with close-cropped black hair and a silver whistle perpetually dangling around his neck. He rarely employs said whistle, because his voice dwarfs his size, powered by whatever limitless battery lives inside of him.

He's trained the soldiers of several nation's armies, his speed and accuracy more than making up for his wiry frame.

He hands out our training knives, which are blunt and flexible, but still hurt like hell if someone gets a good poke on you.

My torso is already dotted with ugly purple bruises from the last time I sparred with Leo. So is his, proving the old adage that "nobody wins in a knife fight."

Leo grins at me, gripping the handle of his knife overhand like Professor Howell taught us.

"So glad we get to do this again," he says. "I think it's good for a friendship if both people know there's a level of mutually assured destruction in trying to murder each other."

"I think I could get you," I say, grinning back at him. "I'd just wait for my opening, which would be you trying to make some dumb joke—"

Faster than I can blink, Leo swipes his knife toward my belly. I leap backward, the dulled blade still catching and tearing my gym shirt.

"You dick!" I say. "I've only got two shirts."

"Only one shirt now," Leo chortles, circling around me. "Don't worry, you can borrow one of—"

I interrupt him with a quick slash toward his cheek, then a stab downward at his shoulder. Leo twists with eerie speed, narrowly avoiding my knife.

He really does have phenomenal reflexes. You wouldn't think it on a guy his size, but Leo is the most athletic person I've ever met, and it absolutely translates to fighting.

I think I've gotten ten times faster just from training with him.

"Tricky, tricky." Leo shakes a finger at me, laughing his irresistible laugh.

Thanks to Leo, I'm also immune to taunts. His shit-talking game was honed on the basketball courts, where making your opponent lose his cool is a near art form.

"Come on, you big baby," I goad him, taking a couple feints in his direction. "You wanna dance, or you wanna fight?"

"Both." Leo grins, charging me and slashing his knife every which way like a coked-up Michael Meyers.

I try to keep my free arm in a guard position in front of my chest and stomach like Professor Howell showed us. As Leo jabs at me, I chop his wrist with my forearm and counter with a stab to his side that makes contact. As I twist away, Leo slashes me down the back.

"Ow, you fucker!" Leo complains, rubbing his side.

"Same to you!" I say, feeling my back to see if the dull blade drew blood.

We're both sweating in the stifling heat of the Armory.

It's the warmest autumn I've seen at Kingmakers. The castle doesn't have air conditioning, relying on the thick stone walls to keep us cool. Even Professor Howell looks dewy just from watching us spar.

"Come on, use your blocks!" he barks at us. "This isn't boxing—you let your opponent make contact in a knife fight and you'll find your guts in a pile on the floor."

"He has such a way with words," Leo says, slashing at me again.

"A modern poet," I agree, successfully parrying.

When Professor Howell finally calls a stop, Leo and I race for the water fountain to drink a gallon or two each. We shove our heads under the faucet, then shake the water out of our hair, making a mess all over the mats.

"Clean that up!" Professor Howell yells at us.

"I was going to," Leo says to Professor Howell, then to me, "I was *not* going to."

"Here," I say, chucking him a towel.

"Thanks, buddy," Leo says, mopping up the mess.

Leo really is my best friend at Kingmakers. He might be my best friend anywhere, which is a funny thing to say about someone who doesn't know your real name.

I've wanted to tell him the truth a million times.

Leo is a good man. I think I can trust him.

But I promised my mother I wouldn't confide in anyone outside our own family.

It's just too risky. The relief of sharing my secret would be nothing compared to the devastation if someone betrayed it.

Even though I can't confide in him, Leo has been more of a comfort to me than he could ever understand. His relentless cheerfulness is the only thing that keeps me going sometimes. I've never seen him lose his optimism, except during our first year of school when he was on the outs with Anna.

Leo runs off a belief that things will turn out for the best.

My mom is powered by an absolute refusal to quit.

And what about me? What motivates me?

I suppose it's a sense of duty. My family is everything to me. I can't let them down.

"What are you thinking about?" Leo asks me, flopping down on the nearest stack of mats.

"Just thinking how slow you've gotten . . ." I tease him.

"Compared to you I'm the fucking Flash, old man!" he laughs, deliberately poking the biggest bruise on my arm.

Dean and Bram drop down on the mats next to Leo.

"Why is it hotter than the gates of hell in here?" Bram complains, wiping his forehead with the back of his arm. His shirt is soaked through with sweat in the front and the back.

"Shakespeare called it Halloween Summer," Dean says, proving yet again that he's surprisingly well-read.

"Americans call it Indian Summer," I say. "I dunno if that's racist."

"Probably," says Bram. And then, turning his scowl on me, "How come you're being all chummy with that Malina brat? I thought you knew what a fucking snake her father is?"

"I don't care about her father," I say.

The biggest lie yet.

"You should," Bram says darkly.

I can feel Dean watching me.

There's a strange dynamic between us these days. Dean's a lot more chummy with Leo since he and Cat visited the Gallos in

Chicago over the summer. I think the feud between their two branches of the family is finally at an end.

I wasn't there to see it, 'cause I have to lay low over the summers so that nobody who knows me as Ares sees me anywhere they shouldn't. Or vice versa, for anyone who would recognize who I really am.

On top of that, I don't think Cat trusts me, which means Dean doesn't trust me either.

It's nothing specific. Just too many little things that I'm sure Cat has noticed.

"I like Nix," I say to Bram. "She didn't do anything to you. So quit giving her shit."

"It's not me you have to worry about," Bram says. "Her own cousins hate her fucking guts."

"Oh man, I wonder what that feels like?" Leo says.

Dean laughs—still a relatively new sound, coming from him.

"What kind of a dick hates his own cousin?" he says.

I push up from the mats, feeling jealous even though I know how stupid that is.

Dean is a better friend to Leo than I am, because for all his flaws, at least he's honest.

"Where are you going?" Leo asks.

"I've got a free period next," I say. "I'm gonna study."

The perfect excuse for any occasion.

In actuality, I think I'll wander around for a while feeling like shit.

I LEAVE THE CASTLE GROUNDS, intending to go for a walk in the woods. Instead, I'm drawn toward the shooting range by the whoops and howls of students engaged in some apparently highly stimulating task.

Curiosity draws me on until I'm in the middle of the field that abuts the west wall where the targets are set up for long-range shooting.

Careful not to cross the line of fire, I tramp through the dry, golden grass, joining the raucous cluster of Freshmen.

I hadn't heard any gunfire.

The silence is explained when I see Professor Knox and Nix Moroz facing off with bows instead of rifles.

Both Nix and the professor are firing at the same target set far down the range. The professor goes first, his bald head gleaming in the late-afternoon sunshine. He pulls his string back taut, the thick muscles of his right arm and shoulder straining against his black t-shirt.

He lets the arrow fly. It crosses the seemingly-impossible distance to the target, hitting it near-center.

"What are they doing?" I ask a kid with a thick mop of reddish hair and several Hibernian F.C. patches sewn onto his trousers.

"Trying to shoot through the professor's wedding ring," the kid says, in a thick Scottish brogue. "I can't even see the damn thing from here."

I squint my eyes, looking for the gleam of a tiny circlet pinned to the middle of the target. I can just make a glint that might only be a trick of the sun.

"How can they even see that?" I say.

"Fuck if I know." The boy shrugs.

Nix takes her turn after the professor, holding her bow steady in front of her, coolly looking down the shaft of her arrow. Though she's using the same seventy-pound-draw compound bow as Professor Knox, she's able to pull the string back without a tremor.

She really is strong.

Confident, too.

I see no nervousness on her face. Just keen focus as she squints her sea-green eyes against the glare of the sun, slowly exhaling as she releases the arrow.

It flies straight and true to the heart of the target.

I don't see the shaft pierce the ring, but it must, because Nix immediately whoops in triumph, and Professor Knox tosses down his bow, saying, "Are you fucking kidding me?"

The Freshmen were too invested in the competition, and are too elated to see a professor bested, to maintain their grudge against Nix. Whoops and shouts break out all over again. Several students slap her on the back.

Nix grins, her teeth blinding in the sunlight.

She catches me watching her.

Giving a little chuck of her chin, she tosses back the errant strand of kinky red hair that's fallen over her eye.

"What are you doing here?" she says.

"Just passing by. I heard the shouting."

"I'm going to get my ring," Professor Knox grouses. "Don't any of you fucking shoot me."

He stomps off down the range, highly incensed at his loss.

"Why are you shooting bows?" I ask Nix.

We usually only practice with handguns, ARs, and sniper rifles.

"I said a bow could be better than a sniper rifle for a stealth job," Nix says. "The professor said they're no good over a hundred yards, especially for small targets. So I challenged him."

"You challenged him?" I say. "In the first month of school?"

"Yeah." Nix shrugs. "I knew I could hit it."

"What was the bet?"

"An A in his class," Nix says.

"What if you missed?"

"An F," she laughs.

"Why would you make that bet? You'll get an A anyway if you know how to shoot."

Nix shrugs. "It's more fun this way."

Nix's joy in her win is irresistible. I find myself smiling back at her without meaning to.

Her hair is flaming corona around her head. She's wearing the usual gray gym shorts, but her ass and thighs fill out the material in a way that's not at all typical.

On impulse, I ask her, "You want to come for a walk with me?"

"Might as well," Nix says. "He can't fail me for skipping class anymore."

She leaves the bow with the Scottish kid, and we tramp off across the field before Professor Knox can come back and stop us.

"I'm sweaty as hell," Nix says.

The tiny curls around her hairline are sticking to her forehead, and her skin looks less bluish, more golden in this light. The sun brings out little glints of gold in her green eyes and in the red of her lashes.

Nix has a complete lack of self-consciousness that I find strangely restful. Since I'm constantly monitoring what I say, what I do, and how I'm coming off to people, it's refreshing to be with someone who seems utterly themself, for better or for worse.

Proving my point, Nix asks bluntly, "Why'd you come looking for me?"

"I wasn't," I say. "I just heard everyone shouting."

Snatching up a long strand of dry grass, Nix twirls it between her fingers, tilting her head and watching me closely with those narrow eyes that seem more animal than human.

"Sometimes I feel like you're sitting by me on purpose. Walking with me on purpose," she says.

I'm transparent as glass. She can see right through me.

My face is getting hot, and I tell myself to pull it the fuck together. I'm a shit spy if I crack under two seconds of interrogation.

"Do you not want me to?" I say, trying to keep my tone casual.

"No." Nix shrugs, tossing the grass aside. "I like it. God knows, I can use all the friends I can get."

"Me too," I say.

Nix laughs. "You don't like being a third wheel to Leo and Anna?"

Fuck, she really is perceptive.

"How do you already know everything about everybody?" I demand, trying to turn the tables on her.

"Not everything," Nix sighs. "That thing with Hedeon was a mind-fuck. How could parents act that way toward their kids? Whether they're blood or not."

Nix is striding along beside me at a rapid pace, her long legs easily matching mine. Her cheeks flush with outrage. I saw her face when Hedeon was talking — despite only knowing Hedeon a short time, her sympathy overpowers her.

"Was . . . was your father not harsh with you?" I ask her.

I can't imagine Marko Moroz as supportive and affectionate, even though I know, theoretically, his daughter is the center of his world.

I expect Nix to be offended by this question. She's been forced to defend her father every day since she came here. I ask anyway because I really want to know.

Nix answers as honestly as ever.

"My father isn't perfect," she says. "He has an ego. And a temper. He hates to be challenged. We get in fights—screaming, shouting, throwing things. He demands nothing less than total loyalty, from me and his men."

I can feel my lip curling—I'm well aware of that particular characteristic of Moroz. I have to force my face smooth, as if this is new information, impersonal to me.

"You've never seen a more devoted father, though," Nix says. "He spent every minute with me after my mother died. I was only three years old. I don't actually remember her. I tell him that I do, but the image I have of her face . . . it's just what I've seen in photographs. I don't remember her voice, or what she was like. I rely on him to tell me."

I swallow hard. I know for myself how quickly those details fade, even when you're much older, even when you think you could never forget . . .

"He took me everywhere with him," Nix says. "He showed me how to run, climb, shoot, fight. He never treated me as inferior because I was a girl. I was always his heir, always expected to grow to be just like him. And that . . ." she sighs. "Is a blessing and a curse. Because of course I'm not *exactly* like him. One person can never be just like another."

I let out the breath I've been holding, shaken and confused.

Every time I talk to Nix, I feel like she's relating the exact thoughts swirling around in my brain. She's voicing my own deepest fears and insecurities, reflected back through the open mirror of her face.

I, too, am supposed to be just like my father.

And I *want* to be. I want it desperately.

I just don't know if I am.

"You don't think we're destined to be like our parents?" I ask her. "Almost every culture has an idiom that says it's inevitable. '*The apple doesn't fall far from the tree*'; '*a fish's child knows how to swim*'; '*like river, like water . . .*'"

"Who says that last one?" Nix asks me.

"It's Catalan. Zoe told me—Cat's sister."

"I like it." Nix smiles. "But no river is the same, and no body of water."

We've reached the edge of the forest that separates the fields and vineyards on the north end of the island from the village on the south. You can follow the road through, or you can diverge onto the many paths that lead through the trees, down into the river bottoms.

"Do you want to run for a while?" Nix asks me.

"Okay," I say.

I'm still wearing my gym clothes and a beat-to-shit pair of Ares' old sneakers. I could get new shoes, but it's been helpful these four years to wear his clothes whenever possible, to read his books, and carry his school bag. A continual reminder of the role I'm supposed to play, so I don't accidentally slip into being myself.

Nix likewise sports the plain white t-shirt and gray sweatshorts the school provides, the white knee socks only coming halfway up her long shins.

"Come on then," she says, throwing a teasing smile back over her shoulder. "Try and keep up."

Runaway — AURORA
Spotify → geni.us/spy-spotify
Apple Music → geni.us/spy-apple

She sprints off along a side trail, her thighs flashing under the hem of her shorts, her coarse, wild hair streaming behind her.

It's cooler in the shade of the trees, and darker. Nix is fleet as a deer. I can only keep sight of her from the brilliant red of her hair and the white flag of her shirt.

I can't tell if we're running or racing—if she wants me to catch her, or she's trying to get away.

I sprint full-out, wondering if this is a test. Wondering if her heart is hammering as hard as mine as my pounding feet chase after her.

My sneakers churn up the scent of pine needles and dark earth. As I follow her trail, I can smell Nix as well. A perfume of salt water, clean sweat, and the warm red scent of her hair—like fox fur, wild strawberries, sandstone . . .

Nix leaps over fallen logs, darts around the pine trees. Her laughter echoes through the woods.

She's a white stag. Catching her will win me some prize: a wish granted, a door to another world . . .

I hear a rushing sound—we're coming to the river.

I run faster, sure that Nix will stop up ahead. I don't want her to stop, I want to overtake her.

I sprint forward, the taste of iron in my mouth, almost close enough to grab a handful of her hair . . .

She halts so abruptly that I almost skid into her.

"We're here!" she pants.

Her face is red, her shirt drenched in sweat, as is mine.

We've come to a waterfall.

The ground drops away ahead of us, the river plunging ten or twelve feet down a broken rock face to a cool, green pool below.

"How did you know this was here?" I ask her, my breath wheezing in my lungs. I don't think I've ever sprinted so far.

"I found it the first week," Nix says. "Haven't you been here?"

I shake my head. I'm embarrassed to admit that Nix may have explored more of the island in her first month than I have in three years.

"Come on!" she says. "We can wash off."

Without waiting for a response, she pulls her shirt over her head.

The bra beneath is transparent with sweat. I can clearly see her nipples, stiff with exercise, and the full outline of her breasts. Her stomach is flat and hard. When she strips off her shorts with equal nonchalance, I see that her panties have ridden up in the cleft of her pussy lips. She turns, revealing a firm, round ass the color of milk.

It takes me way too long to look away.

My heart is still thundering like we're in full sprint.

My cock swells inside my shorts. I mentally order it to stop, because Nix will see, and also there is no fucking WAY I'm going to get a hard-on for anybody with the last name Moroz.

This unexpected surge of arousal reminds me exactly who she is, and what I'm supposed to be doing.

I can't be attracted to her. That's fucking insane.

I haven't been attracted to anyone for a long time. Every time I saw a beautiful girl at Kingmakers, I stuffed that emotion deep down inside me. Lying to my friends is hard enough. I knew I couldn't possibly keep up the facade in a romantic relationship.

It's been so long since I allowed myself to feel arousal that I almost thought I'd extinguished it. I thought I might be as asexual as everyone believes me to be.

And now, in an instant, lust comes roaring back.

Nix is a wild thing, a force of nature.

I feel like an animal that wants to bite and claw and fuck. I want to chase her down, throw her against those rocks, and mount her.

Nix is already scrambling down the rocks. Every move she makes is incredibly erotic, stripped of her clothes. Those mile-long legs, that firm, dewy flesh, the hint of ribs when she turns and the flex of her ass when she drops down to the pool . . .

She pops up out of the water again, droplets sparkling in the thick twists of her hair.

"Come on!" she shouts up to me. "It's not even cold!"

I take several deep breaths, trying to get control of myself.

Then I strip off my clothes, leaving them next to Nix's.

The rocks are slippery with moss. I half-climb, half-slide down, dropping into the pool before Nix can notice the bulge in my boxer shorts.

As soon as I'm in, Nix leaps on me, dunking my head.

We wrestle under the water, my thighs slipping between hers.

I can't believe how erotic it is to tussle with a girl who can fight back. I have to work to overpower her, I have to exercise a level of aggression I never thought I'd use on a woman.

My cock is iron, red-hot even in the cold water. It throbs when her leg presses against it.

Nix dunks me and then I dunk her, until we're both choking and sputtering and laughing.

She dips her chin under, deliberately swallowing a mouthful of water.

"Are you drinking that?"

"I'm thirsty! Anyway, running water's clean," she says.

I'm thirsty as hell myself. Trying not to think about dirt or bugs, I swallow a mouthful. It's cold and clean, with a faint mineral taste.

Nix dives and swims across the pool, her pale figure undulating beneath the dark water, her bright hair floating in a cloud around her.

Russian mermaids are called *rusalki*. They're the malevolent spirits of girls who die near water. Perhaps they leapt in a river to escape an unhappy marriage, or they might have been forcibly drowned by a father who discovered his daughter pregnant with an unwanted child. They haunt waterways, luring young men into the deep where they entangle their prey in their long red hair and drag them down.

It's said that the *rusalki* can alter their appearance to match the tastes of the men they intend to seduce.

I never believed in such a thing . . . until this moment.

Nix hauls herself up on the rocks, her back arched, her long legs outstretched, her skin slick and glistening.

If ever a figure had been formed to suit my preferences, it would be hers . . .

My cock is raging hard below the water. I press on it with my palm, trying to stifle its stiffness, only succeeding in sending a sickening jolt down my legs.

Nix stretches luxuriously on the moss, pointing her feet all the way down to the tips of her toes, hands clasped over her head. Her nipples jut upward, hard enough to cut glass.

My mouth is watering, my heart pounding.

Tearing my eyes away, I mutter, "Don't you want to swim anymore?"

"Of course I do!" Nix says, rolling back into the water.

Thank god.

She paddles around, agile as an otter. At home in the water.

I feel a stab of longing, remembering endless summer days in the warm turquoise ocean around Syros. Easier times. Better times.

"I wish all our classes were outside like Marksmanship," Nix says. "I hate being cooped up indoors."

"Right now I agree with you," I say, looking around at the sun-dappled ground and the thick pads of green moss blanketing the rocky pool. "You may change your mind come winter."

"I grew up in Kiev," Nix laughs. "I doubt it will bother me. A walk-in freezer seems balmy by comparison."

I open my mouth to say that St. Petersburg is nearly as bad, and then I snap it shut again, realizing my idiocy. I haven't had a near-slip like that in a long time—not since I fought Dean and lost control of myself.

Keeping up the front with Nix is even harder than with my friends.

She's too blunt, and the flow of the conversation is too rapid. I can't predict what she'll say next, so I can't plan my responses.

I was wrong about her, I can see that already — her candor is no act. She's not trying to manipulate me, not trying to appear as anything but herself. She embraces what she is, even when it doesn't align with what her father wants.

She's more honest than I've ever been, even before I had to take on this identity.

"We should head back," I say. "It's gonna get dark. I don't want to have to run all the way back."

"Sure." Nix shrugs easily.

She climbs out of the pool, water streaming down her body, flesh paler than ever from the chill. Her soaking wet underwear might as well be painted on—I can see everything. I'm hit with another hot, raw flush of lust, and I grit my teeth, turning away.

Nix dresses quickly, pulling her clothes on without bothering to even shake dry. Her curls are already springing up again in wild, tight corkscrews that point in every direction.

We're quiet as we walk back through the woods in the direction of the school. I don't think Nix is tired—I'm not sure what could possibly tire her. But she seems calm. Peaceful. Her red hair flares brightly every time we pass under a patch of late-afternoon sunlight. She tilts her face up into the sun, absorbing every last bit of it.

I can't stop watching her.

11

Ivan Petrov

St. Petersburg

Twenty-nine Years Ago

Dominik asks me to meet him in the War Room of the monastery, which was once the chapel where the monks knelt in prayer—or whatever they were actually thinking about. The church is a power structure like any other, and the similarities between my brotherhood and theirs are no coincidence.

This monastery has been in our family for generations. The Petrov motto is carved in stone over the gates:

Fides Est In Sanguinem

Loyalty In Blood

My brother is the only blood left to me. Our mother has been dead a decade, our father passed last year. I might have killed him, indirectly, with the stress of my takeover. It wasn't my father I had to subdue—it was his unruly and disloyal army of soldiers, who had no respect for him, and were just as much a danger to us as our enemies. Maybe even more so.

I killed Rurik Oblast the night I was released from prison.

He knew it was coming, and he tried to flee to Kotka. I cut off his hands, the old punishment for thieves, and drove a dagger through his spine at the base of his neck, the penalty for traitors. I sent a finger to his family so they'd have something to bury. The rest of him I burned.

Oblast's friends tried to launch a mutiny amongst my men, but I expected that. Marko, Dominik, and I slaughtered everyone that dared to raise a hand against us.

Then we turned to my enemies.

Every family in St. Petersburg that was supposed to pay homage to the Petrovs was brought to heel. I rained down terror on their heads, forcing repayment of every last ruble that should have been turned over to my father's accountants as our tariff on the whorehouses, the gambling rings, the drug dens, and the extortion rackets within our boarders.

And then, I began to expand.

I took back the territory that had been stolen from us. Then I took more in reparation. I brought family after family under my boot: the Sidarovs, the Veronins, the Markovs.

My father ceded the position of *Pakhan* as soon as I was released from the prison camp. But he did not approve of my methods or my ambition. He particularly hated my alliance with Marko Moroz, a Ukrainian with no ties to the Petrovs, or anyone else we respect.

"Our allies stood by and did nothing while the vultures picked our bones," I told my father.

"You ought to turn to your uncles, your cousins . . ." he pleaded with me.

I kept the best of my relatives: Efrem, Oleg, Maks, and Jasha.

But the others—those who stole from us, those who lied to us, those who conspired with our enemies—those I drove out into the winter snow like they were strangers to me.

"I'd rather have a true friend over false family," I told my father.

Now the men that live in the monastery are my hand-picked soldiers. Those I know and can trust with my life. Whether I recruited them in the prison camp, on the streets, or from the ranks of distant relatives, it makes no difference. I promote off merit, not blood relation.

I was almost glad to lay my father in the ground. I grew tired of his ceaseless complaints.

He brought us to the edge of ruin, then bemoaned the measures necessary to haul us back again.

The bonds of family can be chains weighing you down.

My father wanted the love of his men. It made him weak.

I'm not interested in love—I'm interested in achievement. I want the whole of St. Petersburg under my control.

I will admit, the alliance with Marko Moroz has come at a cost. It's a deal with the devil, and the devil always takes his due.

I knew from the beginning he would not be an obedient lieutenant. We agreed to work as partners, neither of us in authority over the other. I take control of St. Petersburg, and he takes a hefty portion of the profits, so that when he returns to Kyiv, he'll be flush with cash for his own takeover.

I'm beginning to think it's time for him to go.

The more I learn of Marko, the more I see that he is a coin with two sides. A coin that can be flipped by the slightest breath of air.

His warmth and humor are a real part of his personality. Equally real is the demon that lives behind his eyes. Sometimes the demon sleeps . . . and sometimes it wakes.

My methods are brutal, but they are never emotional. I do only what is necessary to secure my business, nothing more.

Marko behaves as if everyone in this world has personally offended him. His punishments are out of proportion—unpredictable and cruel in a way that will certainly come back to haunt us.

I rein him in when I can, understanding that he is no attack dog on a leash. I don't have control of him.

I'm certain that's what Dominik wants to discuss with me tonight—the consequences if we continue to partner with someone who is, at his core, irrational and violent.

I meet my brother in the War Room at precisely the agreed-upon time. Dominik is already waiting, sitting on the edge of the vast meeting table, running his fingertips repetitively over the deeply-carved scrolls in the woodwork, as is his way when he's stressed or nervous.

We don't resemble one another, not really. I'm dark and he's fair, I'm broad where he's lean. I take after my father's side of the family, he after our mother's. Dom is young—not fully grown. Still, he's thoughtful and focused. He's never let me down. I trust his judgment. Whatever he tells me tonight, I'll listen.

"*Privetek, brat,*" he says. *Hello, brother.*

"You look serious," I say.

He smiles slightly. "This from the man whose face is only capable of one expression."

"Don't exaggerate," I say. "I've got at least two."

I'm trying to put him at ease, but Dominik runs his hands through his sandy hair, taking a long inhale.

"Brother," he says. "We have to end our partnership with Moroz."

"Time will do that for us," I say. "He intends to return to Kyiv within the year."

"He should go now," Dom says flatly.

I can tell from his pallor and the nervous energy in his hands that this is no idle conversation.

"What happened?" I demand.

"We went to see Isay Chaykovsky. He had our stolen guns in the freezer of his restaurant, just as you said."

"Yes." I nod, already knowing this from Efrem.

"He knew he was fucked," Dom says. "He was crying and begging. I told him he would have to hand over the title on the property, just as you ordered."

I wait, arms crossed over my chest.

"But then . . ." Dom says, "his daughter came running out of the office. She threw herself on top of her father. She thought we were going to kill him."

I frown.

"I told her to go back to the office. Moroz stopped her. He tilted up her chin. And said she could save her father right then if she stripped naked and got down on her knees."

I'm opening my mouth to speak, but Dom holds up his hand to forestall me.

"I told Moroz, that's not how we do business. I sent her back to the office. I made Chaykovsky sign over the title while the men were loading the guns back in the truck. Then I heard screaming coming from the office."

I can feel my skin getting hot, anger rising inside me.

"Moroz had her over the desk. I ripped him off of her, but he had already done what he intended." Dom's jaw is rigid, his hands clenched. "She was only sixteen."

"She was ripe," a deep voice says from the doorway.

Marko comes striding into the War Room, the same boisterous smile on his face as always, within the frame of his wild reddish beard. He's been growing his hair ever since we were released from Stark. It now hangs below his shoulders, as uncombed as his beard.

He approaches us without shame or remorse. I don't think he's ever felt those particular emotions.

"This is true?" I ask Marko, already knowing it is. My brother doesn't lie.

"Of course." Marko shrugs. "The girl was pretty. And it's a useful deterrent. Warlords have always known that the best way to subjugate a man is to fill his women with your seed. It's why Genghis Khan has sixteen million descendants."

Marko lets out his booming laugh, slapping his hands against his meaty thighs.

I'm not laughing or smiling.

Dominik glances quickly between Marko and me, probably wondering how Marko even knew we were meeting in here tonight.

I would expect nothing less from him.

"That is not my way," I say to Marko. "It's one thing to bend a man, another to break him. You sow nothing but the seeds of your own demise when you make bitter enemies for yourself. That is the kind of act that demands revenge."

"I'd like to see Chaykovsky try," Marko scoffs. "He's no one and nothing."

"You went there for the guns and the title," I say. "That was punishment enough. We did not agree on more."

"I don't take orders from you, Ivan," Marko says. His tone is casual, and his smile as friendly as ever. But I see the first hint of malice in his eyes—the glint of that demon, waking and beginning to stir.

"I'm not talking about orders," I say. "I'm talking about a mutually agreed-upon plan."

"Plans are a guideline." Marko shrugs.

"Not to me they're not."

I see his jaw tighten beneath the red beard. He exhales through his nostrils, our eyes locked in place: mine dark, his an odd shade of green, like cloudy water in a stagnant pool.

Then he smiles again, breaking my gaze to stride around the room, pretending to examine the oil paintings on the walls and the heavy wooden mantle over the wide, cold fireplace where no wood burns in the grate.

Marko likes to take up space in a room. He likes to stand and walk so you never forget his stature, how easily he could destroy the furniture or overturn even this massive slab table.

"I don't think your brother likes me," Marko says, raising a gingery brow in Dom's direction.

Dominik stiffens. "I never said that."

"You don't have to say it," Marko hisses, the anger leaking out now. "It's in those judgmental looks, in every time you avoid me, in every instance where you run to your brother to tattle!"

He's roaring by the end, beefy fists clenched at his sides.

To his credit, Dom doesn't flinch. He stares at Marko coolly as he says, "You're right. I don't like you. I don't like your methods. And I don't like your personality."

"That's irrelevant," I cut between them. "The cogent point is the one Marko made first: there's no one giving orders among us. And it's time that there should be. This brotherhood grows too large—it requires a single leader. We no longer fit in the monastery."

Marko has stopped pacing. He faces me, arms crossed over his chest "What are you saying?"

"Take the ten soldiers of your choice and your share of the money. Let us part while we are still friends, before anything comes between us," I tell him.

Marko looks at Dominik, his face black with anger.

"Something *has* come between us," he says.

"My brother is only saying what I already feel," I tell Marko.

"Your *brother*," Marko spits, lip raising in a snarl. "A brother is an equal. If anyone in this room is your brother—"

"There's no need to choose," I say, cutting him off once more. I hold out my hand to Marko, looking him in the eye. "You've been a strong partner and a better friend. Let us part that way. When we meet again, it will be as kings of our respective cities."

Marko looks at my outstretched hand. I see the flicker behind his eyes—his demon battling with his more rational brain.

I don't know if he will take my hand or not. He's never been predictable.

At last, he grasps my hand in a bone-crushing shake. I can almost hear Dom's sigh of relief.

"Goodbye then, my *friend*," he growls. "Until we meet again."

With that, he stalks out of the room.

12

Nix

It's near dark by the time Ares and I return to the school, the sky purplish and starless, the pale stone of the castle walls taking on a gloomy tint.

The school grounds are quiet, with only a few students crossing between dorms or walking across the lawn toward the library, their faces difficult to discern in the dark.

We missed dinner. Luckily I've got some snacks stashed away under my bed, or I might starve to death in a single night after all that exercise.

A brief silence has fallen between Ares and me, after easy conversation all the way home, centered on our classes and the upcoming first event of the *Quartum Bellum*.

The quiet is companionable.

I've never been so tired, and I've never had so much fun.

I love being out in the woods by myself. Having someone with me was even better. And not just any person—someone whose speed and stamina matched my own.

Ares fascinates me. Every time I peel back a layer of his reserve, I find something unexpected beneath—something stronger and more intense than I anticipated.

Everyone thinks he's some gentle giant.

I don't think he's gentle at all.

I only think he's careful.

I don't know why he's holding back, but I want to see more.

I look at Ares, more handsome than ever in the twilight.

He has a long face with a straight, patrician nose, a sharp jaw, and a deep cleft in the chin. The curve of his upper lip reminds me of my bow. The dark stubble on his cheeks is rich and velvety. His hair, dark with a few lighter streaks from the sun, has dried windswept. The faint scowling line between his eyebrows never seems to entirely fade away. It's not a mark of anger—more like stress or worry.

"What are you thinking about?" I ask him.

"Nothing," he says. "Only that I should probably—"

He breaks off with an infinitesimal jerk of his head, like a hound sighting a rabbit. I look in the same direction, toward the Armory, but I don't see anything.

"What is it?" I ask him.

"Nothing," he says. "Only . . . I thought you might like to see the hall of winners in the Armory. Since you were curious about the *Quartum Bellum*."

"Sure," I agree.

My legs are already jelly. What's another few minutes of walking?

We cross the lawn, the grass dark as ink now that the sun is all the way down. Only a little soft, golden light leaks from scattered windows. No floodlights illuminate the Kingmakers grounds.

Ares leads me into the annex of the Armory. He seems to be looking around, like he isn't quite sure of the way, though he must know the school ten times better than I do, this being his fourth year.

"It's right in here," he says in a strangely hushed tone.

Up ahead, someone else is speaking, low and intent, like they don't want to be overheard.

I hesitate, not wanting to interrupt the two figures up ahead, one tall and one short, engrossed in conversation. But Ares hurries on, saying loudly, "Cat! Hedeon! What are you two doing?"

Cat Romero and Hedeon Gray startle, their gazes tearing away from the wall of photographs.

"It's alright," Hedeon says to Cat. "I don't mind if you tell them, too."

Cat examines us, her dark eyes liquid and glimmering in the golden lamplight of the corridor. She's frowning slightly.

It's Hedeon who rushes on, his voice tight with excitement, "Cat thought the girl in this picture might possibly be my mother..."

We all turn to look, irresistibly drawn—even Cat and Hedeon, who had already seen the photograph before.

I see a girl no older than me, with dark hair and deep blue eyes. She's extremely beautiful, only more so because of the expression of wild triumph on her face. Something about her—maybe the sensual edge to her beauty, or the air of recklessness—reminds me of Sabrina Gallo.

The girl is the winning Captain of the *Quartum Bellum* in her Sophomore year, and then again , the next picture over, as a Junior—an achievement even I know to be exceedingly rare.

The losing Captains, all male, glower at her furiously.

"Why would you think that's Hedeon's mom?" Ares asks. He sounds skeptical and confused.

I glance between the girl's face and Hedeon's. "She does look a bit like him..."

"Not really," Ares says. "Just 'cause she's got dark hair and blue eyes..."

Hedeon's face falls. He examines the photograph again, searching for evidence to counteract Ares' disbelief.

It is true, their features aren't entirely alike—the girl has a soft, oval face, with a narrow nose and gently arched eyebrows. Hedeon's bone structure is rougher, his jaw broad and his nose, before it was broken, more Roman in shape.

Still, children don't look precisely like one parent. Or either parent, sometimes...

I read the name beneath the photograph. "Evalina Markov... Who is she?"

Now Cat speaks up in her soft but penetrating voice.

"I looked her up. She lives in St. Petersburg. She's married to a man named Donovan Dryagin. They have three children." She pauses a moment, her eyes fixed on Ares, not Hedeon. "She's related to Neve and Ilsa Markov—you know them, don't you?"

"Yes, of course," Ares says, in a slightly strained tone. "I took Snow's boxing class with Ilsa last year. She's one of the only female Enforcers."

"Her older sister Neve already graduated," Cat says, explaining to me now, and maybe Hedeon, too. "But Ilsa's still here. We could ask her—"

"No!" Ares interrupts. "You can't do that!"

"Why not?" Cat inquires calmly.

"Because think what you're accusing this woman of! Getting pregnant at Kingmakers, which is completely against the rules, then having a secret baby and giving it away without her family knowing—"

"How do you know they're not aware?" Cat demands.

"Because obviously Hedeon's parents don't want to be known!" Ares cries, throwing up his hands in disgust. "Look, I'm sorry, Hedeon. I know you want to know where you came from, but you could really fuck up this woman's life if she hasn't told her parents or her husband . . . if it's even her at all! You could accuse someone based off what, a guess? The fact that you both have blue eyes? A lot of people have blue eyes."

Hedeon's look of disappointment is heart-wrenching. At the same time, there's truth in what Ares is saying—when you dig up a grave, you're sure to find bones.

Cat is frowning, arms crossed over her chest. I'm not sure if she's annoyed that Ares is poking holes in her theory, or if she doesn't like him dissuading Hedeon.

Hedeon can't stop staring at the photograph.

"How is she related to Ilsa Markov?" he asks Cat.

"Ilsa's grandfather and Evalina's father were brothers. And guess what Evalina's father's name was?" Cat says, throwing a triumphant glance at Ares.

"What?" Ares says dully.

"Hedeon Markov," Cat replies, in the tone of a slamming book.

Ares shrugs like that doesn't prove anything, but Hedeon and I both gape at Cat, suitably impressed.

Cat says, "I could see a girl, forced to give away her baby, wanting him to have a family name, since he wouldn't have her surname."

The silence in the annex is profound, all of us pondering if this could possibly be a coincidence.

At last, Ares says to Hedeon, "Well . . . what are you going to do?"

"I don't know . . ." Hedeon replies.

He looks stunned, and almost dreamy.

"Just . . . be careful," Ares says desperately. "Think about it first."

Ares and I leave Cat and Hedeon in the annex.

As we walk north toward our respective dorms, Ares seems strained and distracted.

I can't help but wonder why he's so concerned about Evalina Markov.

"Don't you think Hedeon has a right to contact his parents?" I ask Ares.

Ares turns on me, already agitated before the words have even left my mouth.

"Nix, you know what these old mafia families are like. Especially one or two generations back. This woman is married, with her own children. If Hedeon's her son, he'd be the oldest of all of them. Do you know what a mess that makes?"

"The truth isn't messy," I tell him. "It's just the truth."

Ares shakes his head at me.

"The truth is *always* messy," he says. "That's why legends are lies. In real life, there's no perfect narrative where the good guys and the bad guys all get what they deserve, and everything works out in the end..."

I can feel my face getting hot.

My father's stories always have the ring of legend to them. A clean narrative arc, and a moral at the end... usually my father getting his just reward for being particularly brave or particularly cunning...

His stories mean everything to me. Especially the ones about my mother.

"Something can be true, *and* a good story!" I cry. "Maybe Hedeon's mom would love for him to call her up, maybe she's been waiting..."

"Waiting for what?" Ares shouts back at me. "If this woman gave her baby away, she knew where he was the whole time. If she wanted to contact him, she would have done it."

We're standing at the junction point where Ares is supposed to go east to the Octagon Tower, and me west to the Solar. Yet we're standing here, both way too upset over something quite different than what we're shouting into each other's faces.

I know what I'm angry about.

The question is . . . why is Ares so mad?

No time to ask him. Ares gives me a brief and grudging, "Good night," before turning and stalking off toward his dorm.

I'm left standing there, with the nagging suspicion that Ares followed Cat and Hedeon into the annex on purpose.

13

Ares

I fucked up royally with Hedeon, and with Nix, too.

Throw Cat in the mix while you're at it.

I saw her and Hedeon walking into the annex together and I knew, I just fucking knew, that Cat was going to spill the truth. Call it a sixth sense, or simple intuition that those two wouldn't be walking around together at 9:00 at night for no reason.

My only solace is that while Cat may have guessed Hedeon's mother, she doesn't seem to know his father just yet. But I'm afraid it's only a matter of time.

Cat is so fucking relentless.

I panicked. I didn't know how to stop what was happening right in front of my face.

And now I've made myself look suspicious, in front of Nix no less.

I was never meant for all this sneaking around.

My mother is pissed when I tell her.

"I should have let Rocco Prince skin her alive in the library," she grouses, fully annoyed with Cat's meddling.

I know she doesn't mean that. Well—not entirely, anyway.

"What do you think I should do about it?" I ask her.

"Stick close to Hedeon. If he talks to Ilsa Markov, try to convince him not to spill what he knows."

"What about Cat?"

"Stay away from her. She's got the worst kind of radar—you don't want to be on it."

My mom is in a hell of a mood. She's stalking around the library, flinging books into bins willy-nilly. It's the middle of the night, no other students around. Still, it's unlike her to behave so recklessly, tossing off her Miss Robin demeanor like a stifling fur coat, the real Sloane emerging from underneath.

"What's wrong?" I ask her.

"Everything," she seethes, raising her hands as if she'd like to strangle someone. "Dom called me today. Abram Balakin has finally seceded his position in Moscow. Danyl Kuznetsov is taking over as *Pakhan*."

"Why does that matter?" I ask, confused.

Danyl was Abram's lieutenant. He's been eagerly anticipating Abram's retirement, and his promotion was expected by all the Bratva bosses.

I've never met Danyl, but I know Dean Yenin owes him two years' service when he graduates from Kingmakers—payment for Danyl's sponsorship when Dean applied to the Heirs division.

"Danyl is calling another meeting of the high table," my mother explains. "He's insisting that *all* the *Pakhans* attend."

My stomach twists. That means they'll expect my father to be there. We already sent Dom in his place last year. The bosses are getting suspicious.

"You think Danyl's doing this on purpose?" I ask.

My mother paces restlessly.

"Most definitely," she says. "He's buddied up with Foma Kushnir. Foma's been tracking our withdrawals from the Gazprombank. He knows something's up."

"Yeah, he thinks Dom's stealing money," I snort, remembering how Bodashka Kushnir accused my cousin Kade of treachery and embezzlement.

"They're not stupid," my mother warns me. "They're putting it together."

My head is pounding, my blood pressure at a constant high for three fucking years now. I don't know how much more I can take.

Forcing my voice steady, I ask her, "When's the meeting?"

"The first week of January."

I'm trying to think strategically, the way my mother would think.

Slowly, I say, "Dean knows Danyl, and he used to be friends with Bodashka Kushnir, though I don't think they're as close anymore. If Danyl plans to make a move, Dean could keep us informed . . ."

"How are you going to ask him that as Ares?"

"I'm not gonna ask him—I'll tell Kade to do it. Dean likes him. He defended him to Bodashka last year."

My mother considers this carefully before nodding.

"Talk to Kade. Don't let Dean know you have anything to do with it. And for god's sake, don't let Cat hear about any of it."

If only it were that easy to hide things from Cat Romero.

14

Ivan Petrov

Twenty-one Years Ago

The party on the HI SO Terrace is intended to celebrate the birth of my son, though no one in Russia would ever call it a baby shower.

I've become familiar with many American traditions since marrying Sloane. She clings to few of them, considering herself a citizen of nowhere and a resident of anywhere she pleases.

Still, she likes to compare Russian customs with American.

This is her nature as a chameleon: observing and adapting the practices of those around her, until she might convince you that you'd grown up next door to one other.

She finds the Russian superstitions around pregnancy and birth highly amusing.

She laughed when my soldiers firmly refused to acknowledge her burgeoning belly, even when they bumped right into it in a cramped hallway.

"They don't want to invite the eye of the devil on your unborn baby," I informed her.

"I think he already has the devil inside him," Sloane said, giving me a wink. "Do you remember what we were doing when we conceived him . . .?"

I remember that night well. Sloane and I had just liberated four million in unmarked American bills from an armored truck outside of Gatchina. Robbery is not a usual part of our business, but Sloane had gotten a tip on the unusually large cash transfer, and she was intent on intercepting it.

I had never seen her as energized as she was that night. She insisted that we go, just the two of us, and she organized the entirety of the heist. I let her take the lead for once, watching her work with the skill and precision of a master.

Once we had the money, we hauled it up to the penthouse suite of the Astoria hotel, bribing the clerk for the use of the service elevator.

Sloane spread the money out on the bed, then stripped naked and lay on top of the pile of bills, offering me her body and the cash as our anniversary present.

We had been married four years.

I never expected an heir from her. Dominik had a son to carry on the Petrov name. And I knew how Sloane valued her independence and her physical prowess.

Yet, I must admit . . . every time she showed me her cleverness, her ruthlessness, and that wild joy that bubbled up inside of her like an endless fountain, I thought to myself, *What a child we could make, her and I. He'd rule the world.*

She was possessed of a kind of madness that night. We fucked like demons, scattering the stolen money like leaves in a hurricane. I took her in every position, harder and harder as she urged me on.

She dug long scratches down my back, she bit my shoulder so hard that it bled, she rode me like a prize stallion in the final stretches of the Triple Crown.

As I erupted inside of her at last, she cupped my testicles in her hands, stroked her fingertips on the underside of my balls, milking every last drop out of me.

We were drenched in sweat, cash stuck to our backs, the hotel room destroyed.

A few weeks later, she told me she was pregnant.

"I thought you were on the pill?" I asked her.

"I must have forgotten to take it," she replied, in her enigmatic way.

I was obsessed with the changes in her body. Every day I wanted to run my hands over every inch of her, marveling at the fulness of her breasts, the darkening of her nipples, the swelling of her belly.

My lust for her was so intense that I followed her around the monastery from room to room. Nothing ever required more self-restraint than keeping my hands off her when she was in the throes of nausea.

I was rewarded by a libido surge in the second trimester—then it was Sloane who attacked me at odd hours of the day, ripping my clothes off my body and mounting me without foreplay. Her pussy was wetter and warmer than it had ever been, her curves filling my hands in new and satisfying ways. She was a goddess of fertility: I only wanted more of her to worship.

My happiness was violent in the extreme. I felt a new level of protectiveness that probably annoyed her at times.

"Of course I'm going down to the gym!" she scoffed, lacing up her sneakers at eight months along. "Do you think women in olden days sat around eating bon bons?"

"The royals did," I growled. "And you are my queen, after all . . ."

Sloane flatly refused the Russian traditions of the husband not accompanying the woman to the birthing room and the forbearance of buying any baby items until after the infant's safe arrival.

"You know I'm always prepared," she told me. "I'm not giving birth without a single damn onesie in the house."

"Usually the husband buys the baby clothes while the wife is in hospital."

"Not this husband," she said. "You'll be right beside me, rubbing my feet."

In truth, I mostly held her hand, brought her ice water, and terrorized any nurses who dared chastise Sloane for cursing.

She birthed our son as she does all things: with single-minded intensity.

She pushed him out and demanded to hold him at once, before he had even been cleaned.

If I had any question whether my wife possessed maternal characteristics, it was answered when the doctor pricked our infant's foot, making him squall.

"You take one single drop of blood from my son, and I'll answer it with a gallon of yours," she snarled in perfect Russian.

The doctor retreated, hands upraised, mumbling apologies and excuses about hospital policy.

I admired our son's thick head of hair, his lusty screams, and his long frame.

"He'll be tall," I told Sloane.

"Of course he will," she said. "Look at his parents."

She surprised me by nursing him, and by carrying the baby in a sling everywhere she went.

I suppose I should have known that Sloane does nothing by halves. She would never have a baby only to neglect it.

It was her idea to throw the party, though baby showers aren't common in Russia. She said it wasn't a shower, only an opportunity for our friends to offer their congratulations.

It's an elegant affair, held on the rooftop of the SO Sofitel, with strings of golden lights drowning out the stars, a stunning view of Saint Isaac's Cathedral, and the famous cellist Leonid Gorokhov playing a suite in the old style.

Every Bratva family in St. Petersburg is here to pay homage to the new scion of the Petrovs. Even some of the Moscow *Pakhans* have made the journey. They hate missing out on any event, particularly one as posh as this. Sloane may not care much for parties, but she damn sure knows how to throw one.

I believe the real intent of this particular event is to solidify our standing as the most powerful couple in the nation. She knows exactly how it looks, presenting our son and heir to the world. She knows the meaning of the pile of luxurious gifts weighing down the receiving table. She issued a call to the Bratva, and they answered with obeisance.

I make the rounds through the crowd, shaking hands and accepting congratulations from friends, allies, and rivals alike. I kiss the hand of Jori Zaitsev's new bride and accept an introduction to Pavel Veronin's eldest son, who requests a private meeting the following week.

Hilo Stepanski has come all the way from Minsk. He presses a wrapped package into my hand, telling me, "This is a gift for you as well as your son. It's a Rolex from his birth year. You can wear it now, and later you can pass it down to him."

"Very thoughtful, Hilo. Thank you," I say, tucking the package in the breast pocket of my tux. "How is business?"

"Volatile," he replies with a significant raise of his thick salt-and-pepper eyebrows. "Have you heard what Moroz has been doing?"

"Yes," I say shortly, not wanting to mar the festivities with the stain of the dark rumors swirling out of Kyiv.

"Upheaval can be good for business," Hilo says. "But only if there's anyone left alive to do business."

I'm not sorry when Hedeon Markov interrupts us, accompanied by his son Kristoff, his daughter Evalina, and her fiancé Donovan Dryagin. The Markovs are one of the only families who supported me during my bloody battle with my rival Remizov. The Markovs' loyalty will not be forgotten—they will always have a place at my table.

I've already helped Kristoff Markov to secure an appointment as Minister of Culture. I'll offer my assistance to Donovan Dryagin as well, once he marries Evalina.

Hedeon Markov has a broad, taciturn face with a thick shock of snow-white hair combed straight back from his brow. His hands are harder than iron, and he's rumored to use them freely on his wife and children, despite his age. His son Kristoff, barrel-shaped and black-haired, shares his father's dour expression.

Only the daughter displays the famous Markov beauty—or at least, she used to. When last I saw her, she was slim and vivacious, with brilliant blue eyes and a daring manner that earned her several severe looks from her father and brother.

Tonight she looks pale and doughy, leaning on her fiancé's arm as if already exhausted, though the party is just beginning.

She barely glances up as I take her hand.

"Welcome home," I tell her.

Sloane greets Evalina warmly, asking how she's enjoying her time at Kingmakers.

"I've decided not to return for my final year," Evalina replies, quietly.

"Surely Donovan can wait a little longer?" Sloane inquires, with a glance at the tall, stern fiancé.

"It's Evalina's decision," Dryagin says. "I was content to allow her to complete her education."

I see the slight curl of Sloane's lip at Dryagin's magnanimous tone, but she lets it pass.

Her eyes are fixed on Evalina's somber face.

"We're glad to have you back," she says.

Evalina nods. Her eyes land on our month-old son, tightly swaddled and cradled in a sling across the breast of Sloane's gown. His sleeping face peeps out, dark lashes laying against his round cheeks and small mouth making a delicate sucking motion as he dreams of milk.

Evalina's hands make a convulsive, clutching motion in front of her chest, as if she's been afflicted by a sudden pang—heartburn, perhaps.

"Excuse me," she says, turning and heading in the direction of the ladies' room.

Hedeon Markov begins to talk of market futures, barely noting his daughter's departure.

Later, when the party is in full swing, I corner Sloane so I can kiss her behind a potted banyan tree strung with lights.

Wolf — Boy Epic
Spotify → geni.us/spy-spotify
Apple Music → geni.us/spy-apple

"Don't squish the baby," she teases me.

"I think I squished him plenty while he was still inside you."

Sloane's smile turns to a wince.

"What's wrong?" I demand, my voice too rough as my heartrate spikes.

"Nothing," she says. "Only my tits are killing me. He hasn't woken up to eat."

I look at her breasts, heavy and round as a porn star's, when usually they barely fill my hands. The skin is stretched painfully tight over their curved tops, her nipples stiff against the material of her dress.

I take her hand.

"Come on."

She follows me down the staircase to the lower level of the SO Sofitel, which houses several rooms for board meetings and luncheons. I take Sloane into one such room, with a gleaming oval executive table, and a freshly-cleaned whiteboard mounted on the wall.

"I don't want to wake him up," she says.

"We're not going to."

Gently, I put my hands around her waist and lift her up so she's sitting on the edge of the table, her feet resting on one of the plush leather chairs. Then I pull down the bodice of her black velvet gown, exposing one tight, swollen breast.

Her nipples are larger than usual, and darker. The point stands out from the breast, already beginning to leak milk just from the stimulation of air against her bare skin.

Supporting her breast with my palm, I close my mouth around her nipple.

I suck gently at first, lightly massaging her nipple with my tongue.

The milk begins to flow at once, first in a thin stream, then a rich and creamy torrent. Sloane lets out a low moan of relief as the let-down initiates. The moan is distinctly sexual—my cock stiffens inside my dress pants, jutting upward to the waistband.

Her milk is slightly sweet, as if mixed with honey.

I gulp it down.

I drink enough to give her relief but I leave her breast half-full in case our son wakes hungry. Then I move to the other side, still painfully taut and already leaking milk, dampening the velvet dress.

This time Sloane holds her breast, feeding me the nipple. She cups the back of my head, pressing my mouth against her flesh, gasping at the first touch of my tongue.

As her milk begins to flow into my mouth, I reach up under the hem of her gown, running my fingers up the inside of her thigh. Her temperature grows warmer and warmer the further I travel, until I reach the steady-burning furnace of her cunt.

She's already wet, as I knew she would be.

As I nurse from her breast, I rub the ball of my thumb in circles on her clit.

With each gulp, I press a little harder.

Then I slide two fingers inside her. Now there's no mistaking that moan that I know so well. She rocks her hips, riding my fingers like a cock, still clutching my head hard against her breast.

She starts to cum, milk spurting into my mouth.

I keep finger-fucking her, knowing she might kill me if I miss a single stroke.

I rub her pussy until I've wrung every last bit of pleasure out of her, giving her the relief she needs in every possible way.

Only then do I release her, covering her breasts once more.

"Is that better?" I ask.

"Infinitely better," she says, kissing me deeply, tasting her milk on my lips.

Our son slumbers peacefully in the sling between us, unbothered by anything around him.

I rest my hand on his head, marveling how the curve of his skull perfectly fills the palm of my hand, his wavy dark hair softer than featherdown.

Sloane watches me, unsmiling.

"What is it?" I ask her.

"Did you see Evalina Markov's face?" she says.

"What about it?"

"She had melasma—darkening of the pigment in the skin."

"What of it?" I say.

Sloane frowns, cradling our son's warm body in the crook of her arm.

"Usually that happens from pregnancy," she says.

15

Ares

The first challenge of the *Quartum Bellum* takes place directly before Halloween.

Leo is, of course, voted in one last time as Senior Captain. He's trying not to let on how badly he wants to be the first Captain to lead his team to victory four years in a row.

I've never been able to tell him how much that would enrage my cousin Adrik, the former record-setter. Adrik is intensely competitive, maybe even more than Leo or Dean, if you can picture that level of psychopathy.

He's been infuriated by the ongoing war with the Malina. He wants to go scorched earth on them, though he knows as well as I do what their first act of reprisal would be.

My family will never be able to repay my uncle Dominik or his sons Adrik and Kade for how they've stood by us through all of this. Dominik's name has been slandered among the Bratva—he's been accused of embezzling money, overstepping his position, and god knows what else. He swallows it all to protect us, though his honor means everything to him.

Kade and I used to talk about how much fun we'd have attending Kingmakers together. Now I have to pretend I don't even know him.

I fucked up on that too, trying to come to his defense when Bodashka, Valon, and Vanya were harassing him last year. It's infuriating hearing those idiots slander my own family right in front of me. Hearing their "secret plans" of how they'll exploit our weakness for their gain. I'd like to strangle every last one of them in their sleep.

I asked Kade to enlist Dean to help us—to inform us if he hears of any concrete plans from that snake Danyl Kuznetsov. Dean, of course, thinks that Kade is only asking on his own behalf.

I wish I could tell Dean how much I appreciate his kindness to our family, which is in direct contrast to his own self-interest in Moscow.

I wish I could tell my friends a lot of things.

Despite Kade's team being eliminated in the second round last year, the Sophomores apparently feel he did well enough to warrant being voted in as Captain again.

I can at least congratulate him publicly, giving him the same kind of friendly fist bump that a casual acquaintance might offer.

The Juniors, perpetual first-round losers in the *Quartum Bellum,* seem at a loss when choosing their Captain. This year they go for brains over brawn, voting in Jacob Weiss, a slim, bespectacled Spy from a well-known Chicago mafia family.

The real surprise is the Freshman Captain: none other than Sabrina Gallo.

Though not everyone likes her close friendship with Nix Moroz, there's no denying Sabrina's charisma. Within a week of landing on campus, everyone seemed to know her name—certainly all the male students did. The Freshmen may be hoping that all Gallos are born champions. Or they might think that only a Gallo can beat a Gallo.

Leo and Sabrina have been engaging in non-stop shit-talk at every meal. Sabrina fully intends to knock her cousin off his pedestal, and Leo is equally determined to grind her into the dirt, not giving a fuck that she's three years younger and a girl.

"That's true equality," Leo tells Sabrina, grinning at her. "I wouldn't be a good feminist if I let you win."

"Let me win?" Sabrina scoffs. "You'll be lucky if you even catch of glimpse of me as I speed past you to the finish line."

"You don't even know what the challenge is yet," Leo says.

"It doesn't matter." Sabrina shrugs. "I'm nothing if not adaptable."

I'm not listening to them banter.

I'm looking across the table at Nix, who's eating her usual enormous breakfast, but without her typical enthusiasm.

Things have been strained between us since our argument outside the annex. She probably thinks I was being a shit friend to Hedeon, and she's right. I'm not a good friend to him. Or to anyone.

There are no classes today. All students will either be participating in, or watching, the *Quartum Bellum*. We never know what we'll be facing until directly beforehand. Strategizing on the spot is part of the difficulty.

By ten o'clock, every student in the school has assembled in the large field outside the castle grounds. Professor Howell waits for us in his usual drill sergeant stance: legs apart, shoulders square, chest out, hands clasped behind his back.

The air is crisp and dry, with a light, teasing breeze.

I'm relieved to see that Professor Penmark is nowhere in sight. The last QB challenge designed by him was one of the most torturous I've encountered—fitting, since he is our professor of Torture Techniques.

The absence of any visible apparatus is nerve-wracking. Surprises at Kingmakers are never good.

"Good morning!" Professor Howell bellows. "Would the four Captains please step forward?"

Sabrina Gallo, Kade Petrov, Jacob Weiss, and Leo Gallo all take their place before the professor.

Sabrina looks ridiculously self-possessed next to the three older Captains. Ridiculously glamorous too, even in her gray gym shorts and white socks. She tosses her mane of dark hair back over her shoulders, looking boldly around at the assembled students.

Kade bounces lightly on his toes, running a hand through his thick black hair. Kade has a gentler temperament than Adrik, but I'd never make the mistake of thinking he's a pushover. Like Leo, his cheerful demeanor hides an inner fire.

Jacob Weiss is still and watchful, examining each of the competing Captains in turn. He gives Leo a nod when they take their place next to each other. They probably met in Chicago.

Leo flashes his bright white grin to the Seniors, a silent signal that he already believes we're going to win. He knows a good leader never shows anything but full confidence to his troops.

It's Anna Wilk who looks pale and nervous, watching him. I know she wants the Seniors to win even more badly than Leo does—because she can't bear to see Leo disappointed.

"The rules for this first challenge will be slightly unusual," Professor Howell announces.

A ripple of whispers runs across the crowd of students as everyone tries to guess what that might mean.

"Each Captain will select one champion," Professor Howell says. "Only the champion will compete in the first event."

Now the mutters are louder and more excited.

"Be aware," the professor continues. "Whoever you select as champion will not be permitted to compete in any other events of the *Quartum Bellum*. Also, Captains cannot select themselves."

Now the mutter is a full-out babble as students begin shouting their suggestions to their Captains.

I can see Leo frowning, wondering who he should choose.

It's an interesting paradox: you want to pick someone strong enough to win the challenge, whatever it might be. But if you select your strongest competitor, you eliminate them from all subsequent challenges. A choice you might regret in the second and third round.

"Leo Gallo," Professor Howell says. "You first."

Leo doesn't canvas the Seniors to ask their opinion. And he doesn't hesitate. He looks me dead in the eyes as he declares, "I choose Ares Cirillo."

My stomach flips over.

Just what I needed: another massive burden on my shoulders.

"Thanks, buddy," I say.

Leo grins, knowing I'm not exactly thrilled.

"You've got this," he says.

"Your turn," Professor Howell says to Jacob Weiss.

Jacob considers for several minutes, looking around at his team.

I know why he's hesitating: the reason the Juniors have repeatedly lost the *Quartum Bellum* is because they don't have any all-stars in their year. They have no Leo Gallo or Dean Yenin, no "full package" competitor. Jacob is forced to choose between brains and brawn, skill and strategy, without even knowing the terms of the challenge.

At last, as Professor Howell taps his foot impatiently, Jacob says, "August Prieto."

August and his friends give a round of whoops. August is from a Brazilian Narco family. Handsome and popular, he was voted Captain in his Freshman year, but his team lost immediately. Jacob is clearly hoping this will be an athletic challenge and not one requiring much strategy.

"Kade Petrov," Professor Howell says.

Kade takes a deep breath, naming his champion: "Tristan Turgenev."

The blond giant steps forward with a look of resignation. Tristan is one of the Paris Bratva—an Enforcer already almost as tall as Leo and me, though he isn't yet full grown.

He's Kade's roommate and closest friend. Like Leo, Kade clearly wants to use someone he trusts, willing to risk deploying one of his most valuable soldiers early. After all, there's no point "saving the best" for the second and third round if you don't make it past the first.

Now only Sabrina Gallo is left to make her decision. As Professor Howell gives her a nod, she answers without hesitation. "Nix Moroz."

An uneasy murmur runs through the Freshmen.

"Are you fucking kidding me?" Estas Lomachenko says loudly.

Sabrina ignores them all, secure in her authority as Captain. She smiles at Nix, who tries to smile back but only manages to grimace.

"Excellent," Professor Howell claps his hands sharply. "Now, if you'll all follow me to the river bottoms . . ."

We troop downhill in a long, snaking line of students. With the champions chosen, speculation runs rampant on what the challenge might be. I don't bother to guess—we'll find out soon enough.

Leo falls into pace beside me.

"You don't mind being out for the rest of the challenges?" he asks me.

"No," I say. "It'll be nice to relax and watch for once." I throw him a look. "You might be watching, too, if I fuck this up."

"You won't," Leo says.

Even though I know Leo is an eternal optimist, his warmth spreads through me regardless. This is why people will follow him anywhere: Leo makes you believe. In this moment, I believe too. Leo chose me because he knows I can win.

As we reach the shady, sun-dappled river bottoms, I can't help glancing at Nix. We ran through here together. The river is right in front of us—I can hear it though I can't yet see it. It runs east toward the waterfall.

She looks over at me, a glint in her green eyes. I know she's thinking the same thing.

The path is roped off, with scarlet markers every hundred yards through the forest ahead.

Professor Howell calls us to attention once more:

"You'll be running an eight-mile race," he says. "With several obstacles along the route. Spectators, you may spread out along the route, or you can take the shortcut to the finish line. DO NOT interfere with the course or the racers. If you do, your team will be eliminated. Racers, you must follow the red markers. If you attempt to take a shortcut, or you fail to complete any of the obstacles, you will be eliminated."

"Sounds simple enough," Leo says.

"You would *think* so," Professor Howell says, with a suspicious look at the assembled teams.

He knows as well as I do that cheating and sabotage are second nature to most of the students.

I take my place at the starting line, right next to Nix.

She's pulling her insane curls back into a ponytail so thick that she can barely get her hand around it. The elastic band does its best, but snaps after one twist.

"Goddamnit!" Nix curses.

"Don't worry, I've got one," Sabrina says, taking the band off her wrist and passing it over to Nix.

Nix successfully completes the ponytail, though the elastic is straining like a waistband at an all-you-can-eat buffet.

She sees me staring.

"Just . . . zip it," she tells me. "I'm not in control of this hair."

I can't help laughing. "Have you ever tried cutting it?" I say.

"Yes." Nix scowls. "It broke the scissors."

I can't tell if she's joking.

"Ready . . ." Professor Howell says, raising his starter pistol.

Nix, Tristan, August, and I all drop to a half-crouch, looking straight ahead through the trees.

I can't see the obstacles. I have no idea what we'll be facing.

The pistol fires with an echoing boom that sends several birds rocketing up out of the treetops.

Daddy Issues — Sophia Gonzon
Spotify → geni.us/spy-spotify
Apple Music → geni.us/spy-apple

My legs are churning before I even register that we've started.

I dash across the pine needles and soft, springy earth, following once more the bright red banner of Nix's hair. I can see Tristan on my left, and August ahead of all of us, but it's only Nix I'm following, like we're the only two people in the woods.

August is faster than all of us, Tristan the slowest. That means little in the first leg of an eight-mile race. August constantly plays soccer with the other Narco kids, and if this were a simple sprint, he'd surely win. His stamina is a different question.

Tristan Turgenev is in for the long haul. I can hear him puffing along behind me, steady as a freight train.

I feel intensely focused. When I have to wait and worry, my mind runs in circles. But when it's time to act, I know what to do—at least, when it comes to physical tasks.

I see the first obstacle ahead of us: a thirty-foot fishing net strung up on a frame. We'll have to climb up one side and down the other.

August reaches the net first, leaping up and beginning to scale the front side. Nix follows hot on his heels. August climbs steadily at first, but as soon as Nix begins her ascent, the net undulates like a wave.

"Watch it!" August shouts down at her.

"I'm not making it shake on purpose!" Nix calls back up.

When I start climbing, the net jerks so hard that August loses his grip and drops five or six feet before he can scramble for purchase. His face is red and irritated but Nix doesn't give a fuck, she passes right by him, climbing hand over hand as fast as she can. Furious, August grabs her heel and tries to yank her down, half pulling off her shoe.

"No interference!" I shout at August.

"He said no interference from the *spectators*," August spits back at me.

"I don't give a fuck," I snarl. "Keep your hands to yourself."

Ignoring me, August grabs for Nix again.

Nix retaliates by kicking back with her heel, hitting August square in the forehead.

"You fucking *bitch!*" he howls up at her.

While he's distracted, I knock his feet out from under him. He loses his grip on the net, sliding all the way back down to the bottom.

Nix has flipped over the top of the net, descending the other side. We come face to face with each other, me going up and her coming down.

"You don't have to help me," she tells me.

"I'm not," I say.

"Good," she calls over her shoulder, dropping down. "Because I *am* going to beat you."

"We'll see about that," I mutter, climbing faster.

Tristan has reached the bottom of the net. His bulk makes it sway like a gale-force hurricane. I'm seasick by the time I'm halfway down the opposite side.

August is also climbing again, with a heel-shaped mark in the middle of his forehead and a poisonous expression on his face. He's only just reaching the top as I drop down from the net and start running.

I jog down a mile of winding trail before encountering the next obstacle.

I pound after Nix, using her as my pace setter, not really trying to pass her. From our previous run, I've got a pretty good idea of our relative speeds. If she's going as hard as she can and I match her, I'll be close to my redline.

The next challenge is a rig with twelve hanging rings set just far enough apart that you can brachiate from one to the next like a tree-dwelling monkey.

It's fairly straightforward. Nix and I cross over without too much trouble, me catching each ring directly after she releases it.

When we drop down on the other side, Nix pants at me, "Who builds all this?"

"The grounds crew," I say. "There's fifty of them, and they're mostly here for school security. But they do other shit too—tend the greenhouses and the gardens and all that."

"Do they ever have to secure anybody?" she asks, jogging off down the path again, following the red markers hung from the trees.

"Yeah," I say. "Miles Griffin—that's Leo's cousin—he got in pretty deep shit the year before last. They hauled him up to the Prison Tower for a week. And Ozzy Duncan . . ." I break off, not really wanting to relive that particular event. "He got in a lot of trouble, too. The Rule of Recompense is a real thing."

Nix has slowed slightly, listening to me as we run. She frowns.

"Miles Griffin . . ." she says. "I know that name . . ."

I want to swallow my own tongue.

I hadn't realized that Nix would have heard about the deal Miles cut with her father, handing over his drug pipeline to Dieter Prince and Alvaro Romero in exchange for breaking Zoe's betrothal to Rocco Prince.

And Nix definitely doesn't know I was there that night. Miles and I stole the Chancellor's private speedboat, one of the only ways off this island. We snuck over to Dubrovnik in the dead of night, so Miles could meet with Dieter, Alvaro, and Moroz in person and work his persuasive magic to force them to take the deal.

I warned Miles not to include the Malina. I tried to tell him that Marko Moroz is not a partner you want to have.

But Miles was desperate. He was willing to risk anything to free Zoe from her loathsome engagement to Rocco. So he cut the Malina in on the deal—using their American dollars to launder the bitcoin from the online drug deals.

Little did he know, that's not Marko's money.

It's *my* fucking money.

And I want it back. Along with everything else the Malina stole from us.

I should have known that Marko shares his business with Nix. Or at least, the parts he wants to tell her about.

"Miles is Caleb Griffin's older brother," I say, hoping she won't make the connection.

"Hm," she says, her brows still knit together.

"Anyway, quit trying to distract me," I pant, putting on another burst of speed. "I can't talk and run at the same time."

I hear footsteps behind us—August Prieto with fire in his lungs and malice in his heart, trying to overtake us.

We've almost reached the third obstacle: five pillars, before which stand five spherical stones.

I've seen this before. It's part of a typical strong-man competition, and also some of the Highland Games. I've seen it called the Atlas Stones, or the Dinnie Stones in Scotland.

You're supposed to lift the rocks, one by one, placing them atop the pillars.

Each stone is heavier than the one before.

I can't help casting a worried glance at Nix—strong as she might be, someone like Tristan will be at an obvious advantage in this part of the competition.

"Go ahead," I say to Nix, nodding for her to try the lightest stone first, while I start with the second.

Nix braces herself, feet wide apart, so she can muscle up the awkwardly-shaped rock. It's difficult to gain purchase on the smooth sphere.

I'm having the same problem with the second stone. I try several angles before bear-hugging the damn thing and lifting it up to the plinth, which is chest height for me and nearly head-height for Nix.

Grunting, Nix manages to lift her stone. It must weigh at least eighty pounds. The others only get heavier.

Once she's completed the lift, Nix shoves the stone down again so August can take his turn. I do the same with mine, grimacing at how hard it falls to the ground, knowing Nix will have to lift it back up again.

I work my way down the line. Each stone feels twice as heavy as the one before, though I know that's only my own growing exhaustion. The real difference in weight is probably only twenty to thirty pounds per rock. Still, it adds up quick.

By the time I get to the fifth and heaviest stone, I'm guessing it's about two hundred pounds. I have no idea how Nix will lift it, and I have the sick sensation that this might be the end of her race.

Tristan Turgenev has finally caught up with us. He seems to view the stones as a pleasant break from all the hateful running. With an expression of relief, he easily heaves up the stones one after another with no break in between.

August looks like he'd like to kill Tristan. He's still struggling with the fifth stone, having failed to lift it twice. He has to step aside to let Tristan finish.

I go back to the first stone and hoist it up, almost glad I saved the lightest for last.

Task complete, Tristan jogs off.

I should leave too. I linger, wondering if Nix will be able to lift the fifth stone. It took her several tries to get the fourth.

August manages to muscle the last and heaviest stone onto the stand, knocks it off, and sprints after Tristan.

Nix braces herself, breathing heavily, staring at that damned stone like it's her mortal enemy. She hugs it to her chest, driving her heels into the dirt, the muscles standing out on her quads against the tight legs of her shorts.

I can't stand and watch. My team is waiting somewhere along this course, hoping to see me in the lead, expecting me to win.

I start running again, praying for Nix's sake she can do it, even though I'm supposed to be beating her along with everyone else.

The next obstacle is a long crawl under a low-slung net, in which we receive a thick coating of dust and pine needles, and August and I pass Tristan once more.

Then we come to a pool with chain-link stapled over top.

August stares in confusion.

"How the fuck are we supposed to cross that?" he says.

The pool is essentially a shallow wooden coffin, a hundred yards long, filled with water. The only break in the chain-link is at the front of the pool, and then again at the end.

"You've got to swim across," I say.

I'm already dropping through the narrow opening in the chain-link. As far as I can tell, the point of this particular challenge is to battle your claustrophobia. The water is barely deep enough to actually swim. You can come up for air, but just barely—you've got to lay on your back, your face pressed against the metal mesh, with barely enough space for your mouth to open without water rushing in.

It doesn't bother me much—I used to swim in the ocean all summer long when we stayed at our house in Poseidonia. Ares and I even swam through the narrow sea caves on the south end of the island. So I'm able to cross the pool with only two breaks to breathe.

August lingers at the entrance of the pool, a greenish cast falling over his face. He's obviously dreading dropping in. He only does so when a large group of Juniors swarm along the edge of the course, shouting encouragement.

I climb out of the pool, sopping wet, wishing I'd thought to take off my sneakers before I got in. Now they squish with every step.

I'm smiling a little, thinking that if Nix does manage to lift that fucking rock, she'll sail through the next obstacle. She could swim the whole thing without taking a breath.

We must be getting close to the end now. Almost the whole course is lined with students who took the shortcut to the end, some walking back along the route to see who's in the lead. They shout a mix of encouragement and jeers, depending which team they're rooting for.

I check behind me to see how Tristan and August are faring—I can see them jogging along, both soaking wet. Tristan is plodding with the same steady determination as ever. August is the one who seems to be flagging. He made it through the pool, but at the cost of the last of his willpower. As I guessed, his stamina is shot and he seems to be running slower and slower.

I cross the next obstacle—a tightrope—which I have to repeat twice when I slip off two feet from the end.

Tristan falls on practically his very first step across the slack rope, then tumbles off again on his second attempt.

Seeing this, August picks up speed. He manages to cross first try, and now I'm sprinting again, sensing that we're nearing the end. August races after me, catching a second wind.

The thickets of spectators are three deep on either side of the course. They're screaming at me to "RUN! RUN! RUN!".

Up ahead, I spot two twenty-foot towers erected at the base of a short cliff. At the top of that hill . . . a hundred-yard dash to the finish line.

I race to the wooden tower, August grunting and gasping right behind me.

When we arrive, neither one of us knows what the fuck to do.

The towers are hollow, like we're supposed to climb up inside to reach the top of the cliff. But the sides are smooth, with nothing to grip. Reaching out with both hands, I can barely touch each wall.

August spreads his legs as wide as he can, almost in the splits. He tries to wedge himself in place so he can shimmy up like it's a chimney. His legs are so widespread that he can't scoot his feet without falling.

I hear his curses, echoing in the empty tower.

I'm racking my brains, trying to discover the trick.

I know there's a way to get up. I just have to be smart enough to think of it.

Nix comes sprinting out of the woods, her elastic split again, her hair bouncing wildly behind her.

She catches sight of August and me, still trapped in the towers, and her face alights with fresh hope. She's running harder than ever, her gaze darting back and forth between the towers, strategizing before she's even reached us.

She stops in front of me, breathing hard.

"Back-to-back!" she gasps.

"What do you—"

All at once, I understand.

I turn so I'm facing the side wall, letting Nix slip in behind me. With our backs pressed together, we can wedge our feet against the wall. She pushes against me, and I push against her. In coordination, we begin to climb.

"Left leg. Right leg. Left leg," Nix grunts, as we inch our way upward, knowing that if either of us slips, we'll plunge all the way down.

"Ready . . ." I say, when we're almost at the top.

In sync, we each grab the upper ledge of the tower, our legs dropping away beneath us. We haul ourselves up and over.

As soon as our feet hit the ground, we're sprinting for the finish line.

It's between me and her; August and Tristan are far behind us.

Though I can't spare a second to look at any of the Seniors crowded around us, I can hear them all screaming, "ARES! RUN! FUCKING RUN, YOU'RE ALMOST THERE!"

The finish line is right ahead of us.

Nix and I are sprinting flat out, side by side, running harder than we ever have in our lives.

And I'm trying to beat her, really trying.

Until I edge just the tiniest bit ahead.

I'm taller. My legs are longer. I know in that split-second that if I truly run as hard as I can, I'm going to win.

Nix is trying so fucking hard. She's racing against three boys, all bigger than her. Somehow she lifted that stone overhead when it weighed more than she does. She figured out how to get us up that tower. She wants this so badly—to prove herself to every kid at this school who hates her on sight. She wants to be their champion.

I don't need it. She does.

All it takes is one slow step—a slackening of pace that no one could notice.

Nix pulls ahead. She whips across the finish line, inches in front of me, immediately enveloped by the screaming, cheering Freshmen.

I let Leo pound me on the back in a congratulations I don't entirely deserve.

"Well fucking done!" he hollers, thrilled that we'll be moving on to the second round.

Anna, Chay, Dean, Cat, and Hedeon all swarm around me, along with the rest of the Seniors. The mild disappointment at the second-place finish is flushed away in the amusement that August is still trapped at the bottom of his tower, furiously listening to the celebration on the top of the cliff while he waits for Tristan to complete the tightrope.

We all crowd the edge of the cliff, looking down at him. He stares back up at us, sweating and snarling.

Tristan jogs up the path to the tower.

Through gritted teeth, August says, "Come on, go back-to-back with me so we can climb up."

"No," Tristan says, shaking his head.

"What do you mean no?" August shrieks.

"No," Tristan says calmly. "You're faster than me. When we get to the top, you'll sprint past me and win."

August can't argue that point.

"Well, you have to anyway!" he sputters. "That's the only way up!"

"The only way for *you*, maybe," Tristan says.

Crossing to the opposite tower, Tristan lays down on his stomach, his arms and legs outstretched like Superman. With his superior height, he can just wedge himself in place and begin inching his way upward, belly down.

The mixture of laughter and howls is deafening as half the students cheer Tristan onward, the rest in near-hysterics at the sight of August trapped on the ground.

Like the fabled tortoise, the slow and steady Tristan makes his way inexorably upward. He hauls himself over the ledge, then lightly jogs across the finish line.

"There," he says to Kade, wiping the back of his arm across his sweating brow. "We didn't lose at least."

Kade is laughing so hard that tears run down his cheeks. "I can't believe you left him down there," he howls.

"That's what he gets for making me run so fast," Tristan says, his face still pink and sweating.

"You weren't fast," Kade says, holding his sides.

"Fast for me," Tristan grumbles.

Tristan's little sister Lucy and his cousin Rene come running up to congratulate him. They're both Freshmen, and they seem in awe of Nix, who pulled off a stunning first-round victory against the far more experienced champions of the opposing teams.

"You even beat *him*," Lucy whispers to Nix, looking at me like I'm an ogre in a fairytale.

"I can hear you," I tell her.

Lucy blushes almost as pink as Tristan.

"I didn't think you were gonna come back from those stones," I tell Nix.

She shakes her head, surprised at herself.

"It took me six tries," she admits. "I almost gave up."

"Why didn't you?" I ask her.

"Because," she says as if it's obvious. "I never give up."

"Right," I say. "I should have known."

And I really should have.

My whole life I've been intimately acquainted with that kind of woman: my mother is exactly the same.

Several professors have joined the crowd of spectating students. While Professor Howell has jurisdiction over the *Quartum Bellum,* the other teachers enjoy watching the challenges, especially the strangest and most interesting ones.

I see the Chancellor congratulating Sabrina Gallo on a rare Freshman win.

The Chancellor has come to the *Quartum Bellum* before—usually only when it takes place right outside the school grounds, where he has appropriately luxurious seating available to him. I've never seen him walk as far as the river bottoms.

He's standing close to Sabrina Gallo, his black, heavy-browed eyes roaming over her face. The deep, craggy lines on his face are arranged in an uneasy mixture of curiosity and something else . . . something very like hunger.

Sabrina doesn't seem discomfited. She speaks to the Chancellor with the same careless, confident air she applies to everyone, young and old, weak and powerful.

I'm the one with the anxious impulse to drag Sabrina away from him.

Nix follows my gaze, watching the Chancellor's avid conversation with the much younger girl.

"He's taken a liking to Sabrina, hasn't he?" she says quietly. "I thought so on the first day of school, when he let us off so easy."

I force myself to look away, saying, "He's not always a despot. I've seen him be nice to students before."

"What kind of students, I wonder?" Nix says, her red-gold eyebrows drawn together in a line.

"Come on," I say, trying to distract her. "Everybody's going to want to throw you a party."

16

Nix

The elation I feel winning that first challenge is like nothing I've ever known.

I've never been on a team before.

I've never been anyone's champion.

The high-fives and back-slaps and compliments and congratulations are like a mainline drug straight to my brain. I'm floating on a cloud of euphoria, which is all the warmer because Ares doesn't seem to mind that I won.

The fact that we worked together to make it happen is the best part of all.

I admire Ares.

He's disciplined and restrained—two qualities I lack.

He never loses control of himself.

When I was left all alone standing in front of those stones, I could have screamed with frustration. But I knew I wasn't going to give up, and that meant there was no point whining or crying about it. I had to get it done any way I could.

Sabrina is over the moon that we took first place in her very first challenge as Captain. I've never seen her look more gorgeous than in the full glow of gloating.

"I think me picking you as champion really shows my genius," she says, grinning at me with her sharp white teeth.

"Of course you do," I laugh. "Don't ever let anyone accuse you of being humble."

"I never would," she assures me.

"I'm just sorry I can't compete in the rest of the events," I say, frowning. "I mean, don't get me wrong—winning that one was well fucking worth it. But now that I've got a taste of it—I really think we could take the whole damn thing!"

"If we do, it'll be because of you," Sabrina assures me. "You got the Freshmen hyped."

We're getting ready for the party to celebrate our win. Well, the Freshmen, Sophomores, and Seniors are celebrating—the Juniors are in near-mutiny, utterly fed up with their constant losses and ready to lynch August Prieto for letting them down yet again.

Cat Romero is the only Junior who seems indifferent to the humiliation.

"I didn't even have to compete this year," she said happily over dinner.

I ate an entire chicken and a mountain of potatoes. I've never been so ravenous in my life. Then for dessert, fresh-baked blueberry pie with actual whipped up cream, not the shit out of a can ... I think I reached nirvana.

Now I can feel my legs stiffening up like redwood trunks, and I have no idea how I'm going to dance tonight.

Sabrina is, if anything, more excited for this party than she was for the challenge itself.

She's standing at the mirror, somehow managing to improve upon an already perfect face. She's made her eyes all the more smoky and cat-like, her irises a pale silvery-gray in the ring of the dark shadow. Her hair falls in smooth, shining waves that my insane curls could never hope to emulate. Her dress is a liquid silver that reminds me of chain mail. It looks like she poured it on over her curves.

Sabrina's body is insane. I try to avoid watching her change clothes so I don't suffer a heart attack.

"What are you gonna wear?" she asks me.

"This," I say, gesturing to my trousers and sweater vest.

I detest the uniform, but I also hate doing laundry, so I don't change outfits any more than necessary. You can't go to class without your uniform, or to the dining hall. I usually wear a sweater vest or pullover with no blouse underneath, and a pair of trousers with my army boots. It's an uneasy compromise between me and Kingmakers that displeases us both.

"Nix," Sabrina says patiently. "Everybody dresses up for parties."

"How do you know?" I say. "We haven't been to any yet."

"Not here," Sabrina says, "but it was practically my full-time job in Chicago."

"I don't like dresses," I tell her. "I like them on you, but they look stupid on me, like a bear in a bikini. I'm too big."

"There's a million sexy outfits you can wear that aren't a dress," Sabrina persists. Then, with a sly look, "You know Ares is gonna be there..."

She knows we've been spending time together.

Still, I have to squash her insinuation up front.

"He's not trying to date me," I say bluntly. "Nobody in their right mind wants to date the daughter of Marko Moroz, that's pretty fucking clear."

"Did *he* say that? Or are you just assuming?" Sabrina inquires, calmly glossing her lips.

"We're just friends," I tell her stubbornly.

"I've got a lot of friends," Sabrina smiles. "They don't look at me like that . . ."

"*Everybody* looks at you like that." I roll my eyes.

Sabrina is sex incarnate. The way she walks, the way she stands, the sultry rasp of her voice . . . even the Chancellor couldn't take his eyes off her.

"What was he saying to you?" I ask Sabrina. "The Chancellor, I mean."

"Don't try to change the subject."

"I'm not—I saw him talking to you. What did he want?"

"He was just congratulating me," Sabrina says carelessly.

"You should be careful around him. I don't trust him."

"No shit," Sabrina says, snapping her lip gloss closed. "I know what he did to Ozzy's mom, and to Dean. I have no intention of getting on his bad side."

"I'm not sure his good side is a great place to be either," I persist.

Sabrina won't be distracted from her own initial point.

"You should dress up tonight. Really make Ares stop and stare."

"If he likes me, then he likes me looking like this," I say, gesturing to my usual attire.

Sabrina sighs. "Look, I'm not trying to *Princess Diaries* you. I'm just telling you, I know men . . . and it's never a bad thing to surprise them."

I narrow my eyes at her, sizing up the glamorous vision of Sabrina Gallo, wondering what a ten-percent dose of her moxie might look like on me.

"Well . . ." I say slowly. "If you promise not to go overboard . . ."

17

IVAN PETROV
ST. PETERSBURG

Nineteen Years Ago

Gangsta — Kehlani
Spotify → geni.us/spy-spotify
Apple Music → geni.us/spy-apple

I t's late on a snowy December evening.

I'm fucking my wife on a bearskin rug in front of a roaring fire.

I can't imagine a more perfect activity for a winter's night. And she has never looked more stunning.

I've never known a woman more beautiful or ferocious. She bites the side of my neck, her teeth digging into the flesh. I have to pin her down hard in the rough, black fur, still smelling of bear oil and Siberian snow.

We wrestle together, twisting and swapping positions, our naked bodies entwined in the blazing heat of the fire.

This never fails to remind me of the night I met her. The night she tried to kill me.

Never have I fought harder for my life. Not knowing what I was really fighting for—not to save my life, but to live it more fully than I could ever have imagined.

Her flesh glows with an inner fire, not just the reflected light. Her eyes glitter like gems. Her mouth tastes richer than chocolate.

I'm ravenous for her. I trace the mounds of her breasts with my tongue. I lap at the hollow of her throat. I can't stop inhaling her scent, thrusting my face against her neck, and even raising her arms overhead to smell beneath.

"What perfume is this?" I growl.

"No perfume," she says. "Just me."

No scent is more enticing. My mouth is watering, my cock raging to ram inside of her.

"I'm ovulating," Sloane says.

My heart pumps harder, each throb sending a gallon of blood rocketing through my veins.

She licks the rim of my ear, thrusting her tongue inside and then whispering, "If you can hold me down and cum in me, I'll carry another baby for you."

I would never mix my seed with a lesser woman. I want children from her, and no one else.

Sloane has already born me a son, a strong and handsome child, as intelligent as his mother and as disciplined as myself.

Now I want a daughter as beautiful and vicious as Sloane.

We struggle with new intensity, all her skill and trickery in opposition to my superior strength and size.

My wife did not enjoy pregnancy. She hated how it weakened her with nausea. I know this offer is not given without conditions, and it may not be repeated. If she manages to slip my grip, there will be no baby.

She tries to twist away from me. I seize a handful of her hair, yanking her back again. She vaults over my shoulder, throwing her arm around my neck, trying to choke me from behind.

I get my forearm in the crook of her elbow and muscle her arm away, grabbing her wrist with my opposite hand and twisting it.

Now I have her arm up behind her back and I throw her down on the bearskin, forcing her legs apart with my knees.

She's still struggling, fighting like the wild little fox that she is—never submitting.

I see the gleam of wetness between her thighs and I smell that rich, musky scent that inveigles me, promising that if I cum deep inside of her tonight, my seed will take hold.

My cock is raging, standing out from my body like a weapon.

I put one hand on her back, shoving her down. With my other hand, I grip the base of my cock.

I thrust it in.

Her pussy is hotter than the fire, tight and liquid and clenching.

She lets out a shriek that is part fury and part helpless pleasure.

I pump into her, my knees pinning down her legs, my cock driving into her from behind, my hips smacking against the firm globes of her ass.

She begins to moan, rocking her hips, spreading her thighs wider to invite me in deeper. Her hands splay in front of her, fingers gripping the thick black fur.

I want her to moan like that in my ear. I want to feel her breasts against my chest.

I withdraw so I can flip her over to face me.

The moment I do, she leaps up from the rug, ready to sprint away from me. She can't help herself—as good as it feels, she can't resist her impulse to trick me with her supposed cooperation, to escape, and to win.

Roaring, I fling myself after her, wrapping her up in my arms and bringing her to the ground once more.

Now there will be no mercy and no hesitation.

I pin her arms over her head. I drive into her with full force. And I fuck her ruthlessly, her breasts bouncing on her chest, her head thrown back to expose the long, beautiful lines of her throat.

I suck that throat like I could drink her blood through the skin. I bite her neck and her breasts, marking her with bruises to remind her that she's married to an animal, to an equal, to the one man in the world who will never let her escape.

She may be a fox, but I'm a wolf. The wolf takes the fox whenever he likes.

I crush her lips under mine. I pump into her, telling her, "You belong to me, *moya malen'kaya lisa*. You will carry my child."

She lets out the three whimpering gasps that tell me she's about to cum—the only vulnerable sound she ever makes. Then, as her pussy clamps down on my cock, I erupt inside of her, pouring my cum at the very entrance of her cervix, bathing her womb with my seed.

Her pussy twitches and clenches, helpless against the waves of pleasure washing through her.

I don't stop fucking until I've milked out every last drop.

She lays still, limp and exhausted beneath me.

I scoop her up, depositing her on the sofa.

"Don't stand up for an hour," I order. "Let it stay inside you."

For once in her life, Sloane obeys, looking at me with the simmering lust that only appears when I conquer her. She isn't angry that I won—she married me because I'm the only man who can beat her.

I take down a copy of *Hiroshima,* and I lift her head into my lap, saying, "Read to me."

She reads for over an hour, weaving the history of war in the air with her low, enchanting voice. The fire pops and shifts in the grate. The snow batters silently against the dark windows.

I'm warm and more peaceful than I've ever been, wondering if, at this very moment, sperm and egg are meeting inside of her, inches below my hand resting on her belly.

I stroke Sloane's hair, watching her eyelids grow heavy and the book droop in her hands as she succumbs to this most soothing of sensations.

Then the radio crackles on the end table.

Maks says, "Someone is coming to the gate."

Sloane sits up, her dark curls disarrayed in every direction. She blinks, the usual avid brightness popping back into her eyes. She says, "Who would come visit us unannounced?"

It's a rhetorical question. She knows Maks will answer it as soon as he approaches the vehicle. Sure enough, a moment later, the radio crackles again and Maks says, "It's Marko Moroz."

Sloane's eyes meet mine.

She's aware of my history with Marko, though she's never met him. Marko hasn't left Kyiv in several years, and I haven't visited him.

I don't know why he's come here tonight.

After a moment's hesitation, I say to Maks, "Let him in."

Sloane and I retrieve our scattered clothes, subconsciously aware of the time elapsing while Marko drives up toward the monastery, parks, and strides across the snowy yard to our front door. I can almost hear the soft growl of the dogs, who will be held back from attacking by an order from Efrem or Oleg.

At the same moment, Sloane and I finish dressing. We abandon the book, walking down the hall to the front entryway. I pause to smooth back an errant curl from Sloane's face.

"Yes, make sure I look pretty for Marko," Sloane says.

My wife is equal parts playful, mocking, and brilliant. She's never serious . . . until she needs to be. Then there's no one more deadly.

I would never make the mistake of underestimating her.

I'm glad she's here beside me, to meet this man who has been an uneasy shadow over my life since the day I met him in the prison camp.

The stories of Marko's rise to power in Kyiv have reached far beyond St. Petersburg. It was one of the most brutal and bloody coups of the last fifty years. I wouldn't like to believe half of what is now said about Marko—though I wouldn't dare doubt it, either.

I throw open the door.

Marko steps inside, his beard, mustache, and eyebrows frosted with ice, snow dusting his shoulders.

The cold comes in with him, the chill thick on his clothes.

He looks like a Siberian bear standing on hind legs. His fur coat reaches to the floor, his boots dropping melting puddles of slush on the flagstones.

"Ivan!" he cries, holding his arms wide.

I step into them, though I'd rather not, and we embrace.

When he releases me, he turns to Sloane with the look of shock and wonder that no man can hide when he catches sight of her.

"By god," he says. "I heard you were a beauty, but for once the rumors cannot exaggerate. Now I understand how my friend Ivan went from vicious *Vor* to family man."

Sloane holds out her hand to be kissed, a deft maneuver that prevents Marko from attempting to embrace her as well. Her dark eyes size Marko up, cataloging his every word and gesture.

"Would you like a drink?" she says. "This cold will steal your soul."

"I never turn down a drink," Marko says, following us deeper into the house.

Several of our men are occupying the billiards room where the full bar resides. Sloane leads us back to the sitting room, swiftly plucking up the book from the sofa cushion before Marko can sit on it.

"What's your fancy?" she says to Marko.

It's not like her to play housewife—I'm guessing she wants to stay on her feet, free to cross behind us, and free to access the bevy of weapons stashed all over the monastery, including behind a false panel of books on the shelf.

"Surprise me," Marko says with a grin.

Sloane mixes the drinks at the smaller bar. I know she'll make mine weak and Marko's strong.

Marko looks around the room at floor level.

"Where's your son?" he says.

"Asleep. It's past midnight," I remind him.

"Oh, of course, of course," he says. "I won't keep you long . . . wouldn't want your wife to miss her beauty sleep."

I can almost feel Sloane's irritation like a furnace behind me. She despises when men try to make her looks her defining characteristic—as if beauty is the only and highest achievement a woman can reach.

She hands Marko his drink, deliberately spilling a few drops on the thigh of his cargo pants. He doesn't seem to notice.

"Thank you," Marko says, allowing his eyes to rest on her a little too long.

This is a deliberate provocation. If he does it again, I'll cut his fucking eyes out of his head.

Marko turns to me, smiling more widely than ever. "I want to invite you to my wedding," he says. "Though I wasn't invited to yours."

"It was a small and private ceremony," I say. "Dominik and Lara were married at the same time."

"Two brothers wedded on the same day," Marko says, that old jealousy creeping back into his voice. "What a bond you share."

"Congratulations," I say, ignoring that. "Who's the lucky woman?"

"Her name is Daryah Tataryn," Marko replies proudly.

I can tell he's genuinely excited for the match. There's no reason for him to marry otherwise—more than ever these days, Marko answers to no one.

"She's a famous swimmer," Marko says.

"I've heard of her," Sloane perches on the arm of the couch, not too close to Marko and me, and not so settled that she couldn't rise easily. "She swam from Florida to Cuba."

"Indeed," Marko grins. "And that is how we met."

"Swimming the opposite way, were you?" Sloane says.

Marko's eyes narrow slightly. "She's funny," he says to me, turning away from Sloane.

"When will the wedding take place?" I ask Marko, my jaw tight.

"Next week," he says. "That's as long as I can wait. You've never seen such a woman—as strong as a man! And twice as stubborn."

He laughs his loud, booming laugh, then tosses down half his drink.

"I'm happy for you," I tell Marko. "I wish we could attend—unfortunately, Sloane and I are traveling to Denver in a few days' time. We're opening a dispensary."

"I heard you expanded to America," Marko says, nodding slowly. "You were always ambitious, Ivan. I'm glad to see the hunger is still there."

"I hope your marriage will bring you as much joy as mine has done," I say.

Marko finishes his drink, setting his glass down hard on the end table next to the sofa.

"It is good to see you, my friend," Marko says, standing up. He claps me on both shoulders, hard. "Let us not wait so long before the next time."

Then, giving a slight bow to Sloane, "Forgive the interruption, and please enjoy the rest of your evening, Mrs. Petrov."

"Good night," Sloane says shortly.

She doesn't speak again until the door has closed behind Marko.

"He didn't give us enough notice on purpose," Sloane says. "He doesn't want you at the wedding. And he certainly didn't come to St. Petersburg to invite you. I'm sure he's up to something in your territory."

"*Our* territory," I remind her. "And yes, I assumed the same thing."

Sloane looks agitated, folding the throw on the couch and flinging it over the back cushion with too much vigor.

"You didn't poison his drink, did you?" I ask her.

"No," she says. "Though I was tempted."

I put my hands on her shoulders, gently massaging the tense muscle at the base of the neck until she relaxes slightly.

She turns to face me. "I don't like him," she says, dark eyes fixed on my face. "He reminds me of my father—that same edge of madness. He's got one foot in the real world, and one in his own head."

I sigh.

"I wish you were there to tell me that in the prison camp."

Sloane stands on tiptoe to bring her lips to mine.

"It doesn't matter," she says. "Your alliance with him is over. We can be 'friends' at a distance."

18

Ares

Because it's been such a warm autumn, there's no need for the shelter of the old stables on campus. Tonight's party is taking place down on the Moon Beach.

You can't actually swim on the beach—the riptides are too strong. But the crescent of white sand, and the black star-speckled sky overhead, and the crashing waves close at hand, all add to the wild air of two hundred students ready to cut loose.

Dean Yenin and Bram Van Der Berg have organized tonight's festivities. In Dean's usual overachieving way, he's built not one, but four separate bonfires that blaze away like vast torches, calling everyone down from the school.

The air glows smoky red, the popping sparks and the scent of burning pine singing my nose.

I followed Hedeon down here, sticking close by his side as my mother advised.

Music blares from several speakers hung from the trees. Students are already peeling off their shirts in the combined heat of the bonfires. It only makes us look more savage as we dance on the uneven sand.

Uprising — Muse
Spotify → geni.us/spy-spotify
Apple Music → geni.us/spy-apple

I'm surprised to see Hedeon also strip off his shirt, baring the awful scars on his back and arms. Usually he keeps his torso covered at all times. He throws the t-shirt aside with a defiant snarl, looking around like he's daring anyone to comment.

Even his chest is burned and slashed, though not as badly as his back. One of his nipples is missing.

I catch several students peeking at him with shocked expressions. But the more bootleg liquor is passed around, not to mention handfuls of party drugs sold at outrageous prices by a Senior Spy called Louis Faucheux, the less anyone seems to notice.

Hedeon isn't the first scarred mafioso. Bram has plenty of scars from his habit of getting in fistfights with anyone who annoys him, and Dean has a freshly fucked-up back that almost rivals Hedeon's.

It's always been Hedeon's anger that repelled people, not his appearance.

I see that anger burning in his eyes more furiously than ever tonight.

He's watching Ilsa Markov as she dances on the opposite side of the nearest bonfire.

Considering that she lives and studies with almost exclusively male students, Ilsa has a surprising amount of female friends. She's funny, boisterous, and popular, in a way that makes me think half those girls have a crush on her. They're certainly trying to dance as close to Ilsa as possible, with admiring looks at her athletic physique.

Ilsa is a blue-eyed Wonder Woman with a glossy dark ponytail, Amazonian thighs, and extreme confidence. A second circle of boys surrounds her group, led by Bodashka Kushnir and Pasha Tsaplin, who both hail from Moscow and have lusted after Ilsa since long before any of them came to Kingmakers.

Bodashka and Pasha are two of the conspirators who think my family's territory is ripe for takeover since my father's "absence" and my uncle's "betrayal" have left us vulnerable to attack.

I'd like to walk over there right now and smash their heads together. They're drunk enough that I could do it.

But I have to focus on Hedeon instead.

He approaches Ilsa directly, cutting through the group of giggly girls, drawing the angry scowls of Bodashka and Pasha, who had hoped to swoop in any moment.

Ilsa gives Hedeon an appraising look, her eyes roaming over his bare torso. Hedeon stands firm under her scrutiny, arms folded over his chest.

"I didn't think you danced," she says.

"I didn't come over here to dance," Hedeon replies.

"Come to offer me a drink, then?"

"No."

Now a gleam of curiosity flares in those indigo eyes.

"What, then? Arm wrestle? Footrace? Ares knows there's no better foreplay," Ilsa says, shooting me a sly look.

I keep my expression neutral, though I can feel my neck getting hot, and not from the fire.

It's impossible to do anything at Kingmakers without someone seeing and guessing exactly what's in your head.

Ilsa knows the thrill of physical competition. She knows damn well that chasing after Nix gets my blood pumping in more ways than one.

Luckily, Hedeon isn't going to be distracted.

"I want to talk to you," he says to Ilsa doggedly.

"Alright." She shrugs, abandoning her clique of blushing girls.

Ilsa and Hedeon stalk off across the sand to a slightly quieter patch of beach. Neither of them questions why I'm following along after them. Hopefully Hedeon thinks I'm offering moral support.

"What is it?" Ilsa says, standing with legs apart and arms crossed over her chest just as boldly as Hedeon himself.

Ilsa's older sister Neve is Heir. She's made no secret that Ilsa will be her lieutenant. Both girls surely know that in our world, the slightest sign of feminine weakness would be deadly to them. They have to be more decisive, more intimidating, and more ruthless than any man, or the Bratva jackals will come for them, just as they're trying to come for my family.

Hedeon can feel the challenge radiating out of Ilsa just as I can. He's choosing his words carefully. He won't get anything out of Ilsa if he offends her.

"I saw a picture of one of your relatives in the annex," he says. "Evalina Markov—she was a Captain in the *Quartum Bellum*."

"That's right," Ilsa says proudly. "She won twice."

"I saw that . . ." Hedeon says. "But then, she didn't compete in her Senior year. And I thought that was odd."

"She wasn't at school her Senior year," Ilsa replies promptly.

Hedeon licks his lips, trying to hide his eagerness.

"Why?" he says. "Where did she go?"

"She married my uncle Donovan."

I see Hedeon's chest rising and falling rapidly. He's wondering if Uncle Donovan might be his father. Evalina Markov and Donovan Dryagin might have given their baby away to hide the accidental pregnancy, then married afterward.

"Was your uncle at Kingmakers, too?" Hedeon asks, his voice shaking slightly.

Ilsa shakes her head.

"No. Donovan is ten years older," she says. "They were betrothed when she was, I dunno, fourteen or something. He had to wait for her to grow up a little. You know how it was then." She rolls her eyes. "How it still is now, for some families."

Hedeon locks eyes with me.

We both know that means Dryagin can't possibly be Hedeon's father. Dryagin was ten years older, established in his career, and had the blessing of the Markovs. If he had impregnated Evalina over the summer holiday, she would simply have dropped out of school and married him, as she apparently did in her Senior year.

The hasty adoption surely shows that Evalina fell pregnant from someone other than her fiancé.

Now Ilsa is frowning, watching the silent communication pass between Hedeon and me.

"Why are you two so curious about my aunt?" she demands.

"I'm not," Hedeon grunts, with a passable imitation of his usual surliness. "It's Leo who wanted to know. You know he's trying to break the record of all the previous Captains."

"He better hope Adrik Petrov doesn't kill him if he does." Ilsa grins. "I met him once in St. Petersburg—he's pure animal, that one."

It's the first time I've seen Ilsa admit admiration of anyone. I have to hide my smile, knowing how much Adrik would love to hear it.

"So . . . do you want that drink, then?" Hedeon says to Ilsa.

I don't know if he's covering his tracks, pretending to hit on her after all, or if he's as sucked in by her beauty and boldness as Bodashka and Pasha.

"No thanks," Ilsa says, tossing her head. "But . . . you can come dance if you want."

She strides back across the sand, walking as easily as if it were firm ground.

"You gonna go dance with her?" I ask Hedeon.

"No," he says, looking at me like I'm insane. "I'm not gonna grind on somebody who might be my cousin."

"Oh, right," I say, trying to hold back the slightly-hysterical laugh that wants to bubble up inside me.

It's impossible. I let out a snort, and then a full laugh.

To my surprise, Hedeon chuckles too. His laugh is strangely soft compared to his rough features.

"She'd only be like . . . your second cousin," I say, trying to compose myself.

"You've been hanging around Anna and Leo too long," he says, shaking his head at me.

That only makes me laugh harder.

"Anyway, she's not my type," Hedeon says.

"Oh yeah? What's your type?"

Hedeon doesn't answer me. But a few minutes later when we join Dean, Cat, and Bram by the fire, I see him scanning the jostling crowd of students. Looking for someone.

I can't keep an eye on him any longer. Sabrina and Nix have just made their appearance on the edge of the sand.

A dozen heads turn in their direction—in Sabrina's direction, most likely. I'll admit, she's looking particularly stunning in a silver dress that shimmers like scales.

But it's Nix who captures my attention, immediately and irrevocably.

I've never seen her dressed up before.

She still looks like herself. Everything is just . . . more.

She's got her hair braided on the sides, running back along the crown before loosening into curls again. The smoky shadow around her eyes makes her green irises look pale and serpentine. Her cheekbones are sharper, her mouth wide and firm.

She looks like a Viking princess, here to celebrate her victory.

She's dressed all in black—trousers as usual, but this time in a silky material that gleams in the firelight. Her cropped tank top shows a slice of flat, hard abdomen above the waistband of her pants.

I'm drawn to her like a fish on a line, reeled in.

"There you are," I say. "What took you so long?"

"I put on makeup and better clothes," Nix says, with that raw honesty that grabs hold of me every time, like a fist in my guts. "I wanted to impress you."

"It worked," I say. "You're stunning."

"Do you like me better this way?" she asks, looking up into my face to see the truth of my answer, whatever I might say.

"I like you best outdoors," I tell her. "On the beach, in the woods . . . anywhere outside. It's where you belong."

She smiles, letting out the breath she was holding.

"I agree," she says.

"Do you dance?"

"I like dancing. Whether I'm good at it is a different question . . ."

Desire — *Meg Myers*

Spotify → geni.us/spy-spotify
Apple Music → geni.us/spy-apple

I don't know if I'm a great dancer either.

Nix and I seem to move well together, and that's all that matters. Song after song flows by, faster than I can count them. I'm transfixed by the way Nix's hair flares gold, copper, and scarlet in the firelight, and how the smoke mixes with the scent of her skin.

Sabrina has already been snatched up by Kenzo Tanaka, who looks overjoyed at his good luck—until Bram cuts in and steals her away.

Anna and Leo are dancing the way they always do, extremely close together, looking into each other's faces, talking and laughing the whole time.

Caleb Griffin asks Chay Wagner to join him on the sand and she agrees, unembarrassed to be seen with a Freshman since everyone knows she's in a long-distance love affair with Ozzy.

I spot Kade Petrov dancing with Lucy Turgenev. Kade throws several cautious looks back at Tristan Turgenev to be sure Tristan doesn't mind his friend grinding with his little sister in a (mostly) respectful manner.

Tristan is paying zero attention, distracted by Cat's friend Perry Saunders who's hanging off his arm, babbling away at him with an expression of intense admiration plastered across her face. When he tries to escape, several more Sophomore and Junior girls surround him, drowning him in the celebrity adoration that comes from winning a challenge, even in third place.

Hedeon hasn't asked anyone to dance. He's standing at the edge of the sand, sipping a drink, watching everyone else. His face is deeply shadowed, the marks on his body dark as tattoos, almost seeming to writhe in the shifting firelight.

Then Cara Wilk steps into view, waving shyly to her sister. She's dressed simply in a pale blue dress, her dark hair loose around her shoulders. She dips her bare toes into the sand, her shoes abandoned in the grass.

Before she can join Anna and Leo, Hedeon cuts across the crowd of students, roughly shouldering aside anyone who stands in his way. He blocks Cara's path, glowering down at her.

Cara looks up at him, wide-eyed and startled, lips parted.

"Do you want to dance with me?" he grunts.

Cara's reply is so soft that I can't make it out over the music. She must have agreed because Hedeon pulls her onto the sand.

Anna is the ballerina, Cara the writer. Yet Cara has enough of her sister's grace that she slips into a smooth and even sensual rhythm within the rough circle of Hedeon's arms.

Dancing seems to relax her. Within a few minutes, she's able to look Hedeon in the face and answer his questions without blushing too much.

Hedeon doesn't take his eyes off hers, not for a second. His hand rests possessively on the small of her back.

Nix observes their interactions with the same interest as me.

"Opposites attract," she says, smiling slightly.

"Do you think that's true?" I ask her.

"Sure," she says, her eyes locking on mine once more, Hedeon and Cara forgotten. "I'd never want to be with someone with my same flaws."

"What flaws?" I laugh.

"Horrible temper, obviously. Always blurting out stupid things . . ."

"Not stupid," I correct her. "Just honest."

"I'm a grudge holder, too," she admits. "My father never forgives. And I think . . . I'm too much like him."

My stomach clenches. "What would you hold a grudge about?" I ask her.

"I hate being lied to," she says, her green eyes looking into mine, unbearably clear and direct. "It's why I've been so angry with my father since I came here. I thought he was honest with me. And now I realize there's things he didn't tell me. Lies of omission are still lies."

I have the horrible, panicked feeling that she knows. That she's talking about me, not her father.

"Honesty can be difficult," I say, through stiff lips. "Not everyone knows themselves as well as you."

"He knows his reputation, whether he agrees with it or not," Nix says, angrily, bright spots of color in her cheeks. "He could have warned me."

I let out a breath.

She really does mean her dad.

"Well, he let you come here at least."

"I'd like to see him stop me," Nix says, her color only rising.

If anyone could fight Marko Moroz tooth and claw, I think it's his daughter.

"God," Nix groans, as her leg twitches beneath her. "Aren't you sore? I'm fucking dying from that challenge."

"Come on," I say, leading her off the sand, toward the stand of trees surrounding the beach.

"Where are you taking me?" Nix asks, noting the pairs and trios of students who have already crept off this way to find a secluded spot for their intimate activities.

"Don't worry, I'm not trying to seduce you," I say.

Possibly another lie.

I can't take my eyes off her. My cock has been hard all night from every brush of her thigh against mine.

It doesn't help when Nix says in her low, throaty voice, "I'm not worried."

Our eyes meet and slide apart.

"Sit here," I say, indicating the base of an almond tree.

Nix lowers herself down gingerly, her legs unwilling to bend in the normal way.

I take her thighs across my lap. Gently, carefully, I begin to massage her quads. I start down by the knees, rubbing my thumbs in small circles where the muscle fibers meet the kneecap.

"Ohhh, Jesus," Nix groans, her head titled back and her long, creamy throat exposed to the moonlight. "Why does that feel so good?"

"It's one of the biggest muscle groups. Lactic acid builds up . . . feels good to release it."

I work my way upward, using the heels of my palms to run up and down the long strings of muscle.

Nix's legs are firm, but not like a man's. However androgynous she might dress, Nix remains feminine. She's not boyish—just a powerful and beautiful woman.

I haven't touched anyone in a long time.

Nix's warm legs laying across mine give me comfort she can't possibly know.

"Are you a professional masseuse?" Nix laughs. "Your touch is just . . . fucking magical."

I think of my family, where affection was as common as words, in a way that might surprise an outsider.

My father taught me to fight. My mother taught me to shoot. Both were harsh taskmasters, expecting a level of tactical precision that I've often had to hide at school so I don't draw attention to myself.

Yet, they were never violent with me outside of training. My father would rub my shoulders when he knew my traps were seizing up. And my mother would run her fingers through my hair as we watched a movie, like I was still a small child.

We hugged each other. We laughed together.

Our world is cold, but it was never a cold house.

"What's wrong?" Nix asks me, feeling my hands clench on her thighs.

When I don't answer, Nix says, "Are you trying to date me Ares, or are we just friends? I can't read you as well as some people."

Because I confuse her on purpose.

Because I'm not Ares at all.

"We can't date," I say.

"Why not?"

My jaw twitches. "I don't think your father would like that."

"Do you care what *he* wants? Or what *I* want?"

Through the thin silk of her trousers, I can feel her blood rushing, right under my palms. I know her heart is beating as hard as mine.

"What do you want, Nix?" I ask her.

"I want you to kiss me."

I look into her eyes.

Do I even remember how to do this?

I see her lips part, ever so slightly.

I lean forward, closing the space between us.

Right before our lips touch, a spark jumps between us, stinging my mouth. Then I kiss her, and the jolt is drowned in the shocking warmth and softness of her mouth. Every nerve comes alive. The sensation is so much stronger than I remember, overwhelming me.

I plunge both hands into her thick curls. They're coarse and soft, warm as fur wrapped around my fingers. I slip my tongue into her mouth, tasting her for the first time, finding her breath as sweet and smoky as the scent of her skin.

It doesn't matter if I remember kissing, because I've never kissed like this: without rhythm or plan, my heart speeding faster and faster like I'm sprinting downhill.

I rub my thumbs across her cheekbones, feeling the velvet texture of her skin. I push my tongue deeper into her mouth, breathing her in and swallowing her down.

She's gripping the back of my neck, her blunt nails digging into my flesh, pulling me in just as tightly as I'm pulling her.

When we finally break apart, it's only for breath, because we might pass out otherwise.

We're silent and panting, with no idea how much time has passed.

Nix breaks the quiet, laughing softly.

"Alright," she says. "Now I know you like me."

"Yes," I say. "I do."

There's no lie in that.

19

Nix

November passes in a whirl of classes and increased studying for end-of-term exams.

My fellow Freshmen are finally starting to warm up to me in the afterglow of the *Quartum Bellum* win, and Sabrina Gallo's unfailing support of me.

I don't know what I did to deserve a friend like her. I think we recognized each other as kindred spirits on that first day of school: two women who aren't afraid of anything, including getting into a little trouble together.

It's Sabrina's nature to be loyal to her friends—I see that same fierce fidelity in all her family who attend Kingmakers. Leo Gallo will decimate anyone who shows the least bit of snobbery to Ares. Anna Wilk is intensely protective of her little sister Cara, always saving her a seat at mealtimes and checking in with her daily on how her classes are going. And Caleb Griffin has fallen in with fellow Enforcers Tristan Turgenev, Rene Turgenev, and Kade Petrov, the four friends forming a clique that has apparently counteracted some of the rampant bullying in the Gatehouse.

Sabrina's attitude toward her many suitors is a different story. She's been relentlessly pursued by every male with a pulse since she stepped foot on campus. None of them have kept her attention for more than a week or two, leaving a trail of bitter exes and broken hearts in her wake.

She's already burned her way through half the eligible bachelors at school, including a square-jawed boxer called Corbin Castro, the Norwegian Heir Erik Edman, a devastatingly witty Junior named Jesse Turner, and, for a single day, the beautiful but conceited Thomas York.

She caused a near double-homicide by dating roommates Cameron Wright and Joshua Pierce. Then put the final nail in the coffin of any chance of being friends with Alyssa Chan when she dumped Alyssa's cousin Archie.

Kenzo Tanaka lasted the longest—Sabrina seemed intrigued by his rockabilly pompadour, artfully-distressed leather jackets, and encyclopedic knowledge of vintage Harleys. Unfortunately, Kenzo couldn't maintain his bad-boy cool for more than a week, completely losing his head and pinning so many romantic haikus to our door that our garbage can was soon overflowing with unwanted poetry.

"Why do they all turn out to be so boring?" Sabrina moans, as she finds herself single yet again at the end of November.

"Maybe you need to get to know them better," I tell her. "Ares isn't at all like I thought he was when we first met."

"Most guys are about as deep as an oil slick on pavement," Sabrina scowls. "Ares is the exception."

"He might be too deep," I sigh. "Sometimes I think I don't know him very well, even after spending all this time together."

Ares and I have been roaming all over the island together. The colder weather hasn't stopped us for a second—we bundle up and tramp anywhere we want to go.

But I feel like he pulled back from me after we kissed that night down on the Moon Beach.

"Have you fucked him yet?" Sabrina asks, noisily biting into a carrot stick.

We're sitting on our respective beds, ostensibly studying, but actually just shooting the shit.

My books are spread out all around me. Sabrina hasn't bothered to open hers. She's eating a selection of snacks smuggled up from the dining hall, heedless of the impressive mess she's making.

"No," I say, flushing. "And not by choice. He's driving me insane . . "

"Yeah, he's hot as hell," Sabrina agrees, nodding approvingly. "I'm not usually into the strong, silent type, but you can tell he's kinky as fuck under that buttoned-up exterior."

"You think so?" I say hopefully. "I don't know why he's holding out on me . . ."

Sometimes Ares looks at me like he wants to rip my clothes to shreds and eat me alive. But . . . he never actually does it. He's barely kissed me since that first time on the beach.

"Since when are you the type to sit around waiting?" Sabrina says, giving me a sly raise of one inky eyebrow.

"Since fucking never," I say, shoving my books aside.

"That's my girl." Sabrina grins.

I HEAD TO THE LIBRARY, following the advice of Lucy Turgenev, who told me that she saw Ares walking in that direction an hour earlier.

Once inside the still, dry space, I walk all the way up the ramp looking for him. The library is one continuous spiral, with curved shelves set against the wall, so it's not difficult to see who's inside.

I don't find Ares anywhere.

I'm about to leave, assuming I missed him, when he emerges from the pointed archway directly behind Miss Robin's desk.

"Ares!" I call, making him jump.

"Hello," he says, in his deep, smooth voice.

I don't know how one single word can have such an effect on me. The greeting vibrates my whole body like a gong, seeming to hang in the air between us for far too long.

"What were you doing?" I ask curiously.

"The archives are down there," he says, nodding toward the archway with its heavy wooden door still ajar. "I was looking for an organizational chart for the 'Ndrangheta."

"You didn't find it?" I say, noting his empty hands.

"No." Ares pushes back a dusty shock of hair with his forearm. "Just a lot of loose papers and mildewed books."

Miss Robin sweeps out of the archives, pulling the door shut behind her. Unlike Ares, she apparently *did* find what she was searching for—she clutches several crumbling scrolls against her chest, her thick glasses slipping down her nose, her red hair speckled with dust and fragments of ancient paper.

"Someday I'll finish organizing that mess," she sighs. Then, to me, "Can I help you with something, Nix?"

"No, thank you," I say hastily. "I was just . . . here."

I feel silly telling her that I was looking for Ares.

It doesn't help that Miss Robin has a remarkably sharp and inquisitive stare behind those granny glasses. I thought her eyes were brown at first, but now I see they're more of a dark hazel, with a burst of bronze radiating from the iris, inside a ring of olive green.

She's incredibly beautiful. I've seen her before in passing, though not as often, I'll admit, as my fellow students who spend more time in the library.

I've never spoken to her. Her low, husky voice, has that same quality as Ares'—the ability to thrill, to slide over your skin like a physical touch.

I get the sense that she's examining me as I'm examining her. Each of us curious for our own reasons.

I don't know what she's thinking, and I'm glad she can't read my mind.

I'm remembering a rumor I heard once, that there was some kind of romantic connection between Miss Robin and Ares . . .

I thought it was funny at the time—just one of those things people say, jokes and speculation to enliven a boring school day. Miss Robin is in her forties at least, maybe even fifty.

Seeing her now, it doesn't seem as ridiculous. She has a powerful presence at odds with her loose, knobby cardigans and thick stockings.

Not to mention the fact that Ares seems distinctly uncomfortable, glancing back and forth between us.

"We'll let you get back to work," he says, dismissing Miss Robin with little of his usual politeness.

Miss Robin only smiles. "No rest for the wicked," she says.

She strolls past us, carrying the scrolls to the upper level of the library.

"Was she helping you?" I ask Ares.

"Helping me what?"

"Look for the 'Ndrangheta chart."

"No. They didn't have it," Ares says shortly.

A strange tension hangs in the air. I always know when something's off—even if I don't know what, exactly, is wrong.

I fucking hate that sense of misalignment. I hate words unspoken.

So I say to Ares, "Are you friends with Miss Robin?"

He looks at me, eyes narrowed. "Why would you ask that?"

"Some people said . . . that you might like her."

"Jesus Christ." He shakes his head. "No. I don't have a crush on Miss Robin."

"Alright." I shrug. "Just wondering."

"I'm sick of people speculating about me," Ares hisses through his teeth. "This school is a fucking fishbowl. Everybody watching, everybody talking."

"Hey," I say, laying my hand lightly on his forearm. "I'm really sorry. I shouldn't have asked that."

Ares gives his head a shake, as if to throw off his annoyance.

"It's not your fault," he says.

Trying to change the subject in my usual awkward way, I venture, "I wonder what color her hair is really?"

"What?" Ares says, startled.

"Miss Robin—I don't think it's red."

Now he's looking at me like I've got two heads.

"You don't think her hair looks natural?" he says.

"Oh, it does." I nod. "It's lovely. It's more her skin tone—I get a little color in the summer, but come winter I'm pale as a ghost. She looks the same as when school started."

Ares is quiet a minute, then he says, "You really do notice everything."

I laugh. "And yet I can't remember a single thing I learned in my banking class."

Ares picks up his backpack from the nearest table, slinging it over his shoulder.

"So what did you really come here for?" he asks me. "I know you're not here to study."

I aim a punch at his shoulder that he doesn't even bother to dodge.

"For your information, I *was* studying, right before I came here."

We've come out of the library into the chilly afternoon air, the breeze tugging at our hair like a live thing after the stillness of the library.

"What interrupted you?" Ares asks.

"I wanted to see you," I reply simply.

Ares looks down at me, his eyes clear and beautiful beneath his thick, straight brows. "You did?" he says.

"Yeah. I really did."

A smile tugs at the edges of his mouth, showing a glint of his strong, white teeth.

"So how do I look?"

"Pretty fucking gorgeous," I tell him.

"You look like if autumn was a person," he says, taking one wild red curl between his thumb and index finger. "You look like if the woods came alive. And they were extremely competitive." He grins.

"Come walk with me," I say.

"Alright," Ares agrees.

We leave the castle grounds, heading directly to the strip of forest bordering the field.

Though we've walked this way so many times, there's a deliberate intention in our steps that was never there before.

We're not speaking, no need for words anymore.

High — Sivik
Spotify → geni.us/spy-spotify
Apple Music → geni.us/spy-apple

As soon as we step beneath the canopy of a vast sweet gum tree, Ares throws his bag on the ground and seizes me, his hands on either side of my face. He kisses me deeply, the fallen leaves grinding beneath our feet, sending up a dry, sugary scent.

This time, I don't wait to see if Ares will pull back or go further. I slide my hands down his body, touching his cock through his trousers.

I let out a sigh as I feel the thick bulge straining against the wool. He wants me. He absolutely fucking wants me.

It's like I touched a switch. As soon as my fingers graze his cock, Ares throws me down on the ground. We had a late summer and an even later fall—I land in a blanket of thick, crunching leaves. Ares falls on top of me, finding my mouth once more, thrusting his tongue into it as his fingers fumble with at the waistband of my pants.

He yanks my trousers down to my knees, my underwear going along with them. I expect him to touch me with his fingers, or maybe to just start fucking me.

Instead, he puts his head between my thighs and starts licking my pussy.

He eats my pussy exactly the way he kisses—his full, warm lips and his firm tongue attacking me in all my most sensitive places.

He licks all over my pussy lips and around my entrance, pushing his tongue inside of me. Then he finds my clit and dances the tip of his tongue around it until I'm writhing and moaning, grabbing handfuls of his hair and grinding my hips against his face, begging for more.

He flattens his tongue and starts lapping my clit in long, steady strokes. At the same time, he slides one long, thick finger inside of me.

My pussy is on fire. It's never been treated so good.

I've had sex before, but it was quick, secretive sex with one of my father's soldiers. It felt good, but not any better than getting myself off in the shower.

I've never had someone worship my body with their mouth.

I've never felt like I was being eaten alive, while Ares' hands roam over my body like the tentacles of an octopus, squeezing my breasts, sliding down my body, cupping my ass, pushing his fingers in and out of me.

Every place he touches me seems to come alive, warm and throbbing, extending the exquisite sensation of his tongue to all the other parts of me, until I feel like he's licking me up and down the entire length of my body.

Leaves drift down from the gum tree, deep vermillion and five-pointed like stars. They land on my naked body and in my hair, cool against my flesh, smelling peppery-sweet.

I'm in a state of bliss where everything seems brighter and clearer. The bits of blue sky between the red leaves shine as brilliant as jewels. The breeze rubbing the branches together makes a steady, rushing sound like running water.

The blood in my veins rushes at the same pace, spreading warmth to my fingertips and toes, making my whole body throb.

The orgasm comes so slowly at first that I hardly know it's starting. It builds and builds like the crescendo of an orchestra, each pulse stronger than the one before.

Ares thrusts his tongue in and out of me, in time to the clenching waves of pleasure. I'm moaning and writhing, my hands full of leaves as I grasp for purchase on the ground.

He slows his pace as the climax ebbs, but he doesn't stop. He's running his tongue gently over my clit, mindful of how sensitive and throbbing it has become, but not allowing the pleasure to seep away entirely.

He runs his big, strong hands up my thighs, grips my hips, then caresses my breasts again, gently plucking at my nipples.

My breasts are exquisitely sensitive now. His hands are like suction cups, the perfect size to grip every part of my breasts, to pull and squeeze simultaneously.

He's licking me harder now, steadily, and I realize he has no intention of stopping; he wants to make me cum again.

I can't lay back and accept it, I've always been the type to pull my own weight, to give as well as take.

Plus, I touched that thick cock through his clothes. Now I want to see it.

So I flip around, Ares' head still buried between my thighs, now facing the opposite way.

I unzip his trousers, pulling out his heavy cock that fills my hand, warm and throbbing and intensely satisfying to touch.

Ares' cock is as brown as the rest of him, and as excessively sized. It has a slight upward curve, topped with a head like a battering ram. The skin stretches silky smooth over the rigid flesh.

He groans as I grip him, then moans even louder against my pussy as I take the head of his cock in my mouth, dancing my tongue around the connecting ridge. His cock twitches against my tongue, highly sensitive to its slightest movement.

I'm on top of Ares, straddling his face, spreading my thighs wider so he can push his tongue deep inside of me. I'm humping his face, while his cocks slides deeper and deeper into my mouth. The heavy head of his cock hits the back of my throat.

He's thrusting in and out of my mouth in time with my hips grinding against his face. My mouth feels as loose and warm as the rest of me, and even though his cock is even bigger than I imagined, it burrows into my throat relentlessly, like a live thing with a mind of its own.

I'm not gagging—I'm too relaxed. The pounding of his cock is oddly satisfying. I want more and more, deeper and deeper.

Meanwhile, Ares' lapping tongue is bringing on another climax. I can feel it swirling and pulsing, trying to breach its bounds in the pit of my belly. Any moment it will explode outward, washing through me.

I start moaning around Ares' cock, the vibrations of my throat fluttering against the head.

Ares is panting like he's running again, sprinting against me to the end of the race.

It *is* a race, to see which of us will cum first.

Competitive as ever, I'm determined to beat him.

I squeeze my thighs around his face, pressing my clit harder against his tongue.

There's no clear winner this time.

His cock is twitching and pulsing in my mouth, the head fucking my throat, while I cum against his tongue. We're locked together down the length of our bodies, his hands gripping my ass, my fingers digging into the back of his long, powerful thighs.

He cums directly down my throat and I press my clit hard against his tongue, bright flashes of color popping against my closed eyelids—five-pointed and scarlet as the leaves. This orgasm is hot and rushing and intense, my whole body clenching and shaking, as Ares' cum rushes down my throat in three rough bursts.

I pull back from his cock, still swallowing.

I like the way he tastes. His cum is smooth and mild.

Ares comes to lay beside me, his arm a pillow beneath my head, both of us looking up into the canopy of red.

Whenever I went hunting with my father and I saw a deer in the woods and shot, killed, and ate it afterward, I always felt like I imbued part of that deer. By consuming it, I took its energy into my body in a very real way. It made me feel closer to the animals and the trees and the cycle of life that goes around and around in an endless loop.

Now Ares and I have eaten a part of each other.

He's inside of me and I'm inside of him.

Quietly, in that low, deep voice, Ares says, "I love being out here with you. I haven't felt this good in a long time."

"I don't know if I've ever felt this good," I say.

I know I've never been this happy.

20

Ivan Petrov
St. Petersburg

Fifteen Years Ago

The next time Marko Moroz comes to the monastery, I hardly recognize him.

He jumps out of his car, limping to the gates before Maks can even reach him, gripping the iron bars in his massive hands and howling, "IVAN!" at the top of his lungs.

I had already heard what had happened, and I suppose I was expecting him, though not so soon, because by my last intelligence, he was lying in a hospital bed in Kyiv with seven bullets in his body.

I can see the bandage on his jaw where one of those bullets went through his cheek, shattering half his molars before exiting right below the opposite ear.

I know what kept Marko alive. The same thing that brought him here: the thirst for revenge.

I had been playing in the yard with several of the dogs—or at least, to their eyes playing. Really, we were training the latest litter. As soon as my radio crackled, I sent my son into the house.

My son paused, looking at me with those blue-green eyes that have always been so startling in his face. He got my olive skin, and hair a little lighter than mine, more like Dom's. Those eyes must be from some distant ancestor unknown to Sloane or me. They're deeper than ours, and gentler. Too gentle, I sometimes fear.

"Go on inside," I said again sternly. "And take the pups."

Obediently, he scooped up the two fluffy ovcharkas, one under each arm, and ferried them into the house.

He's a good boy. Calm, serious, and already showing flashes of his mother's brilliance.

I don't want Marko to see him.

I nod for Maks to open the gates.

Marko comes lurching up the drive, limping heavily on the leg that received two of the bullets.

"IVAN!" he bellows again, though by this point we're close enough to see each other plainly.

I walk toward him with an ugly feeling of impending doom. Marko has the appearance of a bill unpaid. My own fate coming to claim me once more.

He looks haggard and wild-eyed. Skinnier than I've ever seen him—he must have lost forty pounds in the hospital, or more. He's diminished in all ways. Yet more dangerous than ever.

"IVAN, THEY KILLED HER!" he howls, falling into my arms.

Thinner or not, he's still almost heavy enough to knock me backward.

I can smell the alcohol seeping out of his pores, and the sickly scent of wounds not well-cared for.

"You need a doctor," I tell him.

"You know what I need," he hisses, staring at me with bulging, bloodshot eyes. "And it's no fucking doctor."

"Marko, you better lay down—"

"I'll lay down when I'm dead!" he howls. "They killed her, Ivan, they fucking killed her!"

I heard the night it happened. Marko Moroz and his wife were gunned down outside the Operetta in Kyiv. They had been seeing a showing of *Rigoletto*.

I even know who did it.

Last year, Marko drove a pen through the eye of his former mentor Petro Holodryga. Holodryga had helped Marko take over large swaths of territory in Kyiv, allying his Banderovtsy with Marko's Malina.

No one knows exactly what prompted the argument during what was supposed to be a friendly meeting between the two groups. The Banderovtsy didn't take kindly to their boss becoming a cyclopean corpse. When the dust settled, four of Holodryga's men were dead, shot and stabbed by Marko's Malina during a meeting where all promised to come unarmed.

To no one's surprise, Taras Holodryga, Petro's nephew and the new leader of the Banderovtsy, soon retaliated, orchestrating the drive-by outside the theater. I don't know if he meant to kill Daryah Moroz too. If he did, he sure as fuck should have made sure that Marko was dead first.

"We have to kill him," Marko hisses in my face, pupils black pinpricks in the foggy green. "You have to help me, Ivan."

I can feel my men watching. They're giving us a wide radius so that Marko has the impression of confidentiality.

Though I can't see her, I know Sloane will be watching, too, from somewhere inside the house—likely holding Freya in her arms, as our daughter is particularly attached to her mother at the moment and follows her everywhere she goes.

I know what Sloane would want me to say.

"You want revenge, my friend," I say. "And you deserve it. But you can't rush into this. Your daughter—"

"I'm doing this for her!" Marko cries, his face as red as his beard. "They slaughtered her mother! Nearly left her an orphan! How can I ever look my baby girl in the face if I let this pass?"

I take a deep breath.

Nix Moroz is only three years old, the same as Freya. She will never know her mother. Probably won't even remember her.

What would I do if someone killed Sloane? If someone took her away from us?

Seeing my expression shift, Marko presses his point.

"You owe me, Ivan," he says. "St. Petersburg belongs to you because of me."

"I gave you the lion's share of the profit. I kept my agreement."

"Money comes easy," Marko insists. "I got you power, control. The security to keep your family safe! You owe me the same."

I don't want to start a war with the Banderovtsy. And I don't want to ally with Marko once more—not after everything he's done.

Yet... there's truth in his words.

I do owe him a debt that money can't pay.

And he does deserve his revenge.

You don't kill a man's wife.

What's really holding me back is the knowledge that Sloane will not approve. She wouldn't want me to do this.

Still, I feel that I must.

So for the first and only time in my marriage, I go against the silent advice of my wife echoing through my brain.

I say to Marko, "I'll help you."

WE TAKE six of my men and six of Marko's.

As I guessed, Sloane is not at all happy with my plan. Still, she wants to come with me.

"I don't trust him," she says, her dark eyes furious and resentful. "He'll stab you in the back, Ivan. You know he's jealous—you still have your wife and children."

"And he still has his daughter," I remind her. "So he has something to lose, too."

Sloane frowns, not letting go of my hand.

I don't think I've ever seen her frightened before. Not even when I had her locked in the cells beneath this monastery, when we were not yet well acquainted.

"Why are you smiling?" she demands.

"I was only thinking, if you failed to kill me, there's no fucking way that Marko could pull it off."

Sloane laughs, though I know she doesn't want to.

"Sometimes I think we're invincible, because what you and I have can't be killed," she says. "Still . . . be careful, my love."

I kiss her hard. "Nothing could keep me from coming back to you."

Sloane only agrees to stay with our children because Dominik will be with me to watch my back.

I'm sure he endured a similarly tense parting from Lara. Their youngest son Kade is a curious child who gets into everything, and his older brother Adrik grows wilder by the day.

If all goes as planned, we shouldn't be gone for long.

We meet the Malina in Kyiv, checking our gear for the assault on Taras Holodryga's compound.

It isn't wise to retaliate so quickly. Taras knows that Marko survived the attack. He'll assume that we're coming for him.

Marko insists that Taras thinks this particular house is unknown to anyone but his inner circle. It's a small farmhouse in Baczyna, seven hours outside Kyiv along the Dnister River. The farmhouse has, of course, been renovated to the appropriately luxurious standards of a gangster, but it still sits in an orchard of plum, cherry, and walnut trees, lacking any serious impediments to attack like the stone walls of the monastery.

"He's holed up there with his mistress," Marko snarls. "Like a rat in a hole."

We drive out in the dead of night, surrounding the farmhouse from all sides. With night vision goggles and tactical coordination, it's not difficult to dispatch the four soldiers patrolling the orchard.

One of Marko's men is shot entering the actual house, but it's only a mild injury to the bicep. In less than five minutes we've rousted Taras and his woman from the master bedroom.

Taras looks weak and pitiful, his soft belly hanging over the waistband of his boxer shorts. I can see the lamplight gleaming on his skull through his thinning hair. His pale eyes blink up at us, half-blind without his glasses. Marko finds the glasses and rams them onto his face.

Taras is blubbering and pleading. He has none of the steel of his uncle, and even less of his strategy. Petro Holodryga would never have been foolish enough to fail to kill a rival and then hide in such an unprotected place.

"Go ahead," I say to Marko. "Take your revenge."

Marko towers over Taras, his limp all but forgotten. The devil is raging behind his eyes, fully awake and in control of Marko's goliath body. He deals the man a vicious blow to the mouth that knocks out one of his front teeth. Taras's head lolls limply.

I expect Marko to draw his gun and shoot Taras between the eyes.

Instead, I hear the screams and whimpers of two children being dragged down the farmhouse stairs.

Marko's men throw the kids down on the floor—a boy and a girl, six and four years old at the most. The children are bawling, messy-haired, and dressed in matching pajamas.

Dom throws me a quick, wide-eyed look. His hands tighten on his rifle.

I can see Maks, recognizable even in his balaclava because of the patch over his eye, shifting position behind Marko's lieutenant.

"Who the fuck are they?" I snarl to Marko.

I already know the answer—the woman is screaming and begging, trying to pull away from Marko's soldiers to get to her children.

She's not Taras's mistress—she's his wife. And these are his kids.

"This is not what we discussed," I tell Marko.

He ignores me.

Turning to Taras, he says, "You shot my wife right in front of me. I held her in my arms on the steps of the operetta. I watched her drown in her own blood from the holes in her lungs. Could you possibly imagine how that feels, Taras? No, of course not. A man could never imagine such a thing. He can only experience it."

Marko turns, pointing his gun at the young boy who sits frozen on the weathered wooden boards of the farmhouse floor. He stares up at Marko, tears and mucus running down his face.

Marko says to Taras, his voice soft with anticipation, "I'm going to shoot your son twice in the leg, where you shot me. And then I'll shoot your daughter right below the heart, where you hit Darya. Finally, I'll strangle your wife with my bare hands, till the light leaves her eyes, so you know, you'll truly know, the bitter agony of watching helpless, unable to save the ones you love. And all the while, I want you to beg for mercy. Beg and howl, like I did. And maybe, just maybe, I'll let one of you live."

"PLEASE!" Taras cries. "Let them go, they have nothing to do with this!"

"That's good." Marko nods. "Keep begging, just like that."

His index finger curls around the trigger, the barrel of the gun aimed at the boy almost the same age as my own son.

As Marko's finger squeezes tight, I ram into his arm, knocking the gun askew. The bullet smashes into a vase a foot above the boy's head, and the Glock goes skittering across the floor.

Marko roars with rage, turning directly into the barrel of the AK-47 Dom points at his face.

My men are faster than Marko's, and in better position. While the Malina were subduing Taras' wife and children, my Bratva were already angling around them, ready to draw. They knew I would not allow this to pass.

"Drop your rifles," Dom orders Marko's men. "Or I'll shoot your boss in the face."

Marko stands still, looking at me, not at Dom.

"You made a promise to me, Ivan," he says.

"And I kept my promise. You're welcome to kill Taras. But not his wife, and definitely not his children."

"He has to suffer," Marko hisses. "As I suffer."

"We're not killing his kids," I growl back at him. "I'm not fucking doing that."

"You don't have to do it—"

"*No one* is doing it."

Marko's men have lowered their rifles but not dropped them. They're watching their boss for instructions.

"FUCKING DROP THEM!" Dom shouts at them. "We'll kill every one of you."

Slowly, resentfully, the Malina lay their rifles on the floor.

Now Marko is truly angry. His whole frame trembles with enough force to shake this ancient floor. His teeth are bared in a snarl, his fingers twitching and those blazing eyes fixed on my face.

He wants to charge at me. Maybe even more than he wants to kill Taras.

"You can have your revenge," I repeat. "But only on the guilty. Not the innocent."

I pull the KA-BAR knife from my belt and hand it to Marko, blade in my palm and handle held out to him.

Marko takes it.

His upper lip twitches beneath his ginger beard, his breath coming out between his teeth with a hissing sound.

He grips the handle and lunges, not at Taras, but at my brother. He means to cut Dom's throat—only my brother's quick twist to the right spares his life, the knife slashing open his cheek instead.

I shoot Marko in the knee, dropping him to the ground.

Then I shoot Taras Holodryga, right between the eyes.

"There," I say bitterly. "It's over."

Taras' wife and children are howling.

Marko kneels before me, hand gripping his knee as blood seeps through his fingers.

He looks up at me with burning fury.

"Someday you'll kneel before me, as I kneel before you now," he says, teeth grinding together like stone on stone. "You'll beg and plead for my mercy. And I'll remind you that we could have been brothers . . . that I held out the hand of friendship to you, before you spat in my face."

Marko spits on the wooden boards of the farmhouse, never taking his eyes off of mine.

"It's *because* we were friends that I don't kill you," I tell him. "My debt is paid to you. All bonds between us are cut. You have your city, I have mine—don't come to St. Petersburg again, or there will be no mercy for either of us."

I leave him there, with the body of Taras Holodryga and the unarmed Malina.

I take Taras' wife and children back to Kyiv, depositing them with the remaining Banderovtsy.

Then I find a steady-handed doctor to stitch Dom's face before I take my men home once more.

21

Ares

With her uncanny ability to press on my most vulnerable places, Nix surprises me coming up from the archives with my mother. I knew, I just fucking knew, she would catch some out-of-place detail between us and start scenting around like a wolf on the hunt.

It doesn't help that a small part of me wanted my mother and Nix to meet. I wanted my mom to see her, speak to her face to face, so she would see that Nix isn't some monster, some mini version of her father to be manipulated and wielded like an asset.

My mom couldn't resist engaging in conversation, combing Nix over, looking for those tiny indicators of information that my mother's government-trained father drilled into her during her formative years, until she could write an entire CIA dossier on someone after ten minutes of chit-chat.

I felt guilty as hell putting Nix in that position, oblivious and openly duped. Especially when I had to lie right to her face.

During all the time I spend with Nix, I've been letting myself believe that lies of omission aren't really lies. And the lies I do tell her—my name and where I'm from—don't really matter compared to the deeper truths I lay bare. She knows my genuine feelings, my fears, my likes, and dislikes . . . things that seem so much more essential than my fake history.

Perversely, I liked watching her talk to my mom. I saw my mother look Nix over with the slightly raised eyebrow that indicated she had encountered an object of interest. It would have killed me to see my mom dismiss Nix as boring.

Best of all was the knowledge that Nix had sought me out that day. That she had gone looking all over campus for a purpose that seemed glaringly clear the moment we were alone.

Her eyes roved over me. She had the hunter's determination to bring me down and not go home again starving.

I've been wanting to fuck Nix since the moment she stepped out of the underground pool. Hell, I might even have felt that first flaring lust the moment I laid eyes on her crossing campus. That burst of sudden heat . . . it wasn't all hatred.

I tell myself I can't do it, that it would be wrong to sleep with her under false pretenses.

But every second I'm around her, I'm losing control. It's like the day I boxed Dean—each glance from her eyes, or bite of her lip is like another blow, knocking me senseless. Tearing off my veneer and taking me back to the man I used to be: prince of the West Coast. My father's right-hand man, running his business, preparing to take over someday. Surrounded by women and friends, wealth pouring in . . .

That man had confidence. He didn't have to hide. He never pretended to be weaker, shyer, lesser. He never compromised his integrity with lies.

I want to be myself with Nix, I don't want to be Ares. I want her to know me, not him.

I want to fuck her as myself.

But then I walked into the woods with her, and all my resolve disappeared. Nature is Nix's place. It belongs to her. When I'm in the forest with her, the rest of the world ceases to exist. Nothing outside of us matters, and I'm free to be who I want and do what I want.

I kissed her under that tree, and I had to fucking have her.

I threw her down, the leaves mixing with her hair, and I worshipped her like the goddess she is.

I got down between her legs and tasted her fully for the first time. I've never had so much pleasure just from the sensation of my tongue. All five senses were right there: her rich taste, the velvet texture of her skin, the sight of those creamy thighs wrapped around me, the sounds of her moans, and her sweet scent filling my lungs.

It was heaven. I felt her cumming against my mouth, and I truly experienced enlightenment.

She put my cock in her mouth, and the whole universe melted away. I was in her and she was in me, and everything was as it should be.

Then we walked back to the castle, reality crashing down on me with all the weight of its attendant guilt.

I want to tell Nix the truth. But I can't.

She loves her father. If she knew what we intend to do to Marko Moroz . . . she'd fight us. She'd have to defend him. Just like I would do for my family.

I've already gotten too close to her, let her see too much.

I'm taking stupid risks, and it's all going to blow up in my face.

I'd been down in the archives because my mother had a new idea.

The archives under Kingmakers are vast. Maps are of great use to thieves. Generations of mafia have hoarded every diagram, every blueprint they could get their hands on. Even the properties of other mafia families aren't safe.

We have a remarkable amount of material to look through.

Unfortunately, almost no organization.

The last several Chancellors of Kingmakers weren't academics. Little attention was given to the quality of the librarians.

My mother arrived to a maelstrom of decaying, disorganized mounds. The more she searched, the more daunting the task appeared.

She was trying to drink an Olympic-sized swimming pool one teaspoon at a time.

Still, she never hesitated. She never slowed. She never gave the slightest indication that we might not succeed.

Until last year. Then I finally saw the tiniest cracks start to form as she began to reach the end of the archives without finding what we needed.

We had so few clues. We searched castles, monasteries, fortresses, manor houses, and even old prisons. Nothing seemed to match.

Until my mother thought of mines.

We knew the place was old, and that it had a water source beneath—we had always assumed a moat or river.

She fixed upon the idea of an aqueduct to carry away waste, and she began to search again.

Six potential locations seemed to fit what we knew. She brought me down to the archives to see for myself.

I hardly dared to believe it, but we seemed so much closer than we'd ever been before.

I wanted it to be true ... while dreading what that would mean.

We might finally be reaching the end.

I tell myself to pull back from Nix again, to step back from the line I crossed, but I can't. We're hurtling down this road together, whether she knows it or not.

The Christmas dance is only a few days away.

I ask Nix to go with me.

She says yes, because she was expecting it. We're dating each other in every way but official.

I can't stay away from her. The only time I feel peace is with her. That's the only time the pressure releases. As soon as we're apart, I'm crushed again under the weight of my own lies.

I haven't been going to see my mother as much. If she sees my face, she'll read me like a book.

I have to tell her about the dance, however. She'll almost surely attend herself. Especially since by this point she knows all the staff and has no fear of running into someone who might recognize her like Sasha Drozdov did.

So I visit her the day before the dance, knowing she's sure to give me shit for trying to avoid her.

"Who's that?" she says, pretending to peer through her fake glasses. "I don't recognize you—have we met before?"

"Ha, ha," I say, and then quietly, because a library is one of the only places where you can whisper something without looking suspicious, "You told me not to visit too often, remember?"

"I think you've just been busy," she murmurs, pretending to sort a pile of returned books "Doing such a careful job with your assignment."

I sigh, wondering if there's any point in denying it.

"Do you not want me to take her to the dance?"

"Oh, I absolutely think you should," my mother replies. Her voice is at its lowest and most dangerous.

My heart squeezes in my chest.

I'm not saying I'm afraid of my mother, but I also wouldn't fucking underestimate her.

Cautiously, I ask, "You're not worried that I'm getting too close to her?"

"Oh, I know you are," she says softly, setting down the last book and looking up at me at last. Her eyes are dark and gleaming, steady as they've ever been. "I know you're getting too close to her, Ares. And I also want you to know that I don't care. You can like this girl. You can even fall for her. It doesn't matter."

I lick my lips, my heart nearly rigid now. "Why doesn't it matter?"

"Because in the end, you'll choose your family," she says. "You're my son and I know who you are. You're loyal."

"Yes," I murmur. "I am."

"Loyalty in blood," she says with a slight downward tilt of her chin.

"Loyalty in blood," I agree.

22

Nix

I was hoping Ares would want to go to the dance together. It's one thing to run around the woods just the two of us, and another to dance openly in each other's arms.

I'm also, for my own amusement, hoping that the battle to take Sabrina Gallo to the dance ends in an actual massacre.

I can hardly walk down a hallway next to her without some hapless male making a hurried and desperate pitch.

Sabrina turns them all down.

"Don't you want a date?" I ask her.

"Maybe." She shrugs as if she doesn't care.

I don't believe her. Her irritable mood tells me that she's set her sights on someone and won't be satisfied with anybody else.

The actual day of the dance, she waltzes into our room with a flushed face and an undisguisable air of triumph.

"What is it?" I ask her.

"Nothing." She grins. "Nothing at all."

I have a pretty good guess what's going on, but I don't press. Sabrina loves her secrets.

Meanwhile, I'm trying to decide how to dazzle tonight. I don't just want to look "pretty good for Nix." I want Ares to have the hottest woman in the room on his arm.

I spend an extraordinary amount of time primping, before cracking and begging Sabrina for help. She puts the finishing touches on my face, stepping back to admire the effect.

"Nobody cleans up better than you," she says. "You look hot as fuck."

"Likewise, obviously," I tell her. "But you already know that."

"I do," she says, giving me a wink.

She's definitely outdone herself. She slips out the door looking so sultry that I figure I better start aiming for second place.

Ares meets me at the base of the Solar, wearing a tux so sharp and well-fitted that I think he must have borrowed it from Leo. The deep navy fabric gleams like water at night. It makes his eyes look darker than usual, deeper than the ocean in that handsome, sun-kissed face.

My gown is a rich, dark green. The soft, stretchy material fits me like a second skin. Ares' hands glide over my body as he puts his arm around my waist.

"I've never seen you in a dress before," he says.

"I'm trying something new."

"I can't stop staring," he says. "I'm not even gonna try."

He walks with his arm around me all the way to the Grand Hall, nestled between the two vast glass and iron greenhouses. I notice as I always do how well our pace matches—as if we were made to do this.

Gold — Kiiara
Spotify → geni.us/spy-spotify
Apple Music → geni.us/spy-apple

The Grand Hall is sweltering, the roaring fire in the massive hearth not needed in this unusually warm December. Everyone is drinking the punch twice as quickly as they should, leading to a hectic level of revelry for so early in the evening.

The music is pounding, students crowding onto the dance floor, recklessly swapping partners, and dancing without fear of collision.

Ares has his own wicked gleam in his eye. He throws off his jacket, dragging me out to dance, pressing his blazing body tight against mine. Heat radiates through the thin material of his dress shirt, and his broad chest strains against the buttons. His skin looks very tan against the white. He's had his hair freshly cut down in the village, shearing off some of the sun streaks, showing the soft, dark fade beneath.

The space is packed with students, everyone pressing in so close that heated bodies slide against my back and arms while Ares grinds against me.

I see a whirl of faces, though it's too loud and cramped to actually speak to anyone. I can't even point it out to Ares when I spot Cara Wilk dressed in a diaphanous off-the-shoulder gown, pressed up against the wall while Hedeon leans in close to murmur something in her ear.

Anna Wilk is dancing with Leo, until she grabs his hand and pulls him away somewhere—from the look in her eye, I'm guessing somewhere a lot more private than the Grand Hall.

Cat Romero sits on Dean's lap close to the fire. He's feeding her bites of Christmas cookies taken from the overloaded buffet table against the far wall. She takes each bite from his hand, her tongue slipping out to lick his fingers.

The professors who are supposed to be chaperoning the party seem to have been sucked into the same irresistible mood of bacchanalia. Professor Lyons, the Arsenic Witch, is dancing with Professors Knox and Howell simultaneously. The Chancellor is sharing his flask with Professor Thorn, who looks striking in her backless silk gown.

The Chancellor isn't the only one who snuck in extra liquor—I see Estas Lomachenko passing a bottle back and forth between his Odessa friends and Bodashka Kushnir's Bratva buddies.

Somebody definitely augmented up the punch—maybe several people. The cup Ares brings me tastes like pure sugar and liquor. I gulp it down anyway, feeling an immediate swoop of elation as it goes straight to my head.

Ares seizes me and kisses me, sucking the liquor off my lips.

"I love the way that tastes in your mouth," he growls.

We're dancing again, and this time I can't look at anything but him. He's magnetic, unleashed in a way I've never seen before. He's looking at me the way he used to when we first met, his eyes burning over every inch of me, an intensity in his stare that almost frightens me. I don't see his usual restraint—I see the other Ares. The one who appears only rarely . . . when he begins to lose control.

I want to know that person.

I get us a second cup of punch, watching Ares swallow it down in one gulp. He crumples the empty cup in his hand, his eyes fixed on mine.

He's reckless tonight.

We both want to see where this goes.

He pulls me back into his arms, his large hands tight against my lower back, sliding down to grip my ass. He gropes me, not giving a fuck who sees.

At that moment, Sabrina Gallo enters the dance with Ilsa Markov.

Bang Bang — *GRAE*
Spotify → geni.us/spy-spotify
Apple Music → geni.us/spy-apple

They stand in the doorway, the two dark-haired sirens amplifying each other's beauty.

I've never seen two such sexual women side by side. Like twin stars, they bring the whole room into their orbit.

Ilsa Markov is tall and cap-shouldered, her chin upraised in haughty satisfaction as she surveys the room. The V of her scarlet dress runs all the way down to her navel, the slit all the way up her thigh.

Sabrina Gallo wears black—on the bits of her body covered by her dress. The gown is a marvel of engineering, clinging to her curves in only the most anatomically-requisite positions, before swooping away to reveal startling slices glowing, golden skin.

The two girls stand arm-in-arm, the air between them crackling with overlapping sensuality.

They walk directly to the dance floor, Sabrina slipping her arms around Ilsa's neck. Bodies entwined, they dance slowly, sensually, their hands sliding over each other's curves, their eyes locked.

It's intensely fucking sexy. I'm staring, heat rising in my cheeks.

Ares' torso is pressed against my back, his hands on my hips. He bends his head to murmur in my ear, "You like that?"

I lick my lips, eyes still on Sabrina and Ilsa.

"Sure," I say. "Who wouldn't."

He growls, "Why don't you join them?"

My stomach gives a long, slow lurch. My eyes are locked on the girls, their bodies lithe and graceful as they twine around each other. Their breasts press together through the thin material of their dresses. Ilsa's nipples are hard, visible through the scarlet satin.

Something flares inside of me. Call it the devil on my shoulder, giving me a push.

I walk straight toward the girls.

Ilsa catches sight of me first, stepping back slightly with an appraising look up and down my body. Sabrina turns, the corner of her mouth quirking up in a wicked smile.

The girls envelop me like an oyster, circling around me like a pearl.

They press tight against me in the hot, throbbing space, their bodies sliding easily against the silky material of my dress.

I can't believe how soft their skin is—like the inside of a rose petal. They smell sweet and enticing: their hair, their skin, and their breath.

The girls' delicate hands know exactly where to touch as Ilsa slides her palms up the undersides of my breasts from behind, and Sabrina nuzzles her full lips against my neck from the front.

I'm touching them both, feeling the impossible smallness of Sabrina's waist between my hands, and Ilsa's firm breasts rubbing against my back. I'm inhaling their light, clean scent. But I'm looking at Ares, at his strong jaw, broad shoulders, and brilliant blue eyes. The mix of masculine and feminine is a potent aphrodisiac, skyrocketing my heart rate until I can feel it throbbing all the way down between my thighs.

I've always found women just as beautiful as men—sometimes, even more so. I respect strong women the way I respect strong men. What I would call a "deep sense of admiration" sometimes has a much more heart-pounding flavor.

Ilsa Markov takes my chin between her thumb and forefinger, turning my head toward her. She kisses me deeply, her lips firm and warm, her jaw sharp against my palm as I touch her soft face.

Her tongue glides across mine, fine and velvety. As she kisses me, I feel Sabrina's small, strong hands gripping my hips.

Sabrina turns me. I take her face in my hands, kissing her fuller, softer lips, inhaling her tantalizing perfume, which I've always enjoyed smelling in our room.

Ilsa's hands are on my breasts again, this time her palms gliding all the way over my nipples. She kisses the side of my neck, biting and sucking gently while Sabrina slides her tongue inside my mouth.

Girls' mouths are all the most sensual and delicate parts of a kiss amplified: puffy, pillowy lips, honeyed tongues, and warm breath.

My head is spinning.

I might feel self-conscious if I thought more people could see us, but the press of students is so tight that only the people directly around us are getting an eyeful.

None better than Ares. His stare burns every inch of my skin as he watches me live out a fantasy I've often imagined, without ever really thinking it would happen.

Sabrina kisses me deeply, her hands on either side of my face, her breasts pressing against mine, her thigh sliding between my legs. She lets out a little moan that makes Ilsa's head jerk up, her nostrils flaring.

Isla grabs Sabrina by the hair and pulls her away from me, kissing her ferociously, reminding Sabrina which of us came as her date.

I let Ilsa take her, slipping away back to Ares who seizes me and kisses me much harder than either of the girls.

Kissing Ares after two women makes him seem all the more masculine. I'm acutely aware of his stubble rasping at the edges of my lips, and the intense force in his fingers as he grips me. His frame seems twice as tall, his shoulders immensely broad. His cologne is edged with testosterone.

I've never felt smaller in someone's arms.

Ares' arms are like cables around me, tense and hard. For the very first time, I feel physically intimidated by someone other than my father.

It gives me a thrill.

It makes me want to stay on Ares' good side. To impress him. To please him...

The heat is intense, my legs weak beneath me.

I'm sweating and flushed, looking up into Ares' face, kissing him again with our mouths burning against each other.

"Let's go somewhere," Ares says.

I don't ask him where. I don't really care—I just know I need to be alone with him, right now, with much less clothing between us.

We're pushing through the crowd of students, not looking where we're going. Just as we reach the exit, someone slams into me, drenching me with the icy blast of an entire cup of punch poured down the front of my dress.

Estas steps back, delicately holding the upturned cup between his thumb and index finger.

"Oops," he says.

I'm not sure if he did it on purpose or not. He hates my guts, but also, I really wasn't watching where I was going.

Beat Up Kidz — The OBGMs
Spotify → geni.us/spy-spotify

Apple Music → geni.us/spy-apple

Before I can say a word, before I can even shake the ice out of my cleavage, Ares charges Estas, slamming his shoulder into Estas' chest and knocking him backward through the doors of the Grand Hall.

Ares and Estas go tumbling backward down the steps, already grappling and punching each other as hard as they can. I run through the doors after them, stumbling down the steps in my heels, followed closely by the rest of the Odessa Mafia and at least a dozen other students who saw the fight begin and absolutely want to watch the conclusion.

This is no boxing match—more like a murder in progress.

Ares is on top of Estas, punching him again and again with both hands. His fists drive into Estas' face with a sound like a mallet tenderizing raw meat. Blood spatters in all directions, hitting the skirt of my dress and the trousers of several bystanders.

Ares looks insane. His teeth are bared in a snarl, his eyes blazing. He pulls his bloodied fist back for another blow, though Estas is already a pulverized mess, eyes swelling shut, head lolling.

David Datsuk half-tackles and half-drags Ares off of Estas. Ares flings David aside and shoulders Arkady Chaplin out of the way too, still trying to run at Estas until Hedeon Gray seizes Ares by both arms and drags him backward.

"Fucking knock it off!" Hedeon bellows in Ares' ear. "The Chancellor's right inside!"

That seems to shake Ares out of his daze. He's still snarling, but he stops trying to lunge at Estas, standing upright and shaking off Hedeon's grip.

"You stay the FUCK away from Nix," he shouts at the groaning, battered Estas.

Estas can barely roll over, let alone weaponize any more punch. He spits a mouthful of blood down the front of his dress shirt.

Without thanking Hedeon, Ares grabs my arm and marches me away from the staring circle of students.

He's pulling me along so quickly that I can barely stay upright on my heels.

He's still breathing hard, teeth gritted tightly together and shoulders tense as iron.

The cool night air is sobering me up fast.

"Ares," I gasp. "What the fuck was that?"

"The fucking asshole is dangerous," he growls, his fingers a steel band around my wrist. "He's got a grudge against you, Nix. He wants to hurt you."

"It was just punch," I say, staring at his still-furious expression.

I don't know who the fuck this person is. I've never seen Ares so unhinged, not even in the middle of the *Quartum Bellum* challenge.

"No one is ever going to hurt you while I'm with you, do you understand?" Ares says, grabbing both my arms and forcing me to turn to look at him. "Do you understand me, Nix?"

"Yes. I understand," I say, startled by the wild look in his eyes. Shaking my head, I tell him, "Most people aren't too worried whether I can take of myself. Only one person talks like that—you sound like my dad."

Ares stares at me.

"I'm not like your father," he says.

"I know that. But right now, you remind me of him—protective. And a little bit out of your fucking mind."

Ares starts walking again, taking deep breaths to try to calm down. I can't tell if he's still pissed at Estas, or if what I said offended him.

We've circled around one of the greenhouses. Now Ares turns, heading between the dining hall and the Armory. I don't think he has a destination in mind, he's just walking to cool off.

Several minutes pass before he speaks again:

"What do you think is the dividing line between good and bad?" He looks at me, his expression serious. "What do you think makes someone worthy of friendship . . . or worthy of death?"

He sees me hesitate, lips parted.

"I'm not trying to trick you," he says. "I'm not asking about your father. I just want to know—what's the line?"

I wonder that myself.

When I picture the people I know and love—my friends at school, my father's men, and my dad himself—I can't create a consistent schema for judgment. They all have their flaws. They all make mistakes.

When I ponder what's "right" and what's "wrong," I only know what I'd do myself.

I look Ares in the eye and say, "I'll kill anyone who hurts the people I love."

Ares nods slowly. "So will I," he says.

That sounds strangely like a promise. Like he's warning me.

Grabbing me by the wrist once more, Ares drags me into the Armory.

The gym is deserted, no one dedicated enough to fitness to miss the dance in favor of working out.

The air smells faintly of sweat, rubber, and metal chains.

My heels sink into the mats. I kick them off.

Ares seizes me by the throat, turning my chin up to look at him. He's still burning with this wild energy he can't seem to release.

"You know I don't give a fuck who your father is," he says, his eyes staring into mine. "You know that, don't you?"

"Yes . . ." I say hesitantly.

"Do you feel the same about me?" Ares demands. "You don't care about my parents, where I came from, what I have waiting for me when I leave this place . . . that doesn't matter to you?"

I've known all along that Ares' family is poor and he has no ready-made empire to inherit.

I really don't care. And if my dad cares, if he tried to tell me Ares wasn't good enough for me, I'd tell him to fuck off. Ares is my equal in every way that matters: intelligence, determination, and strength. That's what I care about.

"I've never met anyone as impressive as you," I tell Ares, looking in his eyes. "I want you—not your money or your name."

His eyes blaze and his lips crash down on mine. He kisses me ravenously, crushing me in his arms.

Nightmare — Halsey
Spotify → geni.us/spy-spotify
Apple Music → geni.us/spy-apple

His hands roam over my breasts, pinching my nipples hard. Strong as Ilsa Markov might be, her hands are nowhere near as powerful as Ares'. I flush, remembering how she touched me while Ares watched.

"Did you like watching me with those girls?" I murmur. "That didn't make you jealous?"

"No," he growls, his teeth rasping against the side of my neck. "I fucking loved it. I don't want you restrained, Nix—I want you wild and free and untamed. I want you to have everything you ever desired, and I want to watch you enjoy it . . ."

Heat flares in my belly. My thighs press together under my dress.

I grab Ares' face in my hands and kiss him wildly, pushing my tongue into his mouth. He seizes the shoulder straps of my dress and yanks them down, baring my breasts. He drops his head to my left breast, sucking the nipple hard while he rubs the other between his thumb and forefinger.

I grab the gymnastics rings hanging over my head and I pull myself up a few inches so Ares can take the dress all the way off my body.

He slides it down my legs, and strips off my underwear too, admiring my naked body as I hang from the rings. I'm showing off for him, and I know he fucking loves it. He runs his hands over my breasts, down the curve of my waist, then cups his palms under my ass.

"I love how strong you are," he says. "I fucking love watching you in here. I can't tell you how many times I've watched you stretching or running or hitting the heavy bag with my cock fucking throbbing in my shorts."

He unzips his pants, letting his cock free now. It juts up from his body with just the right amount of curve.

Slowly, I lower down on it, still gripping the rings overhead, my legs wrapping around his waist.

His cock slides into me, thick and pulsing hot.

I let out a long, deep moan.

I've pictured this a thousand times. No imagination compares to the intense heat and pressure of that thick, warm cock filling me up. Wet as I am, and with all my body weight bearing down, it still slides in slow, stretching me with every inch.

Ares groans, cords standing out on the side of his neck.

"Jesus fucking Christ," he moans.

He supports me with his hands under my ass. Slowly, he swings me back and forth, his cock pumping in and out, my hands gripping the rings.

Each thrust seems to take forever. Each pounding impact of that battering ram-head against my interior walls rides the edge of pleasure and pain. It's intensely satisfying, but almost too much.

Pulling myself up with the rings, I slide up and down on his cock, grinding my clit against his flat, hard belly. My thighs squeeze his waist, my heels hooked around the back of his legs. I'm squeezing and clenching, my pussy clamped around every inch of his cock.

"What the fuuuuuck," Ares groans. "Even your pussy is strong . . ."

I laugh.

"Of course it is," I say, leaning over to bite the lobe of his ear. "It's a muscle like any other."

Ares grips my hips and thrusts upward into me.

I let go of the rings so I can wrap my arms around his neck, kissing him deeply.

I strip his dress shirt off because I want to see his body. I want to run my hands over the sprawling tattoo across his chest — the script, the skulls and roses. I want to see the muscles standing out on his arms and shoulders as he fucks me.

Ares sits back on one of the upright benches. I climb on top of him, straddling him in front of the mirror.

Our bodies look insane, dually reflected. As I ride him, I can see my abs flexing, and the round globes of my ass clenching. Ares has a pump like he just bench-pressed three hundred pounds, his chest, shoulders, and biceps swollen and throbbing. Veins stand out on his forearms. Sweat gleams on his skin as if he's been oiled.

I want to fuck him in every position in front of these mirrors. I want to watch us doing what our bodies were made to do—all the exercise and all the training reaching its highest purpose.

I flip around so I'm riding Ares in reverse, my back against his chest, my thighs flexing, and my tits bouncing in the mirror as I pogo on his cock. Ares puts his palm between my shoulder blades, pushing me forward, fucking me hard from behind.

I want more of that.

I stand up, bending over. Ares stands too, grabbing a handful of my hair and wrapping it around his fist. He holds it like the reins of a horse as he enters me again and fucks me hard, his hips slapping against my ass.

Tall as I am, I can't match his long legs. I need to get just a little higher.

I step into the squat rack, my feet resting on the crossbars. I lean forward, bracing myself against the rack with my hands. Now Ares can stand behind me, my ass raised up to the perfect height for his cock, my legs spread wide. He thrusts into me, pounding me hard, making the whole rack shake.

I can see Ares in the mirror, ripped like a Renaissance sculpture, like Michelangelo's most fevered dreams brought to life. Every muscle stands out on his long, lean frame, his fingers digging into my hips, his head thrown back, jaw clenched, teeth bared.

I've never seen anything so sexy.

I'm starting to cum, his cock pounding relentlessly against that sensitive spot on my inner wall, his thick shaft rubbing the base of my clit.

"Harder," I beg. "Fuck me harder."

"I'll fucking destroy you with this cock," Ares snarls.

He pounds into me with all his force.

The orgasm detonates inside of me. It blasts through my body, destructive and hot, incinerating my bones, sizzling through my cells.

Ares is cumming too, roaring out loud and pounding me with all his might. His hands twitch, his whole body shakes as he pours cum inside of me, driving it deep with every thrust.

I'm only vaguely aware of this because I've lost control of my body, I can't think or speak or hold myself up, all I can do is feel this climax to end all climaxes, an orgasm that ought to be named like a hurricane.

If I didn't have the rack to hold me up, I'd fall on my face.

Instead, I collapse backward onto Ares, both of us sweating and shaking on a pile of mats with no clear idea of how we got over there.

"I'd spend a lot more time in the gym if that was the workout," Ares groans.

"Don't forget to wipe down that bench," I tell him.

We both start laughing, helpless and slightly hysterical, clutching abs that are much too sore for any more activity.

23

Ivan Petrov

Present Day

I push up from the floor of my cell, the grit of the bare rock digging into my palms. Those palms are harder than iron by now. They've endured one thousand push-ups per day for three and a half long years.

When I want to do pull-ups, I flip my bed on its end and use the steel crossbar of the headboard.

One thousand push-ups. Five hundred pull-ups. One thousand air squats. Five hundred sit-ups. Broken into intervals like the hours of an invisible clock. That is how I divide my day.

The rest of the time, I read.

Marko provides me with books because he doesn't want me to go mad.

Then I wouldn't be able to provide the monthly check-ins that keep the ransom money flowing. Also, it would spoil his fun.

He's due for a visit any day now. I keep track of how many days have passed, scoring the stone walls with an old nail. Marko's visits aren't regular enough to predict accurately. He does that intentionally. Routine is dangerous, he knows that.

I always knew he was intelligent.

It was the qualities I failed to see that came back to bite me.

I hear Borys and Ihor rotating positions out in the corridor. Borys shined his boots this morning—a sure sign that Marko is indeed about to visit. I know the Malina's routines better than they do, though my cell has no windows, and only a small slit in the door through which my meals pass.

I haven't seen the sky or felt wind on my face since I came to this place.

But I would pass the rest of my days in darkness if I could see my wife one last time.

I've been torn in half. The other part of me is wandering, searching ... longing for me as I'm longing for her.

I know she's looking for me. I know it as well as I know my own thoughts.

Sloane will never give up on me.

And I will never stop trying to come home to her.

I made a promise to her. And I always keep my promises.

I miss my children almost as badly. My only comfort is that they have their mother with them and Dominik to help protect them.

It's Sloane I worry about. She'll drive herself to death looking for me. She'll take any risk. I worry about her survival more than my own.

I can't bear being locked up in here when she might need me out there.

I've never met anyone more capable than my wife. But no one is invincible, no matter what she and I might have believed about ourselves in the hubris of youth. She needs me, and I need her.

We draw life from each other. In the time we've been apart, we've both been slowly dying.

I listen for the sounds of Marko's approach.

I'm buried deep in the earth, in a vast stone tomb, like a pharaoh interred before his time.

I don't know if I'm in a castle or prison, or even in which country we reside. I was shot four times by the Malina, covering my wife and children so they could escape. I woke in this cell, with tubes running in and out of me, with IV bags and monitors, and a doctor called Lyaksandro who tended to me while always ensuring that I was shackled hand and foot to the cot.

The Malina are careful with their most valuable prisoner.

After all, I'm worth $6 million a month, not to mention the priceless satisfaction I provide to Marko Moroz.

He's bleeding my family dry, raking in over $252 million so far. Still, I think he would trade every penny for the pleasure of rubbing his revenge in my face.

That's why he comes for these monthly ransom calls. So he can witness my pain.

I know when his convoy arrives, because I hear the crackle of the radio out in the hallway, and the shifting sound as Borys stands at attention. I don't know if Marko comes by boat, helicopter, or car. I don't know if we're on an island or in the middle of the wilderness.

But I do pick up clues—small, significant clues. And I pass them along in the only way I can.

I'm sitting on my cot, back against the wall, reading *The Devil In The White City* for the third time.

I hear the clanking of electronic locks and the groan of heavy doors creaking open. Then the tramping tread of Marko and his men approaching.

"*Dobroho ranku, ser,*" Borys greets him with an audible salute. *Good morning, sir.*

I already knew some Ukrainian, similar as it is to Russian. Now I know more from listening to Borys and Ihor shoot the shit outside my cell. I know far more than I ever cared to learn about Borys' rotten luck with the ponies, and Ihor's persistent foot rash.

Marko's men are not permitted to marry or even maintain long-term relationships. They have no children, and he deliberately recruits those without close family. He is a jealous god who tolerates no other loyalties.

It does create a cult-like bond between him and his men. They depend on him entirely. But they also squabble bitterly amongst themselves, vying for his approval in petty, backstabbing ways.

Marko thrives on this. He loves to pit them against each other, doling out compliments and mockery in arbitrary and capricious ways.

I can feel Marko's bulk standing outside the door to my cell. I hear the grit of gravel as he leans forward, pressing his eye against the retinal scanner.

Only Marko and his lieutenant Kuzmo can enter my cell. Marko doesn't trust his other soldiers, not with his favorite prisoner. They might be vulnerable to threats or bribes.

The door swings open, Marko's vast bulk filling the frame.

I mark my place in the book before setting it down next to me.

"Another call already?" I say. "How time flies."

It never flies. I count every second, every minute, every hour.

But this is part of the game Marko and I play, where I refuse to let him see the overwhelming hatred that wells up inside of me at the sight of his face. He wants me to rage and howl and beg.

I will never fucking do it.

Marko steps into the cell, looking around as if he's never seen it before.

It's a plain space, blank walls, stone floor. A capsule carved out of the rock, windowless and lit by a single electric panel set in the ceiling. The only furniture is the metal-framed bed and a single folding chair, currently collapsed and leaning up against the wall. My books sit in a stack on the floor.

"Are you done with those?" Marko says, nodding toward the tower of books.

"Yes," I say.

He snaps his fingers, ordering one of his soldiers to exchange the books for a new supply.

My own personal library.

"Any requests for the next month?" Marko says, unsuccessfully trying to hide his smile.

"Yes. *Wolf Hall*," I say.

"I thought you didn't care for fictionalized biographies."

"A man can always learn to appreciate something new."

"I brought this one for you," Marko says, tossing a paperback down on the bed.

The Count of Monte Cristo.

His teeth glint as he grins.

This is a tired joke: he already brought *Little Dorrit, Rita Hayworth And Shawshank Redemption, The Man in the Iron Mask,* and *The Green Mile.*

"Really, Marko," I say quietly. "I almost think you're trying to give me ideas."

"I think you come up with plenty of ideas on your own," Marko growls, giving one last glance around my empty cell.

I've never tried to escape—that he knows of. I'm sure that only makes him more paranoid. He knows me too well to believe that I'm patiently biding my time.

"Chair," Marko barks at his lieutenant.

Kuzmo lifts the chair from the wall and sets it in the center of the room. I take my place upon it, crossing my arms behind my back so Kuzmo can handcuff them behind me.

These security measures are, perhaps, overblown—after all, Marko has four soldiers with him and two more out in the hall. I'm alone and unarmed.

On the other hand, he knows me well.

I'm sure he tells himself the handcuffs are to humiliate me further. The stare that passes between us tells another story.

"Are you looking forward to going home, my friend?" Marko says, his eyes fixed on mine, his pupils dark and dilated in the dim space. "Excited to see your wife again? How lucky that she still *lives* for you to see her."

I don't like when he mentions Sloane. It takes effort for me to hide my anger.

It's nothing but effort, controlling the almost irresistible impulse to snap the chain on these cuffs and tear his throat out with my fingers.

If I had no wife and no children, I would do it. I'd rather die riddled with bullets from his soldier's guns than suffer another minute of his taunts or another month in this sunless torture chamber.

Imprisonment *is* torture, make no mistake about it. Marko may not burn my flesh or break my bones, but he is making deep cuts to my soul, every day that passes. He is trying to twist and break me on the rack of boredom, rage, and loneliness.

"Yes," I say quietly. "I look forward to going home."

Marko is too clever to ever let an enemy as dangerous as me free in the world to seek my revenge. He will never let me go.

My family pays the ransom to buy time, not because they believe him.

His amusement draws out the game.

We play into his enjoyment to drag it on. But eventually he will reach the end of his diversion. When that happens, either he will die, or me.

He's too angry that I have Sloane while Daryah is dead.

In his fury, he has decided that I took his wife from him, not Taras Holodryga.

Taras is a ghost. He's no fitting target for Marko's anger—he can't be punished anymore.

I'm the one alive. The only person left to rage upon.

That's why he comes here every month, to drive the knife in deeper. To satiate himself on the sight of me: filthy, pale, and trapped in here like an animal in a cage.

He takes a sick satisfaction in my phone call to my family.

He listens in every time, wanting to hear the desperation in their voices, and the bitterness in mine.

He's never caught what I actually say to them.

"Bring the phone," he says to Kuzmo.

Kuzmo is the only person Marko trusts, at least to some degree. Kuzmo is tall and well-built—Marko wouldn't respect anyone who wasn't. He has a stern, unsmiling face, a narrow, lipless mouth, and the same close-shaved haircut imposed upon him during his days in Stark prison. The dark stubble on his cheeks and scalp has a bluish tinge, repeated in the steel blue of his eyes. His military clothing has an old-fashioned look, like the Black

Brunswickers. On the wool sleeve of his jacket, I see a single perfect crystalline flake, not yet melted.

Kuzmo rarely speaks, except to bark orders at his subordinates on Marko's behalf. He certainly doesn't engage in any of Borys or Ihor's idle chatter.

He brings the cellphone to me, already dialing my brother Dominik's number.

Dom answers at once, expecting the call.

"Ivan," he says.

"Still here," I reply. "Still alive."

Kuzmo is holding the phone to my ear. I'm not allowed to touch it, even under the scrutiny of all these men.

"Are you well, brother?" Dom says.

"Of course. And you?"

"Very well. Business runs smooth. The deposit will be sent as usual."

"Good, thank you. I keep busy here, too. Reading in the morning. Then," a short pause, "I spend evenings exercising so no opportunity wastes."

"Good, brother. Keep it up," Dom says.

Kuzmo pulls the phone away before I can say anything else.

No matter. I told Dominik what I needed to say.

Marko is watching me as always, meaty arms folded across his chest.

He was always a big man, and he's grown softer with age—a layer of fat over what was once hard muscle. Still, he could break the back of any man here, save for one.

"Until next month, my friend," Marko says.

"I look forward to it," I reply.

Kuzmo unlocks the cuffs.

I return to my place on the bed, picking up my paperback once more.

Marko is the last to depart my cell, closing the door himself with an echoing clang.

The sound is dismal and cold.

But there's a fire in my chest that had burned down to an ember, now stoked anew.

I managed to pass a message to Dom, with a piece of information that might be useful to Sloane in her search.

I do this every month, if I've observed anything about the prison or the guards that might help her to find me.

It's a simple code, the first letter of each word forming its own sentence:

I

**Spend
Evenings
Exercising**

**So
No
Opportunity
Wastes**

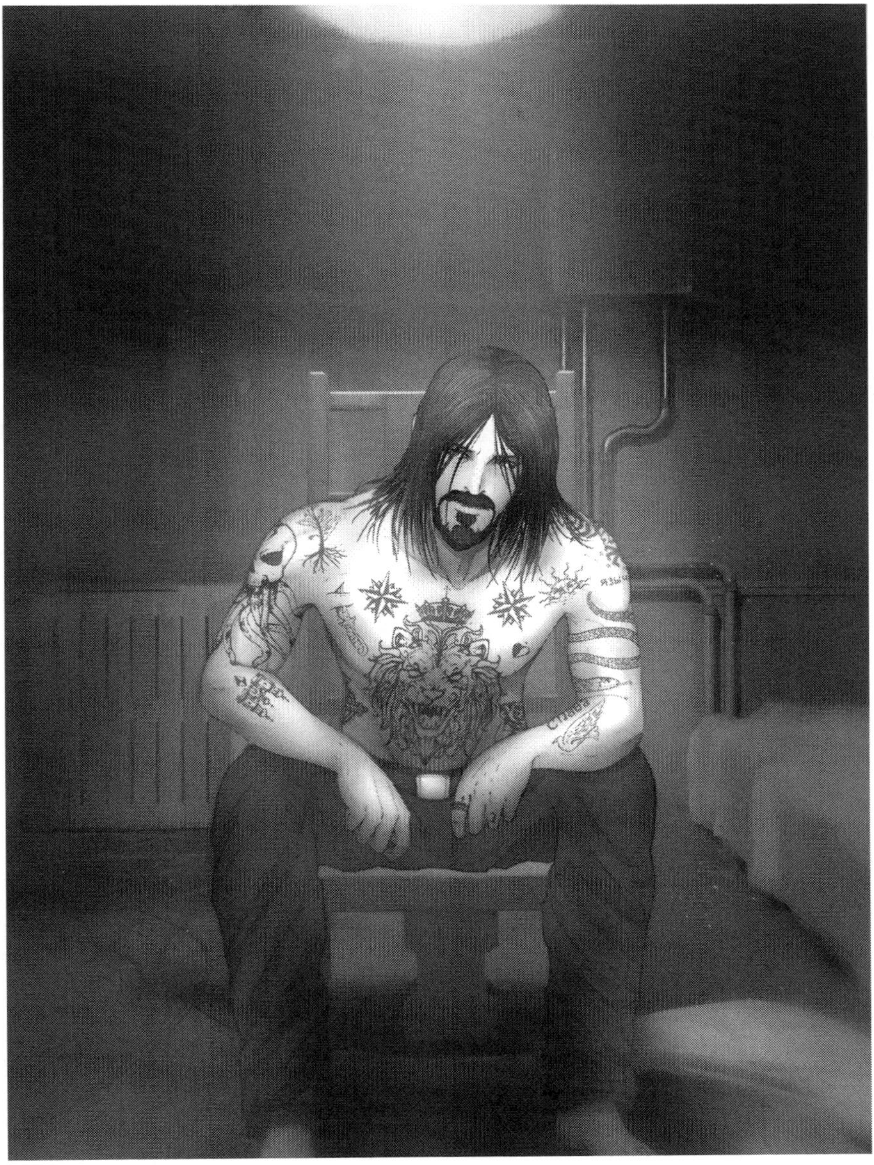

24

Ares

Christmas morning I visit my mom.

I stop by the Solar first to leave my gift for Nix outside her door.

I couldn't get her anything expensive, because after all, Ares is supposed to be poor, but I bribed one of the cooks to make her an entire basket of fresh, hot *verhuny,* the only food she's complained of missing at Kingmakers. The little pastries—deep-fried, crispy, and sprinkled with powdered sugar—smell exactly like funnel cake, which makes me surprisingly nostalgic as well. I hadn't realized I was missing American food.

I also commissioned a basket of blueberry muffins for Hedeon, as penance for making him intervene in my fight with Estas.

I leave the muffins by his door, knowing an apology is less welcome if somebody wakes you up to offer it.

My mom gets a different sort of gift—a photo Freya sent in her last letter, found in the drawer of our father's study in our house in Cannon Beach.

I've returned to that house several times during the summers when I'm not at Kingmakers.

It gives me no comfort, no sense of being at home.

The house is too cold and too quiet. My father's absence an echoing emptiness that no light or sound can fill.

I never knew I could miss someone like I miss my dad.

I never knew how much I relied on him.

He was always there to tell me what I should do. Giving me a sense of security even in a world as chaotic and violent as ours. I always knew he'd keep us safe.

And he did—the night the Malina attacked us, he offered up his own life so we could escape, providing cover while we fled on the boat.

But he didn't die. The Malina shot him, captured him, and dragged him off to a cell in some desolate place, in some unknown country.

We've been searching for him ever since.

We know he's alive because Marko Moroz has been using my father to extort us for every penny the Petrov empire earns.

We siphon off as much cash as we can without the rest of the Bratva noticing. It's our money, but if the high table knows that Ivan Petrov is missing, that he's no longer in control of his territory, they'll descend on St. Petersburg, and on our holdings in America, too.

Dominik has been running St. Petersburg, and Freya has been keeping the dispensaries going, even though she's barely any older than Nix. She has the real Ares to help her, at least. During the summer months, my mother shores up the bulwarks. Come September, she returns to Kingmakers as Miss Robin so she can scour the archives for schematics not found anywhere else in the world.

We've seen where Marko holds my father. The first call was video —my mother insisted upon it to confirm that my father was still alive, refusing to pay a single penny without seeing him in the flesh. Her real purpose was, of course, to gather information.

Marko only showed us the interior of the cell. Even that provided several clues to where my father might be found. The type of stone that formed the walls, the shape of the doorways, the angle of the light . . . all have been studied to the minutest degree when my mother combs over the recording.

And my father himself has been giving us information, disguised by a simple code that, to our knowledge, Marko has never noticed during the monthly calls to Dominik where proof of life is exchanged for another ransom payment. Once a month my father tells us what he's observed, and slowly, painstakingly, we narrow our options, cutting closer and closer to the source.

It was a coded message from two months ago that gave my mother the idea of a mine.

My father had observed a fleck of yellow powder on one of the soldier's boots.

We've tried following Marko and his men. As far as we can tell, only Marko and his lieutenant Kuzmo visit the place where my father is held. The rest of the guards must stay there permanently.

Tracking Marko is no easy task. He leaves from his compound deep in the mountains outside of Kyiv. He flies on his private jet, which is regularly combed for explosives and tracking devices. He's paranoid and reclusive, the growing list of enemies who would want to see him dead causing him to ramp up his security measures by the month.

The only places he goes regularly now are the Four Seasons in Kyiv to meet with his accountant, and wherever the fuck he's got my dad.

Even tracking him to the Four Seasons is dangerous. He saw Adrik's SUV following him once, and he called Dominik, bellowing into the phone, "If you ever fucking try to track me again, I'll cut off Ivan's arm and mail it to you in a box. You take one step toward me, you even think of raising a hand against me, and I'll chuck an incendiary grenade into his cell. Your only hope of getting him back alive is to pay me my fucking money and bide your time."

None of us believe that Marko will ever release him.

He told us five years—that was my father's punishment for his betrayal the night Marko sought his revenge on Taras Holodryga. Five years in a cell, and payments every month.

The closer we get to that five-year mark, the more certain my mother becomes that Marko intends to kill my father, keep the money, and pour out his endless lust for revenge on the rest of us.

So that was Plan A: find my father, break into wherever he's being held, and bring him home. Knowing that if Marko even caught a hint of what we were trying to do, he would slaughter my dad immediately.

Plan B is Nix.

We knew she'd be vulnerable at Kingmakers—out of her father's tight circle of protection.

You can't attack Kingmakers to kidnap a student. But if you're already inside . . .

We planned to take her and trade her life for my father's.

The only reason my mother hasn't done it already is because it's risky—Marko is volatile, irrational. A simple trade might not go as planned. And my mother believes we're closer than we've ever been to finding my father.

I cross the deserted castle grounds.

It's too early in the morning for anyone else to be stirring, after the night of extended revelry at the Christmas dance.

My mom will be awake. She doesn't sleep much anymore.

I crack the heavy library door, entering the cool, dark space.

I know she'll hear me coming in. She'll hear me walking up the ramp, even with the thick carpet underfoot.

Sure enough, she's waiting for me halfway up the ramp, perched on the edge of the desk, a simple black robe wrapped around her slim frame.

She looks more like herself than I've seen in a long time. This is how she dressed normally: in simple, dark clothing. Moving as smoothly as a shadow come to life.

I can just see the tiniest hint of her natural dark brown color coming in at the roots of her red hair. Time for another application. She dyes her hair in the sink of her small apartment at the very top of the Library Tower.

She's not wearing the false glasses. Unencumbered and unshielded, her dark eyes glitter with the full force of their intensity.

"How was the dance," she says.

I hesitate, wondering if she knows I got in a fight.

I didn't see her at the party, though that doesn't mean she wasn't there. She hears all the gossip that passes between students in the library, allowing her to know more of what goes on at the school than the Chancellor himself.

No students today, though. So no gossip.

As blandly as possible I say, "It was good."

Then, to distract her further, I thrust my gift into her hands.

My mother unwraps it, smiling slightly.

"I was hoping for a new Ruger, but it doesn't feel heavy enough . . ." she teases me.

When she sees the framed photograph, her face goes still.

It's a picture of my father and her, dancing at a wedding—I don't know whose.

My father is spinning her around, her hand up-stretched and his arm the axis. My mother's head is thrown back. She's laughing, her skirt flared around her legs like a bloom around the stem of a flower. My father is staring at her like he's never seen anything more captivating. He's grinning like the luckiest man in the world.

"Freya said he kept it in his desk, face-up in the top drawer, so he'd see it whenever he—"

"Yes," my mother says softly. "I remember."

She can't take her eyes off my father's face.

I know she has pictures of him hidden upstairs. But she's looking at this one like she's seeing my father in the flesh, standing before her now.

"There's no one else for me, and there never could be," she says quietly.

"I know, Mom."

She looks up, startled, like she forgot I was there.

"Thank you," she says. "I'll keep this safe for him. It's his favorite."

My stomach twists. Maybe Freya should have left the picture in the desk. Taking something out of my father's office feels like a bad omen—like we don't think he'll return.

Reading my face, my mother says, "Don't worry—I have good news for you."

I swallow hard. "You do?"

"Yes," she breathes, her excitement barely contained in the slight tremor of her shoulders. "I think I found him."

"How?" I say.

"I had it narrowed down to six —"

"I remember," I say, mentally running through the maps she showed me in the archive.

"When he spoke to Dominik last week, he said he saw snow. It only snowed in one place out of the six that day."

Grabbing my arm, she pulls me toward her desk, shoving aside a pile of unsourced books and unfurling a long, crumbling scroll.

"Look!" she points to the blueprint, to the spider-fine script in the corner bearing the name.

Irkolasan Uranium Mine, it says.

The powder on the soldier's boot—yellowcake. Uranium concentrate.

I have to lick my lips before I can speak.

"Where is it?" I murmur.

"Kazakhstan."

My heart is thudding hard against my chest. I can hardly believe it's true. After all this time . . . we could actually go to him.

"What do we do now?" I say.

"We scout the location and plan our attack," my mother says. "We have to be meticulous. If we make a single mistake, if they know what we're doing . . ."

She doesn't have to finish that sentence. We have to break in unheard and unseen—or the first shot fired will be directly into my father's skull.

I let out a shaky breath.

"We won't need Nix, then," I say.

My mother turns to look at me, her gaze sharp and unyielding.

"Nix is coming with us," she says. "As insurance."

Now my heart drops down to my toes.

What my mother means is, if Marko Moroz puts a bullet in my father's head, she'll do the same to his daughter.

I RETURN to the Octagon Tower, the full weight of reality crashing down on my shoulders.

We got what we wanted: we finally found the map.

But that seems so unreal that I can't really enjoy it.

The thing that seems intensely clear and present is the fact that Nix is about to find out that I lied to her—when I rip her out of her bed and fucking kidnap her.

It may be a week or it may be a month until it happens, but she's going to know that I've been manipulating her. That everything I did was for the purpose of destroying the one person she loves.

My chest is so tight that I can hardly draw a breath.

I almost run into Hedeon in the common room on the fourth floor.

"Hey," he grunts, his face unshaven and his stubble dark against his skin. "Did you make muffins for me?"

"I didn't make them," I say. "But I dropped them off. Felt bad about dragging you into that thing with Estas last night."

"Don't worry about it." Hedeon shrugs.

I notice that he's still wearing his rumpled dress shirt and trousers, like he hasn't gone to bed yet.

"Did you sleep in here?" I say, nodding toward the battered sofa.

"Didn't sleep at all," Hedeon says.

The dark shadows under his eyes confirm it.

"What's wrong," I say, "Didn't get enough dances with Cara?"

"Cara is perfection," Hedeon says quietly. "Way too fucking good for me."

He doesn't say it like he's trying to be convinced otherwise—he's just stating a simple truth.

"I think she likes you," I tell him.

Hedeon ignores this.

"Did you see Sabrina Gallo dancing with Ilsa Markov?" he says.

"Yeah." I nod, my cock trying to stir at the memory of Nix sandwiched between the two girls, Ilsa Markov cupping her breasts from behind while she took Sabrina's face in her hands and kissed her . . .

"Pretty hard to miss it," I say.

Hedeon nods. "Everyone was watching. Including the Chancellor."

My stomach does a long, slow flip.

"Well," I say, with a fake chuckle. "He's only human."

"He was talking to Sabrina after the *Quartum Bellum*," Hedeon says. "And he let her off easy the first day of school, after she clocked Estas."

"He didn't punish Nix, either," I say, trying to hide my pounding pulse.

"I think he's got a thing for her," Hedeon insists.

I take three slow breaths, my brain racing behind my dull expression.

"So what if he does?"

"I think he has a type," Hedeon says. "He likes them young. Dark-haired. And wild. Just like my mother."

The silence stretches between us, Hedeon's angry stare drilling into me, with all the heat of his long-suppressed rage.

"If he's your father . . ." I say, "Then what are you going to do?"

With calm surety, Hedeon replies, "I'm going to kill him."

25

Nix

My head is spinning from my hookup with Ares. I've never been so turned on in my life. I felt like I was high, every sense amplified.

And at the same time, I felt more myself than ever.

The whole reason I wanted to come to Kingmakers was to feel free and unrestricted. To find experiences and new relationships.

I'm definitely getting exactly what I wanted, more than I even imagined...

My only concern is that things might be awkward with Sabrina now. I value her as a friend, and I hope I didn't fuck that up by satisfying my curiosity about those sultry lips of hers.

I shouldn't have worried—Sabrina is never awkward, and nothing phases her.

She comes bursting into our room, still dressed in her gown, hair and makeup a mess, apparently just stumbling home from whatever she's been doing with Ilsa Markov.

"Somebody left you pastries!" she announces. "You have to share them with me because they smell phenomenal."

She's already pulling a fresh *verhuny* out of the basket, taking such an enthusiastic bite that flakes of pastry and powdered sugar rain down on the tops of her breasts.

I'm reminded of the simultaneous softness and firmness of Sabrina's body under my hands. My cheeks burn.

Sabrina catches me looking. She grins, licking the sugar off her lips.

"Don't worry." She winks. "You can look."

"I don't want you to think that I—"

"Oh, relax," she laughs. "I know you're crazy about Ares. But a girl's allowed to have a little fun."

"You look like you had more than a little fun with Ilsa," I say, grinning right back at her.

"She's fucking sexy, isn't she?" Sabrina sighs, taking another bite of pastry.

"Aggressive too," I laugh, noting the love bites running down the side of Sabrina's slim brown throat.

"I wouldn't have it any other way." Sabrina passes me the basket so I can enjoy a bite of my own pastry.

I don't need the card to guess that Ares left them. Only he could be that thoughtful.

The *verhuny* are deliciously light and flaky, with a hint of spiced rum mixed into the dough. It's the quintessential flavor of Christmas for me—bringing to mind the twelve-foot tree my father always cuts and hauls home for the holidays, decorated in his clumsy and over-the-top way with huge handfuls of tinsel and fresh holly.

I feel a pang of guilt, knowing it will be his first Christmas without me. He'll have all his soldiers around him, and they're sure to get roaring drunk and probably spend the afternoon axthrowing or some other raucous activity that really shouldn't be done intoxicated.

Still, I know my dad will be lonely. At the very least I need to call him today.

So even though I'd rather go find Ares and give him my own small gift, I tell Sabrina she's welcome to eat the last pastry, and I dress and head over to the Keep to use the bank of phones on the ground floor.

It's early enough that the phones aren't yet packed with students calling home. I only see one Freshman Accountant tearily telling her mom that she misses her, and Tristan Turgenev crammed into a too-small booth, thanking his parents for the gifts they sent.

Wanting privacy, I walk all the way down to the last phone.

I hadn't seen that it was occupied, because the boy sitting in the booth was hunched over, speaking quietly into the receiver. He hangs up as I approach, turning and squinting at me through two heavily swollen eyes.

His face is so battered and bruised that I almost don't recognize him. His two black eyes are little more than slits in a lumpy, misshapen face, his right cheek and lower lip puffed up like beestings. Even his shaved skull bears several ugly goose eggs.

"What do you want?" Estas asks, his voice coming out mushy through the puffy lips. I'm not sure how the person on the other end of the phone even understood him.

"I . . . I was just looking for a phone," I say.

Estas has been a constant annoyance at Kingmakers, stirring up the negative sentiment that swirls around me when anybody remembers my last name. I always felt his grudge was unjust, since my dad promised me he had nothing to do with Estas' brother's death. It seemed like Estas was just looking for somebody to blame and he latched onto me.

Still, the aftermath of Ares' beating is hard to look at. It no longer seems like a proportionate response. I'm grateful that Ares defended me—but I feel guilty that this whole thing has spiraled so far.

"I'm sorry about last night," I say.

Estas just looks at me, the whites of his eyes bloodied around his dark pupils.

"That was my mother on the phone," he mumbles through those swollen lips. "She couldn't hear a thing I was saying because she was bawling the whole time. My father's been in prison all my life. You only get so many conjugal visits—she had my brother, and then me ten years later. No other kids."

I don't want to feel sympathy for Estas.

I don't want to hear about his life.

And I definitely don't want to argue about his brother again. But I'm rooted in place, maybe because for once, Estas isn't trying to physically intimidate me. He's still seated, his voice low and slurred, his shoulders slumped.

"My brother was killed on December eighteenth," he says. "Have you ever seen New York in December? In the summer it stinks, and the winter's cold and sleety. But when they put those Christmas lights up, and the display windows are like dioramas, and people are skating at Chelsea Piers . . . it feels like magic."

Against my will, I picture it: the scent of cocoa and perfume gift sets . . . the bustle of shoppers . . . the sharp slice of skates over ice . . .

"Kyrylo said he'd take me to Rockefeller Center to see them light the giant tree. It's kid stuff, I know, but I was only twelve so I guess I was a kid still. He told me to meet him at the marine terminal. That's where he worked, in the port authority office. He and my uncles all worked there, it's how they smuggled in shipments.

"Kyrylo was the one who made the deal with your father for the Soviet guns. My uncles said he shouldn't do it. They said Marko was sure to fuck them, one way or another.

"But Kyrylo liked your dad. He thought the rumors were bullshit. And anyway, we were family. Whatever Marko might have done in Kyiv, he wouldn't betray his own family."

Estas' lip has split open again from all the talking, but he doesn't seem to notice, even as a thin line of blood runs down his chin.

"Marko was supposed to send twenty crates of AKs. They arrived on the sixteenth. I was there at the marina, waiting for my brother. I saw him open the crates. He broke the seals, used the crowbar to wedge out the nails. Threw off the lids.

"They were empty. He stood there, staring inside the crates. He even ran his hands through the sawdust, like the guns might be hiding underneath.

"I said, 'What's wrong?' and he said, 'Nothing, wait here.'

"He went out back to the alley to make a call. I heard him talking for a long time, low at first, and then starting to shout. He came back thirty minutes later, pale, sweating.

"I said, 'Can we still see the tree?' and he said, 'Yeah, of course, nothing could stop me.'

"He took me to Rockefeller. He wasn't talking much, but I was too excited to notice.

"Two days later, my uncles found him in the warehouse, hanging above the dock, gutted like an animal. Cut from here to here."

Estas traces a line from the divot of his sternum, straight down to his crotch.

"My brother was a big guy. You'd have to be pretty fucking strong to lift him up and hang him."

Estas' eyes are fixed on mine, red and unblinking. He told the story simply, with no hint of embellishment.

Through dry lips I say, "That was six years ago?"

"That's right." He gives one, slow nod.

I'm remembering a December six years past when my father took an unexpected trip. He came home five days before Christmas.

It doesn't prove anything. My father travels all kinds of places all the time.

Still, the image of Kyrylo Lomenchenko burns in my brain: his body hanging over the dock, cut from neck to groin . . .

I've seen my father gut a deer in exactly that manner.

My stomach heaves.

Anyone could have killed Estas' brother. Maybe my father *did* do it, but he had a good reason.

But then ... why lie to me?

"I'm sorry," I say quietly.

I mean, *I'm sorry that happened. I'm sorry you lost your brother.*

Estas just looks at me, through the mask of swollen flesh blanketing his face.

"You really don't know anything he does, do you?" he says.

I want to deny it.

I want to shout at Estas that I know my own father.

Instead, I turn and run out of the Keep.

26

Ivan Petrov

Marko visits me early in January.

We're both in a dark mood.

Me, because it's the fourth Christmas I've missed with my family.

Marko's swirling anger is a mystery to me. He comes into my cell with none of his usual mockery. His face is stone, his eyes blank and dark as a shark's.

He doesn't greet me—he only jerks his head to the folding chair, a silent order to sit down so Kuzmo can cuff my arms behind me.

Once I'm seated, bound in place, he doesn't bring out the phone. Instead, he orders Kuzmo to leave and close the door behind him.

"Are you sure?" Kuzmo asks, with a significant look in my direction.

Marko reacts in an instant, seizing Kuzmo by the throat and slamming him against the wall with all the might of his massive frame. He snarls into his lieutenant's face, "Do you think I can't handle one fucking man tied to a chair? A man who's been locked in here for four fucking years as my prisoner?"

"N-no sir," Kuzmo stammers. "I mean yes, of course you can handle him. I only meant—"

"*Get out,*" Marko hisses at him.

Kuzmo stumbles out of the room, swinging the heavy door shut behind him.

Now Marko and I are truly alone, for the first time in years.

His shoulders are still heaving with rapid, angry breaths. He stares at the wall, trying to recover his calm. Then, at last, he sinks down heavily onto my cot, the metal springs creaking beneath his weight.

"You have a son and a daughter," he says, his rasping voice cutting through the silence.

"Yes," I say.

"Are they obedient children?"

"Sometimes."

"And what of your wife?" he persists. "Is she loyal to you?"

"Always," I say.

Marko doesn't like that answer. He shifts irritably on the cot, his cloudy green eyes fixed on me. His sclera are bloodshot. Vodka seeps out of his lungs with every exhale, acrid in the tight space of the cell.

"I confess," he says. "I thought Sloane would try harder to find you."

Anger churns in my stomach. The cuffs bite into my wrists as my arms flex against the steel.

I tell myself not to rise to the bait. Marko is trying to anger me. He may even be searching for Sloane, trying to goad me into revealing where she might be, and what she might be doing.

Calmly, I say, "All I ask of my wife is that she pay the ransom and keep my business running in my absence."

Marko gives a dismissive snort. His gaze slides away again, pulled back to his own tormenting thoughts. His gnarled hands clench and unclench on his lap.

"We do everything for them," he says. "We capture the world and lay it at their feet. And all we demand in return is fealty."

I think, without saying it, that fealty cannot be demanded. It can only be exchanged between two people, freely and willingly.

Marko has never understood that.

He wants what he himself cannot give.

Because deep down, his only loyalty is to himself.

Perhaps to his daughter as well . . . I've never seen them together, so I can't say. Even if I had, I doubt anyone can guess the deepest priorities of a man's heart.

All I know is that I would offer my body and soul to save my wife, my daughter, or my son.

They are more precious to me than myself.

While my deepest wish is to see them again and hold them in my arms, I would never risk a hair on their heads to make that happen.

I haven't answered Marko, and that irritates him further.

He holds the cellphone in his hand, gripping it so hard that I'm surprised his swollen fingers don't shatter the screen.

"Do you tire of this, Ivan?" he says, jerking his head to indicate the entirety of the cell. "Do you want this to be over?"

He isn't asking me if I want to go home.

We're not playing that game anymore.

"Sometimes," I reply cautiously.

"Are you lonely here? Do your thoughts eat at you? Does your guilt eat at you?"

His teeth are bared, the incisors the color of old ivory. The lid of his right eye twitches.

It strikes me that *Marko* is lonely. His men worship him with slavish devotion—Kuzmo especially. But they are not his friends.

And certainly not his equals.

Marko put a pen through the eye of his last ally. As for me, his oldest friend ... I've become his most hated enemy.

A king has few friends. A dictator has none.

"We all have our demons," I say. "I know mine too well to lose any sleep over them."

"Indeed," Marko says, angry and unsatisfied by my answers. "Well, don't worry, Ivan. This will all be over soon. Only a few more payments to make."

I don't like the sound of that. Marko said it would be five years. I never believed that ... and I certainly don't like the escalation of the timeline.

Marko holds the phone up to my ear, already dialing.

When Dominik answers, our conversation is brief.

"We had a problem with the last transfer out of Gazprombank," he says.

"What a kind of problem?" I ask.

"Foma Kushnir said there were irregularities with our account. He wanted to order an audit."

"What did you tell him?"

"I told him to check with the bank director, to buy us time. Then I had Zima hack in to work his magic. We erased all recurring entries. Cash-flow on Monday is now good. Moroz will get his payment right on time."

"I better," Marko growls, listening carefully.

"Good," I say to Dom. "Thank you for handling that."

Marko ends the call, slipping the phone back into his pocket.

My heart is racing, though I try not to let him perceive so much as a flicker of an eyelash.

Maybe there was a problem at the bank and maybe there wasn't.

Either way, Dominik's actual message is clear:

> **We**
> **Erased**
>
> **All**
> **Recurring**
> **Entries**
>
> **Cash-flow**
> **On**
> **Monday**
> **Is**
> **Now**
> **Good**

27

Ares

I have to track Hedeon everywhere he goes.

I can barely let him out of my sight, in case he decides that's the perfect moment to enact his revenge on Luther Hugo.

The Chancellor thought he covered up his little indiscretion so cleanly.

He seduced Evalina Markov. Impregnated her—accidentally I would assume. When she could no longer hide her belly under baggy school pullovers, he ferried her off the island on his private boat and sequestered her in a hospital in Dubrovnik. Shortly after the birth, he carried the baby away, never to be seen by its mother again.

Evalina Markov flew home to St. Petersburg, surprising her father, brother, and fiancé with her unexpected arrival. She told them she no longer cared to finish her schooling. Donovan Dryagin was only too happy to move up the long-awaited wedding date.

None of the men seemed to notice the difference in her figure or demeanor. Only my mother, having just gone through the same process of pregnancy herself, noted the tell-tale signs: the darker pigment on Evalina's face, the bulge of her slowly shrinking uterus, and the aching breasts that likely were still producing milk the night of my parents' party.

My mother liked Evalina Markov. She had no interest in exposing the girl's secret.

However, she couldn't resist tracking a piece of potentially valuable information. Knowing that Evalina could not have hidden a baby all on her own, she began to search for recent adoptions in mafia families.

It only took her a matter of months to find the Grays. She was surprised to discover that Kenneth and Margaret Gray had adopted not one but two baby boys that same year. The timing made obvious which one belonged to Evalina.

From there, it was no difficult task to confirm the father.

My mother kept that secret for eighteen years.

She keeps entire ledgers full of such leverage. It's her nature to maintain blackmail and contingency plans on everyone. Most of it will never be used.

But in this case, three and a half years ago, we needed a favor . . .

Luther Hugo was just the man to provide it.

My mother arrived on the doorstep of his private compound in Monaco, informing him that he now had a long-lost niece . . .

He railed against the idea of allowing her on campus. For all his wealth and experience, nothing is more valuable to Luther Hugo than Kingmakers. His father was Chancellor before him, and his grandfather before him. The Hugos' sigil of the golden skull is found on the university's seal. By ruling the school, Luther rules the rising generation of every powerful mafia family across the globe.

I'm sure that's why he went to such great pains to hide his illegitimate son.

If the Markovs discovered that he impregnated their daughter, he would have lost his position as Chancellor. To say nothing of the physical reprisal her family and the Dryagins would have sought.

So he hid the baby carefully, counting on Evalina's shame and misery to keep her quiet.

He thought he got away with it.

Until my mother and Luther's son came back into his life in the same year.

I'm not sure why he allowed Hedeon admission. My mother asked him that question once—he said it would have looked more suspicious if he denied the application. But hearing Hedeon's story of how the Chancellor placed him in the Heirs division over Silas Gray, I think it was nothing more or less than pride. The Chancellor couldn't resist seeing his son face-to-face, and he couldn't bear the idea of his blood in a subordinate position.

Still, his fear of scandal is as powerful as ever. If Hedeon makes public what he knows, the Chancellor will surely expose my mother as well.

So I stalk Hedeon, trying to guess whether he truly intends to follow through on his quest for revenge.

It's the worst possible task, because I am going through literal physical withdrawal for Nix. Not just for sex, though I'm dying to fuck her again. It's her scent, her throaty laugh, and even the incendiary reaction that occurs in my brain when I catch sight of the particular shade of red in her brilliant hair. I need it all.

While I'm following Hedeon, I instruct Kade to do the same with Danyl Kuznetsov and his minions, by way of Dean Yenin.

We have to watch Danyl even closer than Hedeon.

The meeting of the high table did not go well. The *Pakhans* didn't bother to hide their displeasure that once again my father sent Uncle Dom in his place. Danyl whipped them into a frenzy, demanding a video conference with Ivan at the very least.

Dominik shut them down, departing Moscow under a cloud of barely-veiled threats.

As an additional bad omen, Bodashka Kushnir dropped out of Kingmakers, taking the supply ship back to Dubrovnik right after the dance.

I can't help but think his father must have summoned him home. Which can only mean that the Foma Kushnir and Danyl Kuznetsov have plans they intend to execute before summer.

Meanwhile, my mother intercepts me on the way to Advanced Interrogation Techniques, my first class of the week.

She almost never speaks to me outside the library so I know at once this is no simple social call.

"Adrik says the mine looks good," she says. "He's seen military Hummers going in and out of the tunnels. The mine's supposed to be decommissioned. But it's definitely in use."

"Kazakh military?" I say. "Or Malina?"

"He thinks both," my mother says, eyes glinting. "I'm going there myself to check it out."

"I'll come with you," I say at once.

"No—I'm leaving this afternoon. You stay here and keep an eye on Hedeon—if he blows this whole thing up, then Luther will fuck us over out of spite. We can't have anyone raising an alarm while we're still making arrangements."

I stare at her hard.

"Don't even think of doing it without me," I say.

She holds my eyes, unblinking.

"I would never do that," she says. "He's *your* father and *my* husband. We'll bring him home together."

"Keep me updated," I say.

I have a contraband cellphone, though not from Miles Griffin—I never trusted that he wasn't monitoring the calls and texts on his clandestine network. Like my mother, Miles never misses an angle.

My mom and I have been in contact with Dom and Freya via our own phones. Because it's difficult for me to find privacy on campus, Freya sends the complex or non-time-sensitive information via letters.

I can speak to my mom the same way. But as she turns to leave, already wearing a pair of trousers and a light coat, much more streamlined than Miss Robin's usual cardigans, I feel a stab of fear for her.

As awful as the last few years have been, I knew my mother was secure on Visine Dvorca. Now she's venturing out in the world again, with more fire in her eyes than I've seen in a long time. I'm worried what might happen to her.

The week passes achingly slow.

We're in the doldrums of January, thick in some of the most dense and convoluted classes I've taken in my entire time at Kingmakers.

Worse, a flu is sweeping through the students, something that seems to happen every year despite our isolation.

Almost everybody in the Octagon Tower catches it, including Leo and me.

It takes me four or five days to recover, during which time I live off tea and toast from the dining hall. Luckily Hedeon caught it too, so I don't have to drag myself too far to keep an eye on him. Leo hates laying around, so he pretends to be recovered, though he still sounds like an asthmatic seal. Hedeon looks like walking death—he's been so sick that he hasn't even been trying to "accidentally" sit by Cara at every single meal.

Every minute I'm expecting a call or text from my mom. When she does update me, her messages are encouraging but vague. She met up with Adrik and they're gathering information, trying to make absolutely certain that we've found the right place. We'll only get one shot at this.

I'm dying to see Nix. My constant excuses to her so that I can keep tracking Hedeon are really starting to piss her off. She thinks I don't want to see her, when in reality I could peel my own flesh off my bones out of sheer desperation.

Finally my mother texts me late in the afternoon, telling me to find a private spot so we can speak.

As soon as I call her, she says, "It's time."

The word "time" vibrates in my ear like a bell. I'm frozen in place, hearing my lips say, "You found him? He's there?"

"I'm certain of it," she says, quietly.

I've never been so excited and so scared. All the clarity of what we're doing here comes rushing back to me.

"What do I have to do?"

"Marko is here, and Kuzmo too. We need one of them to open the cell door—you can guess which one I'd prefer."

"I'll call in my favor with Miles Griffin," I say. "The timing is perfect—Marko is due to see his accountant at the Four Seasons. Miles could meet him there."

"Set it for tomorrow night. Take the Chancellor's boat and meet me in Dubrovnik. Dom, Adrik, and Freya will pick us up with a plane. Don't forget the scuba gear."

"Do I tell Hugo I need to borrow his boat?"

My mother laughs. "Let it be a nice surprise for him."

I leave the cluster of bare-branched trees in which I sequestered myself, walking in a daze across the chill, snowless ground. I almost plough into Nix, who's striding with her usual aggressive speed, bright patches of color whipped into her cheeks from the wind.

"There you are!" she cries. "What are you doing way over here? It's fucking freezing."

"Artillery class," I lie. "What about you?"

"Environmental Adaptation," she says, abruptly adding, "Are you avoiding me?"

"No, of course not. I'm sorry, I've just had so much—"

"Oh, save it," she says. "Do you want to see me tonight or not?"

She tilts up her chin in her usual forthright way, demanding an honest answer of me. Her nose has a slight upward tilt to it, like a ski jump, which prevents her features from ever seeming truly severe.

I'd love to run my finger down that adorable curve.

But she'd probably bite my hand off.

"I want to see you," I tell her. "Badly."

I know it's wrong, but I can't help myself. I want one last night with Nix where she looks at me with those fierce green eyes, and kisses me with that relentless hunger, and blurts out one of her awfully penetrating comments that makes me feel like she pulled another private file out of my brain, rifled through, and read it back to me in question form.

I don't know what's going to happen tomorrow night.

All I know for certain is that things will never be the same between Nix and me.

She'll know that I lied. That I used her. That I was her enemy all along.

After tomorrow, she'll fucking despise me.

So tonight might well be our last night together. And I'm not missing it, not for anything, not even if it's fucked up to do this to her.

Hedeon shouldn't be a problem, he could hardly hold his spoon up at breakfast. I bet he's asleep by 8:00.

"Meet me at the underground pool tonight," I tell her.

I want one last look at my *rusalka* in her natural habitat.

All that afternoon and evening, I can hardly sit still.

"What's up with you?" Leo rasps, still barely able to speak.

"Gonna see Nix tonight," I mutter.

"That's great, man. I'm really happy for you," Leo says.

God I wish I deserved that congratulations.

I fucking hate what I'm about to do to Nix. I regret that I ever allowed things to go this far. But at the same time . . . how in the fuck can I regret anything at all? I'm crazy about her. I can't wish we never met.

I have no choice in any of this.

I have to help my father. That one goal has been the center of my universe for three and a half years now. I can't stop this close to the finish line. I can't even slacken my pace—not for a single step, not even for Nix.

So that night, I watch while Hedeon picks at his dinner, his eyes ringed with dark circles. He says, sleepily, to the table at large, "I'm going to bed, I feel like shit."

"Good night," Cara Wilk calls from across the table.

Hedeon doesn't even look up.

I look across at Nix, catching her eye and mouthing, "One hour."

She grins.

I spend that time in the Octagon Tower, making absolutely certain that Hedeon really went to sleep and won't come wandering out looking for tea or another blanket.

I'm mildly concerned that Kenzo Tanaka might wake him up when he goes to bed.

"You planning to stay up studying?" I ask Kenzo, seeing the pile of books spread across the common room table.

"I'm gonna sleep right here," Kenzo says, nodding to the blanket stolen off his bed, and the artfully arranged cushions on the sofa. "I'm the only one in this whole damn tower who hasn't caught the flu yet, and I sure as fuck don't want whatever strain is trying to kill Hedeon."

Inwardly rejoicing, I head back to my room to grab my swimsuit.

Leo's out with Anna, who apparently doesn't share Kenzo's fear of germs. She hasn't stopped swapping spit with Leo for a single day, though apparently her constitution is stronger—she hasn't caught so much as a sniffle.

Pulling on the rest of my clothes to counteract the cold, I hurry down to the Armory.

I don't see Nix in the water yet. The shimmering, pale green surface of the pool is as smooth as a mirror.

I strip off my clothes. Then, following a strange impulse that wants nothing between my skin and the water, I pull off my suit, too, before descending the steps.

Compared to the chilly, windy night, the underground pool feels warm as blood. I walk down into the water, the pale limestone steps rough against the soles of my feet.

This pool is a hundred meters deep at least. We took scuba lessons here our first year at Kingmakers.

I've sunk all the way down to the bottom, the column of water as heavy as a building on top of us.

The floodlights set in the walls only illuminate so far down. They can have a blinding effect, shining upward. Anything could be beneath my feet.

At that very moment, something seizes me by the legs and yanks me down.

I'm so surprised that I don't even close my eyes. The saltwater burns as I stare into the pale, unearthly face of Nix Moroz, her crimson hair floating around her head in a corona.

I Feel Like I'm Downing — *Two Feet*
Spotify → geni.us/spy-spotify
Apple Music → geni.us/spy-apple

She's completely naked too, her pale breasts with their rose-colored nipples freed of all gravity, assuming a shape of impossible symmetry. Her flesh glows pearlescent in the lights, her eyes greener than they've ever been.

She reaches out her hands to me, slow and sensuous under the water. She takes my face between her cool fingertips, bringing her mouth to mine.

Salt seeps into my mouth as I kiss her. Her mouth tastes all the sweeter by comparison.

Our naked bodies slide against each other as if we're oiled down every inch of our skin. We're floating suspended, swirling around in a slow circle in the ghostly green light.

Her wild curls float around my face like tentacles, tickling my bare arms and even my back, as if each lock has become sentient and teasing.

My lungs are burning, my heart is on fire.

And still I haven't even considered that I might need breath.

It's Nix who gives two strong kicks of her legs, rocketing us upward.

I gasp, the air as fiery as if I had never drawn breath before.

I blink salt out of my eyes, dazzled all over again by the crisp perfect lines of Nix's face without the blurring effect of the water.

She kisses me again, my thigh sliding between her legs as she treads water in place. The churning motion rubs her pussy against the top of my thigh. I press against her, making her moan into my mouth.

"Let's never leave," she murmurs. "I hate when you're busy. I hate when I'm not with you."

"I hate everything that pulls me away from you," I tell her, seizing handfuls of her wet hair and kissing her harder.

When I release her, Nix dives down below the water. I feel her warm mouth close around my cock.

I arch my back slightly, so I can float instead of kick.

I look up at the limestone ceiling a hundred feet overhead, dripping down into stalactites like melting vanilla ice cream. Below the water, Nix sucks my cock.

She comes up briefly for air and I kiss her again. Her mouth tastes saltier than ever, from the water and from the precum leaking out of me in this warm bath.

I feel utterly relaxed, floating in more ways than one. Each time Nix dives down to take me in her mouth again, I give in more fully and completely.

I want her to drag me all the way under. I want to stay there with her forever.

I don't care about the world on the surface. I don't care about anyone who lives in the sunshine and the wind. I want to be in the cool blue-green shadows, where the creatures are as bright and vivid as Nix, and time means nothing—no day and no night.

I give in to her ... and I start to cum in her mouth.

Each surge of pleasure is as long and as endless as a wave sweeping across the ocean.

I have no idea how long she's been under there. She might have broken an Olympic record for all I know.

At last she floats up to the surface, her iridescent green eyes peeking up at me before the rest of her face breaks the water.

I kiss her again, wanting to feel how swollen her lips and tongue have become.

"Let me do you," I say.

"I don't think you can hold your breath as long," she says.

"Fucking drown me, then."

I dive below the water, flipping over on my back with my head between her thighs. I plunge my tongue upward between her pussy lips, nibbling at her, tasting her. There's no gravity, no stiffness, no awkward angles. I can eat her pussy any way I want, floating below her.

Only the need to come up for air prevents me making her cum in record time.

I take three deep breaths, then dive down again. With no sense of taste or smell, I focus on the pressure of my tongue against her clit, and the velvet-warm texture of her pussy when I slip my fingers in and out of her. I start to play with her ass too. The water is just enough lubrication to slowly work the tip of my middle finger into her ass as I lap at her clit.

When I surface again, Nix is too rabid to wait any longer. She wraps her arms and legs around me. I thrust into her, my cock only just recovering enough to rise to the occasion again. The interior of her pussy brings it all the way to life as she squeezes me hard, her pussy ten times warmer than the water.

We're locked together, spinning and floating in the water, able to assume any position like astronauts fucking in space. We couple and break apart and couple again. Sometimes we rise to the surface, sometimes we sink ten feet below.

I don't want air. I don't want sun. I don't want anything but her.

She starts to cum, each clench around my cock as slow and endless as the waves of my own climax. With little friction between us, each thrust of my cock against her clit seems to drag out another pulse of pleasure, without draining her entirely.

Meanwhile, my second climax is building—a river rushing faster and faster against a dam. Any second it's going to burst.

Nix wraps her legs tight around me and her arms around my neck. She slides all the way down my cock, giving one last extended clench, her arms shaking, her whole body trembling as she squeezes me with all her might.

I erupt inside of her—an underwater volcano that could turn this whole fucking pool to steam. I'm cumming and cumming, my strangled yell echoing off the stone walls. I can't stop, I'm pumping upward in her, I'm kissing her, biting her lips, biting the side of her neck.

It goes on forever, until finally it's over.

We're both floating, still connected, neither one of us wanting to let go.

"I love you," I say. "I want you to know that. Now, tonight."

She looks at me, searching my face.

"Is that true?"

"It's the truest thing I've ever said."

"I've never been in love before," she says. "But I don't know what else to call this feeling."

She kisses me again, hungry as ever.

I don't care if this is wrong.

I don't care that I have no right.

I need her, and I love her.

I WALK BACK to my dorm room. It's so late that Leo will likely be asleep already. I'll have to creep in without waking him.

I sneak through the common room first, though Kenzo is snoring so loudly on the sofa, I doubt anything short of a vuvuzela would wake him.

I pass Hedeon's door. On impulse, I press my ear against the wood, expecting to hear long, rasping breaths.

Instead I hear . . . nothing.

He's probably just deep asleep. Maybe with the blankets over his head.

Still, I can't help the cold dread that seeps into my lungs. The sense that I did something wrong . . . and now I'm about to be punished.

I shouldn't have met up with Nix. I shouldn't have fucked her again. Karma demands payment.

Hurrying back to my room, I rifle through my drawers as quietly as possible, searching for a lock pick. Leo is asleep on his back, arms and legs sprawled wide, paddle-sized feet hanging off the too-short bed.

At last, my fingers close around the silver pick. It glitters in the dim light, pointed as a knife.

I hurry out of the room, slipping down the dark hallway once more to Hedeon's room. Trying not to let the pick scrape in the lock, I jimmy the tumblers until the door pops. I crack it open, hoping I'm about to see the slumbering lump of Hedeon in his bed.

Both beds are empty.

Panic rising, I run to the bed and yank the blankets back like Hedeon might somehow have flattened himself to the width of a pancake. The bare mattress blazes back at me.

Now my heart is really racing. I have to find him. Right this fucking second. It might already be too late.

I sprint down the stairs of the Octagon Tower, flushed with dread, paranoid that an alarm might start blaring across the empty campus any second. Like a flood of burly grounds crew might come pouring in from every direction.

I'm running for the Keep. I don't know where Hedeon went, but I have a pretty good idea where the Chancellor should be. His private quarters are on the top floor, next to his office. I know he's here tonight—I've been checking his berth regularly to make sure he hasn't snuck off the island in his private boat.

I run up the stairs of the Keep, making a swift detour out of the stairwell on the second floor as I hear someone coming down. I'm hoping it might be Hedeon chickening out, or the Chancellor strolling down, safe and sound. Peeking out, I see Professor Lyons instead, slipping out of her white lab coat and folding it over her forearm as she descends the steps. She must have been working late, probably mixing up one of her custom chemical compounds for an upcoming class.

I wait until she passes, then sprint up the remaining flights.

I only slow when I reach the luxurious oriental carpet running toward the Chancellor's office. My feet pad silently along, the wall-mounted sconces casting distinct pools of light onto the floor, with dark wells between.

I plan to creep up to the Chancellor's apartments. Until I hear a sudden scuffling and a crashing sound that brings me sprinting through the doors at top speed.

Hedeon and Luther Hugo are grappling in front of Hugo's immense fireplace, silhouetted against the roaring flames.

Hedeon doesn't look sick anymore—he looks possessed. His hands are locked on the Chancellor's shoulders, half his shirt slashed away, baring the gruesome scars running down his right arm to the flickering firelight.

The Chancellor is wearing black brocade pajamas, as if Hedeon dragged him out of his bed. Despite being forty years older than Hedeon at least, the fight is not nearly as uneven as one might expect. Hugo still retains a portion of his once-great strength. Driven by desperation, he grapples with his son, the tendons standing out on his neck, his bared teeth glinting in the black beard.

It won't matter. Neither skill nor experience will overcome Hedeon's rage tonight. Not even the dagger on the floor between them—stained with Hedeon's blood—is going to save the Chancellor. Slowly, inexorably, Hedeon is dragging Hugo toward the open grate, as if he intends to fling him into the fire.

Neither man has noticed me. They're aware of nothing but each other's sweating, snarling faces.

I run at Hedeon, grabbing him from behind and trying to drag him away as he did to me when I almost murdered Estas.

"Stop!" I bellow. "You can't kill him!"

Hugo dives on the knife and snatches it up, wildly swinging it toward his son's throat.

I block the strike with my forearm, with a deftness that should earn me an instant A in Professor Howell's class. Seizing the outside of Luther's hand, I twist his wrist over, forcing him to drop the knife from his boneless fingers.

Luther swings his other elbow around, knocking me across the jaw. I dive at him, taking out his legs and bringing him down to the floor. We grapple with each other, his limbs hard as petrified oak, the strength of his long years baked into the muscle. But age has no stamina—it's two o'clock in the morning, and Hugo is fighting for his life against two much younger men. He's flagging.

I pin him down on the carpet, my knee in his back and his arm twisted up behind him.

"Get something to tie him up!" I bellow to Hedeon.

Hedeon has picked up the knife. He's holding it overhand, his dark blue eyes fixed on his helpless father. His own blood stains the blade, garish evidence of Luther Hugo's utter disregard for his safety.

"Don't," I say, in a warning tone.

I know Hedeon wants to rush forward and plunge that knife into Hugo's back. Maybe cut his throat for good measure, like Hugo did to Ozzy's mom.

"He deserves it," Hedeon says, his voice dull and emotionless. "He left me with those people. Dropped me off like unwanted luggage. Left me to be tortured. Or even to die."

"I know," I say, trying to keep my voice steady. "But you can't kill him, Hedeon. You'll be executed."

"I don't care," Hedeon says, his eyes flat and unmoving. "I've never felt alive in my whole fucking life."

"You can't do this," I say again, torn between threatening, begging, and trying to reason with him. "I can't let you."

"He has to pay," Hedeon says. "It's the only thing that kept me going, year after year. Thinking that someday I'd find my parents, and I'd kill them for what they did to me."

"Don't you want to know the whole story?" I ask, desperately. "Don't you want to know what happened?"

"I know what happened!" Hedeon shouts, his anger flaring up again. "I know what he did to her, and I know what he did to me."

He clenches the knife in his hand, but he doesn't rush at us. Not yet.

Luther has stopped struggling beneath me. He's waiting, listening. I'm not stupid enough to loosen my grip—the old viper's only waiting for his chance to strike.

I haul him up, dragging him to the throne-like chair set behind his desk, and throwing him down on it.

"Don't fucking move," I tell him, "or I'll help Hedeon hack you into pieces and throw you into the fire."

The threat has no effect on the Hugo's stoic expression or his dark, glittering eyes, but it seems to placate Hedeon somewhat.

He slashes through the curtain ties with his knife, using them to bind the Chancellor to the chair.

Now we stand in a strange inverse of the usual power dynamic in this office: the Chancellor cowed and at the mercy of two students. Or at least, pretending to be cowed.

Hedeon strides over to the corner behind the desk, rips down the photograph of Evalina Markov, and brandishes it in Hugo's face.

"Who is this?" he demands.

"Evalina Markov," the Chancellor says, calmly.

"And what was your relationship to her?"

"She was a student here," Hugo replies.

With one ruthless swipe, Hedeon slashes Hugo's face from temple to jaw. The Chancellor doesn't even flinch, only letting out a grunt as blood patters down on the silk thigh of his pajamas, disappearing on the black brocade.

"Answer my questions fully and truthfully, or I'll cut off your nose next," Hedeon hisses. "Do you know that's how Kenneth Gray used to threaten me? He'd pick some little piece of me—a finger, a toe, an earlobe, and say, 'You don't need all ten toes to be a soldier. You don't even need both eyes . . .' "

"Kenneth is maudlin," the Chancellor says, dismissively. "He always was."

"How did you know the Grays?" Hedeon demands.

Hugo's upper lip curls in disgust at the idea of being interrogated by two students. But he isn't stupid enough to keep stonewalling Hedeon. After a moment he says:

"Kenneth and I attended Kingmakers together when my father was headmaster. His wife Margaret was younger. I knew her family too. I used to visit her father in Oxfordshire. He'd always bring out the best brandy, offer me his favorite gun when we went shooting. The Vanbrughs are social climbers. He hoped I might take an interest in one of his daughters. Margaret would only have been too willing to offer herself.

"No chance of that—she had the face of overbred horse, as you know. She was no prettier at twenty than at forty. I wanted nothing to do with her, though I kept visiting whenever I needed anything from Connor Vanbrugh, stringing them all along, enjoying the ass-kissing.

"I had no intention of marrying anyone. Eventually Margaret gave up and Connor offered her to Kenneth Gray.

"I barely kept tabs on them. I heard once from Kenneth that Margaret was infertile. After seven or eight years he considered divorcing her, but he didn't want the headache from her father."

I'm watching Luther closely, making sure he isn't trying to twist out of the curtain ties or reach some hidden button with his toe that might call the grounds crew. Hedeon shifts impatiently, caring less about the Grays than about his own, direct history. He's still brandishing the knife, more than ready to cut another chunk out of Hugo.

"Then you met Evalina," Hedeon prods.

Luther hesitates, not wanting to confirm what he's kept hidden so long, even if Hedeon obviously already knows it.

Hedeon slashes him again, this time across his chest, opening a gash in the pajamas and Luther's flesh.

Luther turns not to Hedeon but to me, narrowing his eyes and hissing, "We had a deal."

Hedeon looks at me sharply.

"What does that mean?" he says.

Now the tip of the knife is pointed in my direction, not Luther's.

"I made a deal with Hugo to come to Kingmakers," I say, trying not to give too much away. "It has nothing to do with you. But that's why I can't sit back and watch you murder him!"

"You're not going to stop me," Hedeon informs me.

We'll see about that.

For now, I only say, "Ask him for the whole story. He won't be any use to you once he's dead."

Meanwhile, out of the corner of my eye, I'm searching for my own weapon. I don't want to hurt Hedeon, but if it's a choice between him and my father . . . I know who I have to pick.

A gold letter opener lays atop a neat stack of correspondence.

Hedeon doesn't notice it. Through he's vibrating with rage, he can't keep his eyes off his father's craggy face, deeply-lined and vulpine in the glow of the firelight.

Hedeon asks, "Did you love her?"

Hugo pauses, this time I think for a different reason—he's not sure how to answer.

"She captivated me," he says at last, his rough voice scraping against my skin like sandpaper. "I had seen the girls come and go in their short skirts . . . but Evalina was something else. I wanted her. I wanted to touch her, hold her, possess her."

Hugo's eyes glitter like a dragon crouched over a hoard of gold.

"You seduced her," Hedeon says.

"She wanted it just as I wanted it," Hugo says, with no hint of shame. No, he's smiling beneath the dark beard, reveling in the memory. "Men desire beauty, women desire power. My name, my presence, was just as powerful an aphrodisiac to her as those long, shapely legs and those full breasts were to me."

Hedeon's fingers twitch on the handle of the knife. He wants to cut Hugo again, though technically Hugo is doing exactly what Hedeon asked.

"She was barely eighteen," Hedeon says.

"What a convenient number eighteen is," Hugo sneers. "Transforming a girl into a woman in a day."

"You took advantage of her," Hedeon snarls.

"I wasn't the first. Remember that she was already engaged to a man barely any younger than myself," Hugo scoffs. "She was no virgin when we met. Dryagin bored her—at least she enjoyed fucking me."

"Was the pregnancy accidental?"

"Accidental and unwanted for both of us," Hugo frowns. "But Evalina showed her usual stubbornness. She waited to tell me until she thought it was too late to do anything about it. I would have cut you out of her body until the last day of the ninth month, but Evalina wouldn't consent, and she certainly wouldn't have kept quiet if I'd forced it. I'd have had to kill her, too."

"Why didn't you?" Hedeon demands.

"I should have," Hugo says.

I don't believe him. Hugo can pretend indifference all he wants, but the picture hanging behind his desk all these years tells another story.

"So you took her to Dubrovnik," Hedeon prods.

Hugo nods. "I waited as long as I could. Some of her closest friends were beginning to whisper. We induced labor early. Evalina was in hysterics—she thought you might die. It would have been better for everyone if you did."

Hedeon's face is impassive, Luther's coldness having no effect on him. Hedeon has never felt wanted, never felt loved.

"Once you were born, I had her sedated and I took you out of the hospital. I should have thrown you off the sea cliff. Instead, I brought you to the Grays."

"Why?" Hedeon barks. "Why them?"

"They wanted a child. I knew Margaret would be particularly partial to a baby with Hugo blood, even if it was tainted by illegitimacy. Kenneth was amenable. Until . . ."

"Until what?" Hedeon says.

I already know the answer.

"Until Kenneth realized he had a son of his own," Luther says. "His own flesh and blood, born from some waitress in Westminster. Margaret Gray was furious—she didn't want to take his bastard into the house. But he wouldn't relent, particularly since she had just pressured him into accepting the other child."

"Silas is Kenneth's biological son," Hedeon says, a look of understanding coming into his face.

"Indeed. And, to all accounts, a more impressive son than mine," Luther snorts.

"Silas is a fucking automaton," I snap.

"Oh, I wouldn't say that," Hugo raises one black and silver eyebrow. "A blunt instrument, yes. But I've heard he enjoys what he does."

"He certainly enjoyed torturing me," Hedeon says, quietly.

Hugo shrugs. "Would you prefer to grow up weak and ignorant? A civilian . . . a *software engineer*?" he sneers. "You're mafia in blood, from both sides. I placed you with a wealthy and well-connected family. I did my duty by you."

"You put me in hell!" Hedeon cries, the firelight reflecting in his eyes.

I can see Hedeon tensing, like he plans to run at the Chancellor. Quickly, I say, "Did Evalina Markov know where you took Hedeon? Did you ever tell her?"

Luther's eyes are drawn, irresistibly, toward the photograph of Evalina, abandoned by Hedeon on the desk. Evalina smiles up from the frame—young, triumphant, ignorant of the fate in store for her.

"No," Hugo says at last. "I never told her."

There's no roar of rage, no warning—Hedeon runs at the Chancellor, and I have no chance to grab the letter opener. I barely catch Hedeon's wrist as he stabs at Hugo's throat. Hedeon and I wrestle over the knife, the blade swinging wildly back and forth between us, once almost plunging into the Chancellor's shoulder, and once sweeping in front of my face an inch from my eye.

Now is the moment where I have to choose: my friends or my family. Mercy or loyalty.

My scramble with Hedeon is brutal and brief. I don't want to hurt him, but I can't let him kill the Chancellor. I hold nothing back. Perhaps Hedeon does—because I'm able to wrench the knife away from him and pin him down, both of us breathing hard, my cheek scraped and his nose bloody, but neither of us seriously hurt.

Maybe he doesn't want to kill Hugo as much as he thought.

"Look," I pant, "I'm really fucking sorry about this, but I don't have a choice."

I slash another cord from the drapes and tie his hands just like we did to the Chancellor.

"Those curtains are two hundred years old," Hugo says, irritably.

"Time for some new ones, then," I snap.

Hedeon isn't fighting me anymore. He's given up—on pretty much everything, from the look of it.

He only gives me one resentful glare as I cut Hugo free.

"And what am I supposed to do about this?" Hugo says, standing from the chair, sneering in the direction of the temporarily subdued Hedeon. "Pretend like he didn't try to kill me?"

"Yes," I say, testily. "I doubt you want to blow this thing up any more than I do."

Hedeon is still watching the Chancellor mutinously.

"Try that again," Hugo says to him, quietly, "and you won't find me so easy to surprise."

"You won't see anything but oblivion," Hedeon hisses back at him.

Not wanting the two of them to exchange any more words, or Hugo to consider more options for reprisal, I frog-march Hedeon out of the office—quietly pocketing the keys to Hugo's cruiser on my way past the desk. I don't want to have to come back for those tomorrow.

Hedeon is letting me lead him along, not struggling. I can tell he thinks the idea of me holding him captive is fucking ridiculous.

"What's your plan now?" he says. "Keep me tied up the rest of the year so I don't go blabbing about your weird secret deal with Hugo?"

I don't have to keep Hedeon incapacitated the rest of the year—only until tomorrow night when I leave. But even that is going to be extremely difficult since I don't have a private dorm room. I consider taking Hedeon to the library to lock him up in the archives, but my mother isn't there to keep an eye on him.

I decide to simply take him to his own room, trusting that Kenzo is still on plague watch.

The Octagon Tower is so silent that the air seems thick and buzzing. I hustle Hedeon along, already starting to feel a sense of relief as we near his door.

Until Leo rounds the corner, heading back from the bathroom. He halts in the hallway, not sleepy enough to miss the fact that I'm marching Hedeon along with his hands tied behind his back.

"Uh . . . what the fuck are you doing?" Leo asks.

"That's a great question," Hedeon replies.

I shove Hedeon into his room, having no choice but to allow Leo to follow. Leo closes the door gently behind us, folding his arms over his broad chest and saying, carefully, "Is this consensual, or . . .?"

"No, it's not fucking consensual," Hedeon snarls.

Leo looks at me with an expression of mingled amusement and genuine concern.

"What's going on, Ares?" he says.

I take a deep breath.

"I'm not Ares. My name is Rafe Petrov. My father is Ivan Petrov. He's been imprisoned for three and a half years. Tomorrow, I finally bring him home."

Leo and Hedeon stare at me with near-equal expressions of astonishment.

"Okay . . . that is not what I was expecting you to say," Leo remarks.

Despite the fact that the night has been a fucking disaster, and I've now involved two more people in this mess, I feel the strangest sense of lightness, like my bones have been replaced with helium.

I'm finally telling the truth.

Hedeon frowns.

"Then who the fuck is Ares?" he says.

I tell them everything, starting at the beginning. I speak for almost thirty minutes uninterrupted, pausing only to set Hedeon free from the curtain ties.

When I'm finished, the stunned silence is even longer than before.

Leo breaks it by saying, "I'm coming with you."

Now I'm the one who can't speak. I just told Leo that I've been lying to him since the day I met him. That his roommate "Ares" doesn't even exist. And now he wants to leave school to help me assault a near-impregnable compound.

"I don't think that's a good idea," I says.

"Why not?"

"Because there's a very good chance that we're all going to end up dead."

Leo shrugs, tucking his hands in the pockets of his sweatshorts.

"Less of a chance if I'm there," he says.

"I'll go with you, too," Hedeon says, quietly.

"Why do *you* want to go?" I say, feeling like the whole world is tilting sideways.

"Well, for one thing, I think Hugo's gonna try to murder me back if he gets the chance," Hedeon says.

"Wait, what?" Leo interjects.

"But mostly," Hedeon continues, ignoring Leo, "I want to get the fuck off this island. I want to do something. And the only thing I planned for the last twenty years was kill my fucking degenerate father. So if I'm not going to do that . . . I'm going to need a new option."

This is not what I expected, and it's too much to process all at once.

All I can say is, "Look, I really appreciate it, but—"

"Don't bother arguing," Leo says. "What, are you going to tie both of us up in here? Don't be stupid. You're taking us with you, you don't have a choice."

As much as I'd like to keep arguing, Leo is right.

28

Nix

Breakfast is an odd affair.

Estas Lomachenko nods to me in the line for pancakes —not exactly friendly, but as if he no longer minds us breathing the same air in the same space.

The bruises on his face are still healing. I don't think he's softened towards me because of the beating from Ares—I think, strangely, telling me the full story of what happened between his brother and my father has unburdened his soul. He's not blaming me for it anymore.

Maybe because he saw that I believed him.

I never did call my father that day. We haven't spoken since before Christmas.

I'm sure he's furious.

Well, I'm pretty fucking angry, too.

He lied to me when I asked if he killed Kyrylo Lomachenko. Straight up lied to me. He could have told me it was complicated, that he had his reasons . . . I wouldn't have judged him. But I would have known the truth so I didn't look like such a fool defending him to my own fucking cousin.

While Estas seems to have relaxed his hatred of me, Ares is behaving more strangely than ever.

He looks simultaneously exhausted and wired—dark circles under his eyes, unshaven face, and a jitteriness to his movements like he's already had several cups of coffee this morning.

He sits by Leo and Hedeon instead of by me, which feels intentional.

Ares can be so hot and cold, so intimate and then so closed off.

We've shared moments where I felt more connected to him than anyone on the planet. And then he pulls back again, and I'm left with that nagging sensation that he's hiding something from me. That he's not telling me everything.

It's starting to make me feel . . . really fucking sad. Like I'll never truly know him. Like this is all I'm going to get.

Maybe I'm paranoid because of what happened with my father this year—thinking that I knew him so well, only to discover that he has a darker side he never showed me.

Or maybe I'm becoming less naive, and I'm realizing that the same is true of Ares.

He could be just as twisted as my father.

I don't know what to believe anymore.

I don't know how to feel secure when it's clear that I suck at choosing who to trust.

Sabrina drops down in the empty chair next to mine, wearing her most comfortable pullover, with her hair piled up in a messy bun atop her head. She hasn't brought a tray with her, since she mostly only drinks tea or coffee in the morning.

"Not sitting with Ilsa today?" I ask her.

Sabrina and Ilsa have been spending practically every second together since the dance. I've barely seen her outside of class.

"We split up," Sabrina says, taking a strip of bacon off my plate and biting into it.

"I'm sorry," I say.

"Ah, it's fine. She's too jealous," Sabrina shrugs. "Plus, she's constantly trying to get me to come to the gym with her. Squatting my bodyweight is not a life goal for me."

"Working out together can be fun," I say, with a quick glance at Ares.

He either didn't hear or he doesn't agree, because he doesn't smile back at me. My stomach sinks a little lower.

"Not for me it's not," Sabrina says. Then, grinning, "Unless you count sex as a workout."

Ares pretends not to hear this, either.

He doesn't speak one word to me all through breakfast. So I'm surprised when he catches up with me on the commons, intercepting me on the way to History.

"Hey," he pants, jogging up to me. "Can you meet me again tonight?"

"Alright," I say, hesitantly. "When?"

"10:00."

That's later than we usually meet. I frown at him.

"Is something wrong?"

"No," he says, not quite meeting my eye. "Why would something be wrong?"

"I don't know. You just seem . . ."

I don't know how he seems. I can't decipher his expression. It's not quite nervousness. Not quite excitement.

"I'll be waiting outside the Solar," he says.

"What are we going to do?"

"It's a surprise."

He smiles now, but it's tense and strained.

Something's wrong.

I hope he'll tell me what's going on if I meet him tonight.

If he doesn't . . . I don't know how much more of this I can take.

29

Rafe Petrov

I don't want to bring Nix with me tonight.

I'm considering just leaving her here.

I'm the one who has to take the boat and meet my mom and Freya in Dubrovnik—if I show up without Nix, there's nothing they can do about it. We can attack the mine and take our chances.

But then, if something happens to my father . . . it will be my fault. Because I didn't bring our insurance.

On the other hand, if something happens to Nix . . . that will be my fault, too.

I'm pulled in two directions, tearing down the center line.

I don't know what the fuck to do.

It doesn't help when my mother calls me in the middle of my International Investment class. I feel the phone vibrating in my pocket, and I make a quick excuse to run to the bathroom and sequester myself in the furthest stall, picking up on the last ring.

"What is it?"

"Dom's not coming tonight," my mother says.

"What do you mean?"

"Danyl Kuznetsov, Foma Kushnir, and six of their men just showed up in St. Petersburg. They haven't come to the monastery yet, but they're clearly snooping around. Zima says they're in the Diamond District right now."

"So . . . are we waiting, then?" I ask.

"No," my mother says, grimly. "We can't wait any longer. Danyl is clearly determined to pull the lid off this thing. Whatever happens today, he's going to run back to Moscow to run his mouth. Kuzmo's at the mine, Miles is waiting at the Four Seasons. The wheels are already in motion. We're seeing it through."

"Will Adrik still be there?"

"Yes. But we're short Dom and four of his men."

"I can bring two," I say.

"Who?" my mother asks, confused.

"Leo Gallo and Hedeon Gray."

"What happened?" she demands.

"A little... conflict with Hedeon. But it's handled," I assure her.

"Is the Chancellor alive?"

"Yes. Annoyed, but alive."

I can feel her disapproval radiating through the phone.

"And you're sure they haven't told anyone... sure they can be trusted?"

"Yes."

"Alright. Bring them."

ALL THROUGHOUT THE DAY, I go back and forth a hundred times on whether or not I can bring myself to kidnap Nix.

Picturing her face when she realizes the truth...

I can't fucking take it.

At the same time, we're finally about to get my dad. We've worked years for this moment. Sacrificed everything we used to love in our lives.

If I show up without Nix... my mother's disappointment and rage will be just as bad.

The hours seem to drag by interminably slow. Then all of a sudden it's dinner time, and I can't eat a single bite. I'm looking across the table at Nix, at her confused and unhappy expression when I can barely form a sentence to speak to her.

Then dinner is over, and we're racing toward 10:00, with barely enough time for me to make the simple preparations I need to accomplish.

I meet Kade behind the Keep at 9:30. I expect him to come alone, but instead he's accompanied by Dean Yenin.

Without preamble, Kade says, "I told him everything."

"*What?*" I hiss. "You had no right to do that."

"Yes I did," Kade says, his expression stubborn. "This has affected my family almost as much as yours. Dean's my friend. I trust him."

Dean regards me coolly, one blond eyebrow raised.

"I should have known you were a Petrov when you knocked my fuckin' head sideways," he says.

I take a deep breath, trying to remain calm while panic spirals inside me. This thing is already out of control and it's barely even started.

"Look," I say to Dean. "I appreciate how you've helped Kade, and the information you gave us about Danyl Kuznetsov. But this isn't your concern."

"Yes it is," Dean says. "I owe service to Danyl. I've allied myself with your family instead. I'm already involved. I've given you my loyalty—I need yours in return."

My nails dig into my palms.

"You understand the risks in this—"

"Yes," Dean says. "I understand."

I sigh. "Alright. Leo and Hedeon are coming—meet them inside, at the door by the tapestry." I give Kade the Chancellor's keyring. "In fact, wait for me inside the staircase so nobody sees you." I swallow hard. "I've got to go get Nix."

The walk across the dark lawn to the Solar seems to take forever. My stomach is twisted up in so many knots it might as well be macrame. I'm sick with guilt, so fucking sick I could choke on it.

The sight of Nix already waiting for me at the base of the Solar is like a slap to the face.

She looks so hopeful as she turns those clear green eyes on me. She smiles up at me, saying, "So what are we doing?"

My throat is too tight to even swallow.

I say, "I'll show you. Come on."

She walks along beside me, trusting as a lamb.

I'm really fucking hoping she'll come along quietly. I don't want to have to physically subdue her.

I already feel like I'm going to vomit.

"Are you okay?" Nix asks me, her coppery eyebrows drawing together. "You look . . . stressed . . ."

"I'm fine," I mutter.

"What's in the backpack?"

"Just . . . come on," I say.

We're coming up to the Keep. I need to get Nix inside, to the stone staircase that leads down to the Chancellor's boat.

Tipped off by my tension, Nix is starting to become less amenable to this "surprise" excursion.

"What exactly are we doing?" she presses.

"I'll show you, it's right in here," I say, holding open the door of the Keep so she can pass inside.

Nix is still following me, but slower now, as we approach the small, recessed door that leads down below the school.

This is not an area that students visit. Only Luther Hugo has the key to this door. Or, I should say, only Kade has it now.

"Ares," Nix says, standing in place and refusing to go any further. "You're kind of freaking me out."

"Come on," I say. "It's right through here."

"What is?" Nix demands. "Tell me what we're doing, because you look weird."

"I can't," I say.

I don't want to tell her any more lies.

Nix narrows her eyes at me. Something in my face, something in the way I'm standing seems to tip her over the edge from wary to frightened. She tenses up, then takes one swift step, trying to run away from me.

Too late.

I grab her by the arm, yanking her back, wrapping my arm around her throat, clamping my other hand over her mouth.

I didn't want to have to do it this way.

I didn't want to do it at all.

But I have no choice.

Slowly, I start to apply pressure to her neck, holding her still while she rages and struggles against me.

She's clawing at my arm, kicking with her legs, squirming in my grip, trying to scream against my palm.

She's strong.

But I'm so much stronger.

I bear down on her throat, cutting off her air so I can subdue her without injuring her any more than necessary.

I murmur in her ear. "I'm sorry. I don't want to hurt you . . . but you have to come with me."

I start to drag her over to the door.

Only to be intercepted by Sabrina Gallo.

Sabrina steps in front of me, arms folded over her chest, gray eyes fixed on Nix, who's still bucking and kicking—though weaker now—trying to wrench out of my grip.

"I don't think she likes that," Sabrina says, coldly.

"Oh, fuck," I mutter. And then I call out, louder, "Leo!"

The door cracks open. Leo pokes his head out. "Need some help?" And then, his eyes fixing on Sabrina, "Oh, shit."

"Oh shit is right," Sabrina says, eyes narrowing at the sight of her cousin. "What the fuck are you two doing?"

I'm still dragging Nix toward the stairs, not wanting to be interrupted by any more unwanted guests.

Sabrina looks between me and her cousin. She's trying to calculate exactly what the fuck is going on, but she's coming up empty. Uncertain, she darts after us before the door can close in her face.

I enter the dark stone staircase, Nix finally going limp in my arms from the extended headlock. I loosen my grip enough for her to breathe, but not enough for her to squirm free.

Kade, Dean, Hedeon, Leo, and Anna all wait in the gloom. A pile of scuba suits and a dozen tanks lean up against the wall—Leo faithfully bringing everything I asked. And something I wasn't expecting.

"What's Anna doing here?" I demand.

He shrugs guiltily. "I tell her everything."

"You should have told me yourself," Anna says to me, with a stern look. "I thought we were friends."

"We are friends," I say. "Or at least, I hope we still are."

"Why'd you bring Sabrina?" Kade asks me.

"No one brought me," Sabrina says, eyes darting from person to person as she tries to make sense of the madness. "I saw Anna leaving our dorm dressed like a fucking cat burglar, and I was curious. I thought you guys were doing something fun without me."

"We are," Leo says, bluntly. "So go back to your dorm."

"I'm not going anywhere! And I'm especially not leaving Nix," Sabrina says, with a furious look at her half-choked roommate.

"Sabrina's too young to come with us," Leo says to me. "Plus her dad will murder us."

"I don't fucking want her," I say.

The minutes are slipping away. We're on a tight schedule—I don't have time to deal with Sabrina Gallo, or any other interruptions.

With no clear understanding, but an intense desire not to be left out of anything exciting, Sabrina declares, "I AM coming with you, and if you try to stop me, I'll wake the whole goddamned school up."

I round on her, still supporting the limp and dazed weight of Nix.

"I don't have time for this!" I shout. "I've got to go right now. So come or don't, but get the hell out of the way."

Sabrina looks startled, then intrigued.

"You're not taking Nix anywhere without me," she says.

"Hurry up then," I say.

With that, I throw Nix over my right shoulder and start jogging down the stairs.

Leo, Anna, Dean, Hedeon, and Kade scoop up the suits and the heavy metal canisters. Sabrina grabs several canisters of her own and trails after me.

The stone steps spiral down, down deep under the school. Sometimes the tunnel flattens out, sometimes it descends steeply. Sometimes we can hear water running behind the walls.

Our footsteps echo all around us. Once or twice someone stumbles behind me, the passageway gloomy and lit only by the flashlight Kade carries.

I'm careful where I put my feet. I don't want to drop Nix.

At last we come to the berth where the Chancellor hides his private cruiser. Long, gleaming, and shaped like a bullet, it's painted black so he can come and go from the school at night without anyone noticing.

I've stolen it once before.

Tonight I won't be bringing it back.

I carry Nix on board, binding her hands and feet and cuffing her to the railing for good measure. She's starting to rouse as I do it, and she stares around at Anna, Leo, Hedeon, and Sabrina with an expression of absolute betrayal.

When she turns her gaze on me, there's far more than hurt in her expression. Her eyes burn with pure fury.

30

Nix

I sit on the deck of the boat, bound hand and foot, while Ares steers us out of the limestone cave, out onto open water.

It's cold and windy, the waves rough and black, tossing the speedboat like a cork. I can see the strain on Ares' arms as he steers us through the wild currents and unexpected rocks, away from Visine Dvorca, out into open ocean.

No one is speaking because we all understand that distracting Ares at this moment might lead to us being smashed to bits in the frigid January sea.

Though I'm silent, my mind is working a thousand miles a minute.

I'm looking from face to face of each of these people I considered my friends, everyone I trusted at this school. Understanding now that they were lying to me all the while. Conspiring against me.

Kade, Dean, and Hedeon are huddled in conversation inside the protected shelter of the bulkhead. Leo and Anna are up at the wheel with Ares, helping him watch for obstacles in the water.

Sabrina sits on the deck a few feet away, watching me.

Once Ares has us pointed toward what I assume is Dubrovnik, he lets Leo take the wheel.

He comes to speak to me, tall and upright, the wind whipping his dark hair around his face. He hasn't shaved in a day or two. Stubble shadows the hollows of his cheeks and jaw, and the cleft in his chin. His shirt, damp with salt spray, clings to his chest.

"Don't be scared," he says.

"I'm not scared," I hiss at him. "I'm fucking furious."

I yank hard on the cuffs binding my wrists together, that clamp me to the railing. The chains rattle, the metal biting into my flesh. The railing makes a sharp, splintering sound as it jerks against the wood.

Ares' jaw tightens, but he makes no move to release me.

"I'm sorry it has to be this way," he says.

"That's no fucking apology," I reply.

"I had no choice."

"Oh shut the fuck up, you had a thousand choices."

Now he frowns, his dark brows coming down low across his eyes.

"Maybe I did," he says. "But I can't see this ending any different."

All I can think is how fucking stupid I was.

All the things I must have missed.

I knew from the moment I met Ares that he hated me. I could feel it radiating out of him.

I've always had good instincts. But I ignored them. I pushed aside the things that seemed strange, that didn't make sense. And why? Because he was handsome? Because he paid attention to me? Because I was lonely, and I needed a friend that badly?

Because he made me feel things I never imagined feeling . . .

Things that keep coming back to me now in flashes, bright and beautiful and intensely sensual, protesting that they were real, that they meant something, while the chains around my wrist declare the opposite.

"Who are you?" I ask him, furiously blinking back the burning tears that want to flood my eyes. "You're not Ares Cirillo."

"No," he says. "I'm not. My name is Rafe Petrov."

The pieces fall into place.

Kade Petrov. Rafe Petrov. And . . .

Miss Robin. That beautiful face, those brilliant eyes, that low, husky voice like a thrill across the skin . . . so similar to Ares. To Rafe, I should say . . .

"She's your mother," I murmur.

"Yes," Rafe nods. "She's Sloane Petrov."

"You lied to me all along. From the day we met."

"Yes," he says. And now I see a flicker of guilt in his eyes, but I don't fucking care. I don't care if he feels bad about it.

"So what is it, then?" I say. "Revenge? My father killed someone you love, and now you're going to kill me?"

"No!" Rafe cries. "No one's killing you. No one's going to hurt you, Nix."

"Liar," I say, bitterly.

"Look," Rafe says, gripping a handful of his own hair before roughly pushing it back. "Marko has my father. He's been holding him prisoner, extorting us for money. We're finally getting my dad back. I had to bring you as insurance. But I promise you Nix, no one is going to hurt you. I won't let that happen."

"You're not going to hurt me. You're just going to kill my father in front of me. Is that right?" I ask him.

Now Rafe's face darkens with that shadow that I've seen before. When I've caught glimpses of who he really is.

"He has to pay for what he's done," Rafe says.

"I won't help you," I say, through gritted teeth. "I'll fight you. I'll stop you if I can."

"That's what I thought you'd say," Rafe replies.

That only makes me angrier. He thinks he knows me, while he lying to me the entire time. Well, I might surprise him still.

My mood is as black as this sunless ocean. Every person I've ever cared about has lied to me, used me, and made a fool of me.

First my father, then my friends, and finally Ares. I mean Rafe. Fuck, I can't even wrap my brain around this.

He's the deepest cut of all.

I really thought he loved me.

I've never felt so connected to someone. I thought we were bound together by a thousand links, every shining moment that we spent together another clasp between us. Now it all seems tainted and tarnished, false as nickel and fragile as paper, tearing apart in my hands.

I see Sabrina arguing with Leo up in the bow of the boat. The cousins are snarling at each other, their words lost to the wind. Anna tries to interject and Sabrina snaps at her too, though usually the two girls are on excellent terms with each other.

Finally Sabrina stalks away from them, crossing the deck and dropping down next to me, no space between us.

"They won't let me untie you," she says, irritably.

I ignore her. The handcuffs aren't the issue.

"What are you mad at me for?" Sabrina says. "I found out about all this the same time you did."

I'm not disposed to believe anybody's story right now—certainly not anybody in the process of kidnapping me.

Still, Sabrina *did* try to stop Rafe hauling me off down the stairs. She followed us onto this boat because she was worried about me—and because she loves to be in the thick of drama.

"Are you going to help them?" I demand.

"Probably," Sabrina admits.

"Well fuck off, then!" I snap.

Sabrina sits quietly for a minute, not offended, but obviously considering what to say to me next.

At last she says, "It's impossible to be neutral in our world. You have to pick a side. Are you sure which side you want to be on?"

"I'm not going to turn against my own father," I hiss.

"And Rafe won't turn against his," Sabrina says. "So I guess you'll both immolate yourselves for your dads."

I look at Rafe standing at the wheel again—a stranger in name, but achingly familiar in the shape of his broad shoulders, his lean frame, and his shock of wind-tossed hair.

My chest is burning, my eyes are burning.

I've never had to struggle so hard not to cry.

Is he tearing apart inside, like me?

Does he feel like he's dying, minute by minute?

Or was this easy for him all along?

"Just leave me alone," I mutter to Sabrina.

"Alright," she says. "But I'm not actually leaving you. I'm here with you, as much as them."

Right, I think. *Until it's time to kill my dad.*

WE PULL into the port of Dubrovnik.

Rafe unlocks the handcuff tying me to the rail, and the ones between my feet, but leaves my hands bound.

"Will you come along quietly?" he asks me. "I don't want to have to gag you."

"You've gagged me plenty of times before," I say.

The muscle at the corner of his jaw twitches.

"I'm sorry," he says. "I shouldn't have been intimate with you."

"Is that what we were?" I say. "Intimate? Or was it just me who was intimate, and honest, and real, while you were a fucking lying snake."

Now Rafe's anger flares to match mine. He seizes me by the front of my shirt, bringing our faces close together.

"I've told you things I never told anyone in my life," he growls. "I felt things with you I've never felt. I fell into you like a well and I'm still fucking falling. I never lied when I said I love you."

"Just about everything else!" I cry.

"I don't care about anything else!" he shouts back at me.

Someone clears their throat on the dock. I see three people standing watching: a tall young man with a shock of wild black hair and a ferocious expression, a slim, dreamy-looking girl with eyes dark as bruises in her pale face, and Miss Robin—or, Sloane Petrov, I suppose I should call her.

It's plain as day that this woman is no librarian. I'm not sure how I ever believed she was. She's dressed in black, her hair no longer red, now a deep midnight shade that mirrors her companions. The glasses are gone. She stands taller, straighter, radiating that dangerous energy I intimated the first time we met. Now her power is unleashed, like a shade taken off a lamp.

"Let's go," Sloane says.

Rafe takes my arm. I try to shake him off, but he pulls me along with that unnerving strength he tried so hard to conceal.

I see Kade grin at the black-haired young man, passing him a couple of scuba tanks.

"Are you getting shorter?" the man says, grinning back at him.

I'm guessing this is the famous Adrik Petrov—famous at Kingmakers, at least.

"You fucking wish," Kade says, sizing up their relative heights in a glance. "You're lucky if you've got a solid inch on me still."

"I've still got several inches on you where it counts," Adrik says, winking not at Kade, but in the direction of Sabrina Gallo.

Sabrina rolls her eyes, picking up the last two scuba tanks.

Adrik holds out his hand to take them from her.

Ignoring him, Sabrina leaps lightly down to the dock.

Adrik narrows his eyes, following close after her.

He doesn't know Sabrina likes the hunt herself. Showing obvious interest is the quickest way to bore her.

I'd be amused to see how this will play out, if I didn't have more pressing things on my mind. Like where the fuck we're all going, and what these people plan to do when they get there.

We all load into two SUVs. I'm in the first car with Sloane, Rafe, Hedeon, and the dark-haired girl.

The girl slides into the backseat next to me, with Rafe on my other side.

"I'm Freya," she says, quietly. "Rafe's sister."

This is not how I wanted to meet Ares' family.

I blush, remembering the stupid fantasies I had of meeting the Cirillos on some beautiful Greek island. Being welcomed into their home.

I was such a fucking fool.

"Rafe wrote to me about you," Freya says.

Her large, dark eyes are similar in color to Sloane's—a deep amber color with rings of forest green. Their character is entirely different, however: there's nothing sharp in Freya's gaze. Rather, she's looking at me with a level of sympathy that pains me.

"I didn't know you existed," I say, trying to hide my hurt, and failing miserably.

We're speeding through the dark streets of Dubrovnik. Time seems to collapse and extend like a spring. Each moment is painful and jarring to me, and yet it all streams by too fast, because I don't want to arrive wherever we're going. Too soon we pull up to a private airfield outside the city. I can see a jet waiting on the tarmac—one similar in size to my father's.

"Are you going to tell me where we're going?" I ask Rafe.

"Almaty," he says.

That means nothing to me.

"In Kazakhstan," he clarifies, while explaining nothing at all.

"What's in Kazakhstan?" I say, blankly.

"My father," Rafe replies. "And by the way, *your* father is traveling in the opposite direction, from there to here. So whatever reckoning is coming to him, he should be safe at least for tonight."

That shouldn't comfort me—the Petrovs obviously intend to kill my dad as soon as they get the chance.

But I am relieved to hear that we won't be seeing him now.

A hundred things could happen between tonight and tomorrow.

31

Rafe

We fly to Almaty, where we meet eight of my father's men, including Timo Sidorov, his *Avtoritet* since Efrem died.

Timo embraces my mother, clasping her on both shoulders.

"It's good to have you back, *gertsoginya*," Timo says.

"By morning, we'll all be back where we belong," my mother says.

"God willing," Timo agrees.

"God doesn't get the credit for this one," Adrik says, disembarking from the plane. "Not after we did all the fucking work."

"Careful," Timo says, with a paranoid glance skyward. "You might need his help still."

My phone pings in my pocket. I check the screen.

"Marko just landed in Dubrovnik," I say. "Miles has eyes on him."

"Good," my mother nods. And then to Timo, "Let me see what you brought."

Timo throw open the trunk of his military Jeep, displaying an impressive array of firearms.

"You brought the C4?" my mother asks.

"Of course," Timo nods.

"Good. Let's get going, then."

We already briefed Leo, Anna, Hedeon, Dean, and Sabrina on the plane. Our plan is simple: we're going to attack the mine at two points. Half of us will drive in through the tunnels, while the other half will attempt to traverse the underground waterways used to remove waste from the mines.

The waterways are complicated and labyrinthine. They'd be impossible to navigate in the dark, with only one tank of air. Except that we have a map. As long as we don't take any wrong turns, and as long as none of the tubes are too narrow for a body to pass through, we should be able to swim all the way up to the heart of the mine.

This is the most secretive way inside.

Those going in through the tunnels will take a more direct route, one we know for certain can be traversed. But they'll be vulnerable to attack by Marko's men.

"I want you to swim in," my mother says to Freya and me. "Take your friends. Adrik, too. I'll go in through the tunnels with the others."

"What about Nix?" Sabrina asks.

"She's going with you," my mother says.

"You plan to drag me along underwater?" Nix says, holding up her handcuffed wrists.

"You'll swim, or you'll run out of air in that underwater maze and drown in the dark," my mother says, calmly. "And if you don't cooperate, I need you to remember that your father has kept my husband prisoner for three and a half years. You're only breathing right now because I think you might be of use to me. The moment you become a hindrance instead of a help, I'll snap my fingers like this," she gives one crisp click of her finger and thumb, "and that will be the sound of a bullet entering the back of your skull. Do we understand each other?"

"I understand," Nix says.

My stomach is one solid knot.

I know better than anyone that my mother means exactly what she says.

But if she tries to hurt Nix . . . I can't let her do it.

I'm almost relieved we're splitting up, even though I know Adrik and Freya are just as loyal to my mother—and just as dangerous to Nix—as any of my father's soldiers.

"Perhaps you should swim as well," Timo says to my mother, quietly.

He's worried she might be injured or killed in a direct assault. We'd better not rescue my father at all, if the first piece of news we give him is that his wife is dead.

My mom isn't having it.

"I'm the best shot of any of you," she says, sternly. "I'm going in through the tunnels. Now remember—watch out for Kuzmo. We need him alive. Or we need his eyes."

One of the pieces of information my father passed to us was that the locks are operated by retinal scan. And as far as he knows, only Kuzmo and Marko himself can open his door.

Miles lured Marko away. Kuzmo is still inside that compound.

We need to find him and shove his face up against that door.

"Alright," my mother says. "We'll take this Jeep and you—"

She's interrupted by my phone buzzing loudly in my pocket. I pull it out, seeing the last name I want to see on the screen: Miles Griffin.

I answer the call.

"What is it?"

"He left," Miles says.

"What do you mean he left?"

"I mean, he was walking up to the hotel, we were ten feet away from each other, and he turned around and left. Didn't say a word to me."

"Where the fuck is he going?" I cry.

"I have no idea."

Predators have a sense for traps.

My mother told me that.

I wheel around to face her, seeing that she already heard both sides of the call.

"What do we do?" I ask her.

"We go in. Right now."

"What if Marko called them?"

"I don't care if he has," my mother says, fiercely. "It's now or never. We're getting Ivan back."

We pile into our respective Jeeps, my mother heading for the tunnels, our car driving to the point in the Ile river where we can access the outflow pipe leading up into the mine.

As we jostle around in the back of the Jeep, Nix catches my eye. Her face is pale and rigid. We're both thinking the same thing, without either of us speaking aloud:

Marko Moroz could be on his way here right now.

"Am I going to grow another set of arms swimming in this shit?" Adrik says, eyeing the outflow pipe distastefully.

"The mine is supposed to be decommissioned," Freya says, fitting her mask onto her face.

"It isn't, though," Adrik says. "Even if they're not actively digging, they're still extracting yellowcake from the ore. And selling it to god knows who."

"Well," Freya shrugs, "The Geiger counter says it's no worse than an x-ray. And you're wearing a wetsuit."

We're all wearing wetsuits. Even Nix, who didn't hesitate in donning hers—not with Adrik scowling at her.

He only stopped glaring at Nix when distracted by Sabrina Gallo zipping her very tight wetsuit over her hourglass figure. I've never seen Adrik stunned to silence over a girl. Usually he gives them about the same amount attention as he pays to speed limits and unpaid parking tickets—a mere passing glance.

Sabrina is too intrigued by the mission at hand to pay attention to Adrik in return. She scans the map of the waterways, following the route I marked out in red.

"Don't worry," Adrik says. "We've got a list of the turns."

"I don't need a list," Sabrina says. "Left, left, center, right, left, right, right, center, left, center, right, right, left, center."

She rattles off the directions flawlessly, without glancing down.

Adrik stares at her, then snatches the map away to check if she's correct.

"You're still not the smartest cousin," Leo tells her.

Anna looks pale and strained, staring down at the dark water.

I know why she's nervous—Leo almost drowned in the sea caves below Kingmakers our first year at school. Actually, it was Dean who almost drowned him. As the cousins have reconciled since then, I'm guessing we won't have to worry about overt sabotage. Only all the other things that might kill us down there.

"Do you remember how to use the regulator?" I ask Nix.

"Yes," she says, snatching it out of my hand. "Probably better than you do."

She aced Environmental Adaptation, with a higher score on her SCUBA exam than I managed to scrape in all four years.

"Fair enough," I say, fitting my own mask in place.

We drop down into the water: first Adrik, then Kade, followed by Sabrina, Dean, Leo, Anna, and Hedeon, then Nix with me right behind her, and Freya bringing up the rear.

Freya is a strong swimmer. Still, I keep glancing back over my shoulder to make sure she's right behind me.

The water's freezing, even through the wetsuits. My headlamp only illuminates a small radius in front of me.

Right from the start, the tubes are narrow and congested. Claustrophobia kicks in hard as I realize it's impossible to turn around. We can only keep moving forward, or painstakingly back up, bit by bit. And if someone were to become wedged behind me, like a cork in a bottle, there would be no going back at all. I'm glad only Freya is behind me, and not someone bigger like Leo or Adrik.

We have to shove ourselves through some of the narrowest junctions, the rough stone chutes catching and yanking at our tanks, as well as the waterproof bags in which we've stowed our guns and ammunition.

I'm mentally counting the turns.

Around the third junction, our train stops as Adrik hesitates at the head. I wait, stuck between Nix and Freya, unable to see what's happening. When I come to the turning point myself, I realize the problem: instead of three branches to choose from, there's four. The map we took from the archives is inaccurate.

Adrik presses ahead anyway, choosing the second branch. But I know it's only a guess—we could be about to lose ourselves in the maze with only one tank of air each.

By the time we come to the eighth junction, which again doesn't match the map, my heart is starting to race. We're more than halfway through our air. We need to surface soon, one way or another.

Adrik is trying to swim faster, though that's impossible with the tightness of the tubes. For all our sweating and struggling, we crawl through the waterways at a snail's pace.

In the pitch black, there's no way to know if we're ascending or descending, doubling back or moving in a steady direction.

We've taken more than the fourteen turns we expected. As far as I can tell, Adrik has taken us in approximately the right direction each time—assuming these waterways roughly correspond to those on the map. But we should have reached the center of the mine by now.

At last, with less than a quarter tank left, the tunnel widens out ahead. We've come to an underwater chamber with a flat grate overhead. Adrik takes out his saw and begins to work on the hinges of the grate.

It's impossible for us to tell how much noise we're making—I'm hoping the water is muffling the worst of it. We don't know what's directly overhead.

Adrik saws away at the rusted hinges.

Our air dips lower and lower.

I can see that Leo is already in the red, though he's keeping quiet about it. Anna notices too, passing him her regulator so he can take a full breath.

I check Nix's gage. Calm and steady, she's got plenty of air still in the tank—much more than me. I bet her heartrate is barely over 80. I smile beneath my mask.

Adrik finally cuts through the hinges. Slowly, carefully, he pushes up the grate. His head breaks the surface of the water for the first time in over an hour. He peers around, then motions for us to follow him up.

We haul ourselves out of the water into an empty stone chamber, black as the heart of a whale.

My body feels heavy and clumsy, exhausted from the swim in tight quarters. Still, it's incredibly luxurious to be able to stretch and move in any direction. We strip off our suits and fins, trying to remain as silent as possible. Our every movement echoes in the stone chamber.

I can't hear a thing from outside this room—not the sound of soldiers or gunfire or even the crackle of a radio.

My mother had a longer drive to the entry point of the tunnels, but I'm guessing she's well on her way inside. She's got heavy firepower with her. I only hope it's enough to match whatever defenses Marko's men have in place.

"Do you think the others made it in?" Kade asks, shaking water out of his hair.

Right at that moment, an echoing boom shakes the chamber. Bits of rock and dust rain down on our heads.

"Yeah," Adrik says. "I'm gonna guess that's Sloane."

Leo unzips his bag, pulling out his rifle.

"Let's get going," he says. "Before we miss all the fun."

Sabrina retrieves her own rifle.

"You know how to shoot that?" Adrik says.

Sabrina swiftly slaps a magazine into the stock, then pulls back the slide to chamber a round.

"Yeah," she says. "I'm good."

Nix is the only one of us without a gun.

Hopefully, she won't need one—she should be the least likely of any of us to get shot. Assuming Marko's men recognize her. And assuming they know how to aim.

Adrik seizes Nix by the arm, pulling her to the front of the pack. He points his rifle right at her spine.

"You lead the way," he says. "And if you get any brilliant ideas about yelling out or trying to run off . . . I'll cut the cord to your legs."

I shove my way between Adrik and Nix, standing between her and the gun.

"Don't touch her, and don't fucking threaten her," I snarl.

Adrik stares at me like I've lost my mind.

"She's not your girlfriend," he scoffs. "She'd shoot you in the back right now if she was the one holding the rifle."

I look at Nix. Her stare is as furious as I've ever seen it. But I don't believe she'd shoot me.

"I don't give a shit," I say. "No one touches Nix but me."

Adrik shakes his head in disgust. "You've been Ares too long," he says.

That stings.

Do I really seem so different to my cousins, my sister, my own parents?

Do they think I'm not one of them anymore?

"Nix goes in front," I say, "I'll be right behind her."

Now it's me with my gun pointed at her back. I see her stiffen, with hurt or with outrage.

It doesn't matter. She's safer this way.

Because no matter what she does, I'll never pull the trigger.

32

IVAN PETROV

The explosion shakes my cell—a deep, booming thunder that I know could only come from underground.

I'm on my feet in an instant, running to the door.

Borys and Ihor are in a panic out in the hall, shouting to each other.

Marko's men are not well trained. They don't know what to do in a moment like this.

I, on the other hand, know exactly what's happening.

My wife is here.

I don't know where she is, or what she's doing, but I know she's coming for me. And these two idiots in the hall better pray they don't get in her way.

I hear the crackle of Borys's radio and frantic shouting in Ukrainian as several soldiers try to talk over each other.

All I can make out is:

Attackers in the tunnels!

Someone put—

Send Mikhail and Gendray to the—

Then Kuzmo comes running down the hallway with two more men. I peer through the slot, watching. I see his look of relief at Borys and Ihor standing guard, at the closed door and empty hall.

"Don't move from your post!" he orders the soldiers.

"Are they here for him?" Borys says, the nervousness in his voice like a live wire, exposed.

"I don't know," Kuzmo says, stiffly. "They could be looking for Marko."

Marko isn't here. He received a text message right in the middle of our monthly visit, and he left Kuzmo to handle my phone call to Dom. Kuzmo has been lurking around all evening, which means Marko took the plane or chopper or whatever they fuck they used to get here, leaving Kuzmo with no ride home.

That gives me an idea.

If Sloane is coming, I have no intention of waiting for her in here.

This cell is a bottleneck, the worst possible place for a conflict.

"Kuzmo!" I call. "Bring me your phone. I need to speak to Marko."

I hear Kuzmo's boots crunching on the stone floor as he stops pacing, then turns to look in the direction of the cell.

Kuzmo is Marko's most faithful servant. He's a good right-hand man: loyal and precise in following instructions.

But at the end of the day, he's a dog with a master. He responds to authority.

In my most commanding tone, I call out, "He'll want to take this call. It concerns his daughter."

Kuzmo hesitates a moment longer, torn between the imperative to never enter my cell, and the possibility that harm might come to Nix Moroz because he didn't listen to me.

I stay silent.

Then I hear three rapid steps toward my cell, and the grit of stone as Kuzmo leans forward, pressing his eye against the retinal scanner.

The lock clanks open.

"Stand back from the door!" Kuzmo orders. "Don't fuck with me, Ivan."

I stand back, calm and quiet as ever. I sit down on the folding chair, allowing Kuzmo to cuff my hands behind my back.

Kuzmo stands in front of me, his *boyevik* Mykah right next to him with his rifle pointed at my chest.

"Why do you want the phone?" Kuzmo demands. "Do you know who's in the tunnels?"

"I'll only speak to Marko," I say, stubbornly.

Sweat gleams on Kuzmo's shaved scalp, even in the chilly cell. He doesn't know whether to face the attackers in the tunnel, stay close to me, or allow this phone call. I think it's his own desire to hear his boss's voice that compels him as he pulls out his phone.

All the while, slowly and quietly behind my back, I'm dislocating my thumb.

This is a trick I learned at the age of eighteen. It was much easier to do then, before my fingers thickened and my joints stiffened. I haven't attempted the maneuver in twenty years. Yet I find I can accomplish it still, with only a popping sound that I disguise by clearing my throat.

Kuzmo's fingers tremble slightly as he finds Marko's number. When your men fear you too much, they make stupid choices.

Gripping the steel manacle with the fingers of my left hand, I pull my right hand free, keeping it hidden behind my back.

"Don't move," Mykah says, his barrel pointed at my face now. "Don't even breathe."

Something funny about all these soldiers and all their guns: I don't think they're actually supposed to kill me. Shoot me, maybe. Stop me from escaping, most definitely. But I don't think Marko wants me to die at any hand but his own.

Kuzmo holds the phone up to my ear.

Foolishly, he's stepped partway between me and his *boyevik*.

I wait as it rings twice. Then, right as I hear the rough, familiar voice of Marko Moroz saying, "What is it?" I bite down hard on Kuzmo's hand.

Shimmy Shimmy — *El Michels Affair*
Spotify → geni.us/spy-spotify
Apple Music → geni.us/spy-apple

I seize his thumb between my teeth, crunching down through muscle, tendon, bone. Kuzmo shrieks and tries to rip his hand away, which only tears the flesh more. The phone goes flying. I take my own newly freed hand and grab him by the front of his shirt, wrenching him sideways so that when Mykah tries to shoot me in the leg, the bullet hits Kuzmo in the back of the thigh instead.

I spit out a chunk of Kuzmo's flesh, grabbing him in both hands now and flinging him at his soldier. They crash against the cell wall in a pile.

I'm already running, wrenching the rifle out of the Mykah's hand and jamming the barrel in the crack of the cell door, half a second before the soldiers on the other side can pull it shut.

I yank the gun like a lever, pulling the trigger the whole time, sending a spray of bullets out like a fan. I hear the grunts and thuds as at least two soldiers fall to the ground. Then I ram the door with my shoulder, shoving it outward and hitting the third soldier with the full weight of the metal door. He stumbles backward, hands up in a useless protective gesture. I shoot him in the chest, feeling a small pang of regret as I realize it's Borys, who used to be my favorite of the guards.

Ihor, my least-favorite, slashes at my legs from behind with an old-fashioned trench knife, taking a chunk out of my calf. He's bleeding in at least three places from the spray of bullets I put in him, but he still lunges at me from the ground, dragging his useless legs, swinging his knife wildly. I kick him in the face, which probably hurts me more than him, seeing as I'm barefoot. I finish him with two shots to the chest, which definitely hurts him more.

Kuzmo and Mykah are scrambling to get out of the cell. I kick the door shut right in their faces, locking them inside. The irony of this is not lost on me.

"I'm sorry Kuzmo," I say. "I'd open the door for you, but I'm afraid you'd have to pluck out your eye and pass it to me through the slot."

I can hear his snarl of rage and incoherent cursing in Ukrainian. He hammers at the door with his fists, something I often longed to do myself, but always refrained because I wouldn't give Marko the pleasure of watching me lose my fucking mind.

But now I'm ready to lose it.

I'm ready to wreak the havoc these cretins deserve.

They kept me chained in that cell for three and a half years. One thousand, two hundred, and sixty-eight days away from my family, away from my home.

I'm going to slaughter every one of them standing between me and my wife.

I strip the soldiers' bodies of guns, knives, and ammunition, as well as a pair of boots that are only a little too small for my feet.

Then I begin to run down the tunnel of the prison that I've never actually seen.

33

Nix

"Come on," Adrik says, looking over the map once more. "If we came up here, in the center . . . I think we should go this way."

"How do you know?" Dean says. "We don't know where they're holding Ivan."

"I'm guessing," Adrik snaps. "Do you have a better idea?"

Hedeon isn't listening to the argument. He's walking the opposite way, out of the chamber, following something he seems to hear rather than see.

"Stay together," Leo calls, but Hedeon ignores him, pulled onward by whatever's drawing his curiosity.

"For fuck's sake," Rafe mutters. He follows after Hedeon, which means I'm following too, since Rafe has a firm grasp on my arm.

Hedeon is a long way down the dark corridor already. We jog to catch up to him, Rafe hissing, "Hedeon! What are you doing?"

Hedeon turns to face us, still looking around in the gloom.

"Do you hear that?" he says.

Now that we're standing quietly, out of the echoing chamber, I do hear it . . . distant and steady, a faint churning sound. Running water.

"I think there's another river," Hedeon says.

"That's not on the map," Rafe says.

"Well, the map's shit," Hedeon replies, with a shrug.

Rafe can't argue with that.

We keep following the sound of water, taking two wrong turns before we double back and find the source: an underground dock with a boat tied up against the pull of the river.

A dock guarded by three armed soldiers.

They fire at us, the first bullet hitting the wall a foot from my ear, sending several shards of stone flying across my face, cutting my cheek.

Rafe yanks me down.

Adrik comes running up the tunnel, Leo and Anna close behind him.

"What the fuck are you doing?" he shouts, already taking position to return fire.

"We might have found another way out of here," Hedeon says.

"We don't need a way out! We just fucking got in!" Adrik snarls.

Leo takes the opposite side of the tunnel, firing back in tandem with Adrik. Anna watches their bursts of fire and the returning shots from the soldiers, her eyes darting back and forth as she waits for a split-second pause. Then she darts out of the tunnel, chucking a flash grenade over by the dock.

Even at this distance, and even with our eyes closed and our ears covered, the explosion is deafening. Anna stumbles back into the tunnel, reeling from the oscillation in her inner ear. I see her as a dark silhouette against the blinding afterimage still etched on my eyeballs.

Adrik recovers first, leaping up and running out to the dock, shooting the first and second soldier before they can even take their hands off their ears.

Leo gets the third, dropping him before he can swing his rifle around at Adrik.

Rafe stays close to me the whole time, guarding me with his body and his gun.

I feel horribly exposed, unarmed and obviously not safe from these soldiers who might know me if we were standing face-to-face, but seem perfectly happy to shoot my fucking head off from a distance.

I want Rafe right next to me. I want his warmth and his bulk in front of me.

I hate to admit it, but I'm scared.

I've gone shooting plenty of times, but I've never been surrounded by gunfire, echoing off the stone walls of a dark and claustrophobic space. I've never had a bullet whiz an inch past my ear.

I've never been so deep under the earth, away from any light or breeze or living thing.

Rafe looks down, seeing my hand clutching his forearm.

"I'll stay right by you all the time," he promises.

I let go of him, angry at myself for showing weakness. Angry for needing him.

"Come on," Adrik says, impatiently. "Back this way."

We rejoin Dean, Sabrina, Freya, and Kade, who have already scouted the opposite direction.

"This way!" Kade says, excitedly. "I think we found the cells!"

Sure enough, Kade leads us back to a bank of four prison cells with no windows, only thick metal doors bisected by a tiny slot to pass food or drink.

The electronic locks are mounted by what looks like retinal scanners. There's no way to know which cell belongs to Ivan, and no way to open them without the right set of eyeballs.

I'm not sure that's an issue anymore: the hallway is littered with the bodies of three soldiers—my father's men. I recognize Jan and Borys. Borys lays on his back, eyes open, mouth agape, hands still open in front of his chest as if trying to push someone away.

Now I can't stop the tears that run down my face without warning. Borys was like an uncle to me. He used to time how long I could hold my breath in our indoor pool at the compound, and he showed me how to make pizza dough from scratch, with yeast and flour and honey.

At the same time, I see the bleakness of the cells, and the horrible darkness of these underground chambers. I know that if I were captive here, I would shoot my way through anyone to escape.

I'm torn, continually torn, because I can't actually be pulled in two directions at once.

I see Rafe's obvious excitement, the heartbreaking hope on his face as we stand right where his father must have been.

And I see my friend dead on the floor.

"I think there's someone in here . . ." Kade says, bending to peer through the slot in the door.

"NO!" Freya shouts, grabbing his shoulder and yanking him back.

At that moment, someone fires through the door. Kade tumbles backward, hand clasped to the side of his head, blood pouring through his fingers.

Roaring in fury, Adrik shoves the barrel of his rifle through the slot and fires into the cell in all directions. Then, not bothering to check if he hit the occupant, he drops to his knees next to his brother and hauls him up.

Kade is pale and reeling, but still conscious.

Adrik yanks his hand away from his head, grimacing as he surveys the damage.

"It's just your ear, you dumb shit," he says. His words don't match the deep relief on his face as he sees that Kade is only missing the upper portion of his right ear. He's bleeding everywhere, but it's a hell of a lot better than a bullet to the head.

"I take it that means Ivan got out on his own," Dean says, surveying the carnage in the hallway.

"Yes, and I can guess where he's going," Rafe says.

We can hear distant gunfire now, and another echoing explosion.

Sloane is still fighting her way up the tunnels, drawing most of Marko's men in her direction.

"Can you walk?" Leo says to Kade.

"I think so," Kade says, pale and sweaty-faced and embarrassed, blood pouring down the right side of his neck.

Leo puts Kade's arm around his shoulders, hoisting him up.

"I've got him," he says to Adrik.

We hurry down the hallway again, following the direction of the gunfire.

Adrik scouts ahead, Sabrina close behind him like a slim, dark shadow. She holds her rifle ready. I'm a little disturbed to see how naturally she takes to all this. I've never seen her eyes brighter or her expression more focused. She's thrumming with excitement.

I, on the other hand, feel like I'll vomit if I so much as open my mouth.

The violence keeps spiraling and spiraling. There's no happy ending here—whoever lives and whoever dies, I lose friends on either side.

We hurry toward the irregular bursts of gunfire, taking a wrong turn that leads us into a cavernous space full of old, rusted mining machinery, vast and ancient-looking as dinosaur bones.

We turn back, into a cramped corridor where we collide with a dozen of my father's men.

Seven Nation Army — *The White Stripes*
Spotify → geni.us/spy-spotify
Apple Music → geni.us/spy-apple

Our groups run into each other in an instant maelstrom, two storm fronts colliding.

The chaos that ensues is difficult for me to follow. Under the flickering halogen lights, I see Rafe fire at one of my father's soldiers called Andriy, then grapple with Kristyan. I turn to find a gun pointed right between my eyes. All I can do is stare into the face of a soldier I've never met, who curls his finger around the trigger, until Kristyan shouts, "No, that's Nix!", and wrenches the gun away, before being shot in the side himself by Freya Petrov.

Hedeon's rifle jams and he drops, it, pulling a Glock from his belt instead. He shoots a soldier in the chest, then takes a bullet in the thigh, dropping to one knee.

Sabrina is seized from behind, only to have Adrik Petrov drive a knife into the soldier's chest. He rips her out of the dying man's arms. Sabrina wrenches the knife from soldier's body as he falls, driving it into the back of the man attempting to throttle Anna Wilk.

The metallic stench of blood fills the tunnel. I don't know who's winning or losing.

Then I hear a snarl unlike anything I've heard before. I see a man, already covered in blood from head to foot, his bared teeth a slash of white in the grisly mask of his face. His long hair is filthy, his tattooed chest bare except for the belts of ammunition slung across it. He holds a knife in each hand, the wicked blades already wet on their tips like venomous fangs. He charges into the fray, cutting and slashing and stabbing like he has six arms instead of only two.

The soldiers fall before him like grass beneath the scythe.

He rampages through them, his bull-like body whittled down to pure muscle and sinew, not an ounce of fat on his frame. His dark hair is matted, longer than his shoulders, his face bearded, eyes wild with bloodlust.

In the space of a breath, everyone in military uniform is dead.

We stare at this monster, at his snarling teeth and dripping knives.

Then Rafe says, "Dad!", and he runs to him.

Ivan Petrov drops the knives, sweeping his son and daughter into his arms.

His bloodstained hands sink into their hair. He pulls their faces against his.

I can't look at the expression on his face.

I have to turn and stare at the stone wall, filled with a shame I can't express.

The reunion only lasts a moment. Ivan embraces Adrik and Kade as well, saying, "Is Sloane in the tunnels?"

"Yes," Freya says.

"Then we'll save the introductions for another time," Ivan says, his gaze sweeping over Leo, Anna, Hedeon, and me, before he urges us all on.

I don't know if I imagined a flicker of recognition when those dark eyes passed over me. I'm supremely relieved that there's no need for us to speak at the moment. Ivan Petrov is frankly terrifying, and I'm staying as far back in the group as possible.

Rafe rejoins me. I can see the blazing relief in his face, a lightening of his step that makes me realize what a burden he was carrying all this time. His fingers tremble slightly as he clutches his rifle.

My chest is burning with the most complicated set of emotions I've ever known: immense guilt, mixed with happiness and sorrow.

Our eyes meet. I hope Rafe can see that no matter the circumstances, and without considering what might happen next, I'm glad he has his father back.

We're running toward the steadily increasing sound of gunfire, Kade walking on his own, his ear still bleeding but his rifle in his hands once more. Hedeon can't even stand—he's supported between Dean and Leo, his pant leg darkly soaked.

This mine is massive—endless tunnels and chambers.

My father never showed me this place. He told me that he took me to every warehouse, every nightclub . . . and yet, it's obvious he doesn't only keep Ivan Petrov captive here. If it's an old uranium mine like Adrik said, I can guess exactly what goes on here.

None of the uses for black market uranium are at all palatable to me. Another blow to my image of my dad.

We reach the main guardhouse at last, the entry point where my father's men drive in through the tunnels.

Sloane has made it all the way inside, but she's pinned down at the base of the guardhouse, the tires blown out of her Jeep, all the windows shattered. It appears that only four of her men are still alive, including the one called Timo. He crouches next to her, shooting up at my father's soldiers who surround them on three sides.

Dean sets Hedeon down against the wall, tearing a strip off the bottom of his shirt and tying it tight around Hedeon's thigh.

Watch Me Burn — Michele Morrone
Spotify → geni.us/spy-spotify
Apple Music → geni.us/spy-apple

Our group fans out, attacking my father's men from behind.

The Malina splinter, shot at from two sides. The bulk of them retreat up the tunnel to regroup. I stay right behind Rafe as he fights his way closer to his mother.

I see Olek, one of my father's *brigadiers*, stand up in the guardhouse, pointing his rifle directly at Rafe. I scream, "RAFE! Six o'clock!"

Rafe wheels around, Olek's bullet cutting a groove out of his shoulder as Rafe's shot hits Olek right in the chest. I stare, horrified, as Olek slumps over, his head crashing through the guardhouse window.

Meanwhile Ivan shoots two, three, four Malina, before sprinting across the open ground to his wife, heedless of bullets flying around him, sliding into her behind the body of the Jeep, seizing her and kissing her with a ferocity that would tear apart a more delicate woman.

Sloane kisses him back, blood smearing from his mouth to hers, their hands clutching each other's faces, their bodies melded together like they could never be parted again.

I've never witnessed anything so intimate.

I can't look away.

They gaze into each other's eyes as Ivan growls, "Remember what I told you, my little fox: nothing could keep me from coming back to you."

As one, Ivan and Sloane turn, raising their rifles to their shoulders. Side by side they start to hunt.

It's like watching a pack of wolves wheel upon their prey. Time seems to slow as the Petrovs reign down retribution on the Malina. Ivan, Sloane, Rafe, Freya, Adrik, and Kade—each one tall, dark, and utterly ruthless, moving with inhuman speed and coordination. They slaughter every soldier remaining in the chamber. Even Sabrina looks awed as Adrik fires two perfect shots to the chest and one to the head of the last man standing.

Silence reigns for exactly five seconds.

Then two more Hummers come roaring up the tunnel, loaded with men. My father stands upright inside the open top of the lead Hummer, an M240 mounted to the hood. He catches sight of Ivan Petrov and his face distorts in a snarl of rage. He opens fire, spraying bullets across the chamber.

"BACK!" Ivan shouts.

We sprint back up into the protected cover of the mine, back to the room filled with rusting equipment. Dean is dragging Hedeon along, with Leo's help.

Ivan is scanning the hulking machinery, looking for the best vantage point to hunker down and fight. Sloane stops him.

"Can we get out this way?" she shouts to Rafe.

I see the swift calculation on his face: the assumption that the boat at the underground dock must be able to travel all the way out on the river.

"Yes," he says. "I think we can."

"Good," Sloane replies. She pulls a detonator from her pocket and flips up the cover over the switch.

"Are you sure we should—" Timo says.

Sloane hits the switch.

Instantly, three separate explosions rocket through the tunnels, each one seeming to amplify the next. We're already running again, back down past the cells, as rock thunders down in an avalanche behind us.

I can't help looking back over my shoulder, horrified that my father might have been buried by boulders or blown to bits. I know that's what the Petrovs are hoping.

But someone is still behind us, evidenced by the bursts of gunfire hitting the walls and ceiling overhead.

We're back to the chamber where we came up through the grate in the floor. Then we're running down the tunnel toward the dock...

Until my father roars, "I'VE GOT YOUR NEPHEW!"

We all stare at the filthy, bloodied faces around us. I see Rafe, Sabrina, Dean, Hedeon, Leo, Anna, Adrik, Ivan, Sloane, and her four surviving men.

In the mad dash, Kade Petrov fell behind.

Without hesitation, Sloane seizes me by the arm and shouts back, "AND I'VE GOT YOUR DAUGHTER!"

She begins to drag me back down the tunnel.

I let her do it.

She hauls me back to the stone chamber where I see my father, covered in dust, the side of his face bloodied, holding a Glock to the side of Kade's head. The gun presses against Kade's ruined ear. He looks like he might pass out from the pain.

My father's expression upon seeing me is enraged to the point of madness.

"NIX!" he bellows.

Sloane's grip tightens on my arm, her fingers digging into my flesh. I'm not trying to break away from her. I'm standing perfectly still.

"Send her over here now, or I'll put a bullet in this boy's head," my father snarls.

"I would," Sloane sneers back at him, "but I don't exactly trust you."

I can hear Ivan, Rafe, and the others coming up behind us.

Likewise, a half-dozen of my father's men have made it out of the collapsing tunnels. Some are limping, some are coughing, all are covered in bits of blasted rock, dust, and blood.

Our two groups face each other, each with a hostage.

My father is staring at me like he can't believe what he's seeing. His fingers twitch on the gun, his body tense as he fights the impulse to shoot Kade or fling him aside, to run at me.

"What are you doing here, Nix?" he says, hoarsely.

"What are *you* doing, Dad?" I reply, my voice cracking. "What is this place?"

He shifts his bulk, his right eyelid twitching as it always does when he's stressed or angry.

"You know the mine," he says, gruffly. "I told you about this."

"No," I say, flatly. "No, you didn't."

"Well what does it matter!" he shouts. "I was going to show you. This is all for you someday."

The thought of owning this dark underground place, those prison cells, makes my skin crawl.

"I don't want this," I say.

"What the hell are you talking about!" my father roars.

His whole hand is shaking now, the barrel of the gun jittering against Kade's ear. Kade's skin shines like wax.

"Don't hurt him," I say, nodding toward Kade. "Let him go. He's my friend."

"He's your *friend?*" my father howls, outraged. "Have you lost your mind? These are your worst fucking enemies, Nix! That's Ivan Petrov! It's his fault your mother is dead! His fault she was never avenged!"

"You had your revenge," Ivan says, his voice colder than frost and harder than steel. "We killed Taras together. Then you tracked down his wife and children and you slaughtered them, too. You killed his uncles and his cousins. There's barely a Banderovtsy left alive."

"AND IT STILL WON'T BRING HER BACK!" my father bellows, his face redder than his beard.

My stomach is churning.

We killed Taras together . . .

Then you slaughtered his wife . . . and his children . . .

That wasn't part of the story, when my father told me how he tracked down the man who killed my mother, battled him hand-to-hand, then cut his throat and let him bleed out on the floor.

There was no Ivan Petrov in that tale.

I never heard the Petrov name before I came to Kingmakers.

And there was certainly no mention of murdering children.

Obfuscations, elisions, deceit, and lies...

Every moment that I look at my father's face, he becomes less familiar to me, less the man I thought I knew. I begin to see the monster he is to everyone else...

"You lied to me about Kyrylo Lomachenko, too," I say. "You killed him. I know you did."

My father's breath is coming through his teeth in hissing gasps.

"Who are you to judge how I do business," he seethes.

"Let go of Kade," I say, again. "This is over."

"It will never be over," he replies, his eyes slipping away from my face, fixing on Ivan Petrov instead.

"Do you want your daughter back or not?" Sloane snaps. "Put that fucking gun down."

My father's eyes dart from Ivan to me, and back again.

He snarls, "Bring her to me."

Then, he tosses his Glock to one of his soldiers, and drags Kade to the center of the chamber, standing directly over the grate.

"I'll take her," Rafe says, quietly.

He passes his own rifle to Sloane, so he's unarmed except for the knife at his belt, just like my father.

Sloane opens her mouth to argue, but Rafe cuts across her, repeating sharply, *"I'll do it."*

He takes my arm. His hand is warm and steady.

Rafe walks me toward my father, the opposite of a bride being given away on her wedding day.

When we stand before him, my father at last releases Kade. Kade stumbles back toward his brother. Adrik grips his rifle, obviously struggling with the impulse not to open fire as soon as Kade is out of the way.

I'm supposed to cross to the other side like Kade did.

I'm supposed to join my own family.

But all I can think of is Sabrina's words, echoing in my head:

Are you sure what side you want to be on?

My father or Rafe?

The Petrovs or the Malina?

Rafe looks at me. His eyes are as clear and blue as I've ever seen them—a reminder of sea and sky in this sunless place. He relaxes his grip so my forearm slides through his fingers, until my hand is resting on his palm.

We gaze into each other's eyes. There's no lying when you speak without words.

I turn my hand, linking my fingers through his.

Then I say to my father, "I'm not coming home with you."

He looks at my hand, holding tight to Rafe's.

"What are you doing?" he rasps.

"I'm going back to Kingmakers. I'm staying with Rafe."

My father isn't shaking anymore. He's gone deathly still.

"You choose him over me," he says. "This boy over your own father."

"Yes," I say. "I do."

Rafe's hand tightens in mine.

I know for certain he's not letting go—no matter what happens.

My father's men grip their rifles. The Petrovs do the same. The Malina are outnumbered, fourteen to seven. They don't want to fight. Still, they'll obey my father to the end.

The Petrovs are longing to kill every last one of them, especially my dad. And maybe he deserves to die. But I'm hoping this one time, we can all walk away.

"It's over," I say to my father.

I turn away from him, back toward my friends, back toward the Petrovs, and most of all toward Rafe.

Nothing happens for the space of a heartbeat.

Then my father gives a strangled howl. He rips the knife from his belt, swinging it down.

I turn in slow motion, the arc of my spin intersecting with the trajectory of my father's knife—the blade plunging directly toward my heart.

Until Rafe lunges between us, turning his shoulder into the knife.

The blade sinks into his flesh. It cuts deep, all the way to the hilt.

Rafe doesn't even seem to feel it. He's already pulling his own knife from his belt. He swings it upward, faster than a whip, slashing directly across my father's throat.

My father gasps.

Before he can move, before he can even begin to bleed, Rafe slashes him again and again and again, cutting him across the belly, through the groin, and backward across his neck, cutting him to pieces like a carcass in a butcher shop.

The cuts are strategic, merciless, and utterly devastating.

There's no hesitation in Rafe's face. No regret. I see the man I've caught glimpses of before. I see Rafe Petrov unleashed.

My father collapses, spurting blood from a dozen gashes.

I sink to my knees, sobbing, grabbing for his hand.

I lift that hand, heavy as a bear paw, and try to hold it against my face, to feel his rough palm one last time.

My father looks into my eyes.

His teeth clench and he makes a furious, gargling sound, his fingers scrabbling, clutching at my throat. Then those cloudy green eyes roll upward, and his hand falls away from my neck, dropping to the ground.

I look up at Rafe, who killed my father. Who saved my life.

He looks back at me, tall and dark and the calmest I've ever seen him.

Silently, he holds out his hand to lift me up.

I don't know who fires first, or if it's even intentional. It might have been Stepan Pavluk, who after all is only a bookkeeper, and should never have been brought to this place.

I only hear the pop of a finger convulsing against a trigger, and then I see Leo touch his side, a startled look on his face, blood blooming on his shirt.

Then everyone is firing, and Rafe throws me facedown on the grate, covering me with his body.

The chamber echoes with shots from all directions, heat and noise and bits of hot stone raining down on me, like I'm strapped to a pallet of fireworks all exploding at once.

And then we're running again, and this time it's not because we're being chased—everyone is dead behind us. We're running to the boat because Leo and Hedeon and Kade are all bleeding badly, and the mine itself is groaning, tunnels still collapsing from the C4 charges detonated by Sloane. The whole thing is about to fall down on our heads.

We run to the dock, piling into the speedboat as Adrik casts off. This time we count to be sure no one is left behind: Sabrina, Adrik, Kade, Ivan, Sloane, Freya, the four Petrov soldiers, Leo, Anna, Dean, Rafe, and me.

Then we're speeding down the dark river, the stone tunnel so close that we have to crouch low in the boat, still hearing the crashes and echoes of falling rock behind us.

We pass through a dark cavern, the ceiling suddenly soaring overhead, the water glittering black, the motor loud in the empty space.

Anna's scream echoes off the walls as there's a splash right behind us, and she shouts out, "LEO!"

Leo has fallen in, sinking below water darker than ink.

The boat is already far past where he fell. Adrik cuts the motor, trying to circle around. Dean dives off the boat, stroking hard for the place where Leo disappeared.

Sloane takes the headlamp off the front of the boat, aiming it across the water.

I see Dean's pale blond head dive under again and again as he searches for Leo. I'm about to jump off the boat myself when he pops up once more, this time dragging something heavy.

Anna leaps into the water too. Together, they haul Leo back in.

He's gray with cold and shock.

Adrik starts the motor again, roaring off down the dark river.

We speed faster and faster, recklessly close to the stone walls.

Then, like a cork out of a champagne bottle, we pop out into dazzling sunshine and cold, fresh air.

34

Rafe

We take Leo, Hedeon, and Kade to the hospital in Almaty.

I have a pretty nasty puncture in my shoulder that requires a dozen stitches, and Timo needs a bullet dug out of his calf, though he doesn't mention it until we're at the hospital, as it wasn't bothering him too much and he didn't want to make a fuss about it.

The Kazakh doctors are wise enough to take my mother's wad of bills and use the language barrier as an excuse not to ask any questions.

My mother insists that they fully examine my dad, to make sure he's not in any worse condition than might be expected after his prolonged imprisonment.

It's strange to see how much he's changed. Even after he's showered and shaved off the beard, and cut his hair above the shoulders, there's a new hardness to his face, a leanness to his frame carving out each muscle to its most extreme shape.

He can't take his eyes off my mother. They refuse to part from each other, even for a moment. I've never seen her cling to him like this, never letting go of his arm or his hand, never taking a step from his side.

I feel the same about Nix. I don't let her out of my sight, afraid that she might be far more fragile that she looks, ready to shatter any second like hot glass under cold water.

I think she's in shock.

She sits silent and pale, all brightness wiped from her face.

Everyone else has cleaned up and changed clothes. She still sits in the outfit she chose so hopefully for our date, her clothing filthy with dust and stained with her father's blood.

When my parents return—my father clean-shaven and my mother wearing her favorite leather jacket and boots once more—Nix looks up at them both.

"How much money did he take from you?" she asks. "I'll pay you back every cent."

My father looks at her, his eyes dark as flint.

"Money can't repay what was taken," he says.

Nix trembles under his stare, but she holds his gaze.

"What can I offer, then?" she says.

"You can offer yourself," my father says. "Your mind, your body, your soul, your loyalty, your life . . . to my son."

Nix turns to look at me, and for some reason, it's harder for her to meet my eyes. She bites her lower lip, her head bowed, hair hanging down over her face.

I cross the space between her and tilt up her chin so she has to look at me.

"I want you," I say to her. "I want your wildness. I want your passion. I want you to love me the way you love the wind and the water and the outdoors. I want you to be untamable, except by me. I want you to be my wife."

She takes a deep breath, holding my gaze at last.

"Yes," she says. "I will."

"You'll come to America with me. We'll rebuild everything your father tried to destroy."

Nix's lower lip trembles. I'm sure she's thinking of her home outside of Kyiv, the acres of land, the sprawling compound that will sit empty, abandoned, without her or her father or any of his men.

"Will you miss Kyiv?" I ask her.

She shakes her head, slowly.

"It will always be empty, whether I return to it or not. Home is the people you love, not a building, not a place. I want to go home with you, Rafe."

I love the sound of my name on her lips—my real name.

I grab her by the shoulders and I kiss her, the hardest I've ever kissed her.

She belongs to me now, fully and completely.

No lies between us.

Only the brutal truth.

Our fathers were friends, and then enemies. Now the house of Moroz is destroyed, and the Petrovs live on. Nix is one of us.

"Until Rafe buys you a better ring," my father says.

He pulls the gold ring off the pinky of his right hand, slipping it onto the third finger of Nix's left.

She turns her hand so the inscription catches the light:

Fides Est In Sanguinem

Loyalty In Blood

WE HAD INTENDED to take Dean, Hedeon, Kade, Anna, and Leo back to Kingmakers as quickly as possible, hoping to sneak them back onto the island to avoid the uproar of leaving without permission.

Unfortunately, three of the five were in no state to travel until they'd recovered several days in the hospital.

In the meantime, my father had to travel to Moscow to clean up the disastrous mess made by Danyl Kuznetsov's visit to St. Petersburg.

Dominik was hauled before the high table, after killing Danyl and five of his *bratoks*, and shooting Foma Kushnir.

Dom argued that Danyl attacked first, intending to kill Dom and his men, then frame them for murdering my father and siphoning off the earnings of his empire. Danyl was under the mistaken apprehension that my father was indeed dead. With Dom out of the way, Danyl and Foma hoped to take control of St. Petersburg, exiling my mother to our holdings in America.

It was clear that several members of the high table shared Danyl's beliefs, because they were thoroughly shocked when my father strode into the Bolshoi Theater, very much alive and angrier than they had ever seen him.

Several tense and volatile hours followed while my father argued with the other *Pakhans*. They were furious that his imprisonment had been kept secret, and even angrier that Danyl had been killed. My father retorted that their treachery justified the secrecy, and that Danyl Kuznetsov got precisely what he deserved.

It was lucky that Bodashka Kushnir had not been killed, or his father Foma. The fact that they were still alive, and captive at the monastery, was a useful bargaining chip.

In the end it was decided that my family would pay a settlement to the Kuznetsovs, that the Kushnirs would take over Danyl's old territory in Moscow, and Dominik would retain St. Petersburg.

"In fact," my father tells Dominik, once we're all back at the hospital in Almaty, "I think it's time you considered it your own. You've been *Pakhan* in all but name for a long time."

Dominik frowns, the scar on his right cheek crinkling where it runs past his eye.

"I don't care about a title, brother. The monastery will always be your home."

My father shakes his head. "It belongs to you, Dom. St. Petersburg belongs to you. I raised my children in America. I made that their home."

He turns to face Dean Yenin, who's sitting next to Leo's bed, a book open on his lap, trying not to listen in though of course he can understand everything being said in Russian.

"You owed two years to Danyl Kuznetsov?" my father asks.

"I did," Dean says.

"I've agreed to pay a stipend to Danyl's widow to compensate for the loss of her husband. Your service transfers to me," my father explains.

Dean nods slowly.

"You helped my son to find me," my father says. "I consider your service completed in full. If you want to join us in Oregon, we'd be glad to have you. But you're free to choose."

A look of stunned relief spreads across Dean's face. I know those two years weighed heavily on his shoulders—especially once he fell in love with Cat. He wanted to be free to start his life with her, and he hated the anvil around his neck, impossible to shake off.

"Thank you," Dean says. "I'm honored by your offer. I'll consider it carefully."

My father nods, then turns to Hedeon.

"I offer the same to you, if you want it—a place with the Petrovs. My son has told me that you may not wish to inherit from the Grays."

Hedeon gives a rough shake of his head. "I don't want anything from them," he says.

"I apologize if our arrangement with Luther Hugo caused you pain," my father says. "If you still want to know Evalina Markov, I could facilitate that meeting..."

"No," Hedeon says. "No, thank you."

I can't tell if he's trying to protect Evalina from the backlash that might ensue, or if his confrontation with Luther Hugo was so deeply disappointing that he no longer wants to meet his mother.

Hedeon and Leo are both cleaned up, bandaged, and recovering, but while Leo has regained all his usual boisterousness, Hedeon is as withdrawn as I've ever seen him. He barely joins in the cheerful conversation that bounces from bed to bed in this wing of the hospital that we've completely taken over.

I corner him when the nurses bring everyone dinner.

"Are you going back to Kingmakers?" I ask him.

He shrugs, picking at his food. "I suppose."

"Hugo will only let you all back on campus if he thinks his secret is safe."

Hedeon makes an irritated sound. "I don't want anyone to know he's my father any more than he does." Then he stops, registering what I said. "Aren't *you* going back?"

I shake my head. "Only to drop you all off. Then I'm going home with my parents and Nix. You could come with us."

Hedeon considers. I can guess what's really pulling him back in the direction of the school—and it sure as hell isn't Hugo.

He asks me, "Do you feel happy now that you got what you wanted?"

I look at my parents who are eating and talking with Freya and Dom, my father's arm around my mother's waist.

"I'm at peace because we have my father back," I say. "But I'm *happy* because of her."

Hedeon follows my gaze away from my parents towards Nix, who's crowded on the empty bed next to Leo's with Anna and Sabrina on either side of her, smiling faintly for the first time in several days.

Hedeon's eyes linger on Anna's face. I'm sure he's thinking of features very like hers, only a little different in color...

"I'm going back to Kingmakers," he says. "Might as well finish. Only a few months left."

"I think that's the right choice," I say, trying not to smile.

Once everyone is done eating, I ask Nix, "Do you want to come for a walk with me?".

"Yes," she says. "Only it looks freezing out there..."

"It is," I assure her. "But I got you this."

I hand her the coat I bought in the Zeliony Bazaar that morning. It's a deep rust color, covered in black and cream embroidery, with soft strips of sable around the hem, cuffs, and hood.

When Nix pulls up the hood, covering her brilliant hair, she could almost be Kazakh herself. She has the narrow eyes and high cheekbones you often see in Eastern Europeans, especially those with Mongolian or Tartar ancestry.

"You look beautiful," I tell her. "Like a fox."

That's what my father always calls my mother—*moya malen'kaya lisa. My little fox.*

The gold family ring glints on Nix's finger. It gives me a possessive rush, reminding me that she belongs to me now. I want to get her another ring, a necklace, earrings, bracelets . . . I want her draped in golden chains, naked otherwise, tied up on my bed . . .

As we step out onto the street, Nix takes a deep breath of the frigid air, her face relaxing, her exhale streaming out of her lungs in silvery plumes.

"I don't like hospitals," she says.

"Neither do I. Even when we've taken over the whole wing."

"When do we leave?" she asks me.

"I think tomorrow."

She sighs, creating another frosty cloud that swirls around her face.

"How are you doing?" I ask her.

"I don't know," she says. "Maybe a little better."

Nix and I have been going for walks every day for hours at a time. We have to, because I have so much to tell her. We have to re-do every conversation we ever had, when she asked me about my childhood and family and my life before Kingmakers. I'm giving her all my answers again, fully and truthfully this time.

Nix is getting to know me at the same time as I'm finally understanding myself.

I always wondered if I had it in me to live up to my parents.

I wondered if I could be a man like my father.

When the moment came, when I faced Marko Moroz on my own, I knew exactly what to do.

Because I *am* like my father. I always was.

Just like my father, all I needed to become the man I wanted to be ... is the right woman.

I would do anything for Nix.

I CAN do anything for her.

I'm invincible when I'm with her.

I take her hand, our fingers entwining, the gold band nestling between my third and fourth finger.

"Do you want to walk?" I ask her. "Or would you rather skate?"

Nix smiles fully for the first time this week. "Let's skate," she says.

I take her to the Medeu rink, perched high in the mountains outside Almaty. The endless expanse of smooth, gleaming ice has just been resurfaced, with barely a skate mark across. The air is so thin that I feel slightly giddy, especially with the loud Russian pop music echoing off the fir trees.

Nix laces her skates, eager to be on the ice.

I take her hand and we push off, gliding over the mirror-like surface, swift as birds.

It's almost illegal to not know how to skate in Russia.

My father used to flood the grounds behind the monastery. Adrik, Kade, Freya and I could skate almost as soon as we could walk. We played hockey with Timo and Zima.

I tell Nix all this. It feels euphoric speaking to her like this, without having to twist or deform a single detail.

"I played hockey too," she grins back at me. "My fa—"

She stops, her mouth open before she closes it quickly.

"It's okay," I say. "You can talk about him."

Nix is silent for a moment.

I don't want to ask her this, but I have to:

"Do you resent what I did?"

I killed her father right in front of her. He was trying to hurt her, but still . . . I can only imagine what she must be feeling.

Her eyes are as wet and gleaming as the ice. She fights to hold back the tears, to keep control of herself.

"I don't resent you," she says. "I feel . . . I feel like I started to lose my father the day I stepped foot on that ship. I lost the part of him that never existed in the first place. But still . . . even then, once I started to realize . . ."

Her cheeks are burning red and her shoulders heave as she tries to hold back the hurt that can't be contained.

"Even after . . . I never would have believed that he'd . . ."

I stop skating grabbing her and pulling her against my chest so she can sob without embarrassment, her face hidden from view.

For the first time she cries not for her father, but for what he tried to do to her. For how he turned on her when he believed she had betrayed him.

I let her exhaust herself against my chest, while I rub slow circles on her back with the palm of my hand.

When she looks up at me, her face tear-streaked and swollen, she says, "Everything I believed about him was only a fantasy. Even this great love he had for my mother . . . I can't help but think that if she was still alive, if she saw all the things he's done, she would have hated him. And if she didn't agree with him, if she didn't do exactly what he wanted, he would have hated her, too. She's only perfect in his memory because she didn't live long enough to disappoint him. His idea of love is so fucking narcissistic . . ."

I swallow hard.

"I'm sorry I ever lied to you, Nix. I promise you, I'll never do it again, not for any reason. I'll tell you the brutal truth, as long as we live."

"I know you will," Nix says. "You never wanted to lie, it's not your nature." She laughs, softly. "To be honest, you're not even very good at it. There were a hundred things I would have noticed if I wasn't so infatuated with you."

I laugh along with her, remembering how miserably I failed at not falling in love with her.

Nix and I start to skate again, the cold air drying the tears on her face, brightening her eyes once more until they glint like green glass.

Nix grabs both my wrists and we spin around the axis point of our linked hands. The dark green fir trees and the ice-blue mountains whirl around us like a carousel.

When we leave the rink at last, we don't return to the hospital. Instead, I take a room at the Excelsior. We're ripping off our clothes before the door even shuts behind us. Her lips are cold and her mouth is warm as I kiss her. Her freezing hands touch the burning flesh of my chest and stomach.

I take her hands and hold them to my mouth. I breathe into her cupped palms. Then I take her cold fingers into my mouth and I lick and suck them warm.

I reach down and touch between her thighs, over her underwear. She's wet all the way through her panties. I slide my fingers back and forth in the cleft of her pussy lips, feeling how slippery the material has become. Then I push my hand down the front of her panties and feel that velvet skin, slick with wetness. She has the most perfect natural lubrication, like warm baby oil. I drench my fingers in it, then slide them inside her, making her moan, making her knees buckle beneath her.

I take my cock out of my pants and I put it down the front of her underwear, rubbing it between her pussy lips, sliding it back and forth against her clit. She's so wet and warm that it feels like I'm already inside her. She rocks her hips, sliding her pussy back and forth against my cock, the elastic underwear holding it pressed tight against her.

I want her aching for me, I want her dying to have this cock inside her.

When my cock is covered in her wetness, I order, "Get down on your knees and suck me clean."

Nix drops to her knees, her mouth as swollen and sensitive from kissing as her pussy lips. She opens her mouth, allowing the head of my cock inside. I cup the back of her head in my palm and I push my cock deeper, feeling her tongue slide beneath the head and down the shaft.

"See how good you taste," I growl.

I fuck her mouth, gently at first, then a little harder. My lubricated cock slides all the way to the back of her throat. My balls are already heavy and tight with the built-up load of several days.

I withdraw from her mouth, pulling her to her feet. I kiss her deeply, tasting her pussy on her lips.

I want more.

I push her down on the bed, diving between her thighs. I tear her underwear off her, baring her shell-pink pussy lips beneath the tuft of rose-gold hair.

I could eat that pussy for hours. Her scent is sweet and earthy, like fallen leaves. Her texture is warm, melting honey. I lick up and down her slit, I gently suck on the nub of her clit, I push my fingers in and out of her. I reach up and caress her breasts, massaging and tugging on her nipples until she's flushed pink all across her chest, down her belly, and up her thighs.

The inside of her pussy is swollen so tight I can hardly get a finger inside. Her clit is aching. She's right on the edge, dying to tip over.

I look down at her face, supporting my weight on my arms, my heavy cock laying across her hip from her thigh up to her bellybutton.

"You want me inside you?" I ask.

"I *need* you inside me," she gasps.

"Beg me for it."

"Please Rafe, fuck me, I'm dying for you . . ." she moans.

My name is such a thrill on her lips. I can't get enough of it.

"Say my name again."

"Rafe!" she cries. "I need you Rafe!"

I plunge my cock inside of her, one hard thrust all the way in.

She screams out, her nails digging into my back.

I bite the side of her neck in return, my cock sliding in and out of that perfect warm pussy grip, her strong thighs squeezing my hips.

She's already starting to cum, she can't hold it back even for a minute.

Her pussy twitches around my cock, she spreads her thighs wider, begging me to fuck her harder and deeper.

My cock hits that place all the way inside her, that back wall that would be painful if she wasn't intensely aroused, every millimeter of her pussy swollen and spongy and exquisitely sensitive.

"Harder," she begs me, "Fuck me harder, Rafe."

I'm slamming the whole bed against the wall, the headboard thundering against the plaster as I fuck her with all my strength.

She's screaming out, louder than I've ever heard.

She needs this relief, and so do I.

I've never fucked her as Rafe. I've never fucked her without guilt.

This is my fiancée. Her body is mine—not just tonight, but forever. I can take her as many times as I want, in every possible position.

As soon as she's done cumming, I flip her over and take her from behind. Then I fuck her up against the window, her breasts pressed against the cold glass, her hands splayed like starfish on either side of her.

My balls are boiling, my cock raging hard.

I've never felt so unleashed. I'm finally exactly where I want to be, doing exactly what I want to do.

We knock over the lamp, the bulb smashing as it hits the floor.

I don't give a flying fuck. I'll destroy this entire room. I'll burn this fucking hotel to the ground. What I won't do is stop, not for a single second.

I pull her down on my lap on the spindly desk chair, its wooden legs groaning beneath our combined weight. I bounce her up and down on my cock, her tits bouncing in my face. I lick the sweat off her breasts. I take her nipple into my mouth and I suck hard, feeling her pussy clamp around my cock as she starts to cum again.

"I'm going to fuck you like this every day of our lives. Inside. Outside. Everywhere we go . . ."

"You promise?" she gasps.

"Only if you cum for me. Cum all over that cock . . ."

"Aghhhh!" she screams, her head thrown back.

I explode into her, my balls contracting, spurt after spurt of cum pumping up inside of her.

"You're mine," I growl. "All mine."

She falls against my chest, her arms around my neck.

I hold her tight against me, my cock still inside of her, with no intention of ever letting go.

35

Nix

After a week of recovery, Leo, Hedeon, and Kade are finally ready to fly back to Dubrovnik.

Adrik Petrov drives us from the airport down to the dock where the Chancellor's boat still waits. We're returning at night to try to avoid the uproar of students witnessing us sneaking back onto the island, though it can hardly have passed unnoticed that we've all been missing for a week.

"Just tell anyone that asks that you were holed up in your room with the flu," Leo says.

"Yeah? And how's Hedeon gonna explain why he's hobbling around like an old man, and why Kade's missing half an ear?" Dean snorts.

"You better just worry how you're going to explain to Cat how your 'quick and simple field trip to help Ares' turned into a week-long excursion that almost got us all killed," Anna says to Dean.

"Don't remind me," Dean says, miserably. "She's gonna fucking kill me."

"Don't worry," Anna says, sweetly. "I'm sure you won't even see it coming when she does."

As we pile out of SUV, Adrik grabs Sabrina by the arm and pulls her back.

"When am I going to see you again?" he growls.

"What makes you think you're going to see me again?" Sabrina says, tossing back her mane of dark hair.

"I AM going to see you again," Adrik informs her. "I was simply offering you the courtesy of choosing the time and place."

I can see the temptation to smile tugging at the corners of Sabrina's full lips as she attempts to scowl instead.

"I'll think about it," she says.

"Not good enough," Adrik retorts. "I'm picking you up on this dock on the last day of school. Wear something nice."

"That would be a first for both of us," Sabrina snorts, with a contemptuous look at Adrik's torn jeans, t-shirt, and uncut hair.

She turns away from him, ready to board the boat, but Adrik can't stand letting her have the last word. He seizes her arm, whips her around again, and aggressively kisses her.

Then he lets go and stalks off back to the car.

Sabrina is stunned to silence—perhaps for the first time in her life. She stands there for a moment with a slightly dazed expression, then follows Anna and Leo onto the boat.

"That good?" I ask her.

"He's definitely ... something," Sabrina replies.

I can't help grinning, thinking how nice it would be if Sabrina became a Petrov, too. Assuming her and Adrik don't kill each other first.

The ride back to Visine Dvorca is much more pleasant, by virtue of not being handcuffed to the railing. On the other hand, without the distraction of kidnapping and romantic betrayal, navigating the treacherous currents around the island is stressful. The water is so rough that Hedeon gets sick over the side of the boat, and Rafe looks traumatized by the time we finally pull into the Chancellor's private berth once more.

"I'm never fucking doing that again," he says.

While the others intend to finish the school year, Rafe and I only returned so he could navigate the boat, and so I could pack everything in my dorm room. We plan to leave on the supply ship in a few days' time.

Rafe is anxious to go back to America with his family. I don't think any of them will feel this is over until they're all back in their mansion on the sea cliffs of the Oregon coast.

I'm equal parts nervous and excited to join him there.

I haven't spent much time in America.

But after all, I came to Kingmakers to meet new people and become more independent. Even though I stayed less than a year, I'd say I accomplished those goals more than I ever could have imagined.

And anyway, I meant what I said to Rafe: home is with him. I want to be wherever he is. Inside, outside, all over the world . . .

The long, limestone staircase back up to the Keep reminds me uncomfortably of the mine. I don't know if I'll ever enjoy being unground after that particular experience.

By contrast, the interior of the Keep feels deeply nostalgic, from the scent of the dusty carpets to the golden glow of the lamps in the wall-mounted sconces. I'm glad to be back, if only for a short time.

"Thank god we made it back for the *Quartum Bellum,*" Leo says.

"Oh Jesus," Kade groans. "Don't remind me."

Anna asks, "What did Adrik say about you trying to beat his record?"

Leo grins. "He said he'd never forgive me if I win. But he won't respect me if I lose."

"That's as close to a blessing as you're gonna get from him," Kade laughs.

"If you hadn't pulled Leo out of the water, it would have been down to Kade and me," Sabrina says to Dean, sourly.

"Well, I sort of owed it to him," Dean says.

Leo gives Dean a fist bump. "We're even. 'Til the next time I need your help."

As we come out onto the dark lawn, we all stand awkwardly in a group, hesitant to part ways after a solid week in each other's company.

Leo, warm and affectionate as ever, pulls Rafe into a hug.

"What should we call you now?" he says. "Is it still Ares while you're here? Or just Rafe?"

Rafe smiles, his face more relaxed than I've ever seen it.

"I don't care what you call me," he says. "As long as you call me."

Anna hugs him, too. "You can count on that," she says.

"Oh, get the fuck over here," Rafe says, pulling Dean into a hug too, and then Hedeon. I think he holds onto Hedeon the longest of anyone.

"Come see us in the summer," Rafe says.

"I will," Hedeon promises.

Then, finally, we're all walking to our respective dorms. Kade and Hedeon split off in the direction of the Octagon Tower. Dean heads to the Undercroft to grovel for forgiveness with Cat—I assume he'll be successful, as I've been told he has some experience with that.

Leo is walking Anna to the Solar, strolling along a few yards ahead of us. Sabrina stays on Anna's other side, trying to avoid Leo's teasing on the subject of Adrik Petrov.

Rafe likewise escorts me, his arm around my waist. I lean against his shoulder, looking up at the stars.

"Do you think you and I ever looked at the same star at the same time?" I ask him.

"I'm sure we looked at the moon at the same time."

I laugh. "It's funny to think that the Oregon moon and the Kyiv moon are the same."

"The wind that touched your skin might have blown all the way across the world to me," Rafe says. "Maybe that's why you smelled so good to me, the moment I got near you."

We stop on the grass so he can kiss me.

When we break apart I say, "You know . . . I kind of like the way we met. It will be something to tell our kids someday."

"Yes," Rafe says. "Only we'll tell them all of it, the whole thing. The good, the bad, and everything in between."

"That's right," I nod. "The truth is always the best story."

EPILOGUE

Nix Moroz
Cannon Beach, Oregon

September

Home — Edward Sharpe
Spotify → geni.us/spy-spotify
Apple Music → geni.us/spy-apple

Rafe and I collect the real Ares Cirillo from the Portland airport.

I wait in the pickup lane while Rafe runs in to get him.

The two young men walk out together—both tall, tan, blue-eyed and dark-haired. My heart gives a lurch at the bizarre mirror effect: as if I'm looking at the old Ares and the new one simultaneously. One dressed in worn blue jeans and a plain wool sweater, a gentle expression on his face. The other in a new leather jacket and a fresh haircut, grinning happily at the sight of his friend.

I jump out of the car to greet them.

Ares shakes my hand, giving me a lopsided smile.

"I've heard so much about you," he says.

"Likewise," I reply, and I can't help laughing. Ares laughs with me, understanding at once what I mean.

Rafe looks chagrined. "Wondering which one of us you actually fell in love with?" he says to me.

I slip my hand in his and kiss him on the corner of his mouth, where his stubble rasps against my lips.

"Don't worry," I say. "You were yourself all along."

We climb back in the car. I try to let Ares sit up front with Rafe, but he absolutely refuses, holding the door open for me until I return to the front seat.

"I could never take shotgun from a lady," he says.

His voice is softer than Rafe's, his manners unassuming. It makes me realize how much Rafe was acting at Kingmakers. How much he inhabited a character. Since we've come home to Oregon together, I've seen the full extent of his confidence, his boisterousness. How he throws himself into the Petrov business. How much energy he has when he's not weighed down by stress and sorrow.

My happiness blooms with his.

I love living with the Petrovs.

You would think so many big personalities in one house would be overwhelming, but in fact, it's invigorating. I love the noise and the energy. The sprawling mansion currently houses Ivan, Sloane, Freya, Rafe, me, Timo, Zima, and now Ares, as well as four overgrown Ovcharkas and two pups.

Dominik, Lara, Kade, and Adrik were here up until last week, and Sabrina Gallo came to visit on her way back to school, though neither she nor Adrik would admit that they purposefully came at the same time to see each other. This despite the evidence of disappearing for long periods of time, then returning in a distinctly rumpled state.

Leo visited us earlier in the summer. He left before the other Petrovs arrived, probably intimating that Adrik still hasn't forgiven him for knocking him off the pedestal of *Quartum Bellum* champions. Sabrina and Kade may not have forgiven him, either.

I haven't been lonely for a minute in America, even when Rafe is working. Freya and I go for long walks along the beach early in the morning. She's incredibly well-read, and likes to make Mount Rushmore lists for the best fictional villains of all time, the best surprise endings, and the best science-fiction predictions.

Ivan has been teaching me how to train the Ovcharkas. We kept horses in Kyiv, but no dogs or cats, because my father was allergic. As soon as Kira birthed her two puppies, Ivan gave me the pick of the pair. I chose the rowdiest of the two, the one who wouldn't stop chewing on his brother's ear, and named him Okeanu. Ivan teases me that I'll have to perfect my Russian because that's the only language the dogs understand.

Much as I love Rafe's father and sister, to my surprise it's Sloane I bond with most.

We go shooting together. I've never seen a more terrifying marksman.

"My father taught me," Sloane told me, carefully cleaning her Beretta before packing it away in its case. "He was CIA. Special Activities Division—covert ops, paramilitary operations, that sort of thing. Brilliant. Incredibly talented. Until he lost his fucking mind."

"Really?" I asked, instantly curious.

"Yes. He ruthlessly trained me from a young age. Took me all over the world, constantly on the run from the countless enemies trying to hunt us down. It took me much longer than it should have to realize that most of those enemies existed only in his head."

"Oh . . ." I said, my stomach sinking like an elevator.

Sloane looked at me, her eyes very like Freya's for a moment.

"When I met Marko, he reminded me of my father. And when I met you ... you reminded me of me. Determined. Tenacious."

My cheeks flushed.

"I couldn't ask for a better compliment," I said.

"Our fathers shape us," Sloane said, zipping her case. "But it's our husbands who determine what we truly become. And us them. A couple is the sum of both of you together—as strong as you are together. As happy as you are together."

"I've never seen a couple as powerful as you and Ivan," I said.

"I hope you and Rafe will surpass us," Sloane said. "In your own way and your own time."

I think of that now, as Rafe drives Ares and me the ninety minutes back to Cannon Beach, to the mansion on the cliff that I've already come to know and love so well.

I look at Rafe's profile, the set of his jaw and the stormy green-blue of his eyes, and I think I could never choose a better partner, even if I had a thousand years to search.

When we pull up to the house, Freya is sitting on the porch swing reading a book. Her straight, dark hair is brushed to a glossy sheen, and I notice that she's wearing a particularly lovely summer dress with puffed sleeves and a peasant bodice, her bare feet tucked up under her on the padded swing.

Ares Cirillo falls silent in the back seat.

As we unload his suitcase from the trunk, Freya sets down her book, watching us.

Ares climbs the steps, setting down his case and holding out his hand to shake.

"Good to see you again, Freya," he says.

"Are we back to handshakes, then?" she says. "Has it been that long?"

Though I'm standing at the bottom of the steps, I'm almost certain Ares is blushing.

"No," he says. "That was stupid."

"You're not stupid," she says. "Too slow to visit, maybe. But never stupid."

She steps forward and Ares puts his arms around her, pulling her against his chest.

The hug is so long that Rafe and I exchange a look, and then a second look. We're both grinning like idiots. I try to wipe the smile off my face before Freya catches me.

Timo has made dinner for us all. He's an even better cook than he is a soldier. His homemade gnocchi and grilled peach salad beats anything I've had, even in the nicest restaurants down by the beach.

The only person who eats more than me is Zima, Ivan's technology expert. He spends most of his days in front of his computer rig munching things that came wrapped in cellophane, yet he still remains skinny as a bean. I've long since decided that the laws of thermogenesis must not apply to him.

Sloane and Ivan are just as pleased to see Ares as the rest of us. They ask after his family, the bittersweet recounting of his sisters' dance recitals and his mother's new job tinged by the absence of Galen Cirillo.

"What's your plan now?" Ivan asks Ares. "I miss you working for me. Rafe has to go to Las Vegas once a week to keep an eye on the new manager."

Ares casts a quick look at Freya, then down at his peach salad.

"I was thinking I'd go to school for real. Maybe Cambridge."

Ivan likewise glances at Freya, raising an eyebrow as he comes to understand.

"Ah," he says. "Well, I'd be happy to pay your tuition. It's the least I could do."

"Thank you, but I have a scholarship," Ares smiles. "And you did pay me very well for running the dispensaries—even from Kazakhstan."

Freya hasn't looked up from her own peach salad, but her cheeks are pink and she seems extraordinarily pleased with the view of her plate.

After dinner, Rafe pulls me into the hall.

"Come for a ride with me," he says.

"I'd love to," I say.

I climb on the back of his Indian FTR, that even Sabrina had to admit was pretty fucking boss, despite the stigma of being built within our lifetimes.

Rafe revs the engine, the bike coming to life beneath us, the vibration thrumming through my bones. We speed away from the house, my arms wrapped tight around his waist, our bodies leaning together as one.

We roar down the coastal road.

I love the wild, rocky beaches of Oregon. I love how much it rains, and how deeply, richly green it is everyplace you look.

I press my face against Rafe's back, smelling the salt in the air, the rich leather of his jacket, and the intoxicating scent of his cologne.

We've only been driving a few minutes when he pulls into a small neighborhood along the cliffs. It's not as fancy as where his parents live—the yards are overgrown with untamed gardens and untrimmed trees, the roofs covered in moss. The houses are small, cedar-plank sided with ramshackle decks. We've stopped in front of a cabin so covered in honeysuckle vines that I can hardly see the house at all.

"What do you think?" Rafe asks.

"I love it!" I tell him, honestly. "It looks like we're in the middle of nowhere. But we're five minutes from Shake Shack."

Rafe laughs. My growing obsession with American burgers has toured us through every grill in a fifty-mile radius.

"I want to buy this house for you," he says. "I thought we could live here when we get married in the spring. If you really do like it."

I can't speak. My heart is beating too hard.

The cabin is right on the edge of the cliff. From the back deck, we'll be able to watch the sun set over the ocean. A set of rotting wooden steps leads down the cliff to the beach.

"We'll fix those," Rafe says, nodding in the direction of the top step clinging to the rock face by a single nail. "We'll fix up the whole house. I'll make it exactly how you want it."

"If you're in it," I say. "That's the only thing I care about."

Dean Yenin
Visine Dvorca

December

Cat comes to visit me in the professor's quarters in the old buttery.

I'm not actually a professor—I'm just the boxing instructor. Taking Snow's old job for one year while Cat finishes her schooling.

I want to stay close to her.

She comes to see me every evening, and spends most nights curled up on my chest on the narrow single bed. Her roommate Rakel doesn't mind—she's having a torrid affair with Jacob Weiss, so she enjoys having the dorm room in the Undercroft to herself.

Cat gasps when I open the door.

"What happened to your face?"

"Oh," I touch the tender bruise under my right eye. "It's that little shithead from Coney Island. He just keeps trying his luck."

Cat tries to hide her smile. "Looks like it worked today. He got you pretty good."

"I knocked him on his ass," I assure her. "But I'm sure he'll try again tomorrow."

"He's persistent."

"He's a lazy, arrogant asshole," I say. "If his head were any bigger, it wouldn't fit in the ring."

"Hm," Cat says, not bothering to hide her grin at all anymore. "Reminds me of someone. I can't think who . . ."

"I was never lazy!" I protest.

"I doubt he is, either, if he's survived four months in your class," Cat says, reaching up on tiptoe to kiss me.

"You think I'm too hard on them," I growl.

"All I'm saying," Cat murmurs, starting to unbutton her blouse, "is that if you want to take out some of that frustration . . . I'm right here . . ."

An hour later, we're both laying on the floor, naked and sweating. Cat sprawls across my lap, her bottom as pink as her cheeks.

She's right . . . I do feel much better now.

I'm stroking her hair in that soothing, petting motion she loves so much.

I can see her ribs expanding with slow, steady breaths. I think she's falling asleep, until she surprises me by rolling over, looking up into my face.

"Do you like teaching?" she asks me.

I think about my boxing classes—about the thrill I get when one of the students does something right for a change. Even that kid from Coney Island.

"Yeah," I say. "I like it."

"Would you be disappointed if you couldn't finish the year?"

I frown at her, confused.

"I'm only here because I thought *you* wanted to finish."

"I did. But now I'm worried it might not be safe," Cat takes a deep breath. "For the baby."

I stare at her for a moment, not quite understanding. Then the racing of my heart jolts my brain.

"Are you serious?" I whisper.

"Very serious," she says. "And very sure."

I scoop Cat up in my arms, holding her tight against me, squeezing her hard but not too hard. My eyes are burning, my heart pounding, my throat too tight to speak.

"We're gonna have a baby?" I croak.

"Yes," she says, "Sometime in June."

I can't stop hugging her. I can't let go, even for a second.

"You should have told me!" I cry. "I wouldn't have spanked you."

"Don't be ridiculous," Cat snorts. "I made sure you weren't too rough."

"What about the—"

"That's fine, too. It won't hurt him."

"Him? You think it's a boy?"

She laughs. "I don't know. I mean . . . I have a feeling. An inclination. But it's just a guess."

I nuzzle my face against her hair, breathing in the clean scent of her scalp. I need to smell her to calm myself down, because I'm experiencing a mixture of joy, excitement, and terror so acute that I feel like my heart might explode.

"I'm so, so glad," I tell her. "I wish it were June right now."

"Me too," Cat murmurs. "But I'm sure it will come soon enough."

She is getting tired now, I can hear it in her voice.

I lift her up in my arms and take her to the bed. She may be carrying my child, but it's still easy for me to carry her petite little frame and set her down gently on the mattress. I cover her with the blanket, sitting on the edge of the bed and stroking her hair until she's fast asleep.

I'm as awake as I've ever been.

I can't stop imaging this child—what he'll look like, what he'll sound like, what he'll think and feel. What will he want, and will I be able to give it to him?

I've barely learned how to love Cat the way she deserves. I still make mistakes.

What if I fuck up with my child? What if I damage him forever?

I stand up from the bed, my stomach churning. I snatch up my phone, taking it into the other room so I don't wake Cat.

Then I call Snow.

He picks up on the third ring. It's 5:00 p.m. in New York, six hours earlier than here.

"Dean," he says, in that deep, gravelly voice—rough on the surface, but warm underneath.

"Snow. It's good to hear your voice."

"Likewise, my friend. Are you and Cat coming to see us soon?"

"Well . . ." I say. "If we do, there will be three of us coming . . ."

Snow catches on quicker than me. He chuckles.

"Congratulations, Dean. There's nothing like having a child. You'll see."

My skin feels hot and cold at the same time. I grip the phone tight against my ear.

"How do I do it?" I ask. "I don't know how to be a father."

"In some ways it's like being a coach or a mentor," Snow says. "But in some ways it isn't. A coach is there if you want them. If you don't want the goal anymore, then they don't coach you. A father does whatever it takes for his son to achieve his goals. A coach praises when the goal is met. A father always shows that he's proud of his son. You build your child up, and never tear him down, because you love him. And that makes it harder—because you're not controlling where they go. You don't control their goals. Be the kind of father that accepts your son's decisions."

I nod slowly, though Snow can't see me.

"That's how I want to be," I say.

"Most of all," Snow says, "a father never gives up on his son. Your child may struggle at times. He may scream at you, hate you, push you away. But you will always be there to help him when he needs you most."

"Yes, I will be," I say, fervently.

The baby in Cat's belly may barely be formed. But I already love it. I already know I'll protect it with my life.

"Snow," I say. "You were more than a coach to me."

I can picture his rough-hewn face as if he were standing across the room from me.

"And I'll always help you, Dean," he says. "However I can."

Zoe Romero
Berlin, Germany

June

I PACKED several dresses for Chay's wedding, but none of them seem right once we reach the opulent hotel where the ceremony will be held.

I've never seen such an eye-popping array of color, pattern, and texture—as if it were designed by Liberace after a vacation in Wonderland.

I'd expect nothing less from Chay. "Subtle" and "understated" are the dirtiest words in her dictionary.

Now my wardrobe choices seem underwhelming. Chay said the dress code was "somewhere between the Oscars and the Met Gala."

I attended the Oscars with Miles just last year. Chay told me that the black gown I wore was, "nice, but a little boring."

I plan to spend the afternoon shopping on Kurfurstendamm to find something more impressive to wear, but Miles forestalls me before I can leave our room.

"I've got something that might work," he says.

"You brought a dress?" I say, trying not to smile. "That's daring, even for you. Though you do have incredible legs..."

Miles grins. "Yeah, I bet you'd love to see that. Sorry to disappoint—this dress was always for you."

He covers my eyes with his hands, walking me through the main room of our suite into the bedroom.

"Is this just a ruse to get me back in that bed?" I say.

"Possibly," Miles says. "Depends how much you like your gift..."

He pulls his hands away, revealing a strapless gown artfully displayed on the coverlet, with a pair of matching silk gloves, a belt, and high-heeled shoes in precisely the same shade of shocking pink.

I stare at the dress, hands over my mouth.

"You didn't..." I whisper.

"It's not the real one," Miles says, quickly. "I mean, I'll buy that for you if you want, but it's so old it would fall apart if you tried to wear it. I had a replica made. It's all peau d'ange silk, just like the original, and look, the lining's black satin. The palms of the gloves are even suede, just like in the film."

"How on earth did you remember?" I say.

Three years ago, I told Miles that my dream dress was the one Marilyn Monroe wore in *Gentlemen Prefer Blondes*. I used to watch that movie all the time with my *abuela*.

I've never mentioned it since.

"I remember everything you say to me," Miles tells me, his expression serious.

It's true—Miles never forgets. He never misses details. He never fails to come through.

"How do you do it?" I say, shaking my head at him.

"I do it because you matter to me," Miles says. "I wouldn't forget about you any more than I'd forget about breathing."

I can't breathe right now. My chest is too tight. The dress is so beautiful. It's a dream come to life—something I never expected to actually touch and hold.

"Put it on," he says.

The silk is smooth and cool as water running over my skin. I pull on the dress, turning so Miles can zip the back, carefully navigating the oversized bow at the waist.

I step into the shoes, don the gloves, and stand before the full-length mirror so we can both admire the effect.

The pink silk blazes against my skin. The dress fits me to the millimeter.

"How in the fuck did you get my measurements!" I cry.

Miles just laughs. "That was the easy part," he says.

I snap a picture of myself so I can send it to Chay. She texts me back immediately, in all caps, so I can almost hear her screech of delight:

> THAT IS THE HOTTEST YOU'VE EVER LOOKED! What a perfect wedding present for me ;)

Miles laughs reading it.

"I thought it was more a gift to myself, but I'm glad Chay's happy."

I grab his face between my hands and kiss him.

"*I'm* happy," I tell him. "Extremely happy."

We take the elevator down to the reception. Miles looks irresistible in a cream-colored suit with his dark curls freshly washed and his face clean-shaven. I'm already counting the minutes until we can go back up to our room.

We're seated amongst a profusion of peonies, dahlias, and overblown roses, in brilliant shades of fuchsia, orange, and crimson.

Anna and Leo sit directly in front of us, Leo grinning brighter than I've ever seen. The reason is obvious—his hand rests on Anna's belly, which stretches the limits of her tight black dress.

"How was the flight over?" I ask her, squeezing her shoulder in sympathy.

"Miserable," she says. "One of these babies is a real fucking asshole."

"Maybe both of them!" Leo says, with undisguised excitement.

Even as I watch, the side of Anna's belly visibly distends with a well-aimed kick.

"I don't know if they're gonna let me back on the plane," Anna says. "I'm so big that I look like I'm due tomorrow."

"I think Cat actually *is* due tomorrow," I say.

"I wish she could have come," Anna says. "And I envy her only having to push one baby out."

"Yeah, but she'll have to go through the whole thing again if she wants another," Leo says. "This is like a two-for-one deal on the pregnancy."

"Easy for you to say!" Anna says, smacking him on the shoulder.

Leo just grins and pulls her close.

"Sorry babygirl. Twins on both sides of our family — it was pretty much guaranteed to happen."

Cara Wilk drops down in the seat next to her sister, panting slightly.

"Oh good, we're not late!" she says. "I broke a heel on my shoe."

"Don't worry," Hedeon says, sitting down next to her. "Those sandals are even prettier."

He puts his arm around Cara's shoulder so she can snuggle against his chest.

I can't help smiling, seeing that Hedeon has matched his tie to Cara's pale blue dress.

Hedeon moved to Chicago so he can see Cara over the summers when she comes home from Kingmakers. He's been working with Leo and the rest of the Gallos. Well—the rest of them except for my husband.

Miles and I are perfectly happy in Los Angeles. We've been developing a TV show for Netflix—my version of *The Sopranos*, centered around teenagers from mafia families.

"Just don't put anything in the script that will get us in trouble," Miles told me.

"You mean, don't call their high school Kingmakers and put it on a secret island?" I teased him.

"Well . . ." he raised an eyebrow. "It does make for a good setting . . ."

I love working with Miles. Our strengths and weaknesses perfectly complement each other. His ambition is boundless, and he'll do anything to reach our goals. I'm the rudder that helps steer him away from some of his more fantastical ideas toward those that might actually work.

"Oh!" Cara gasps. "Here she comes!"

In true Chay fashion, she walks down the aisle to the pounding refrains of some German rock band I've never heard of.

Her father is wearing his leather Night Wolves jacket over a pair of artfully-distressed jeans and studded boots. He holds Chay's arm, grinning broadly.

Ozzy steps up to the altar to wait for her. He's dressed in plaid pants, combat boots, and a sleeveless suit jacket that shows the tattoos running down his arms. An oversized orange peony protrudes from his buttonhole. His mohawk has been spiked up to its most astronomical heights. He looks dazzled, utterly stunned at the sight of his bride.

No one can outshine Chay tonight. She's got the bouffant of Texas beauty queen, the makeup of an 80s hair band, and a dress that trails ten yards behind her. The layers and layers of exploding tulle are dyed in descending sunset colors: fuchsia, salmon, tangerine, scarlet, indigo, and purple.

She practically runs down the aisle to Ozzy.

Ozzy's dad performs the ceremony. He keeps it short and simple.

"Ozzy was in love with Chay from the moment he laid eyes on her. Chay took a little more convincing."

We all laugh.

"But I think it's clear to see that no couple could be more excited to finally tie the knot. Ozzy, you're damn lucky to have this girl. And Chay, no one will ever be more devoted to you than my son. I know the two of you will never be bored together. And god help anyone who stands in your way!"

Before he can give the order, Ozzy seizes Chay, bends her backward, and kisses her as if he's waited years to do it.

We all whistle and cheer, Caleb Griffin throwing handfuls of rainbow-colored petals on the couple as he'd been instructed to do as the flower boy.

Right at that moment, I feel my phone buzzing in my handbag.

With a premonition of what I'm about to see, I pull it out, scanning the screen. Just as I hoped, it's a message from Dean:

> *Baby was in a hurry. We barely made it to the hospital in time. Cat handled it like a champion—Levi Yenin is 7 lbs. 6 oz, 22 inches long. So fucking happy to have him here.*

I'm crying from the very first word.

Miles reads over my shoulder, his arm around my waist.

"I told you," he says. "We gotta hurry up if we're gonna give that kid a cousin."

LEO GALLO

Chicago

Two Years Later

I'm dressing for Sabrina's engagement party.

After two years of arguing over whether they'll live in St. Petersburg or Chicago, she's finally agreed to marry Adrik Petrov.

They're holding the party on the rooftop terrace of LondonHouse. It's a black-tie affair, which means I have to remember how to tie a goddamn bow tie.

I've been fucking with it for twenty minutes now, not wanting to admit that I'm going to have to ask Anna to work her magic yet again.

She's already dressed, playing with the twins downstairs before we have to leave them with the sitter.

I know she's excited to see Cara, who just completed her last year at Kingmakers, and is finally home for good. Cara's only here a month before she and Hedeon embark on their six-month backpacking trip across Asia. I guess Cara feels like Kingmakers wasn't quite enough inspiration for the novel she's been writing the last two years.

I'm equally excited to see Rafe and Nix, Freya and Ares, and Kade Petrov. It's been too long. We're all so busy and so scattered across the globe—it takes a wedding or a funeral to bring us all together. I know which one I prefer.

Giving up on the ridiculous bow tie, I head downstairs to beg for my wife's help.

I almost trip over the twins, who barrel across the hallway at top speed, Athena chasing after Archie, both brandishing wooden swords.

"Don't run with those!" I bellow after them, but they're shrieking too loud to hear me.

It's hard to tell them apart from behind, since they're both crowned with a bush of dark curls, and they're both equally filthy and feral unless Anna has just lifted them out of the bath.

She may have done so—Athena was wearing the bottom of a pair of pajamas, and Archie the top.

I search through the main floor of our house, looking for Anna.

We bought this gothic mansion right before the twins were born. I was starting to get nervous that Anna wouldn't find a place she liked. She was adamant that she didn't want any gleaming, modern condo on the lake, no matter how pretty the view. Her tastes were shaped from an early age by her father's house.

The Astor Street mansion has everything she likes—dormers and gables, high ceilings, cavernous fireplaces, an overgrown garden, leaded glass windows, and an abundance of ghosts.

The twins love it. They're continually getting lost in the maze of ancient rooms, popping out again in unexpected places as if they've found a secret passageway through the walls.

I love it because it suits Anna so well. She only becomes more ethereal and elegant with each year that passes. She's as timeless as this house, and as beautiful.

At last I find her in the music room, setting a vinyl on her mother's old record player.

I see her long, silvery sheaf of hair laying over her shoulder, and the backless silk gown she's chosen for the evening.

She hears my footsteps behind her and turns to face me, the skirt of her shimmering black dress twisting around her legs like the bloom of a calla lily.

As she looks up at me with those ice-blue eyes, I'm hit with the strangest sense of déjà vu.

All at once I remember a dream I had, my first month at Kingmakers.

Anna and I were only friends then. Best friends, and nothing more.

I was already in love with her, but didn't know it yet.

My heart stops in my chest as I remember every detail of that dream:

A mansion even grander than my parents'.

Two little twins, running through the room.

My wife in an elegant black dress.

When the woman turned, I saw that it was Anna.

That was the moment I realized that no vision of my future could ever be complete without her.

I knew I had to have her. But at the time, it seemed it could never happen.

There are crossroads in life where you can either choose the cold truth you see in front of you, or you can choose to chase the impossible dream.

It's only by believing in that dream, and pursuing it, that you can turn it into a living, breathing reality.

You must chase the dream to live the dream. Otherwise, it will only ever be an ephemeral fantasy in your mind.

Thank you for coming with me to Kingmakers ♥ Have you read Ivan & Sloane's story? →

SLOANE HAS ONLY FAILED AT ONE THING... TRYING TO KILL IVAN 🔥🔥🔥

READ IVAN – FREE KINDLE UNLIMITED

PETROV FAMILY TREE

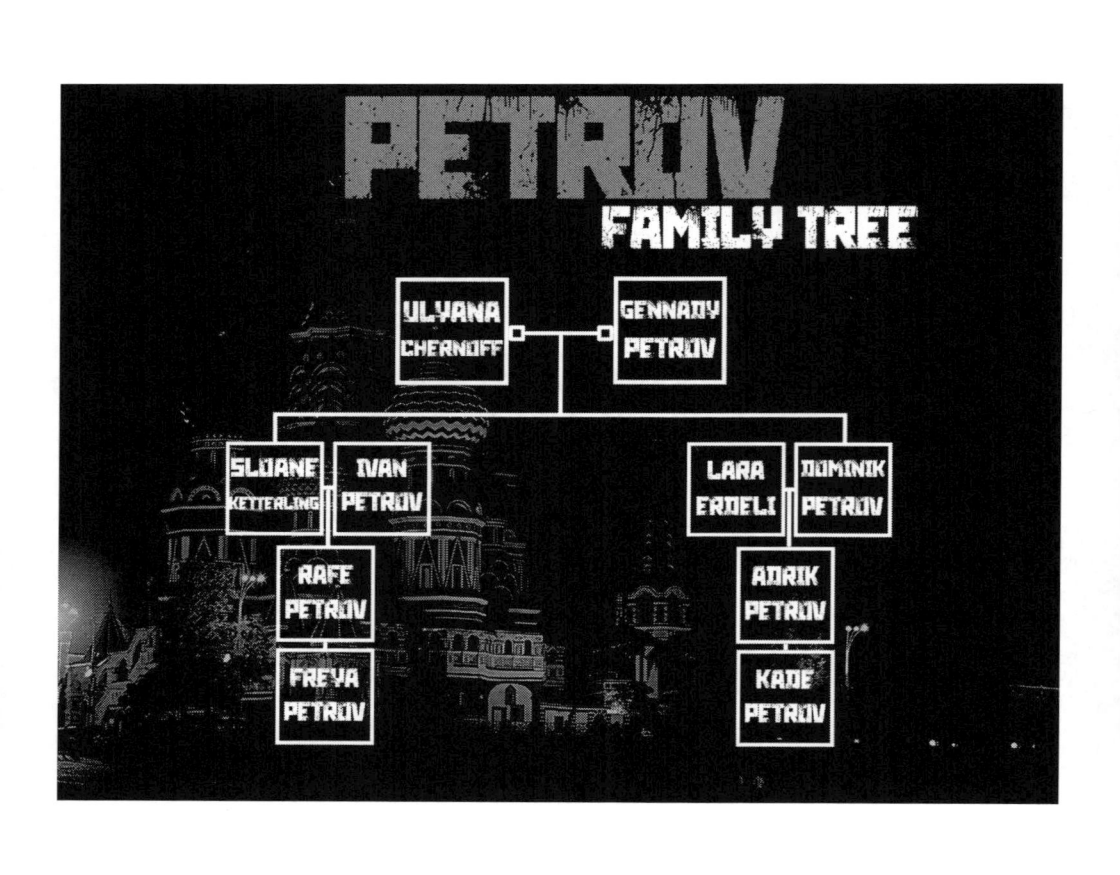

- **Ulyana Chernoff** — **Gennady Petrov**
  - **Sloane Ketterling** — **Ivan Petrov**
    - **Rafe Petrov**
      - **Freya Petrov**
  - **Lara Erdeli** — **Dominik Petrov**
    - **Adrik Petrov**
      - **Kade Petrov**

MARKOV
FAMILY TREE

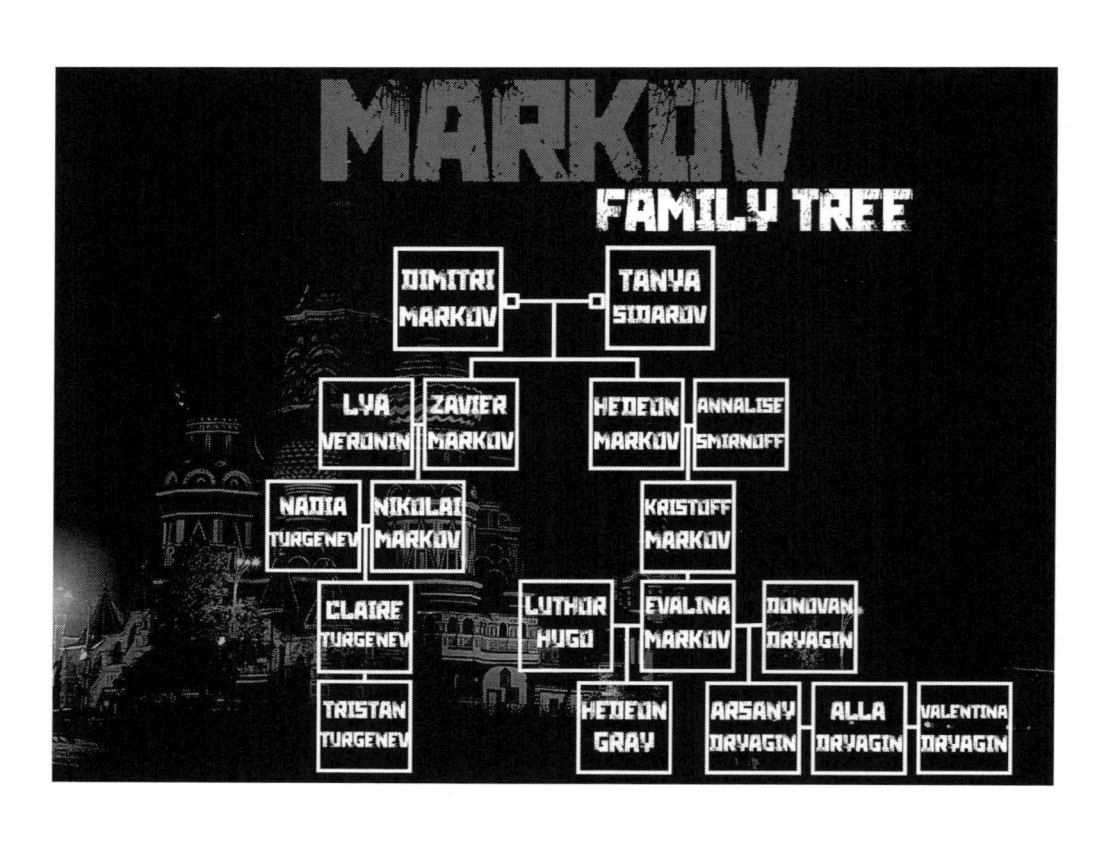

- **DIMITRI MARKOV** — **TANYA SIDAROV**
  - **ZAVIER MARKOV** — **LYA VERONIN**
    - **NIKOLAI MARKOV** — **NADIA TURGENEV**
      - **CLAIRE TURGENEV**
        - **TRISTAN TURGENEV**
  - **HEDEON MARKOV** — **ANNALISE SMIRNOFF**
    - **KRISTOFF MARKOV**
      - **EVALINA MARKOV** — **LUTHOR HUGO**
        - **HEDEON GRAY**
      - **EVALINA MARKOV** — **DONOVAN DRYAGIN**
        - **ARSANY DRYAGIN**
        - **ALLA DRYAGIN**
        - **VALENTINA DRYAGIN**

HAVE YOU MET ALL THE PARENTS?

CALLUM & AIDA – BRUTAL PRINCE
MIKO & NESSA – STOLEN HEIR
NERO & CAMILLE – SAVAGE LOVER
DANTE & SIMONE – BLOODY HEART
RAYLAN & RIONA – BROKEN VOW
SEBASTIAN & YELENA – HEAVY CROWN
SERIES PAGE – BRUTAL BIRTHRIGHT

THE HEIR
SOPHIE LARK

THE REBEL
SOPHIE LARK

THE BULLY
SOPHIE LARK

THE SPY
SOPHIE LARK

WELCOME TO KINGMAKERS!
WHERE THERE IS ONLY ONE RULE...

THE HEIR – MARCH 2021
LEO GALLO (SON OF SEBASTIAN & YELENA)

THE REBEL – MAY 2021
MILES GRIFFIN (SON OF CALLUM & AIDA)

THE BULLY – JUNE 2021
DEAN YENIN (SON OF ADRIAN YENIN)

THE SPY – JULY 2021
*********** (SON OF *****)

KINGMAKERS SERIES PAGE

SOME CHARACTERS FROM MY UNDERWORLD SERIES WILL BE BACK AS WELL . . .

CAN I ASK YOU A **HUGE** FAVOR?

Would you be willing to leave me a review?

I would be so grateful as one positive review on Amazon is like buying the book a hundred times. Your support is the lifeblood of Indie authors and provides us with the feedback we need to give the readers exactly what they want!

I read each and every review. They mean the world to me! So thank you in advance, and happy reading!

CLICK TO REVIEW

Amazon Bestselling Author

Sophie lives with her husband, two boys, and baby girl in the Rocky Mountain West. She writes intense, intelligent romance, with heroines who are strong and capable, and men who will do anything to capture their hearts.

She has a slight obsession with hiking, bodybuilding, and live comedy shows. Her perfect day would be taking the kids to Harry Potter World, going dancing with Mr. Lark, then relaxing with a good book and a monster bag of salt and vinegar chips.

The Love Lark Letter
Click here to join my VIP newsletter

Come Join All The Fun:

Rowdy Reader Group
The Love Larks Reader Group

Follow for Giveaways
Facebook Sophie Lark

Instagram
@Sophie_Lark_Author

Complete Works on Amazon
follow my amazon author page

Follow My Book Playlists
Spotify → geni.us/lark-spotify

Apple Music → geni.us/lark-apple

Feedback or Suggestions for new books?
Email it to me: sophie@sophielark.com

Made in the USA
Columbia, SC
28 July 2021